Praise for the N

THE K

A RIT

"Sexy and funny. Donovan takes the marriage-of-convenience plot and gives it a fun update that will leave readers grinning....these characters are filled with genuine warmth and charm." —*Romantic Times BOOKreviews*

"*The Kept Woman* is an excellent read and I highly recommend it." —*Fresh Fiction*

"Kept me entertained from beginning to end. *The Kept Woman* is a winner of a read in my book!"

—*Romance Junkies*

"Susan Donovan has a real knack for looking at ordinary life and its many foibles in a uniquely clever and humorous way... Be prepared to settle in for a few hours of smart, sexy, hilarious fun with *The Kept Woman*."

—*BookLoons*

HE LOVES LUCY

"A great book…terrific." —*Fresh Fiction*

"A fun and sexy 'feel good' story and a must title to add to your current romance reading list." —*BookLoons*

"A story of rioting emotions, wacky weight challenges, and lots of love. This is one story you will be sad to see end. Kudos to Donovan for creating such a believable and realistic story." —*Fallen Angel Reviews*

MORE…

"*He Loves Lucy* has everything: humor, sweetness, warmth, romance, passion, and sexual tension; an uplifting message; a heroine every woman...can empathize with; and a hero to die for." —*Romance Reviews Today*

"An extraordinary read with intriguing characters and a wonderful plot...fantastic." —*Romance Junkies*

"Lucy is a humorous delight...fans will enjoy this fine look at one year of hard work to find love."
—*Midwest Book Review*

"A great romance...a top-rate novel...with its unforgettable characters, wonderful plot, and excellent message, *He Loves Lucy* will go on my keeper shelf to be read and re-read a thousand times...Donovan has proven that she will have serious star power in the years to come."
—*Romance Reader at Heart*

TAKE A CHANCE ON ME

"Comic sharpness...the humorous interactions among Thomas, Emma, and Emma's quirky family give the book a golden warmth as earthy as its rural Maryland setting. But there are also enough explicit erotic interludes to please readers who like their romances spicy."
—*Publishers Weekly*

"Donovan blends humor and compassion in this opposites-attract story. Sexy and masculine, Thomas fills the bill for the man of your dreams. Emma and Thomas deserve a chance at true love. Delightfully entertaining, *Take a Chance on Me* is a guaranteed good time."
—*Old Book Barn Gazette*

"Full of humor, sensuality, and emotion with excellent protagonists and supporting characters...a wonderful tale. Don't be afraid to take a chance on this one. You'll love it."

—*Affaire de Coeur*

"Impossible to put down...Susan Donovan is an absolute riot. You're reading a paragraph that is so sexually charged you can literally feel the air snapping with electricity and the next second one of the characters has a thought that is so absurd...that you are laughing out loud. Susan Donovan has a very unique, off-the-wall style that should keep her around for many books to come. Do NOT pass this one up."

—*Romance Junkies*

"Susan Donovan has created a vastly entertaining romance in her latest book *Take a Chance on Me*. The book has an ideal cast of characters...a very amusing, pleasurable read...all the right ingredients are there, and Ms. Donovan has charmingly dished up an absolutely fast, fun, and sexy read!"

—*Road to Romance*

"Contemporary romances don't get much better than *Take a Chance on Me*...such wonderful characters! You want sexual tension? This book drips with it. How about a love scene that is everything that a love scene should be? There's humor, a touch of angst, and delightful dialogue...*Take a Chance on Me* is going to end up very, very high on my list of best romances for 2003."

—*All About Romance*

KNOCK ME OFF MY FEET

"Spicy debut...[A] surprise ending and lots of playfully erotic love scenes will keep readers entertained."

—*Publishers Weekly*

"Donovan's blend of romance and mystery is thrilling."

—*Booklist*

"*Knock Me Off My Feet* will knock you off your feet... Ms. Donovan crafts an excellent mixture to intrigue you and delight you. You'll sigh as you experience the growing love between Autumn and Quinn, and giggle over their dialogue. And you'll be surprised as the story unfolds. I highly recommend this wonderfully entertaining story."

—*Old Book Barn Gazette*

"From the beginning I was hooked by the author's fast-paced writing and funny situations...I highly recommend this debut book by Susan Donovan. You'll just have to ignore the ironing and vacuuming and order pizza for the family until you've finished being knocked off your feet by this saucy, sexy romp."

—*A Romance Review*

"Hilarious...full of sass and sizzle."

—Julie Ortolon, *USA Today* bestselling author of *Don't Tempt Me*

St. Martin's Paperbacks Titles by Susan Donovan

The Girl Most Likely To...

The Kept Woman

He Loves Lucy

Public Displays of Affection

Take a Chance On Me

Knock Me Off My Feet

THE GIRL MOST LIKELY TO...

Susan Donovan

St. Martin's Paperbacks

THE GIRL MOST LIKELY TO...

For information address St. Martin's Press, 175 Fifth Avenue, New York, NY 10010.

ISBN: 0-312-93951-5
EAN: 978-0-312-93951-9

Printed in the United States of America

St. Martin's Paperbacks edition / January 2009

St. Martin's Paperbacks are published by St. Martin's Press, 175 Fifth Avenue, New York, NY 10010.

10 9 8 7 6 5 4 3 2 1

This book is dedicated to Steven R. Ivory,
with gratitude and love.

ACKNOWLEDGMENTS

This novel exists because people believe in me. I thank everyone at St. Martin's Press for their patience, especially Matthew Shear, Jennifer Enderlin, and my editor, Monique Patterson. I thank my agent, Irene Goodman, for cheering me on when I needed it most. I thank the many readers who said they couldn't wait for my next book, and, by the way, would it be coming sometime this *century*? Thanks for hanging in there, everybody.

I am honored to have friends and family who continue to walk with me on this journey, especially Steven and my best friend Arleen, along with Gran, Conor, Kathleen, Suzie, Marilyn, Shawn and Cameron, Paul, Kim, Catherine, Liz and John, Matt, and Sean and Diana. I thank the network of people who did something (or a lot) to get me to the settled place I am today—Jehanne, Kathy, Lou, Matthew, Pam, Lisa, Ron, Dana, Bernice, Sharon, Sylvia, and Kenmo Trinlay Chodron and my fellow students at the TMC. Last, I thank the various plumbing and heating professionals, concrete and masonry workers, electricians, locksmiths, roofers, cabinet and flooring contractors, and landscapers who have helped me transform my little house into a home. I am abundantly blessed.

This book is a work of fiction. I took liberties with Baltimore street names and geography to suit my story. The town of Persuasion, West Virginia, and its residents exist only in my imagination. Thank you to Madeline Bowman's parents for placing the winning bid at the 2006 Potomac Classical Youth Ballet Silent Auction, allowing me to use their daughter's name for a fictional character.

ONE

Four shirtless construction workers posed on the roof like suspects in a police lineup. But because of the direction of the afternoon sun—and the fuzziness of her twenty-year-old memory—Kat couldn't tell which was the father of her child and the only man she'd ever loved.

She squinted, raising a hand to block the glare. *Him?* No. The man on the far left was too short and stocky. Even at sixteen, Riley Bohland had been over six feet tall. *That one?* No. Riley's hair had been curly and dark and his shoulders much broader, even as a kid.

Then recognition hit her with a thud, pinning her feet to the wet West Virginia clay. Her breath went shallow. She broke out in goose bumps from head to toe.

"Is he up there?" Nola's whisper was squeaky with excitement, and she gripped Kat's upper arm so hard it hurt. "One of them is staring at you! Is that Riley? Is that him? Holy shit, this is going to be pure, Grade-A drama!"

As the man in question cocked his head and frowned down at them, a hammer hanging useless in his hand, Kat nodded her silent reply. *Oh yeah, that's Riley Bohland all right—the bastard—all grown up, filled out, and still walking around advertising the fact that God had Supersized his order of good looks, and it really pisses me off.*

Nola put her lips to Kat's ear. "You said he was cute, but seriously, hon, you could have gone into a little more detail."

Kat's homegrown heart pounded under her Parisian bra as she stared at him. This wasn't going to be as easy as she'd imagined. Why couldn't Riley have gone flabby over the years like a normal guy? Not that physical appearance was the measure of a man, but why did he have to be so well preserved? He was still long and lean, without an extra inch anywhere. His arms were corded with ropes of muscle. A pair of beat-up jeans hung low on his spare hips.

The instant he dropped the hammer and started down the ladder, Kat's whole world shifted. Suddenly, her righteous return felt all wrong. The glamorous Fifth Avenue makeover that had thrilled her yesterday seemed embarrassingly over-the-top up here in the Allegheny mountains. The three-inch stiletto boots that looked so sexy on the city sidewalk were sinking into the muck.

"I think I might black out," Kat mumbled.

"Man up, sister," Nola said. "This is the moment you've been waiting for. Do what you came here to do."

Riley's work boots left the last rung of the ladder and hit the mud with a *splat*. He turned. He took graceful, confident strides in Kat's direction. One step. Two. Spine straight. Chest rock-solid. Long arms relaxed.

Lips curled in a sneer.

"I'll be in the car." Nola ran away faster than a scalded dog.

Three steps. Four. Five.

Kat fluffed her razor-precise hairstyle with her perfectly manicured fingers. This was it. Riley's face came into focus. She could see those impossibly blue eyes blaze with an intensity that made her stomach flip. She'd practiced this a million times. She could do it. Sweet revenge was within arm's reach. Kat took a deep breath, steadied herself, and prepared to drop the bomb on the man whose selfishness had forever determined the course of her life.

Without warning, a big, black SUV drove right in front of Kat, splattering mud from her bangs to her Blahniks. She let out a yelp of shock, which was accented by muffled obscenities from inside the car.

As she tried to wipe some of the glop from her eyes, her brain seized with panic. Her makeup! Her hair! Her clothes! *This can not be happening.*

Riley walked right up to her. He moved so close that she could smell him—a potent mixture of memories, sweat, and rage.

"Where the *hell* have you been?"

"Uh, Baltimore." Kat let go with a nervous laugh, still wiping her eyes. She told herself that she must be having the mother of all bad dreams. She'd be waking up any minute.

Riley leaned closer. Even through her gunked-up eyelashes, she could see every day of thirty-seven years of life on that chiseled face. She watched his nostrils flare. If this was a dream, it was a very detail-oriented one.

Riley bent down so that his nose nearly touched her own. From behind straight, white, clenched teeth he asked, "*What in the name of God have you done with my son?*"

TWO

Riley shouldn't know about her son. How could he? *No one* from her past knew about Aidan, not even her own mother. There was something very wrong here.

Kat took a moment to regroup. According to her plan, she was, at this moment, supposed to be informing Riley Bohland of his paternity and watching him fall to his knees with the weight of his loutishness. And she was supposed to be doing that while looking hot enough to scorch the man's eyeballs.

But instead, she was covered in slime and had just been denied the right to utter the punch line she'd perfected with twenty years of practice in front of mirrors! And store windows. Every shiny surface she'd ever encountered, really. *I was pregnant the day you dumped me, you lying, selfish jerk.*

Construction noise had stopped. Kat realized she had an audience for what was shaping up to be the most completely fucked-up moment of her life, which was saying something.

The driver of the SUV slammed his door shut. "Very sorry, ma'am," he said.

"Tell me my son's name." Riley tightened his fists

at his sides. His body trembled with tension. "Is he healthy? Is he happy? What have you done with my goddam *boy*?"

Kat closed her eyes, feeling the tears mix with the mud and mascara. She choked out an answer. "His name is Aidan. He's twenty and in his second year at Johns Hopkins."

Riley said nothing. He gave a slow, disgusted shake of his head, then spat in the mud. "You're the coldest bitch on the face of the earth and I will never forgive you for what you've done to me." His voice was flat. He turned away.

Apparently, their big reunion was over.

"Forgive *me*?" Kat waved her muddy arms as she shouted at his back. "What do you mean, you'll never forgive *me*? I don't forgive *you*! Riley, stop! Get back here! How did you find out about Aidan?" He kept moving. "Don't you dare walk away from me! Wait!"

He didn't wait, which was almost a relief, since she had no idea what to say next.

Riley called over his shoulder, "Leave your contact information with your dad so my lawyer can find you."

Kat's arms collapsed at her sides. She went numb for an instant, just before the anger rushed in, hot and bitter and spreading its familiar vigor through her mind. She could not allow Riley to turn his back on her today, just like he'd done when she was sixteen. Twenty years ago, in the span of a single afternoon, she learned she was pregnant, got tossed out of school, kicked to the curb by her boyfriend, and sent away by her parents. Every minute since had been tough as hell, but she'd clawed and fought and survived so that one day—*today*—she could blow into town and get satisfaction. She deserved it. Riley Bohland owed it to her. Her parents owed it to her. The whole stinking, stupid, nothing town of Persuasion, West Virginia, owed it to her! *And this is all I get?*

Nola returned to her side and patted her shoulder. "I think he really dug your outfit," she said.

Madeline Bowman may have put on a few pounds since tenth grade, but Kat decided she looked a hundred times better without the freakishly big high school hair she once had. Madeline chatted away while escorting her two guests to their rooms at the Cherry Hill B and B, which, she wanted them to know, had been under her proprietorship for the last six years. Madeline was so pleasant that she even told Kat not to worry about the clumps of mud she was depositing on the polished oak staircase.

"I almost died when you walked in the front door, Kat! Oh my God! I had no idea that was you making the reservations on the phone! I suppose you're using your married name these days?" Madeline unlocked the door to Nola's room, got her settled in first, then escorted Kat down the hall to her suite. She lowered her voice to a whisper. "I have to admit that I'm just *dying* to know what happened to you! We always expected to see Kat Cavanaugh's face on a milk carton, or on *America's Most Wanted*. But obviously—" She scanned the splattered velvet of Kat's pencil skirt. "You were off to the big city, having some sort of amazing life that no one back here knew a thing about! You were always such a brain in school. I bet you went to Harvard and made a million dollars or something!" She opened the door. "I'm sure this isn't as glamorous as you're used to, but it's the nicest accommodations in town, by far. It's our honeymoon suite!"

Kat let Madeline's entire hyperactive soliloquy go without comment, including the obvious question of who in their right mind would want to honeymoon in Persuasion. She looked around the room. A cozy sitting area was done in a mix of overstuffed modern pieces and Victorian tables, all arranged around an ornately carved mahogany fireplace, which Madeline was quick to point out had been upgraded to gas. Next, Madeline demonstrated the convenience of the small kitchenette with its coffeemaker, refrigerator/freezer, and microwave. The bedroom was next on the tour, and Madeline opened a set of double doors to reveal an antique four-poster bed so high off the ground that it required its own step stool. Kat made a mental note not to attempt to scale that sucker after a couple glasses of wine. Then came the generous bathroom, with a double sink, a shower, and a deep antique claw-foot tub with brass faucet.

Kat smiled to herself. This room ran just shy of two hundred a night and it didn't even faze her. She'd been stinking rich for only three months, but as it turned out, she was a natural at it. Who knew?

"Thank you, Madeline. It's really nice."

"So, you're married?"

The woman was obviously on a mission. "No. I've never been married."

Madeline didn't bother to hide her confusion. "So what did you do—change your name?"

"Something like that."

"Is that your Jaguar out in the parking lot?"

"Yes."

"So you live in New York City?"

"Nope."

"But it has New York temporary tags from a dealership in Manhattan."

Good God! "Yes, it does."

Madeline's brown eyes flashed; then she looked at her feet, embarrassed for her shameless curiosity. Kat knew it had to be mind-blowing for a missing person to suddenly pop up, twenty years after her disappearance, rich and fabulously dressed and driving a brand-new Jag. At least she prayed it was, since that was the whole point.

"I can't wait to relax in this fabulous bathtub, Madeline. Is there a dry cleaner in town where I might be able to take my clothes?"

Madeline perked right up. "Oh! Just leave everything outside your door and I'll take care of it. I can even get your boots cleaned, if you'd like."

Kat glanced down at the recently acquired burnt caramel suede designer boots, now coated in sludge the color of dried blood. "I'd appreciate that."

"We got a lot of rain the last couple days."

"So it seems."

Madeline smiled slightly, turned to go, then changed her mind. "There's towels in the cabinet." She began shifting her weight from foot to foot and cleared her throat. "Look, I'm sorry for being nosy. It's just that—well—it was always a mystery why you and Riley never got together again. I mean, you were so totally in love! Everyone knew it! Your leaving just about killed him. He ditched so much school he flunked out, but I guess that's old news to you. We all figured you'd come back for him one day, and here you are! That's why you're here, right? You've come back for Riley?"

Kat wasn't sure she'd heard correctly. Her leaving

just about killed *him*? She had trouble seeing that, since Riley had chosen such a sensitive way to break up with her. *Go away, Kat. It's over.* She never got to share the news about the baby.

Kat prepared to answer Madeline. She raised her chin, straightened her back, and reminded herself to tuck away the old hurt. She was an expert at it. "Seriously, Madeline. I hardly think it's my fault that Riley Bohland never bothered to finish high school."

Madeline screwed up her face in bewilderment, then exploded with laughter, her eyes sparkling. When she regained her composure, she said, "Of course he finished, silly. He just had to repeat that one year."

"Well. I'm glad for him." She really was. At least maybe when Riley was too old and stiff for life on the construction crew, he could go to community college, like Kat had, and put his perfectly good brain to use. Riley was always able to coast by on charm alone, but he'd also been blessed with a relentless mind. Even when he was a kid, that mind would spin and twist until it grabbed on to something and made sense of it. Kat had always admired that in him, and she'd been pleased to see the same keen intellect at work in her son.

Well, Riley's son, too.

Madeline stared at Kat, deep in concentration. She jangled the master key ring in her hand. "So you were out at the construction site today? Is that how you ruined your beautiful clothes?"

"Yes, unfortunately."

"So you've already tracked him down?"

Kat noticed the strangest combination of worry and glee on Madeline's face, and she racked her brain for the specifics of how the tenth-grade food chain had once been structured. Kat herself was just a nerdy tomboy, preferring books and old movies over mascara and mousse. But Madeline Bowman had been a pom-pom princess and the queen of the Sadie Hawkins dance, the kind of girl Kat steered clear of whenever possible. People change, of course, but Kat figured it was best to keep the details of her visit from her graciously nosy hostess.

"Riley and I spoke briefly. The owner of the Sunoco told me he worked out there on Saturdays."

Madeline's eyebrows arched high on her forehead and she continued to stare. Eventually she cleared her throat. "Uh, so you haven't even gone back to Virgil's house yet?"

"No. That's on the agenda for tomorrow. My parents are going to be very surprised."

For a long moment, Madeline stared at Kat like a doe in the oncoming high beams. "Oh, my," she finally whispered.

"Yeah. The three of us haven't exactly been close."

Madeline blinked a few times, not able to hide her discomfort.

Kat couldn't say the reaction surprised her. The mere mention of Virgil Cavanaugh's name had always gotten some kind of awkward response. What could people say? *Your father is such a beautiful human being!*? Not hardly.

Madeline suddenly gave a crisp nod, pursing her lips so tight that Kat could see deep lines around her mouth. She quickly removed two keys from the ring and handed them to Kat, explaining that one was for the front door of the B and B and the other for her suite. "I'll let you relax, then," Madeline said, already scurrying to the door, avoiding eye contact.

"I'm serving dinner at six thirty, and I'll set the table for you and your friend."

As Madeline slid into the hallway and shut the door, Kat groaned with relief and rubbed her forehead, coming away with a palm dusted with dirt. What she needed was some silence, a hot bath, and a nap. Maybe then she could start to figure out what kind of new-and-improved mess she'd just made for herself by coming back to people who had never loved her and a place where she'd never belonged.

And to think, just three days ago, over a two-hundred-dollar bottle of champagne in the Four Seasons bar, this had all sounded like such a good idea.

Why now?

That's all Riley could think on the drive home. He cranked down the window of the old pickup, hoping that a blast of autumn air would smack some sense into him, but all it did was make him shiver. He was obviously nowhere near sensible, because he felt alive in a way he hadn't in years. All he could think about was Kat's shiny strawberry blonde hair, those big golden eyes, her sweet pink mouth. All he could hear was that raspy girl voice that cut him to the quick with the weight of memory. God help him, but he'd wanted to touch her. It took everything in him not to walk over to her, grab her, and kiss the bejesus out of her before he told how much he hated her.

Because he did hate her. There was no doubt about it. And he'd once loved her with everything he had in him. He couldn't figure out why the hell she decided to pick this particular moment to rise from the dead and throw his life into chaos—yet again. What did she want? Did she want to apologize for denying him his right to be a father to his own child? She sure didn't look apologetic.

Did she want money for the boy's college? God knew he'd gladly hand over everything he had left, but Kat didn't appear to be hurting for cash. She'd come rollin' through the holler in a brand-new Jaguar, for God's sake, posing in a getup that belonged on a Paris runway. Was that really fringe on those boots that went way up past her knees? She looked like a slutty fur trapper!

Riley laughed out loud, remembering that the last time he'd seen Kat, she'd been in Kmart jeans and Converse sneakers. She'd looked normal. She'd looked cute and sweet and perfect, and his sixteen-year-old hormones told him he should lay her down in the backseat of the Nova and devour her.

That didn't happen, because no matter what his hormones were telling him, his daddy had just informed him that he was too young to be so serious about a girl, and if he didn't break it off with Kat immediately, he'd lose his car and the right to play varsity sports. So Riley said what had to be said. And Kat's cute and sweet face turned to stone. She walked away without a word, and he never saw her again.

Until now.

Riley pulled into the drive and hopped out, wincing not only at the squeal of the old truck door but also at the sheer weight of his own stupidity. Sometimes he wished he'd never learned any more of the Kat Cavanaugh story, that he'd been allowed to go through life never knowing why Kat left, or that he had a child out there in the world he couldn't locate. But about a year ago he'd been given just enough information to turn his world inside out, to scrape out his guts and make him question every damn thing he thought was true.

For a year now, he'd been carrying around the ugly suspicion that on that day twenty years back, Kat had asked to meet him out on the quarry road for the sole purpose of telling him she was pregnant. But before she could even get the words out, he'd broken up with her. He'd been cold about it, too. It was the only way he could do it.

Riley grabbed the mail from the box out by the street, shaking his head at the memory of that day so long ago. He'd flunked a chemistry test and been benched for showing up late for basketball practice—twice. He remembered how Big Daddy got right up in his face and accused him of storing his brain in his Fruit of the Looms. Big Daddy had been right, of course, but only partially so. The truth was, Riley was In Love—in his mind, soul, *and* Fruit of the Looms.

He had to laugh at the reasoning prowess of his sixteen-year-old self. He'd had it all figured out. He'd break up with Kat temporarily to get Big Daddy off his back, then patch things up with her in a couple months. The pitiful truth was, Riley hadn't even made it through that first evening without Kat! He was banging on the Cavanaughs' door by nightfall. But she'd already gone.

He dragged his thoughts out of the past and headed up the curved brick walkway, his eyes automatically scanning the ungainly majesty of the old Queen Anne house. The mansion might still be considered the showplace of Persuasion, but all he saw was loose roof tiles, crumbling mortar, and the world's largest second mortgage. Riley's steps eventually took him under the shadow of the huge house, and his eyes adjusted to meet the gaze of the most loving, dependable girl a man could want. His face broke into a smile as he called out his usual greeting: "Hello, my beauty! How was your day?"

As always, Loretta waited for her man from the top step of the big front porch. Her eyes sparkled with adoration, her sleek hair gleamed in the afternoon light, and her tail thumped hard against the porch floor.

Riley reached down and rubbed her stone-hard head, then pulled gently on one of her droopy ears, a gesture that always produced a grunt of pleasure from the old hound.

"She named my boy Aidan. Can you believe that irony?" As he pushed open the front door, Loretta howled to hold up her end of the conversation. "No joke. Turns out Kat was sentimental enough to name our child after Big Daddy but never even bothered to inform me there *was* a child. Can you kindly explain that oversight to me?"

Loretta let loose with another plaintive wail.

"Don't you think that once in twenty years the woman's heart might have melted enough—just enough—to tell me I had a son?"

Almost immediately, the front door opened and shut behind Riley. He didn't even have to turn around to know who it was.

"What you fixin' to do now that she's back? You got any beer?" Matt walked right on through the cavernous foyer and straight into the kitchen, not waiting for his brother to answer him on either count.

Riley shook his head in annoyance as he sorted through the mail. His little brother hadn't lived in the Bohland House since he graduated from college but still traipsed in and out like he did. "Don't you have a refrigerator in that swanky loft of yours?"

"Yep, but there's no beer in it."

Riley heard the pop of a bottle cap and rolled his eyes. He had half a mind to call the cops on Matt. He'd do it, too, if his brother weren't the chief of the Persuasion Police Department.

Riley threw down the mail and followed Matt to the fridge. "You know, seriously, it wouldn't kill you to knock, Matt. What if I was in here all tangled up in a game of nude Twister or something?"

Matt took one long gulp of beer after another, staring at his brother over the length of the bottle. Eventually, Matt let out a sigh of relief, slammed the empty on the counter, and patted Riley's arm. "I didn't know our girl Loretta was into freaky shit like that." Matt then belched loudly, moved into the parlor, and flopped on the settee.

Riley grabbed a couple more beers and went in after him. "Hilarious. Take off your boots, man. They're covered in mud."

"Right." Matt unlaced his work boots and set them on the wood floor by the couch. "Look, I gotta tell you—I really feel bad about spraying Kat Cavanaugh with muck like that." Slowly, Matt turned his head to look at Riley, and after a moment of tightly wound silence, the two burst out laughing. Loretta joined in.

"You did that on purpose, dickhead."

"No, I swear I didn't! I wasn't paying much attention to Kat, to tell you the truth. I didn't even realize it was her I nailed until I got out of the cruiser." Matt grabbed one of the fresh beers from the coffee table. "I'm not ashamed to tell you that my focus was on the brunette in the Jaguar. I'm lucky I didn't run Kat flat over."

Riley shook his head and took a swig of beer.

"Hey. Aren't you on call? Should you be drinking?"

"Shut up," Riley said.

"I thought you weren't supposed to drink when—"

"Shut the hell up, man."

Matt shrugged. "Fine. Well, Kat looked good. Real good. She must be loaded."

Riley laughed and took off his own boots. His feet were achy and wet and he needed a shower. What he really needed, he knew, was a mercifully slow night on call and for Carrie to forget to contact him for about a week. He didn't have the patience to deal with her now. Lately, she'd been teetering on the line between ex-fiancée and completely psycho ex-fiancée. He sure as hell didn't want her to find out that the infamous Kat Cavanaugh had materialized. It could be the ticket to push ole Carrie right over the edge.

"I'm thinking about becoming a Buddhist monk."

Matt hooted with laughter at Riley's lament, and Loretta howled right along for support. "Hey, man, before you go taking a Norelco to your noggin, you should know that Lisa Forrester's been asking about you every day. Remember her? The second-shift dispatcher with the belly ring I was telling you about?"

"Wow, Matt. You sure can pick 'em." Riley was trying to take another sip from his beer bottle when Loretta head-butted his forearm, sending a slosh of foam onto the area rug.

"See? Even the dog knows you're not supposed to be drinking on call."

"Hey, Matt?"

"I know. I know. Shut up. And here I am, not only trying to find you a love connection but working construction for you nearly every damn weekend—and this is the thanks I get?"

"Thanks, Matt." Riley didn't have the energy for a clever retort.

"Well, as much as I'm enjoying this conversation, I gotta scoot." Matt straightened from his slouch, then grabbed his boots and his beer. "I just wanted to make sure you were cool. You know, not oiling up Daddy's old twelve-gauge or something stupid."

"Thank you for keeping our community safe."

Matt got to his feet. "Just so you know—Madeline informed me the women were staying at Cherry Hill."

Riley nodded. "Figured as much."

"You know what that means, right?"

Riley slowly raised his head, checked out his brother's expression, and closed his eyes against the realization. *"Fuck."*

"Hey, I know Madeline's a gossip. But she's a nice woman, and she makes a mean lasagna. It didn't work out with us, but I still think you should ask her out—you know what they say about the sexual needs of divorced single moms."

Riley opened his eyes, ignoring Matt's ridiculous suggestion. "No chance Madeline would forget to tell Carrie that Kat was here?"

Matt snorted. "Are you on drugs or something? She tells Carrie *everything*." The two women were friends, after all.

"Great."

"Look, Bro." Matt cleared his throat. "Are you, uh, you know, thinkin' about going over to the B and B for a little friendly chat with Kat tonight?"

Behind his brother's smirk, Riley knew there was real concern. Matt and Carrie were the only people who knew Riley had a son, and Matt was clearly worried about how all this would turn out. "She named him Aidan. Isn't that a riot? And she says she's been in Baltimore."

"Hole-eee God." Matt's eyes went wide. "Big Daddy would've loved that shit." He headed toward the kitchen but stopped after two steps. "Baltimore? As in Baltimore, Maryland?"

"Do you know any other Baltimore?"

"Huh." Matt gave a slow nod of comprehension. "That would go a long way toward explaining why we never found her in California."

"Yeah, it would. Wrong end of the continent and all that." Riley had been given wrong information about Kat's whereabouts and he couldn't safely say if it had been deliberate or not. But it wouldn't surprise him if it was. With a deep sigh, he rose from the sofa to see his brother out. They'd nearly reached the front door when Matt suddenly spun around, eyes bright with anger.

"What the hell's wrong with you, man?" Matt shoved him in the chest.

"What the f—?" Riley stared at Matt in disbelief. He couldn't remember the last time his brother laid a hand on him. "What was that for?"

"Kat just came back from the dead, man!" Matt waved his arms around. "You're going to finally get to meet your kid! But you're moping around like you just found a boil on your ass or something! What is *with* you? You're like some zombie-assed robot!"

Riley's head snapped back from the force of his brother's words. Matt was pissed. Over something that was really none of his business. "I don't want to get into this right now, all right? I've got a lot on my mind."

Matt laughed bitterly. "You never want to get into *anything.* Nobody knows what you've got on your mind because you never want to share nuthin' with nobody."

"Drop it, Matt. This is not the time for an intervention."

"Fuck you, too! Here's the thing—and you know what I'm about to say is true—you didn't say a damn word when Daddy died. Do you realize that? You didn't cry. You didn't talk about him. Nothing."

"Jesus, Matt."

"And you won't talk to me about the problems with the building money. You haven't talked about your kid in months. You don't talk about crazy Carrie. So now Kat is back and you say *nothing.* And I know what's next—you're gonna wallow around in one of your megafunks and not come out of this tomb except to work."

"It's the way I am."

"That's just dandy," Matt said, his voice dripping with sarcasm. "But here's the thing. I swear to God, that you're wound so tight, you're going to explode on me one day—just *snap*—and the next thing I know I'll be getting a report of a twenty-seven-eight in progress at the Bohland House."

Riley calmly reached around his brother's body and grabbed the carved brass doorknob. "Thanks for stopping by."

Matt let out a hiss of air. "Hey, asshole. I grew up here, same as you, and there ain't no 'stopping by' involved." He yanked open the heavy door himself.

"And just 'cause Big Daddy made you executor of his estate don't mean this house isn't as much mine as it is yours, so don't go gettin' all high-and-mighty on me like this is your own stately manor house and you're the Earl of Persuasion or some shit like that. It might deflate your head a bit to remember that our great-granddaddy paid for this place with bootlegging profits he kept under his mattress, for crying out loud!"

Riley would've laughed if Matt's words weren't so true and didn't slice down to the raw core of his guilt. Matt had no idea that his trustworthy, honest, straight-and-narrow big brother had mortgaged their ignoble inheritance to the hilt and, barring some miracle, they'd be in foreclosure by the New Year.

Riley swallowed hard and waited for the transition he knew was coming. Matt's M.O. had always been the opposite of his own. His little brother would blow his top, then cool off, and never hold a grudge. Riley envied that sometimes. So he watched as, true to form, the hurt and anger drained from Matt's face.

"I'm sorry, Matt," Riley said. "I don't mean to be a jerk."

"And I had no business going off on you like that." Matt slapped Riley's upper arm affectionately.

"It's cool." Riley hated himself for not telling Matt the truth, and swore in silence that he'd come clean about everything. Soon. "I'm not shutting down, Matt. There's just a lot going on right now."

Matt bit his lip. "Kat showing up like this has got to be hard to deal with."

"It is."

"I hear you."

Riley tried to produce a smile as affable as his brother's. "Hey, look, you're right—this is your home as much as it is mine, and if I'm in the middle of a game of nude Twister with the belly-ring babe when you walk in, then so be it."

Matt nodded a few times, then began to frown, as if something just made sense to him. "Baltimore? Are you sure?"

Riley shrugged. "That's what Kat said."

"But her mom claimed she was in California."

Riley sighed. "BettyAnn was either setting me up, or she was out of her head on the pain meds. That's all I can think."

Matt sighed. "Daddy always said you couldn't trust a Cavanaugh."

"I think he was referring to Virgil."

"No doubt. See ya."

Just as Matt's boots crossed the threshold, Riley's pager filled the foyer with a shrill *beep beep beep beep beep.*

"Busted!" Matt said with a grin, slamming the door behind him before Riley could ask him what a twenty-seven-eight was.

THREE

Life got complicated for Kat at about 9:30 P.M., October 3, 1987, out on the quarry road, on a blanket spread out in the grass next to Riley's rust-bucket Chevy Nova. It wasn't the first time they'd enjoyed such a swanky date—it was closer to the 157th time. Mostly, they'd get out there and do nothing but talk, discussing everything from the cosmos and Carl Sagan to Lisa Lisa & Cult Jam. Sometimes, they'd get carried away with those hot and sweet kisses Kat was sure had never been equaled in all of human history. Then Riley would be sure to get his hand up her shirt or down her pants, and she'd be making a beeline for his button fly. But they'd made a pact with each other. Either she would slow him down or he would slow her down, because as much as they wanted each other, what they really wanted was to graduate from Cecil H. Underwood High School with excellent grades, go to good colleges, and get out of Persuasion forever—together. Every one of their dreams depended on it.

Kat turned off the faucet in the claw-foot tub, then eased herself down into the bubbles, leaving her nose just above the waterline. She obviously needed to talk with Riley, tell him everything. But after his questions about Aidan, she had to wonder how much Riley already knew and how he could have possibly found out.

He knew how this whole mess started, of course. On that chilly October night, the two of them burned with the wonder of each other. Their big plans—along with basic common sense—were suddenly no match for the beauty and intensity of that first taste of sex. *Just this once, Kat. Oh God, I'm going to die if I can't get inside you.* In those minutes—all five of them—nothing mattered but the spark they'd ignited between them, the lava of lust, the head-exploding, skin-on-skin confirmation that they were meant for each other, for all of time.

Three months later, Kat got her wish to leave Persuasion, but there was no fanfare to mark the occasion. She left home on a bitterly cold January evening—just walked right out the front door of her house with her mother's blessing and the image of her father's ugliness still fresh in her mind. She was outside the city limits in a little over an hour, curled up in the passenger seat of an 18-wheeler delivering lumber to Baltimore, sick as a dog the whole way. She had eighty-three dollars in her pocket but was rich in luck.

Kat let her head sink down below the bubbles. She held her breath for as long as she could, squeezing her eyes shut against the memory. How ignorant she'd been! What would have happened to her if Cliff Turner hadn't been the one to stop for her? It made her nauseous to think how stupid she'd been that night, her thumb out in the wind and her face frozen with tears, just begging for the world to eat her and her baby alive.

She pushed her head out of the water and gasped

for air. Whether a random occurrence or part of a grand plan, the fact was her entire life hinged on the fact that good-hearted Cliff had spotted her on Highway 3, put on his brakes so fast they squealed, and waited for her to run along the shoulder until she caught up.

He'd felt sorry for her; that's why he'd been so nice. He stopped at an all-night McDonald's for her to use the restroom and to get something to eat. He even paid for it. Then, on his way to the shipyard, he dropped her off at his sister's row house in the Highlandtown neighborhood of Baltimore. A skinny woman in her fifties came to the door in pink sponge curlers and a lime green terry-cloth robe. She seemed pleased to see her brother but annoyed that he'd blocked most of the street with his rig and interrupted her coffee date with Bryant Gumbel. All these years later, Kat still smiled when she recalled Cliff's introduction: *This here's my sister, Phyllis. This is Tina and she's a pregnant runaway from Iowa.* Actually, Kat had told Cliff she was Gina from Ohio, and she'd adamantly denied being pregnant, but since all of it was a load of crap, she didn't bother to correct him.

Phyllis put her hands on her skinny hips and looked Kat up and down. "Well, come on in, Tina. Hope you don't have a phobia about birds."

Phyllis made a skillet of ham and fried potatoes for breakfast, but all Kat could hold down was toast with a little strawberry jam. Then Phyllis took her to the upstairs sewing room, where there was a twin bed covered in a faded purple flowered coverlet, one window, and only three parakeet cages, which Kat would soon learn was close to solitary confinement for any of Phyllis' birds.

Kat slept for twelve hours that first day, and stayed for seven years.

She swirled her fingertips in the bubbles, watching them pop and disappear, wondering for the millionth time what Riley had done with his life. He'd never left Persuasion, obviously, but was he married? Did he have other children? Was he happy? Did his family still own that huge old house on Cedar Street? Was Big Daddy still mayor?

And—a question she rarely permitted herself to ask—what happened with her parents? Did her mother ever think about her? Did she ever miss her or cry for her at night? Did she ever regret the way she'd sent her only child away?

Did the beatings ever stop?

The loud pounding Kat heard was not the sound of her memory. Someone was banging on the door.

"Hon! Open up!" It was Nola.

"Kat! Please! It's an emergency!" The second voice belonged to Madeline.

Kat jumped up, sloshing water over the sides of the tub and nearly breaking her neck when she lost her footing. She tumbled onto the bath mat, bubbles running down her skin, then lunged for a towel. "Coming! I'm coming!"

On the way to the door, Kat grabbed her purse, thinking that she could at least save something from the fire. The rest of her belongings would have to burn. Kat was breathless when she finally got the door unbolted and open.

"Sorry to bother you," Madeline said, which struck Kat as an odd way to inform her the place was on fire.

Nola touched Kat's wet arm. "It's your dad, Kat. He's had a heart attack."

FOUR

Kat jolted awake, her eyes scanning an unfamiliar darkness, her heart pounding. Chills ran through her as an inhuman voice cried out in agony.

"La la la la la la bamba!"

She sat straight up in a bed she didn't recognize, flailed her arms until they made contact with a lamp, and pushed in the switch with shaking fingers, somehow managing to keep the lamp from crashing to the floor. Kat blinked against the harsh light, eventually focusing on a pair of beady blue eyes staring right into hers.

"Squaaaaaawwwwww! La la la la la bamba!"

"Oh my God! Help! Somebody help me!" Kat covered her head with her arms and yelled as loud as she could, hearing the beat of what sounded like a million wings above her head, a loud cacophony of screeching, and an endless *scratch-scratch-scratch* of agitated bird feet.

"Didn't we almost have it all!"

"I wanna dance with somebody!"

"Help!"

A door opened. A bony older woman in black spandex leggings and an oversized Cal Ripken baseball jersey appeared next to the bed. "For crying out loud! You'd think you were being attacked by Freddy Krueger or something. These here are just a few harmless budgie boys."

Kat panted, her mind a total confused mess of dream and wakefulness, and it took her a few seconds to realize everything was real. The pregnancy test . . . being told she could only stay in school until she showed . . . Riley breaking up with her . . . seeing her dad and that woman together in the studio . . . destroying the sculpture . . . her mother sending her away . . . the ride in the semi . . . and this lady—what was her name again?—this lady who'd made Kat toast and told her to lie down.

"I'm going to puke," Kat said.

"Not in here you ain't." The woman finished returning all the birds into their appropriate cages and double-checked the latches. "You'll have to learn to keep an eye on Boris, here. He opens his cage and then goes around springing everyone else free, singing Top Forty hits the whole while."

"Where's your bathroom?" Kat knew she had no time for a chat.

The lady pointed into the hall. "Second door on the left."

Kat leaped to her feet and barely made it into the bathroom before she tossed her toast. Her limbs felt so weak that she decided to stay curled up in a ball on the fuzzy pink bath rug for the rest of her life. She raised her head when she heard the shower running.

"You'll feel better once you have a hot shower and put on some clean clothes. You and I are about the same size, so I'll get you something to wear."

Kat was rolling her eyes at the prospect of what fashion choices awaited her when a thin arm went around her waist and a strong hand pulled her to her feet. "We're gonna have a nice long chat, you and me, figure out what's what. But right now, I've got to get over to the Sacred Heart o' Jesus social hall. If I don't show up at least fifteen minutes early, lard-ass Josefina Dubrowski will try to take my lucky seat, and I need every penny I can get my hands on for that start-up IPO next Wednesday."

"Huh?" Kat felt unsteady. She'd understood exactly nothing of what the woman just said, but Kat thought it might have had something to do with Jesus and some kind of birth control. She really should have paid more attention in family health class.

Then the lady did the strangest thing. She kissed Kat on the cheek and gave her a hug. "Knockers up, hon. You're going to be just fine. I'll be home by eleven. *Miami Vice* is on tonight, if you like Don Johnson, and what normal girl doesn't? But don't go opening any of the cages while I'm away, because you're not used to the birdies yet. There's some Tuna Helper on a plate in the oven for you."

The instant the lady closed the bathroom door behind her, Kat was back on her knees on the fuzzy pink rug, the pain of loss in her gut and the words "Tuna Helper" ringing in her ears.

"How long till we get there?"

Nola's question snapped Kat out of the home movie that had been playing in her brain. She was surprised to find herself behind the wheel, and it took her a moment to remember that they were on their way to the hospital to check on her dad.

Kat put the Jaguar in fifth gear and let it loose on the country road, looking around her to get her bearings. The leaves of the Monongahela National Forest glimmered all around her like millions of gemstones in the sunset, and Kat felt guilty that all that extravagant beauty was wasted on her. She hadn't even noticed.

"About fifteen minutes," she answered Nola. When Kat realized what she'd just said, a lump of dread formed in her chest. In that amount of time she'd be at Davis Memorial Hospital in Elkins, where she would encounter a mother and father she hadn't laid eyes on in twenty years. Her father would probably be hooked up to wires and tubes, and her mother would most definitely be hysterical. And the place itself didn't exactly hold fond memories for Kat, since the last time she'd been there was for that fateful visit to the family-planning clinic, where she'd found out she was going to have a family she hadn't planned.

"Are you sure you're OK to drive, hon?"

"I'm great." *Poor Nola,* Kat thought. She'd convinced her best friend to come along for a weekend of sweet revenge. So far they'd come up short on both counts.

"I know this is turning into the road trip to hell," Kat said. "I probably should have thought this through a little more."

Her friend dismissed her with a wave of her hand. "The important thing is you're actually here, right now, dealing with the luggage you've been carrying around all these years. You're brave, hon."

Kat grinned, both at Nola's usual mangling of the language and at her wishful thinking. Bravery had nothing to do with this trip. Kat was here to rub a few noses in the aroma of her success. She wanted to collect a few heartfelt apologies. She wanted to say a few things to a few people and then get on with her life—whatever exciting, adventurous, wonderful life she decided she wanted to have.

"Or is it baggage?" Nola wondered aloud.

"It's baggage."

"Right. Baggage. In fact, on *Oprah* the other day they were talking about how facing your deepest fears head-on is the only path to inner peace and happiness." Nola checked her lip gloss in the mirror, then snapped the visor back into place with a chuckle. "And I thought to myself, *Well, damn!* No wonder so many of us are walking around so fucking miserable all the time. Who wants to do that?"

Kat laughed. Nola had been making her laugh since their first day in English 101 at Baltimore City Community College fifteen years and three husbands ago. None of Nola's marriages had resulted in kids, but she'd long ago volunteered to round out the trinity of mother figures in Aidan's life. It never failed to amaze Kat how normal her kid had turned out, considering that he was raised by an unwed hillbilly teenager, a chain-smoking parakeet lady, and a tough little Italian girl with highly sophisticated street smarts and extremely loose morals.

Kat smiled to herself, thinking maybe that was why Aidan seemed so comfortable around women of any age, shape, ethnicity, or state of mind—he'd already seen it all.

"Now, what I want to know is how come Riley Bohunk was the one who called the B and B with the news about your dad?"

Kat had been wondering the same thing, and shrugged. "He probably heard about it around town, found out where I was staying, and decided to let me know."

"Must be hard to keep a secret in a place this size." Nola fluffed her newly cut and colored hair, and Kat had to admit that her friend looked like a million bucks. After being waxed, tweezed, exfoliated, manicured, foiled, trimmed, and polished within an inch of their lives, they both did. And the actual cost was only about thirty-five grand, including the week in the Royal Suite at the Four Seasons and the retail therapy sessions at Barneys. The XJ7 with the moonroof, the navigation system, heated seats, and iPod interface was a little extra.

"News travels fast around here," Kat said.

"So your parents probably know you're back."

"Oh yeah. I'm thinking that's why my dad keeled over."

Nola stared out the window and craned her neck to see the top of the tree line. "It's real pretty here, Kat. If you like the country, I mean. Personally, I'd go ape shit if I had to live outside of Bawlmer County. I bet you can't find a decent calzone within a hundred miles."

Kat chuckled. "I would imagine you're correct about that."

"Persuasion sure is a weird name for a town, though. What's the story with that?"

Kat couldn't recall the last time she'd thought about the fable. "They teach every elementary school kid that this Scottish guy named Harmon McEvoy got a land grant and settled in the valley in the late seventeen hundreds. When he brought his wife here to join him, she completely freaked, refusing to live so far from civilization and so close to the Indians."

Nola threw up her hands. "Like I said—no calzones!"

"Exactly. So Harmon built her a nice house and convinced her to stay. He *persuaded* her to stay."

Nola pursed her lips and nodded. "Huh. I bet if that Scottish dude looked like Riley Bohunk, then the girl would've lived in a teepee and been damn glad about it."

Kat shook her head, laughing. "You've got to stop calling him that, Nola, or I'm going to end up saying it."

"Well, he *is* a hunk, and if you'd been more specific about his level of hunkiality we'd have made this trip a long time ago, and even though I am no longer interested in men and never will be again under any circumstances, I have to admit—he's hot."

Kat sighed. "He really was something special. So smart. So intense. So gorgeous. Still is."

"Duh. I think we've established that." Nola's hand settled gently on Kat's forearm. "Are you sure you're ready for this, hon?"

Kat tensed, aware that Nola was asking about the encounter with her parents. "I guess I better be, since we're almost there."

"Kat?" Nola adjusted her position in the deep bucket seat to face her more directly. "Did you ever come close to coming back home? I mean, you always seemed so damned independent and sure of yourself, but wasn't there ever a time when you just wanted to come home and tell them everything—where you went, what you were doing, show them Aidan? Weren't you ever even *tempted*?"

More than she'd ever let on, Kat knew. There were times when she'd been knocked to her knees with emptiness. She needed to feel Riley. She needed to hear her mom's voice. One night, when Aidan was about two, Kat waited for Phyllis to leave for bingo and packed up the baby stuff and bolted. Kat made it to the corner of Eastern and Conkling and waited about fifteen minutes for the No. 57 bus that would get her to Union Station, and eventually Persuasion. But she turned around. She pushed the stroller through the neighborhood and went right back up the marble steps to Phyllis' row house. Who was she kidding? She was already home. If home was a place where you were loved and accepted no matter what you did, where there was no hitting and screaming and no secrets except for the ones you held far down in your heart, then the little row house at 456 California Avenue was the only real home she'd ever had.

"Phyllis kept asking me if I was sure I didn't want to write my mom," Kat said. "But she eventually stopped. I guess she figured it was like talking to a wall."

Nola settled back into the plush leather and sighed deeply. "I never really understood that part. I mean, don't get me wrong—it's no coincidence that 'dysfunction' and 'D'Agostino' both begin with a *d*. But we're still a family. Maybe we're all misogynists, but we stick together. I couldn't imagine just cutting myself off from them the way you did."

"I know you can't. And I think you mean 'masochist.' "

"You may be right."

Kat watched the sun begin to slip behind the trees. She cracked the window, thinking that the air would blow away the pain. It did just the opposite. She smelled her childhood. Wet leaves, pine needles, mountain rain, rich soil—and the stink of buried secrets.

This is a private family matter, Katharine, and everyone would misunderstand. . . . Your father is a good man and he never means to hurt me. . . . He's under so much pressure with his art and I know I can get on his nerves. . . . Why don't you run on outside and play? . . . He works so hard to support us. . . . He'll be in a better mood tomorrow. . . .

Kat pulled the Jaguar onto Randolph Avenue and spotted the hospital complex a few blocks away. She gripped the steering wheel hard, hoping Nola wouldn't see her hands tremble. It had been many years since Kat had allowed her mother's voice into her head like that, and it had arrived so sharp and lifelike that Kat almost expected to turn and see BettyAnn Cavanaugh sitting in the passenger seat next to her.

Kat dared to look but was greeted by a scowling Nola.

"You just went white as a sheet and you're shaking. I better drive."

"We're here," Kat told her, swinging into the hospital parking garage. "Let's just get this over with."

Caroline Mathis, M.D., Ph.D., flipped the cell phone shut and took a moment to center herself. As much as she appreciated Madeline's timely updates on Kat Cavanaugh's comings and goings, they certainly wreaked havoc with Carrie's peace of mind. She knew the secret to her success had always been balance—a delicate titration of all elements of her life flowing together in a synthesis of logic and emotion, action and stillness, effort and acceptance. And that's how she'd handle this latest snag in her plans. It never failed. She'd simply breathe the balance in, and breathe it out again.

"That bitch-whore!"

Carrie shocked herself. She hadn't meant to shout that out loud. She must be losing it. She hoped to

God that her voice hadn't carried through her office door. She smacked the intercom button of her speakerphone with the flat of her hand. "Alice? . . . I'm sorry to ask you to do this at the last minute, but could you please cancel my lecture tonight at the Board of Medicine? Something's come up in Persuasion."

Alice was quiet for a moment, then spoke softly. "Are you all right, Dr. Mathis? I thought I heard you yell in there. Is it the diabetes study?"

"Did I yell? Oh no! I just stubbed my toe! Can you believe it?" Carrie jumped from her chair and began to pace in front of the wide bank of windows overlooking the West Virginia State Capitol.

"Would you like me to reschedule?"

Carrie stared, her mind a blur. *That bitch is going to ruin everything! That bitch is going to ruin my entire life—again!*

"Dr. Mathis?"

"Oh yes. Absolutely."

"After the holidays?"

"Good. Good."

"I don't even think the board meets toward the end of the year, so should I try for January?"

Carrie chewed on the inside of her cheek. She chomped down so hard she drew blood, but somehow she didn't mind the pain. It cleared her head.

"Dr. Mathis?"

"January would be perfect, Alice. Thanks."

Alice went quiet again. "Would you like me to come in for a minute?"

Carrie closed her eyes and took a deep breath. Alice meant well. She'd been Carrie's assistant for eight years now, ever since she'd joined the

Department of Health & Human Resources while still working toward her doctorate in public health policy. Carrie knew that Alice had been instrumental in her promotion to executive director of the Division of Rural Health. Alice certainly had provided a shoulder to cry on during last year's wedding fiasco, but deep down, she was a busybody. She was so interested in every single little detail that you'd think *she* was the one getting married in less than three months!

"Actually, I'm on my way out."

Carrie hit the "off" button on the speakerphone and grabbed her jacket and briefcase. She wouldn't even have time to change her clothes before she had to hit the road. If she made it out of Charleston before the evening rush, she could get to Persuasion in a little over two hours.

She truly looked forward to the day that they could end all this "commuter relationship" nonsense. Riley's talents were being wasted in that town, and that stupid clinic would have done nothing but seal his low-class fate. With that in mind, Carrie had already found a dozen potential jobs for him here in the capital city and she was confident he'd eventually come to his senses. With a little luck, she could wrap up her rural diabetes management study right about the time Riley relocated here—and they could put that silly little town and all its history behind them, for good.

Carrie gathered her briefcase and purse, a twinge of guilt tickling at her as it occasionally did. Some people might think it was unethical the way she'd used legislative sleight of hand to get Riley's clinic funding killed. But anyone making that judgment wouldn't understand that she had Riley's best interests at heart. She loved him. She knew what was good for him. She was good for him.

The nurse at the triage desk pointed to a row of mint green fabric curtains, informing Kat and Nola that Virgil Cavanaugh could be found in evaluation room B-4. It took exactly eighteen steps to get there. Kat counted. She laughed at herself for being such a baby about this. Her parents were just like everyone else. Just people. Not monsters. They'd made some serious mistakes a long time ago, but maybe they'd just done the best they could. Kat was no longer a child—she was a grown woman. She could handle this.

Kat gripped the edge of the curtain and pulled it aside. The first thing she noticed was a pale old man on a gurney, his eyes closed and his body still. The humming and beeping of monitors were the only indication he was alive. The next thing she noticed was that her mother was nowhere to be seen.

Kat sat down in one of the small plastic chairs over by the sink. Nola sat next to her.

"That's Virgil, right?" Nola whispered, reaching for Kat's hand.

"That's him."

Kat couldn't take her eyes off the man who lay under the pale yellow blanket. His body looked . . . *reduced* somehow. Virgil Cavanaugh had never been a huge man, but he'd been strong and he'd been mean, and Kat had always thought that his meanness took up space in the world. People seemed to keep their distance from him. The dean at Mountain Laurel had always humored him, because Virgil's name lent credibility to the college's small art department. His students respected his talent but never liked him as a person. It had always been that way.

Kat leaned forward in the chair, trying to get a closer look. Her father's hands appeared knotted and limp, nothing like the powerful and graceful hands that had once made wet clay and hard marble submit to his every whim. His skin was decorated with a web of tiny broken capillaries and sagged from the bone of his cheeks, jaw, and elbows. For a moment, Kat imagined that his meanness had faded along with his youth, or had even disappeared altogether sometime in the last twenty years.

A vision shot through her brain with such force that it knocked the wind from her. She was looking down at her own young hands, knuckles blanched because she held a mallet so fiercely, and she raised that mallet above her head and brought it down on the clay figure of a woman. The woman's face flew across the studio. Kat raised her arms again. And again. And again. Until there was nothing but clumps of clay on the floor.

Kat nearly jumped when the curtain flew open and a big, smiley nurse barreled into the tight space, greeting the women cheerfully before she went to the patient. "Well, Mr. Cavanaugh, it looks like we're going to be admitting you so that you can get a cardiology consult. How does that sound? We'll have you settled upstairs quicker than you can say 'tiddlywinks.'"

A vile hiss seemed to float up from the bed. *"Tiddlywinks, my ass."* That comment was followed by a wheezy cough and then more gravelly words: "No nurse should be as big as a heifer like you. Cuts back on patient confidence."

Kat thought she'd fall off her chair. Nola's fingernails dug into Kat's hand. But the nurse continued adjusting his oxygen line and responded calmly.

"Listen up, Prince Charming. You might be old and sick, but that doesn't give you the right to be a bastard."

Kat gulped. Her father had just rolled his head to the side and allowed his stare to land directly on target. His eyes pierced hers. "Go on and tell her, Katharine—I've always been a bastard. Go ahead. You know the story."

"*Jesus-Hang-Gliding-Christ,*" Nola mumbled.

"I sincerely apologize for him," Kat told the nurse, hearing the weariness in her own voice. It occurred to her that she'd yet to say one word to her father and she was already exhausted by his company. Why had she come here? What the hell had she been thinking? She hated this place, and this place hated her. She already knew with certainty that this whole trip had been a mistake and she hadn't even gotten to the best part yet—her mother. How much worse would it get? Right then and there, Kat promised herself that her next half-tipsy, spontaneous road-trip fantasy would remain a fantasy.

"He's right," Kat said with a sigh. "My father's always been a mean and nasty bastard."

The nurse's eyes got big and she forced a smile. "Well, then. The doctor should be here any minute to chat with you nice people." She swept through the curtain and was gone. It flung open again so quickly that Kat figured the nurse had forgotten something.

The instant the doctor entered the small space, Kat's heart stopped. Forget her dad—she was the one who was going to need a cardiologist. She watched the tall, handsome, dark-haired doctor grab the patient's chart and begin to flip through the pages.

Kat fought to get enough breath to say the word: "*Riley?*"

"Hell-lo!" Nola sing-songed.

Riley raised his midnight blue eyes to Kat. In that split second, she was sixteen, in his arms, laughing, her heart wide open and her whole life ahead of her. But she blinked and the illusion was gone, and she was looking into the eyes of a tired guy in a white coat with a stethoscope slung around his neck, the words *Riley Bohland, M.D.* embroidered in red on the left chest pocket. "He's going to recover," Riley said.

Kat nodded. "I'm glad one of us will."

Their eyes locked. Nothing else existed except the force of that gaze, the power in it. Riley looked away before Kat could decide what it was that she'd caught a glimpse of. Regret? Longing?

Virgil let out a raspy laugh. "Well, looky here—it's Romeo and Juliet after taxes."

Riley clipped the chart to its hook at the foot of the hospital bed and ignored the comment. "All right, Virgil. We're taking you up to the cardiac unit and let them poke around a bit, do some tests. Could be you'll need a catheterization to unblock your arteries. We'll know by tomorrow."

Riley turned to Kat, all business. "Would you like to help him get settled in his room?"

Kat suddenly felt ill. She stood up and motioned for Nola to get to her feet, too. There was no way in hell Kat was going to hang around to comfort Virgil or deal with this cold, hollowed-out stranger who was once Riley. "I think my mother is better suited for that job. We need to be getting back to town."

"She's not here, Katharine."

Something in her father's voice made Kat freeze. She looked at him, scanning his eyes for an explanation of whatever his voice had just revealed. There was nothing.

"Where'd she go? The cafeteria?"

Her question was met by absolute silence. Kat noticed Riley raise his chin and breathe deep.

"Depends on your views, I suppose," her father said. "But no religion I ever heard of offers a cafeteria option for the afterlife—it's usually just heaven or hell. If I had to pick, I'd say heaven, but then, me and the Almighty aren't exactly fishin' buddies, so what do I know?"

It felt like the floor dropped. Or the whole world. And Kat was relieved to feel Nola's steady hand at the small of her back.

So that was all there was. That cold night when her mother shoved some cash into her hand and dismissed her own daughter like she was an annoying Jehovah's Witness—that was all there'd ever be for them. Nothing would ever be fixed. Nothing would ever be taken back. Nothing would ever heal.

Nola tried to direct Kat back toward the chair. "Maybe you should sit down for a minute."

Kat jerked away and took a step toward Riley. She looked up at him, furious. "When? How?"

"About a year ago. Cancer."

"We're not staying." Kat pushed her way toward the curtain. She had to squeeze by Riley to get out of the room, and her hand brushed the front of his upper thigh. She thought she'd die. Or collapse in a heap. But she would never—*never*—let either of those men see her cry.

Her mother was dead. She'd waited too long to come home.

Riley called after her, "Kat! Please wait!"

"Let her go," she heard her father say. "You know she had no business coming back in the first place."

FIVE

The night rain spat down from the sky, and the wind was cold. Kat scrunched into the neck of her jacket as she walked the cemetery rows, holding the flashlight as steady as she could, the beam landing on one headstone after the next.

She found the words she'd been searching for on a large, oddly shaped slab of stone, the letters appearing as shadows on white marble. *BettyAnn Cavanaugh, devoted wife and mother . . .*

As Kat bent at the waist to look closer, the rush of pain forced her eyes shut and her mouth open. She heard a piercingly loud scream, but it was only in her head. No sound came out of her mouth. It hurt too much for sound—there wasn't sound big enough for the sorrow and regret inside her. Her mother was gone. Her mother was pinned down in this dirt, under this bizarre, misshapen headstone, Virgil's artistic vision keeping his wife in her place through all of eternity.

Nola's hand moved along the length of Kat's spine in firm strokes. "I'm sorry, hon. So sorry—"

Kat's insides twisted. She shook her head.

"Let's get you out of the rain." Nola tried to make Kat straighten up. "Come on, Kat. Please. We can come back in the morning and leave her some flowers."

It took a moment, but Kat did stand up. She clicked off the flashlight they'd purchased at the Ace Hardware in Elkins, and shoved it in her jacket pocket. She looked up at the sky, gray clouds moving over an endless blackness. She wondered if that's what it felt like to be dead—just nothing. Black nothing everywhere . . .

Kat's mother pulled the screen door closed between them.

"I'm sorry, Katharine."

"Are you kicking me out because I'm pregnant or because I ruined his stupid sculpture of the governor's wife?"

Her mother's mouth turned down at the corners. "It was his biggest commission since his New York days."

Kat couldn't believe her ears. "Mom! He was screwing her out in his studio! Don't you even care?"

"I've never once questioned your father's behavior and now is not the time to start. It will be better if you go and let me handle him."

Kat clutched her stomach, shaky and speechless. Her mother was trying to get rid of her. Her father was a liar and a brute and didn't love his wife and kid. He never had. Seeing this so clearly made her feel like she had no footing, like she was dangling in space. Utterly alone. With a baby inside her.

"So where am I supposed to go, Mama?"

"We'll think of something." With unsteady hands, she opened the screen door a crack and shoved a wad of bills into Kat's palm, trying to cover up her fear with a thin smile. "Now, run on over to your

aunt Rita's. She knows you're coming. Call me in the morning after your dad's gone to his first class and we'll put our heads together, all right? Now get along."

Kat stared at the money in her hand, then looked up at her mother's gaunt face and hard eyes, knowing with certainty what she'd always suspected—that if BettyAnn Cavanaugh was ever forced to choose between her husband and her daughter, the choice would be an easy one.

"I'm so cold, Nola," Kat mumbled. "So cold all of a sudden."

Nola hooked her arm through Kat's and pulled until she began walking. "Of course you're cold. I'm cold. It's cold outside and now we're both soaking wet. Let's get out of here."

Kat sat motionless in the chair, her eyes staring unfocused into the fireplace. Nola brought her a glass of wine, placed it in her hands, then whisked away wads of used tissue that had accumulated on Kat's lap and around her feet.

"I'm sorry I'm such a mess," Kat said, afraid to look at her best friend for fear of bawling all over again.

"You're not a mess. You're just in shock."

Kat sniffed. "Thanks for going out there with me. I just needed to see for myself."

"I understand."

"Thanks for being here."

Nola was in the kitchenette, clanking around. "Hon, I'm not doing anything you haven't done for me a million times—every time I got dumped, or divorced, or hey, remember that time we found out Joey had been selling my Grandma Tuti's jewelry on eBay? I must have cried for two weeks straight." Nola returned to her chair by the fire. "To tell the truth, I'm kind of enjoying being the stable one for a change."

Kat managed a smile.

"You want me to stay in your room with you tonight? Now that would *really* give Madeline something to gossip about."

Kat laughed. After so many hours of crying, the sound of her own laughter surprised her.

"You're going to be OK, you know." Nola smiled kindly.

Kat nodded.

"You had two moms in your life and you've just lost both of them, and it's got to suck."

Kat nodded again, then grabbed another tissue.

"But you can't feel guilty, hon. How could you have known your mom was sick?"

Kat blew her nose and blinked at Nola. "I could have called."

Nola scrunched up her mouth. "True."

"Or written."

Nola nodded. "Well, OK."

"Or knocked on their damn door! But I was pissed off and resentful and I never wanted anything to do with my parents the rest of my life!"

"There's that," Nola said.

Kat reached for another tissue and laughed. "What a joke—I find out my mother is dead and all I want to do is talk to Phyllis, but she's dead, too!"

Nola scooted her chair closer. "I really miss her."

"That woman was amazing, you know?" Kat blew her nose. "She took me in—a complete nobody off the street. She didn't ask any questions. She gave me and my baby a home."

Nola nodded again.

"And I think she seemed all that more amazing to me because my actual mother couldn't wait to get rid of me!"

"Phyllis Turner had the best heart of anyone I ever ran across," Nola said.

"She really did." Kat raised her wineglass. "To Phyllis Turner—a woman who lived every day proud of who she was, nothing more and nothing less."

"To Phyllis," Nola said, clinking her glass to Kat's. "Whose investment instincts weren't too shabby, either."

They sat for a few minutes in the quiet. Nola put a hand over her mouth to hide her yawn and Kat checked her watch to find it was after eleven. It had been one hell of a long day, for everyone.

Kat stood up. "C'mon. Let's both get some sleep." She walked Nola over to the door. "Would you mind if we hit the road as early as possible tomorrow, before anything else bad can happen?"

Nola looked confused. "What about your aunt Rita, the evil high school principal? Weren't we going to drop in and give her a piece of your mind? Wasn't she on the list of people who owe you an apology?"

Kat chuckled. The list they'd come up with on the drive that morning seemed ridiculous now. "I don't have an extra piece of mind to spare at the moment. Maybe I'll write her a letter when we get home."

"Sounds good." Nola stretched. "Sleep tight, Kit-Kat."

"You, too. Hey! Wait a sec."

Nola turned back, yawning again.

"I won't keep you much longer, but look, I know this is probably going to sound dorky—"

"You've never had a dorky moment in your life, Kat, except maybe for those yellow plastic snow boots you had back in the early nineties."

"Thanks. So what I was wondering is—do you think anyone could know what love is at the age of sixteen?"

Nola moved her head back in surprise. "You're asking for *my* opinion on relationships?"

"Well, yeah."

"Hmm." She scrunched up her mouth. "I guess it depends on the person. I sure as hell didn't know love at sixteen—or at twenty-one or thirty or thirty-seven—so I'm maybe not the best example. This is about you and Dr. Bohunk, I'm assuming."

"Yeah."

"You think it was love?"

"Well, if it wasn't, it was as close as I ever got. Probably as close as I'll ever get."

Nola opened her arms and gave Kat a hug. As Nola pulled away, she focused her rich brown eyes on Kat's. "Hear what I'm about to say. Are you listening?"

Kat nodded.

"Don't you dare give up, Kat. If anybody deserves to be rich, beautiful, and in love, it's you, and you're already two-thirds of the way there."

"Thanks."

"And I know you came here for revenge and all, but leave your options open—you might walk away with something even better. See you in the morning."

Kat locked the door behind Nola and went into the bathroom to wash, exfoliate, tone, infuse, and moisturize her face with the obscenely expensive skin-care system she'd purchased from the spa several days ago. She remembered thinking to herself that nothing was too extravagant if it meant Riley would be rendered weak in the knees at the sight of her glowing beauty. Well, the way she was feeling right then, Riley Bohland could just shove her glowing beauty right up his tight ass.

How could he be so cold and unfeeling to her? Sure, he was angry about Aidan, but hadn't Riley missed her at all? Didn't he care what had happened to her all these years? Why didn't he throw his arms around her—if only out of curiosity?

Kat brushed her teeth, flossed, and turned out the bathroom light, trying to decide if what she felt inside her belly was a heaviness or an emptiness, or if there was such a thing as a heavy emptiness or an empty heaviness, and whether she should look into therapy now that she had the free time and disposable cash for it.

She threw on a cotton tank top and a pair of drawstring pajama pants, then went out into the sitting room to turn off the gas fireplace. OK, fine. Maybe this suite wouldn't be so bad for a honeymoon. It was cute and comfortable, and the bed sure was romantic. Kat guessed that if two people were really in love it wouldn't matter what the surroundings were. After all, an old blanket had once felt like a magic carpet to her and Riley.

Kat swiped what she was sure would be the last tear of the evening from her cheek and climbed up the bedside step stool, allowing her lonesome self to fall into the embrace of the gigantic four-poster monument to romance.

She'd just closed her eyes when she thought she heard a soft knock on her door. She held her breath and didn't move. There it was again. Kat climbed down the ladder and tiptoed into the sitting room. Someone was most definitely knocking at her door.

"Kat," a man's voice whispered. "It's Riley. Let me in."

"I know; I know!" Carrie switched the cell phone to her other ear and cringed with impatience. "I followed him here from Davis Memorial. I'm sitting a block away in my car and, frankly, I can hardly believe what I just witnessed. How could you let him in? How could you do that to me?"

Madeline's voice sounded hurt. "What was I supposed to do—leave him out there on the porch, banging on the door, disturbing everyone? I've got other paying guests here this weekend."

"Fine." Carrie nibbled on the last rice cake in the package, calculating that with rice cakes at thirty-five calories each, she could have just eaten a jumbo-sized Snickers bar and gotten some real satisfaction, then thrown it up. "Just make sure he doesn't stay long."

Madeline sighed. "Carrie, I can't just barge in on people. My guests are entitled to *some* privacy."

That made Carrie laugh. "Little late for the high road, don't you think, Maddie?"

"I'm just saying—"

"Get him out of there."

"How am I supposed to do that?"

"Oh, I don't know! Damn, damn, damn!" Carrie rooted around in her purse until she found the pill bottle, opened it, shook one out and stuck one on the back of her tongue, then swallowed. "Don't forget to leave the kitchen door open so I can use your bathroom tonight."

Madeline groaned.

Carrie snapped closed her cell phone. Right then, she saw a light go on behind the honeymoon suite window. She knew which window it was. She'd stayed in that room many times over the years, whenever the occasion rendered it tasteless to stay at the Bohland House. That's how she and Madeline met. Carrie had been a guest at Cherry Hill many times during the course of the diabetes study. She had been a guest there the day of Aidan Bohland's funeral. A year later, she stayed there for Matt's swearing-in ceremony as chief of police. And she'd been a guest the day of the clinic's groundbreaking, when she'd smiled for the local papers like it was the happiest day of her entire life! But it wasn't.

That illustrious day had been stolen from Carrie a year ago, when Riley was told he'd knocked up a high school skank named Kat Cavanaugh and he had a teenage kid roaming the country somewhere. It had taken Carrie twelve long months to get Riley's head screwed on straight, and nothing—no thing and no one—would stand between her and her happiness again.

Carrie relaxed her neck and shoulders and breathed deep, seeking her peaceful center. She closed her eyes to allow the positive energy to flow through her. She envisioned the bridal bouquet of red roses and holly. She pictured each miniature ice sculpture centerpiece adorned with mistletoe, glowing atop a contrasting red velvet tablecloth. She felt the snowy satin of her dress brush against her skin, the luxurious whisper of white chinchilla at the décolletage and wrists.

Her moment would come in seventy-four days. If it was the last thing she ever did, she would place one foot in front of the other and float her way toward the altar in the cutest little pair of kitten-heeled satin beaded slippers this earth had ever seen.

"That conniving ho!"

Carrie grabbed the phone again. First she paged the love of her life. Six times. No response. Then she called his cell. No answer. Then she called his answering service and demanded they page him with an emergency. She was informed that he'd already changed over for the night to the doctor in Bowden, who was covering for him.

"Do you want the doctor in Bowden?"

Carrie stared at the phone in horror, hanging up without a response because, no, she didn't want the fucking doctor in fucking Bowden. She wanted Dr. Riley-Fucking-Bohland. And she was going to get him.

Kat stood in the doorway wearing pajamas and an expression of bewilderment. Riley decided that without the fringed boots and the haute couture, Kat seemed smaller. Softer. And as lovely as every one of the thousand fantasies that had kept him company over the years.

"Why are you here, Riley?"

He tried not to stare and failed miserably. He stared at the way her hair swept back from the gentle angles of her face, the barely noticeable tremble in her plump lower lip, the delicate movement of the tendons in her neck. He stared at the sweet, small left hand that gripped the edge of the door, noting the lack of a wedding band. He stared at the rounded curve of her breast, the slope of her waist, the flare of her hip. He stared at the ten bare toes that looked so defenseless and pink against the dark hardwood floor.

He breathed deep, the essence of his youth rushing into his nostrils and straight to his brain, because Kat smelled the same. Even after all this time.

Riley shoved his hands in his pants pockets, which accomplished two things—she wouldn't see his hands shake, and it would keep him from doing the most stupid thing he could imagine: crushing her in his arms and never letting go.

"I'm sorry you had to learn about your mother the way you did. And I'm sorry about Virgil, too."

Kat nodded, crossing her ankles and folding her arms in a blatant display of full-body self-defense. "Yeah. Thanks. You know, I always thought a person had to have a heart before they could have a heart attack."

The force of Kat's bitterness caused Riley to tilt his head away. He stared into her familiar face, the delicate jaw now rigid and the honey-colored eyes hard. She might smell the same, but pretty Kat Cavanaugh had become as tough as rawhide.

He waited several moments for Kat to ask more questions about her mother. Kat didn't. She just scowled at him.

Riley blew out air through his mouth. "We need to talk."

Kat stiffened, but she opened the door and motioned for him to come in.

It felt strange to be with Kat in a room where Carrie had stayed so many times. He closed his eyes momentarily in disgust, aware that Carrie had been stun-paging him for the last half hour. He double-checked that his phone and pager were on silent, only to see her numbers flash on the screen for what had to be the fifth time in as many minutes.

"Busy night?" Kat gestured for him to take a seat in one of the chairs.

"No. I got someone to cover for me so I could spend time with you."

One of Kat's beautifully arched brows rose in a question. He could see her pulse pound under the translucent skin of her throat. "Something to drink?" she asked.

"Sure."

Kat took a couple steps toward the tiny kitchen, grabbing a cotton hoodie sweatshirt from the counter as she went. Riley nearly groaned with disappointment when she put it on and zipped it up all the way to her chin. Not very subtle. Now he couldn't look at her throat and her breasts and the flesh of her bare arms.

"Nola and I opened a bottle of red wine earlier. Will that work for you?"

The phenomenon started as a faint rumbling, somewhere deep in his chest. Then it rose to a roar, circling through his trunk and limbs shooting up to his brain. It was unlike anything he'd ever felt, and it was scary, yet exhilarating. Riley wondered if Matt would be able to hear the *snap!* from his place across town.

Riley jumped to his feet, hands flying as the words came rushing out. "It will not work for me! Nothing's fucking worked for me for twenty years! You took my child from me—he was my child as much as yours, Kat. How could you do that? How could you leave with my baby and never even let me know?"

Kat turned back to face him, her mouth open in disbelief. She laughed sharply. "You told me to get lost. Perhaps that had something to do with it."

Riley could not believe this. "Really? And maybe you never bothering to tell me I had a child was the lowest, most despicable thing a person could do to someone else, let alone someone they claimed they loved."

Kat's face flushed red and she stomped toward him. "Right. Fine. I made a serious error in judgment and I apologize. And how about you, Riley? You said you loved me, that we would be together forever; then you threw me away like I was a piece of garbage."

Rage, lust, and loss pummeled Riley's body. He raced from one emotion to the next so fast his brain couldn't keep up. He'd dreamed about this moment for a year—how he'd eventually find Kat and make her accountable for her selfishness. But now that the moment was here, nothing was clear. He had no idea what to say, let alone what he wanted. Because all he wanted was to hold her again, feel her soft weight against him from head to toe, disappear into the sweet, hot scent of her skin, and that would be a huge mistake. It wasn't even an option. He had to gain control of the situation, and himself.

He stepped closer. "I was a stupid kid and I was so in love with you that it scared the shit out of everybody—me, Big Daddy, my coaches, everyone who wanted to see me make something of myself."

A sickeningly sweet smile spread across Kat's face. "How nice for you all, then."

"You don't understand." He stepped closer, but Kat held up a hand to stop him.

"This isn't going to work," she said. "Virgil was absolutely right. I never should have come here. You need to leave now."

"Damn you, Kat!" Riley lunged at her and grabbed

her by the shoulders, locking his eyes on hers. She squirmed to get away from his grip, and though he'd never held a woman against her will before in his life, he felt he had no choice. "Stop it. Just stop it," he said, his heart nearly shattering as he saw the real fear in her eyes. How could she be afraid of him? He loosened his grip and spoke gently. "If you listen to nothing else I say tonight, you have to hear what I'm about to tell you."

He took her silence as his green light.

"That afternoon at the quarry when I broke up with you, I was just trying to get Big Daddy off my back for a little while. That's all it was! It was a stupid thing to do, and I was at your house that night, ready to beg you to take me back, and BettyAnn told me you'd run away for no reason!"

Kat's face went blank. Without warning, she shoved so hard against his chest that he had to step back to keep his balance. His hands fell away from her shoulders.

"She threw me out, Riley. Plenty of things happened that day, but me running away for no reason sure as hell wasn't one of them."

"What she did was wrong." He inched his way closer to Kat as he talked, his hands outstretched, palms up. "But you should have come to me. You should have told me. You could have lived with us and I would have taken care of you and the baby!"

Kat snorted, resting her hands on her lovely cotton-covered hips. "I did come to you, Riley! I tried to tell you I was pregnant! That's the reason I asked you to meet me out on the quarry road."

Riley's chin dropped toward his chest with the weight of that information. "God, Kat."

"And forgive me, but I'm having a real hard time

picturing me and my love child living happily ever after with Mayor Bohland and his boys."

She turned her back to Riley and walked into the kitchenette. He couldn't stop himself. He hated her for what she'd done, but she was so beautiful and he'd once loved her so much—and she was right in front of him in a pair of pajama pants—so he watched her ass move as she walked. She was still such a tight little package of—

"How the hell did you find out about Aidan?" Kat spun around in time to catch his eyes scanning her backside. "Still an ass man, Riley?"

He was still a Kat man; that's what he was. Holy God, this situation was going downhill as fast as his dick was rising.

"Let's sit down," he managed to croak out.

"I don't want to sit down." She frowned at him. "I'm going to pour us both a glass of wine and I'm going to stay on this side of the counter and you're going to stay on that side."

"You're still stubborn."

Kat nodded curtly as she poured the wine into two large goblets, obviously planning what she was about to say. She handed him his wineglass, then clinked hers against it. "Let's toast to my stubbornness, then. And my amazing luck. Because those were the only two things that kept your kid alive all this time, so I wouldn't knock it if I were you. Cheers."

Riley put down his glass without taking a sip. He hated that she was so glib, like she was the only one hurting here. But she was the only person on earth who could tell him what he needed to know, so he swallowed his own anger. "Tell me everything."

She shrugged, sipping her wine. "We're both going to do exactly that. And you're going to start by telling me how you found out about Aidan."

Riley leaned his elbows on the counter, looking up into Kat's golden eyes. He remembered how, in the sunshine, he used to try to count the tiny flecks of brown and green. He used to get lost in her eyes. He was afraid that he still could. "Your mother died of lung cancer last September, Kat. She'd been one of my patients for a while—in fact, she was one of the first to sign up when I got out of residency and began to practice here."

"I can't believe you came back to Persuasion."

"Well, I had no choice." He took a sip of wine. "Money was tight and I accepted a whole boatload of local scholarships to attend med school, with the promise of coming back here to set up shop."

"But you wanted out of here as much as I did."

"Yeah. I wanted out with you. Once you were gone, it didn't matter so much anymore."

Kat gave him a tentative but genuine smile. It was the first he'd seen since October 1987.

"I thought you were a construction worker, Riley. So when you walked into that exam room tonight, I thought I'd die."

Riley laughed. Did he dare allow himself to think she was warming up? "The construction project is the Persuasion Rural Health Clinic—my baby. State grants we'd counted on fell through a few months back, and the whole town has been pitching in to make sure the clinic gets up and running. I was hoping by some miracle to open by Christmas."

Kat nodded. "Good luck with all that. Now tell me about my mom."

Riley ran his fingers along the goblet's stem, choosing his words carefully. "She'd been sick for about six months. As she was dying she asked your dad to leave the room and told me to come close. She told me you'd had a boy and it was mine. She told me you were living in a small town in California, but she died before she could give me any more details."

"California?" Kat's wineglass hung in midair. "I've never been there in my life."

Riley shrugged. "That's what she said. I hired a private investigator out there, and when he came up empty-handed, Matt and I went out to look for you. We followed leads that took us to fifteen states, and I can tell you with authority that you are the country's best-looking Katharine Cavanaugh."

Kat set down her glass. Her mouth was pulled tight, but he could see her hands tremble. "I never saw or spoke to my mom after I left that night. I don't know where she got her information. It was wrong."

"She was right about the child, wrong about the location."

Kat's voice went soft. "Did she suffer?"

Riley nodded. "She was in pain, though we tried to make her as comfortable as we could at the end." He studied Kat's eyes, trying to figure out what feelings lurked behind there. There was certainly something going on. "Did you win your fortune as a card shark by any chance?"

Kat snorted in surprise. "Excuse me?"

"You've developed quite a poker face."

She raised her chin and walked past him to the chairs in front of the fireplace. She collapsed in one and pulled her feet up under her in silence.

Riley returned to his chair and propped his elbows on his knees. He stared at her profile. The same small nose and pouty mouth. The same graceful neck. She had grown into her looks. As a teenager, she had been cute. As a woman, she was flat-out beautiful. And cunning. "How the hell did you make it, Kat? You were only sixteen."

"Like I said. I was lucky."

"How so?"

She avoided looking in his eyes. "I hitchhiked out of town and ended up in Baltimore." As she talked she glanced around the room and down at her perfectly groomed fingernails. "A nice lady took me in, got me hooked up with prenatal care, and got me in a GED program."

"Is this woman a relative?"

"No—much nicer than any relative I ever had."

"Go on."

"So I worked part-time at a flower shop and took evening classes at the community college. She watched Aidan for me. I lived with her for seven years, until I was working full-time and had the money to rent my own place."

Riley felt his eyes bugging out of his head. "Your parents never tried to find you?"

"Never."

"You never contacted them?"

"No. And I used another name so they'd never be able to track me down."

Riley's mouth fell open. "Shit, Kat. You were serious."

Kat still didn't look at him. "I was."

Riley shook his head. "And what about me? Did you ever tell our son about me?"

When Kat's gaze finally connected with his, Riley saw something that went way beyond stubbornness. "I told him I didn't know who his father was."

Kat squared her shoulders, ready for a fight. "I did it to protect him."

A shout of surprise escaped from Riley's mouth; then he felt a deep stab of hurt. This woman had it so unbelievably wrong, for all this time! "For God's sake, what exactly were you protecting him from? His history? His family? Being *loved*?"

Her head snapped back like Riley had smacked her. "You told me to get lost. I did." She swallowed hard. "Is this your way of telling me you're going to sue me?"

Riley blinked in bewilderment. "Sue you for what?"

"Well." Kat looked down at her hands, then returned her gaze to his face. "At the construction site you mentioned that your lawyer would—"

Riley laughed, setting his wineglass on a nearby table. "Kat, sweetheart, the best lawyer in the world couldn't wrangle me any satisfaction out of this huge fucking mess."

"OK." Kat sat up straight, readying herself for whatever more he had to say.

"Because what I want is the twenty years you stole from me, all those years that my son was a baby, then a kid, then a young man. How's a lawyer going to get me that?"

Kat's eyes remained steely, but her chin began to quiver. "I did what I had to do, Riley. I'll be right back." She hopped up and ran into the adjoining bedroom, Riley catching a glimpse of that huge bed as he followed her movement. God, he wanted to throw Kat up on that high mattress and devour her until two decades' worth of emptiness had been filled up with passion. Love.

He still loved her. After all the damage she'd done to his life, he still loved her. It was as if seeing her again flipped a switch in his soul, adjusting the setting back to the way he was when he was sixteen, full of passion and dreams. It was hard to believe, but he'd just lost his temper! He was practically drooling on Kat, he wanted her so badly. He was thawing out. He was coming alive.

Then she was back, standing at his side. "This is the only photo I have with me. It's his high school graduation picture. You can keep it. I put his cell number on the back. I'll send you more."

Riley cradled the wallet-sized photo in his palm, almost afraid to look. The instant his eyes made contact with the image, it felt like the rest of the world peeled away in layers, leaving only the core of his soul—this teenager in a clearly uncomfortable suit and tie, with too-long black curls and intelligent blue eyes. If Riley didn't know better, he'd think he was looking at Matt, circa 1992.

"Oh God," Riley whispered. "That's really my boy."

"I didn't realize how much he looked like you until today." Kat's voice sounded far away as she settled back in her chair. "I have to tell you, I took one look at you at the construction site and—"

Riley's head dropped. He couldn't carry the weight of the grief anymore, and he cried. Kat's hand reached across the space between them and she stroked his knee.

"I am so sorry, Riley."

He looked up, not caring that she saw him this way. "You could have found a way to tell me." He let the tears fall down his face. "You underestimated the hell out of me, and you cheated me out of my own life, *our* life! Who's going to give me back the twenty years I could have had with *you*?"

Kat's eyes got wide.

"Fuck this." Riley stood up. This was no time for caution or reason—he'd spent twenty years hog-tied by caution and reason. Riley glanced once more at the face of his child, tucked the photo into his pants pocket, and did what had to be done.

He pulled her to her feet and held her by her upper arms. "Damn you, Kat." He pressed his mouth to hers. There was so much hunger in his attack that she yelped in surprise. But she gave in. Within seconds they were feeding at each other, clutching at each other, the tears flowing, moans of desperation filling the room.

Kat managed to move her mouth from under his long enough to gasp, "I hate you for throwing me away like you did!"

"I hate you for keeping the truth from me—for twenty fucking years, Kat! How could you *do* that?"

Their mouths went back to work. Kat's hands were all over the buttons of his shirt. She was unbuckling his belt and unzipping his chinos. He had his hands in her hair, then up under the hem of her sweatshirt and little tank top, and his hands were on her breasts. Riley groaned as soon as his palms covered her nipples. He remembered this. His heart and his body remembered this well.

"I used to love you so much," Kat whispered.

"I loved you, too."

"You were my whole life," she said.

"You were mine."

"I'm not sure I should be doing this."

"I *know* I shouldn't."

Riley picked her up and threw her over his shoulder in a fireman's carry. With one hand he grabbed his pants to keep them from puddling to the floor, then staggered through the double doors into the bedroom. He threw her on the bed, ripped off his clothes, and got a leg up on the bed frame so he could dive on top of her.

"I am so fucking angry with you," he said, tearing her pajama pants off her body.

"I hated you! I hate you still!" Kat reached for him, her nails digging into his biceps, her poker face gone. "I was so lonely! You were the only thing I had to hold on to! Do you have any idea how lost I was? I've been lost this whole time, right until right this second. Why didn't you run after me? *Why couldn't you find us?*"

Riley reached under her soft body and gathered her to him. He kissed her. He tried to take away the pain with that kiss, heal her, make everything OK if only for that instant.

Kat pulled her mouth away from his and whispered in his ear, "Please, Riley. Don't break my heart again. I'm afraid you're going to break my heart again."

"Never." He kissed her throat, collarbone, licked the swell of her breasts.

"We're making a mistake." She gasped from the pleasure of his tongue flicking on her nipple. "This will be too hard."

"The only thing that's hard is me." Riley raised up on his elbows and let his cock nudge between her legs. She looked into his face, unsure, vulnerable, and filled with desire.

"I need you inside me," she whispered. "I'm going to die if I can't feel you inside me."

That was all he needed to hear. With a single thrust he was in deep. Immediately, the heat of the pleasure began to burn away layers of pain and uncertainty, and he knew—this woman and her boy were his life. They'd always been. This woman was his destiny.

Riley insisted that the lights stay on. He didn't want one more precious second lost, one image obscured. They were together again—this time it wasn't some fantasy—and through sex and love they would suck the marrow out of their lives once more.

SIX

Kat lay curled on her left side, eyes open just enough to observe Riley move through the bedroom, bending and scooping up pieces of his clothing as he went—grabbing a sock here, snatching his boxers over there, unearthing his slacks from beneath the comforter that had been thrown onto the floor at some point in the night. Kat wished she could smile as she watched him. She wanted to be filled with a sense of warm well-being. She wanted to believe that everything would work itself out, that she hadn't just made the most ginormous mistake of her life.

Since all that was beyond her abilities, she opted to remain very still. She didn't want Riley to know she was awake, because he'd probably want to talk. He'd want to know how she felt and what their next step should be, questions she had no answers for. So she remained quiet and allowed herself the luxury of worry-free looking. As it turned out, watching Riley move around the room, naked and free, his fine, taut flesh on display, was nearly as pleasurable as touching him.

He'd always been put together elegantly. Tall and slim, long fingers and long legs. He moved with economical grace, never a wasted motion. She remembered watching him on the basketball court all those years ago. This body right here in this bedroom was the same body. Taller by a few inches. Leaner. But it was the body she remembered. And the oddest thought occurred to Kat—Riley Bohland would be the only man she would ever see naked at sixteen and then again at thirty-seven.

She didn't want to think of how many women had gotten a look at the goods in the years between.

"Where the hell is my other sock?"

Kat stifled a giggle. Riley's brow had creased in a frown as he mumbled to himself, dragged his fingers through his short black curls, and scanned the room in vain. She watched the muscles in his butt flex and relax with each movement, and her belly grew hot. She wanted him again. In any normal circumstance, she would be in a coma by now. But obviously, there was nothing normal about this morning. She'd come back to Persuasion. She'd found him. She'd told him about Aidan. They'd spent the last seven hours devouring each other in this monstrosity of a bed, like they'd been starving for each other.

"Oh, fuck it." Riley yanked on his blue pinstripe boxers and then his chinos. He zipped the fly but left the belt buckle dangling. He pulled a white undershirt over his head, whipped a tie around his neck, and shoved his arms into the dress shirt, leaving it unbuttoned at the front. He slipped his bare feet into his loafers and stared at the single sock for a moment in puzzlement, then shoved it in his pants pocket. Next, Kat watched him clip a pager, a cell phone, and a digital organizer onto his belt. Even with all the twenty-first-century nerd accessories, Riley Bohland was too damn sexy for West Virginia—or any other state, for that matter.

Kat couldn't help it. She let out a sigh. Immediately, she shifted in bed in the hopes that he'd think her sigh had come from the depths of sleep.

Riley stopped moving. After a moment, she felt him climb onto the bed and lower his face near hers. He put his lips to her ear and whispered, "I'm on call as of three minutes ago." He kissed her cheek gently, lingering to breathe her in. The gesture felt impossibly tender to Kat, and full of affection. She was just about to throw her arms around him when he said, "Gotta go. We'll talk later."

In a flash, he'd let himself out of the suite. Kat sat up in bed, staring absently into the sitting room, wondering if all of Riley's morning-afters were so abrupt. She yawned, reaching under her left thigh to find out what was pressed into her flesh, and her hand came up with the missing sock. She studied it dangling from her fingers, suddenly quite lonely.

Kat flopped back onto the pillow and stared at the ceiling. She might only have an associate's degree, but she'd definitely earned her Ph.D. in life in the last twenty years, and her research results were consistent—men would abuse you, use you, suck you dry, or sell your grandmother's jewelry on eBay, but they would never be all you needed them to be. Virgil Cavanaugh and Riley Bohland were her first—and most effective—teachers. And she'd learned her lessons well.

Yet here she was. Age thirty-seven. Alone in a strange bed and holding one sock.

"This is a disgrace. It's after seven in the morning and he's just now leaving? He didn't even bother to get completely dressed! My God, Maddie—you completely screwed up."

Carrie got no response from Madeline but heard the loud clack and bustle of the B and B kitchen in the background.

"Madeline? Are you there?"

"I'm in the middle of making a batch of cranberry-orange muffins. I'll have to get back to you."

Carrie huffed in disbelief. "Muffins? You're worried about stupid muffins? I am telling you that my man—my *fiancé,* Madeline—just spent the entire night in that woman's room, and you're fixated on a pan of muffins?"

After a moment of nothing but more kitchen noise, Madeline cleared her throat. "Please don't tell me you're still sitting out there. Did you sleep in your car? Because if you did, *that's* fixation."

"Does it matter? I'd camp out on the polar ice cap if Riley asked me to."

"Uh, Carrie?" The sound of dishes knocking around in the sink nearly drowned out Madeline's comments. "I hate to point this out, but Riley is not technically your fiancé anymore. He hasn't been for over a year. And he didn't ask you to pull an all-nighter in your Volvo. Besides, don't you have to be at work soon?"

Carrie could not believe what she'd just heard. After all she'd done for that woman! Apparently, Madeline Bowman had gotten a little taste of sweet success and had turned huffy on her. Carrie switched the cell phone to her other ear and smirked. "So how's it working out with Matt?"

"What do you mean?"

"What I mean is, are you enjoying dating the second hottest man in all of Randolph County? And have you forgotten who got your business where it is today?"

"Hold on a second."

Carrie heard rustling, a door closing, and then silence. Madeline began hissing a loud whisper. "God, Carrie! It's not my place to stop Riley from doing whatever he wants to do. He's a grown man and I'm just a B and B owner, not a prison guard!"

Carrie looked heavenward, summoning patience. She was beginning to regret ever booking this ungrateful cow's inn for the last year's rural health luncheon.

"And I know you encouraged Matt to ask me out after my divorce, but really, it's not like you introduced us—our mothers did that at the sandbox when we were toddlers!"

Carrie gazed out the windshield at the row of adorable little craftsman-style houses, all built before the depression, when the coal mine was in full swing. It was admirable the way the owners had meticulously restored the homes and fixed up the yards.

"Besides, Matt hasn't asked me out in months. He's moved on."

"That's too bad." Carrie had grown tired of this conversation. "Where are you right now, Madeline?"

"In the pantry. The couple staying in the Silver Birch minisuite is already in the dining room, waiting like hyenas for me to finish setting up for breakfast. I didn't want them to hear me."

"I see."

"Can we finish this conversation later?"

Carrie's mouth fell open at what she was seeing.

Her breath began to come fast and hard. Unbelievable! The teen sleaze queen herself had just bounced out of Cherry Hill's front doors, sporting a pair of black yoga pants, a very chic little jacket, and a post-coital grin. Oh, it was Kat Cavanaugh, all right. Carrie had seen pictures of the junior jezebel in Riley's old photo albums. She must have stumbled into money somewhere. Maybe she was a call girl. Carrie made a mental note to warn Riley that he was in the clutches of a professional.

"Carrie?"

"What?"

"I really have to go."

"Did I tell you that I'm setting up a regional health-care conference for the spring? I plan to present my study results at the new clinic's community center."

"Really?"

"Yes."

"That's nice, I guess. I'll talk to you after—"

"As always, you are failing to see the bigger picture, Maddie. The conference will go an entire week." As Carrie spoke into the cell phone, she watched Kat Cavanaugh turn the corner. She was pretty. She had a nice body and a quality haircut. Carrie hated her. She wanted her dead.

"A whole week?"

"Every room in your place will be booked every night." Carrie allowed her target to get a half a block up Main Street, then put the car in drive to follow her, making sure to pull to the curb every couple blocks to stay inconspicuous. "I have guest speakers coming in from all over the East Coast. You could get some valuable exposure."

Carrie checked her watch. She would have to call

Alice and let her know that she wouldn't be in until after lunch, and that they needed to look into the possibility of throwing together some kind of small conference around the time her study results were released.

"All right, Carrie." Madeline sounded defeated. "What do you want?"

"Just the tiniest little favor. It's so small, it's almost nothing, really."

Kat pulled her jacket across her chest, tucking her hands beneath her arms to stay warm. Though the sun was out, she'd forgotten how chilly early autumn mornings could be up in the mountains.

She walked at a steady pace, letting her eyes take in Persuasion's Main Street district, a place at once familiar and exotic. Most of Kat's life had taken place in only two geographic locations: this small Appalachian town and the working-class streets of Baltimore. Her only vacations had been the annual jaunts she took with Phyllis and Aidan to the boardwalk at Ocean City and the lone lost weekend spent with Nola back in 1991 in Virginia Beach, where Nola had met the man who would become her first and shortest-lived husband.

After a quickie wedding and an even quicker divorce, Nola made this request of Kat: "Promise me that no matter how ass-kickin' hot he may be, you will never again allow me to fall for a man with a beer can collection."

Kat hugged herself, taking in the changes of her hometown. It seemed that several of the old brick storefronts had been torn down, and most everything that remained had been spruced up. The old Rialto movie theater was still in business, advertising a teen slasher flick and a romantic comedy. The five-and-dime appeared to be going strong, though it now referred to itself as a dollar store. There were coffeehouses and bookstores where there used to be pharmacies and insurance offices, a yoga and Pilates studio where there'd once been a candy store, and a bustling copy and express-shipping business in the building that used to house Millhouse Fashions. That's where Kat stopped.

She stared into the plate-glass windows, remembering the day her mother brought her here. They'd come to buy the red wool dress coat with the black velvet Peter Pan collar that Kat would wear from third to fifth grades. She'd loved that coat, and it wasn't due to the style, because it was insanely old-fashioned. It was what it represented—one of the few days she'd ever spent alone in her mother's company, with her full attention. On that day, Kat felt treasured, for no other reason than she was her mother's daughter.

Kat closed her eyes to hold on to the memory. But it slipped away, immediately replaced by the dull ache of loss. Today was the first day she'd woken up knowing with certainty that she'd never see her mother again.

Kat glanced up at the sound of laughter. Three college girls were headed her way, all with long straight hair parted down the middle, heads held high, walking the walk of brazen confidence. Kat smiled at them. "Good morning," she said.

"Good morning!"

She looked over her shoulder to watch them head into the coffee shop. In Kat's opinion, the single redeeming feature of Persuasion had always been the campus of Mountain Laurel College, and it pleased her to see that the regular influx of young people had kept the blood pumping in this town for the twenty years she'd been away.

Kat continued on for a moment, then stopped in her tracks. In the display window of Wilson's Gallery of Fine Art, between a hand-woven shawl and a selection of pottery, was a style of sculpture she'd recognize anywhere. A small white card propped against the figure read: *Untitled No. 236, alpha gypsum and polymers, V. L. Cavanaugh, 2007.*

She leaned her forehead against the cold glass and stared. Had her mother died just before he did this? Or had he come back from visiting her in the hospital and headed right to his studio? Either way, Kat could see the pain in the sculpture of a man's hands reaching upward and bursting into flames. As always, she wondered who would buy such a thing and place it somewhere to be admired. A Satan worshipper? Some aging hippie who remembered her dad's place in the Andy Warhol days of the New York art scene?

Kat cupped a hand around her eyes and peered inside, seeing a dozen or more of her father's bizarre creations displayed at various intervals through the gallery. If nothing else, it seemed her father's career was still in full swing.

Kat shoved her hands into her pockets and continued on down the street. She glanced to the right, down College Avenue toward the classic limestone buildings of the campus. It struck her as funny how she'd once fought so hard against her parents' plans for her. They expected her to attend Mountain Laurel on a faculty scholarship, but she stubbornly fought to be allowed to go anywhere but the local college. She laughed to herself softly—she'd sure won that battle, and here she was twenty years later, staring at the quaint campus with longing.

As she strolled on, Kat watched each puff of her breath mix with the cold air. She had no clear idea where she was headed or what time it was but felt the need to keep walking. She no longer felt in a rush to leave town, not after that head-spinning reunion with Riley. She'd shoved a note under Nola's door before she left the B and B: *I went out to get some fresh air. Take all the time you need this morning. We have to talk!*

What they'd be discussing was a bit unclear to Kat at the moment, since she didn't know exactly what had happened last night. Riley seemed pleased enough when he left, but preoccupied, maybe even unsure. Well, of course he was! How else could he possibly feel? How else could *she* possibly feel? How else would two people feel after trying to make up for twenty years of anger, loneliness, and hurt in one night? Without words? Because there'd been very little talking going on, that was for sure. The night had been 90 percent desperate physical need and 10 percent dozing off. The whole surreal business had left her a jumble of sensations, raw and off-balance.

As Kat continued to walk, she took inventory of herself. Her spirit felt sore. Her heart was full enough to burst. And her body was a wreck—insides swollen and hot, lips puffy, right hip bruised from crashing into the nightstand at some point.

But it was her mind that had really taken a beating. It was careening all over the place. Unrealistic hope kept popping into her head, fantasies of herself and Riley—along with Aidan—piecing together some kind of family where there'd never been one. It was a seductive vision. And impossible. Kat knew there'd be nothing left after they'd hacked their way through twenty years of bitterness. Too much to forgive. Too much to risk.

Kat extracted her Dolce & Gabbana sunglasses from her jacket pocket and slipped them on to shield her eyes from the morning sun. She focused on the sound of her shoes tapping against the sidewalk, letting her arms swing free at her sides. It was Kat's policy to never put herself in a position where a man could hurt her. She'd had some good times with men, yes. But she never loved any of them, or allowed herself to believe they loved her. It was a policy that had worked for her.

Suddenly, Kat stopped, realizing where she'd walked. Her parents' house was just a few houses down, on Forest Drive, but she would not be going there. She didn't even turn her head to look. As if on autopilot, she continued walking, stopping only when she arrived in front of what had always been the unofficial heart of town. She stared at the hard-to-miss monstrosity of a house, its redbrick tower rising sharply into the sky, five thick columns along the front porch, the whole structure the same outrageous spectacle it had always been. As a kid she'd heard that the house was featured in most every American architecture textbook because of its unusual combination of design elements. Tourists would sometimes stop their cars across the street and stare, take pictures, or even sketch the house. All Kat knew was that for as long as she'd been alive it had been the Bohland House, her secret childhood refuge, home of Big Daddy Bohland and his boys. And at that moment she stood gawking at it, like a fool, not even sure why she was there or who lived there these days.

Aaaarrroooooogggghhh.

Kat jumped, suddenly aware she wasn't the only one wondering what her business was at the Bohland House: A rickety old dog made its way down the porch steps and brick walkway, harrumphing half-hearted warnings along the way. Kat smiled at the creature, knowing that this couldn't possibly be the same hound Riley had had back when they were kids, but it looked like it could be a descendant. What had they called that dog? Waylon? Willie? All Kat could remember was that Big Daddy always named his dogs after his favorite country singers.

The dog came to a stop at Kat's feet and sniffed, wagging its tail in what must have been the seal of approval to her visit. As Kat reached her hand down to pat the dog's head, a shiny, black SUV whipped into the drive. It took Kat all of one second to realize it was the same vehicle that had splashed mud all over her yesterday at the construction site.

It would look ridiculous if she turned and ran—like she was doing something wrong by being on a public street—but it couldn't be any more embarrassing than staying put. What if Riley was a passenger in that car? Would it seem she was stalking him? Kat gulped and waited for the driver's side door to open.

"Oh my God," she whispered. It was Aidan getting out of that car. But it wasn't Aidan. Kat blinked, trying to get her mind and eyes to cooperate. Of course it wasn't Aidan. So it had to be Riley's kid brother, Matt, who must be into his thirties by now.

Kat waved awkwardly. Matt stared at her, hands in pockets, like he didn't know whether to ignore her or say something. Kat's heart sank. She supposed that's all she was to any of the Bohlands—the girl who stole Riley's son.

Matt lowered his gaze and shook his head slowly. When he looked up, a tentative grin appeared on his face, much to Kat's relief. He walked toward her, the dog running up to greet him with a howl. In a moment, he was close enough that Kat could make out the image of a shield on his navy blue windbreaker, the words *Persuasion Police Department, Chief Bohland* in yellow print below.

Kat couldn't suppress her laugh. The hound dog chimed in so loudly that Kat had to shout over the wails. "So 'Mad Matt' Bohland grew up to be one of the good guys?"

He reached his hand toward hers and shook it firmly, still trying to hold back his smile. "Kat. You're back. And just for the record, I've always been one of the good guys."

"Really? In my mind you'll forever be a twelve-year-old pain in the ass."

He nodded, his grin expanding, then patted the dog's head. "Whisht, Loretta. Now, up!" Matt snapped his fingers and the dog made her way up the brick walkway and onto the porch, plopping down at the top of the steps. Matt turned his attention back to Kat. "So. You here to see Riley?"

"Uh . . ." Kat knew it was a simple question. She must seem like an idiot. But she was so nervous she could hardly speak. "Not really. I mean, unless he lives here. Does he live here? Anyway, I was just going for a walk."

Matt's eyebrow raised in question. "Kinda chilly this morning."

"It feels great. I needed to clear my head." Kat was struggling to sound as nonchalant as possible, but her heart was beating violently. She knew her cheeks had to be screaming red with embarrassment.

Matt stood in awkward silence for a moment. "Riley came to see you last night?"

The words sounded almost like an accusation, and though Matt's face remained friendly enough, it was now a guarded kind of friendly. It occurred to Kat that Matt was protecting his big brother—*from her.*

"He stopped by. We talked."

Matt said nothing.

"We talked a lot."

"Please accept my apology for the mud yesterday."

Kat laughed a little, relieved that Matt had changed the subject, even if he'd done it with no finesse whatsoever. "Thanks. It did kind of ruin the moment."

He winced. "I am really sorry for that, Kat. And I'm sorry about your dad, too." Matt shifted his weight, then gestured back toward the house. "Look, would you like to come in for a cup of coffee?"

"Oh! Well, no. But thanks. I've got to get back to the bed and breakfast. Nola's expecting me."

Matt's gaze suddenly shifted to behind Kat, and his whole demeanor changed. His face lit up with interest. His shoulders straightened. "Nola? That's her name?"

"Nola Maria D'Agostino. She's my best friend from back in Baltimore."

"You don't say?" His smile went full throttle.

"Boo!"

Kat jumped, spinning around to see Nola behind her, cheeks flushed from running in the cold. She jogged in place, rolling her eyes in a not-too-subtle attempt to get Kat to introduce her.

"Nola, this is Riley's younger brother, Matt. Matt, this is Nola."

Matt extended his hand. Nola stopped jogging and extended hers for a shake, but Matt lifted it to his lips, bowed, and placed a soft kiss on her skin instead. "Nola Maria D'Angelo," he crooned. "We finally meet."

Nola's eyes had gone huge. She was speechless.

Kat corrected Matt. "Actually, it's D'Agostino."

"D'Angelo's close enough," Nola said, smiling.

Matt's cell phone began to buzz and Kat decided to take this opportunity to cut the conversation short. "We should probably—"

"Wait." Matt checked the number and ignored the call. "So, how long you two pretty ladies in town for?"

Kat laughed, amused by Matt's direct approach and his West Virginia accent. There'd been a time in her life when she'd never noticed that people here had one, but now it sounded almost cartoonish to her. "Not sure. We'd planned to be on the road by now, but—"

"We've decided to stay," Nola chimed in, nodding with enthusiasm. "We love it here."

Kat frowned. "When did we decide that?"

"Right now," she said.

Matt's phone buzzed again, and before he could delay her escape once more, Kat said, "We really need to get back to the B and B. It was wonderful seeing you."

Kat turned to go, practically dragging Nola with her, and started to run. Kat was suddenly overflowing with a sense of loss. That man back there was *family*—Aidan's look-alike uncle, her son's father's brother, and a stranger. Hell, Aidan's own father was a stranger to him. They were all strangers to one another!

"Slow down, will ya?" Nola panted, pulling on Kat's jacket until she stopped. "I only jogged that one block because I wanted the Bohunk brother to think I was athletic. I gotta walk the rest of the way."

"Oh, jeesh."

"He's hot."

Kat looked at her sideways. "I am almost certain he has a beer can collection."

Madeline had been dreading this sound, but there it was. The heavy oak front door had just opened and closed, and in seconds Kat Cavanaugh and her rude friend Nola Something-or-Other would be coming in here for breakfast. And Madeline would have to smile at Kat like she wasn't getting ready to lie to her.

But truly, it wasn't such a big lie, was it? In fact, Madeline had figured out a way to get the message to Kat without uttering a single untruth. In any case, it wasn't like a little twisting of the facts would alter the course of the universe, right? Besides, if Kat truly wanted Riley Bohland—truly *deserved* him—then she would've found a way to show up a little sooner than she had. Twenty years? What did Kat expect? Did she really think that a man like Riley would pine away for his high school sweetheart for a lifetime, that he'd be single and available after twenty years of neglect? Puh-leeze!

"Hey, Madeline."

"Good morning, Kat," she said cheerfully. To Nola she said, "Hello again."

Kat and Nola were flushed as they swept into the dining room, bringing in a whiff of cold air with them. Madeline retrieved the coffeepot, rolling her eyes as she did so. Kat and Nola were runners? Of course they were. How else could Kat have kept that figure all these years? God—she was such a mouse back in school, totally unaware of how cute she could have been if she'd made the effort. Well, she was clearly making the effort now, and spending serious money doing it. What was it they used to say—*gag me with a spoon*?

Madeline spun around, cheerful once again. "I heard your father is doing well. You must be so relieved!" She set two cups and saucers on the white lace tablecloth, then continued. "The cleaner brought your clothes back last night as a personal favor to me, and I've already placed them in your room so you can pack up." She gestured toward the sideboard behind her. "The eggs, sausage, and hotcakes are in the chafing dishes here, and on the table near the window you'll find a selection of homemade muffins, homemade low-fat granola, fruit salad, yogurt, and a variety of cereals, milk, and juices."

Madeline wasn't such a yokel that she didn't catch the way Nola's dark eyes had flashed when she'd mentioned taking the cleaning to Kat's room. She also didn't miss the way Nola inclined her head as if to say, *Get a load of this hick,* as Madeline took the time to courteously explain the breakfast options. And she didn't appreciate it. Not at all. In fact, she didn't much care for Kat's friend Nola. She seemed a little rough around the edges. She laughed too loud, and she had the annoying habit of calling everyone "hon."

"Thanks for the rundown, hon," Nola said.

"It all looks great," Kat added, smiling.

At that moment, the retired couple staying in the

Silver Birch minisuite decided to end their feeding frenzy, and Madeline thanked them profusely.

She busied herself tidying up but couldn't help but overhear part of the conversation between Kat and Nola, though they were whispering as quietly as their excitement would allow. She heard Kat say something about that old hen Rita Cavanaugh, the perennial principal of Underwood High School. Then, when Kat whispered something about Riley throwing her on the bed, Nola released a series of whispered exclamations that Madeline didn't quite catch, which really hacked her off, because the conversation was obviously getting good. After a few more minutes of mostly unsuccessful eavesdropping, Madeline decided she'd just get the entire mess over with.

"Excuse me, but do you have a minute?"

The women stopped their conversation and Kat nodded politely. "Of course."

Madeline set down the stack of dishes, pulled a chair from a nearby table, and joined them. "I couldn't help but hear you mention your aunt. She's still at the high school, believe it or not. She's got to be close to seventy years old at this point."

Kat shifted uncomfortably in her chair. "Thanks for letting me know."

"Of course." Madeline folded her hands in her lap, summoning the courage to do what had to be done. "Kat, I really don't know how to say this, since it's technically none of my business, and a rather delicate matter . . ."

She could swear that Nola did that thing with her eyes again.

Kat frowned. "What's up?"

"Well, I suppose I should just tell you and not beat around the bush. I mean, no matter how I say this, it's going to be uncomfortable."

"It's already plenty uncomfortable," Nola said.

Madeline managed a smile. "It's about Riley."

Kat's spine straightened, and Madeline could immediately see the fear in her eyes. Briefly, Madeline considered that what she was doing was wrong. Maybe Kat had real feelings for Riley. Maybe there were details of this story she wasn't privy to. Matt had never wanted to talk about any of it, after all, saying that Kat had run off and broken his brother's heart, and it was all ancient history. But Kat was sitting there looking like she was going to faint, and Madeline hadn't even gotten to the good part.

"Did something happen to him? Just tell me. Is he all right?"

Madeline was startled. The poor woman looked spooked. "Oh no! He's fine as far as I know. I just thought that you might benefit from a little background information."

Kat's frown intensified. Madeline watched her take a breath and a small sip of her coffee before she looked back at her. "I'm not all that interested in old gossip, Madeline."

"I see," she snapped. "Well then, I'll just forget the whole thing." Madeline started to stand up, but Nola's hand smacked down on her forearm.

"I'm interested in anything you got, hon," Nola said. "Lay it on us."

Now it was Kat's turn to flash her eyes at Nola.

Madeline cleared her throat. "Well. I'll start by asking you something, and it's only because I don't want to see you hurt."

Kat nodded. "OK."

"Did Riley mention to you that he was engaged to be married?"

Both women stopped breathing. Madeline waited for several seconds before it became clear that no one was going to answer.

"A Christmas Eve ceremony is planned. It's very hush-hush right now, but I can tell you that there is a woman who fully expects to be Mrs. Riley Bohland in less than three months. I just thought you should know. I didn't want you to get your hopes up."

Kat stood abruptly, her chair making a spine-tingling scrape against the wood floor. She ran out of the room and down the hallway, the sound of her thumping up the steps echoing through the downstairs.

Nola briefly glared at Madeline, then got up without a word.

A half hour later Nola and Kat checked out. Kat's hair was still wet and her hands trembled as she signed the bill. Madeline pulled aside the curtain in the front bay window in time to see Nola flatten the sedum blossoms in her haste to back out of the parking lot.

Madeline sighed deeply and shut her eyes for a moment. She reassured herself—yet again—that not a single thing she'd told Kat Cavanaugh was a lie. Not technically, anyway. And she could be proud of that.

SEVEN

Virgil was tired of lying around on his back like a dead fish. The hospital room smelled like day-old cabbage, and none of the nurses were attractive enough to serve as a distraction. He wanted to rip the damn tubes out of his veins, get the hell out of there, and get to his studio. For the first time in years, his hands were itching to do real work, substantial work. Funny how the rest of his body had chosen this particular time to break down.

He tried to get comfortable by turning on his left side, which didn't work because the hospital bed was as snug as a slab of marble. He tried to remember the last time he'd spent the night anywhere other than his own bed. It wasn't when BettyAnn was sick. That he knew. Even at the end, when everyone knew she was dying, he'd get in the car and go home at night. That meant it had to have been all the way back in his New York days, when it wasn't uncommon for him to spend his evenings in an acid-induced fog looking for trouble and women, which, now that he thought about it, was redundant.

Virgil grunted, pulling at an IV line that he'd somehow managed to twist around his butt. Life was strange. One bad acid trip and he ended up taking a temporary teaching post at a no-name college in Appalachia. He only wanted to lie low until the police stopped nosing around. It wasn't his fault that that girl had decided she could fly and chose his fourth-story window as her launching pad.

Virgil coughed. His chest was sore.

As fate would have it, he met BettyAnn his first week in Persuasion—a pretty, soft-spoken girl with a big problem and not a lick of sense. It didn't take him long to see that just paying attention to her made her follow him around like a puppy. She'd worshipped him. And why not? He was a sophisticated visiting art instructor, older than her and famous by Persuasion's standards—one of his sculptures had been featured in *Life* magazine! BettyAnn was so grateful he'd married her that she did everything he told her to. She was a good girl. Sure, they'd had their rough patches, but it had been a marriage that worked—she got what she needed and he got what he wanted, which was something most people couldn't say about their blessed unions.

Virgil was just about to buzz for the nurse when the esteemed Dr. Bohland strolled through the doorway. Virgil studied him, noting how much he'd aged in the year since he'd cared for BettyAnn.

"Good morning, Virgil."

"Nothin' good about it."

As his doctor flipped through his chart, Virgil decided that Riley Bohland had grown into a refined version of his daddy, with more smarts and less brawn. It was the younger Bohland kid who'd turned out to be a carbon copy of Aidan—a charming good ole boy who thought his last name gave him the right to tell people what to do with their lives.

"Has the cardiologist seen you?"

"Of course not. I was simply thrown in here and left to rot. You people just want me for my insurance money."

Riley clipped the chart back to the foot of the bed and sighed. "Maybe we just enjoy the pleasure of your company."

Virgil narrowed his eyes. Riley had a silly grin on his face. It had something to do with Kat; he could smell it. He sometimes wondered what would have happened with Kat and Riley if she hadn't run away. Probably nothing good.

"Did you know Kat was coming to town?"

Riley flinched ever so slightly at the question, then put the stethoscope in his ears and leaned close to Virgil. "Nope. Please hold still for a moment."

It felt like an eternity, but Virgil did what he was told, waiting patiently as Riley pressed the cold metal disc onto his skin and asked him to take a deep breath.

"Anything?" Virgil asked.

"I'm definitely hearing some irregularities. Dr. Zhou will be in to see you shortly, and you'll be in excellent hands."

Virgil grunted. "He sounds like another damn foreigner."

"She's originally from China."

"A woman *and* a foreigner? Jesus! I've hit the jackpot."

"She trained at WVU, same as me."

"Peking, Persuasion—it's all the same nowadays, anyway, right?" Virgil tried to adjust the pillows behind his back so he could sit more comfortably. "This hospital looks like it's run by the UN. My nurse is from the Philippines. You must be the last American doctor in this state."

Riley smiled slightly at that. "Not hardly. I'll be back to see you this evening."

"Hold on a damn minute."

Riley turned, not bothering to hide the fact that this conversation apparently required every bit of patience he possessed.

"I never liked your family much, Bohland."

Riley shoved his hands in the pockets in his chinos and said nothing.

"But you were a good doctor to BettyAnn and I want to thank you for that."

Riley looked shocked. "You're welcome."

"She always said good things about you. She liked you for some reason."

"I'm glad."

"Now, I never got around to asking you this, but what was it my wife said before she died, when she shooed me out of the room that day? Was it a medical question?"

Riley frowned. "I'm afraid I can't say, Virgil."

His face went hot with anger. "Why the hell not? There were no secrets between us. I'm sure she'd want me to know."

Riley shifted uncomfortably. "She asked that I not share it with you."

He shot up in bed so fast that an electrode popped off his neck. "Liar!" His vision began to swim. "My wife never kept anything from me! Never!"

"Calm down, Virgil."

A wall of pain slammed into his chest. His lungs caught fire. "It's happening again," he gasped. "Get the Chinese woman. Quick."

It happened on a Saturday morning when Kat was thirteen, in mid-May. The big lilac bush outside her bedroom window had blossomed. Lush, fluffy purple cones and dark green leaves blocked her view of the side yard and the broken split-rail fence that separated their property from Mrs. Estes'. Because it was warm enough to sleep with the window open, Kat had woken up that particular morning with her senses filled with the deep, sugary sweetness of lilacs—and the familiar sound of her mother being beaten.

Kat pulled the covers over her head and shook. Would this be a short one, or a long one? Should she shut her window so Mrs. Estes didn't hear? Exactly where in the house were they fighting? The hallway? Would she be able to run out the back door without them noticing? Would there be drops of blood on the wood floor? She hated cleaning up blood. She closed her eyes, clasped her hands together so hard it hurt, then bowed her head under her blankets. *Please, God, no blood today. That's all I ask.*

She knew what would come next. On Monday, Kat's mom would have to tell the school that Kat had the flu, so she could stay home for a few days to put ice and Band-Aids on her mom's face and make sure she had aspirin. Kat hated that.

And she hated that she'd have to make meals because her mother would be too weak. Those dinners were always terrible, and not just because Kat wasn't the world's best cook. They were terrible because she would have to take a tray to her mother, who would eat propped up in bed, and then Kat and her father would sit there at the kitchen table, alone, long minutes of silence pierced with his usual warning: *Stop worrying about your mother or I'll really give you something to worry about.*

She hated that he'd come home with flowers for her mom, like that was supposed to make everything all right, and her mom would tell Kat to fetch a vase and put them in water so she could *ooh* and *aah* over them from her sickbed, like the flowers weren't edged with brown and her eyes weren't rimmed in black-and-blue.

Kat hated that her dad would act all cheerful and announce that they were going to the Rialto for father-daughter movie night, where they'd catch the latest Arnold Schwarzenegger flick.

She hated that her mother refused to go to the doctor every time she got beat.

But more than anything, Kat hated that the single most important rule in her family was that none of this ever happened.

On that particular morning, Kat thought maybe she'd had enough of secrets. She got up out of bed, pulled on a pair of light blue seersucker shorts, a pale green T-shirt, and sneakers. She ran a comb through her hair and pulled it back in a ponytail. She decided to put off going to the bathroom, because she didn't want to risk opening her door. Kat pulled her nightstand to the windowsill, pushed the window open as wide as it would go, took out the screen, and climbed through, feet first. There was no way out but through the lilacs, so she jumped into the bush, breaking more than a few branches in the process. She rolled out into the grass, scraped, bleeding on the inside of her thigh, and covered in a sheen of tiny four-petaled purple buds. But she was out of there.

She ran down Forest Drive to Main Street, the soles of her shoes slapping at the concrete, purple specks flying off her like confetti. Based on the fact that the Gerhards hadn't picked up their morning paper, she guessed it was about six-thirty. Riley would still be home, because baseball practice didn't start until nine.

She raced by the Missonis', the Ballingers', and the McClintocks', then took the usual shortcut through the Wilmers' backyard, jumped the chain-link fence, and landed in the row of cedars that fringed the south end of lawn of the Bohland House. Like always, she ran across the lawn to the side of the house, then hopped up onto the large central air-conditioning unit so she could reach the porch railing. She walked along the railing until she could get a foothold on the wide ledge of the dining room bay window, then pulled herself up onto the tile roof. Once she got a handhold on the window frame of the turret, she inched along until she got to the carport, remembering to avoid the three loose tiles on her way to Riley's window.

She didn't bother knocking on the glass because she didn't want to wake up Big Daddy or Matt. She pushed up the heavy old sash and threw her legs over the ledge, landing with a thud on Riley's floor. His room was a disaster, like always, and it smelled like sweaty socks. She took off her shoes and crawled under the covers with Riley, spooning against his back, his solid heat spreading through her like a blanket for her insides. She sighed. He woke up.

"What the—?" Riley flipped over so fast he nearly tossed her out of the bed. "Kat? Holy shit! Big Daddy's gonna skin me alive!"

"Sssshhhh." Kat put her arms around Riley's waist and pulled him close. She felt her body begin to tremble.

"Oh no, Scout. Is he doing it again?"

She nodded, keeping her face buried in his neck. Riley was the only person who ever used that nickname, and it sounded so comforting and safe that she wanted to cry. She took a deep breath of him—he smelled earthy and sweet, and she could detect the lingering traces of bath soap and deodorant. He had probably taken a shower just before bed.

"I'm calling the police this time."

"He'll take it out on me."

"I'm telling Big Daddy, then. Maybe he can talk some sense into him. One day he's going to kill her."

"Please just hold me."

Riley did. He brought his arms around her back and hugged her as tight as she could stand. After a few moments, he raised his hand to the back of her head, and slipped her hair from the ponytail holder. Kat snuggled closer, feeling her ribs against his. She felt her small breasts being squashed between them. She threw her top leg over his and held on, like they were falling through the sky and he was the only one with a working parachute.

When she couldn't hold it in anymore, she cried.

Riley let her, stroking her hair and whispering to her that everything would be all right.

"Who do you love?" he asked.

"Riley James Bohland, forever and ever," she said between sobs.

"Who do I love?"

"Katharine Ann Cavanaugh, forever and ever."

"That's right. And when we get married, we're going to live so far away that Virgil will be nothing but a bad memory. What kind of car do you want?"

"A Jeep with the top down."

"And what's the first house we're going to buy together?"

"The ski cabin in Colorado."

"Then?"

"The beach house in California."

"Next?"

"Our penthouse in New York."

"Are you doing OK?"

Kat nodded, her tears slowing. "I'm always OK when I'm with you."

"Good. How many kids will we have?"

"Two."

"One girl and one boy?"

"Yes."

"Which will be first?"

"The girl."

"No, the boy."

Kat giggled a little.

"And what will we do for the rest of our lives?"

"Be happy."

"That's right." Riley kissed the top of her head. "Hey, you got little purple things all over you."

Kat pulled her face from its hiding place in the crook of his neck and looked up into his blue eyes, so deep they almost looked black. "I fell into a lilac bush."

"How'd that happen?"

She felt kind of silly, but she told him the truth. "I jumped out of my bedroom window."

"You're all wet."

Kat sniffled and wiped her eyes. "Sorry. All my crying must have gotten your shirt wet."

"No. I mean down here on your legs. You're wet."

"I think I got scraped up and I'm bleeding."

Riley tossed back the covers and pulled away so he could look at her. "Oh my God!" he whispered.

Kat stared down at the front of Riley's body and gasped. Something shifted inside her core. The awareness was so deep and intense it was almost uncomfortable. She'd heard about how this could happen to boys, that sometimes guys woke up with hard-ons because they'd had sex dreams. But she didn't know they got *that* hard!

She continued to gawk. A rush of heat moved through her, the likes of which she'd never experienced. Her mouth went dry. Her nipples tingled. All she wanted was to press up against that hardness. Her body insisted she do it.

"Shit, Kat. There's blood all over you."

"I told you I got scraped up."

"No. I'm mean it's smeared all over the inside of your legs."

"What?"

Kat looked down at herself and froze in embarrassment. This could not be happening. Blood had soaked through the crotch of her seersucker shorts and spread out into the fabric. A thin, sticky smear of red covered the inside of both of her thighs.

"I think you started your period."

Kat recoiled, pushing herself away from Riley as she groaned out in horror. What girl would want the boy she loved to see that? What had she ever done to deserve such a terrible fate? She leaped up from the bed, and Riley followed her.

Kat was heading toward the window when he jumped in front of her, blocking her exit. Kat couldn't stop herself—she looked to see if he was still hard. He was. Harder, even. She tried to swallow, but it was like she couldn't remember how.

"You started your period. So what? It's no big deal."

She put her face in her hands and wanted to stay hidden there forever, but Riley peeled her fingers away.

"No biggie, Scout. Seriously."

"No *biggie*? I want to die, I'm so embarrassed! I just came over here because I had to be with you and there is nobody else I could tell and I didn't even check and—"

"It's your first one, right? Here. Let me clean you up." Riley grabbed a towel that was draped over a chair and squatted in front of her. Gingerly he used the towel to dab at her thighs, frowning in concentration as he worked.

Kat looked down at his curly dark head, realizing there was something wonderful and scary about what Riley was doing. He was more comfortable with her body functions than she was. Taking care of her came naturally to him. The fact that someone loved her that much stunned her, and hot tears began to roll down her face.

"OK." Riley stood up, throwing the towel on the floor, avoiding her eyes. "Maybe there's still some of my mom's stuff around here. I can go check."

"Riley?" she whispered.

He turned back toward her. He swallowed hard. "God, Kat."

There was a need in Riley's eyes that she'd never seen before. The space between them suddenly felt charged, alive. Riley had been everything to her through all the thirteen years of her life—playground enemy, teasing dweeb, friend, brother, lab partner, protector, confidant, and boyfriend. By fourth grade it was understood that they were destined to be together always. There had never been any question. But in an instant, all that had changed. Suddenly, this wasn't a game anymore. It was dead serious.

Riley leaned down and kissed her. He'd been kissing her since the sixth-grade carnival, so she was familiar with all his different kinds of kisses—the soft ones, the ones where he tried to put some of his tongue in her mouth, the ones where he made little noises. This kiss was different from all the others. His lips met hers with such purpose that she felt nailed to the floor. His mouth moved on her like he wanted to gobble her up. Her mind was jumbled with images and thoughts—the shame of the blood on her thighs, the shock of his lips, the heat she felt deep inside her body, the outline of Riley's . . . well, his *penis*, all big and hard and looking like it was ready to bust through his red nylon shorts.

The kiss continued. Riley's hands found their way to her bottom, and though they'd never been there before, it felt perfectly natural to have his hands clamped tight, one on each cheek. Oh, she tried! She really did! But Kat couldn't stop herself. As the kiss intensified, she put her shaking hands down inside the elastic waistband of Riley's shorts, encountering prickly hair and the strangest flesh. It was like velvet and metal at the same time. She wrapped her fingers around its fullness, stroked it once, and noticed that it jumped all by itself. She then pulled it completely free of the fabric and cupped it in her palm, stopping the kiss so she could look down at the amazing thing in her hand.

Without warning, Riley's body shook and a stream of white stuff came shooting out of his penis, landing belly level on her T-shirt.

That's the exact moment Big Daddy knocked on the door and entered without waiting for a response. Kat and Riley jumped apart and stood at attention like they were facing a firing squad, which was exactly the case. Kat's mind began to race through everything that Big Daddy must have seen in front of him—his son shoving his private parts back down in his shorts, a girl standing next to a bloody towel, and, worst of all, the evidence of what they'd been up to all over the front of the girl's shirt.

Big Daddy's form seemed to take up every inch of the doorway. He leaned against the frame and crossed his arms over his chest.

Riley took a step forward, partially blocking Kat. "Daddy, it's not what you think."

"Son, I'm a fifty-two-year-old man. I ain't fallin' for the okey-doke here. I know what I see and I know what it is."

Big Daddy's gaze fell on Kat. She wished she were dead as the mayor of Persuasion quickly surveyed her state, then sucked on his teeth. He cleared his voice, and it came out in its usual gruff way, but tinged with sweetness. "Scoot on in the washroom and fix yourself up, Kat."

"Yes, sir." She scooted—gladly—and closed the bathroom door behind her with relief. She could hear the conversation just fine from behind the closed door.

"Daddy, you don't understand—"

"Sure I do."

Kat pressed her ear up against the thick wood. Her knees were knocking, she was so scared. What would Big Daddy do? If he told her parents that she was here, her life would be over. Just the thought of her father knowing anything about this made her dizzy. She always knew that if he ever got the right excuse, her father's fists would find her face just as easily as they found her mother's. This would be all it took.

Kat heard the creak of the floorboards as Big Daddy moved all the way into Riley's room.

"Are you out of your mind, Son?"

"She needed somebody to talk to, Daddy."

"Didn't know talkin' could get so messy."

"I didn't touch her."

"You expect me to believe she just up and started bleeding like that?"

"That's exactly what happened, sir. She started her period."

"What the—?"

Kat could feel the laser beam of Big Daddy's stare cutting a hole right through the bathroom door. She took a step back.

"Virgil's been puttin' a beating on BettyAnn this morning. Kat was scared and she ran over here."

There was an instant of silence; then Big Daddy moved again. "He's doin' *what*?"

"Hitting her. Beating her up. He gets drunk out in his studio, stays there all night fussin' over his stupid sculptures, then comes in and beats the shit out of BettyAnn—like everything's her fault."

Another silent pause. Kat had to put her ear back against the door to hear Big Daddy clearly. "Do you mean to tell me that you've known about this and never came to me?"

Riley's response was just as faint. "Kat begged me not to say anything to anybody, because she thinks she's gonna be next if she tells."

Big Daddy blew air out of his nose and groaned. "Boy, she's damn right she's gonna be next, but only if something's not done to stop him. You better listen and listen good—if you ever hear about anything like this again in the future, you tell me. You understand?"

"Yes, sir."

"I will never be angry if you come to me with the

truth—about anything, no matter how bad it is, and that's a promise. Now, answer me, Son. Did you, or did you not, take that girl's virginity?"

"No!"

"All right, then." Big Daddy shifted his weight and the floor crackled beneath him. "But something happened. I'm not blind."

Kat couldn't hear Riley's answer, but the words had the rhythm of a confession.

Big Daddy's response was angry: "No son of mine is gonna ruin his life by getting a girl pregnant before he's even out of junior high school. It happens, but it's not going to happen to a Bohland. Do you understand?"

"Yes, sir."

"Now go get some of them female pads out of the hallway storage closet and take them to Kat. I'm gonna have myself a nice little man-to-man with Virgil Cavanaugh."

In the two days she'd been back from Persuasion, memories like that one had come hard at Kat, full of detail and out of nowhere. In fact, she was remembering events and conversations she hadn't thought of a single time since the night she'd hopped in Cliff Turner's truck and ended up right here, in Phyllis' Baltimore row house. It was as if Kat's disastrous visit had opened a can of past and pain, and now she couldn't get the lid back on.

The knock at the door forced Kat to remember why she was there. After months of procrastinating, she'd finally called a real estate agent to look at Phyllis' place, and she'd arrived right on time. It didn't take Kat long to show her around—there wasn't a lot to see—and she waited to hear her opinion.

"If you're willing to spend about forty thousand for upgrades, you'll earn six times that at sale, no problem. Just replace the kitchen cabinets and countertops. Install new appliances. Floors. Update the bath. Rip out the old carpet. Paint. Update the wiring and plumbing. The furnace."

Kat nodded, looking past Julianna Dubrowski and her file folder to study Phyllis' kitchen, trying to view the room with an objective eye. No luck. All Kat saw was scenes from her life—baking that chocolate cake from scratch for Aidan's first birthday, the night the pipes under the sink burst and flooded the whole first floor, and the rip-roaring fight she'd had with Phyllis the day Kat told her she'd decided not to apply to a four-year college but to work full-time and move into her own place instead.

No potential buyer would be as sentimental. They'd only see the faded yellow walls, peeling mint-green linoleum, and metallic red countertops from the era of beehive hairdos. It dawned on Kat that the term "upgrade" didn't do justice to the amount of work the real estate agent had just suggested.

"Sounds like we'd have to gut the place."

"Basically, yes."

Kat laughed. "You realize she didn't spend that much to buy the entire house back in 1973?"

Julianna smiled with glee. "Oh, I know! That's the beauty of these vintage Highlandtown row houses, especially the ones across from the park—she could get close to a quarter of a million for it!"

Kat made an effort to return the smile but didn't have the energy. "She won't get any of it, Julianna. She's dead."

The agent's eyes went wide with embarrassment.

"Of course! Sorry. I knew Phyllis Turner. Well, I knew *of* her, anyway. Everyone in the neighborhood did, and everyone was shocked to hear that she passed." Julianna hugged her folder to her chest. "My mother played bingo with Phyllis at Sacred Heart, you know. She said she was unbelievable—could handle two dozen cards at a time. And the birds. We all knew about the birds."

"She had quite a few."

"And frankly, just between you and me," Julianna leaned close and lowered her voice like she was worried the linoleum might overhear her comment, "my gut feeling was the house would be even more of a mess than it is. I'm a little surprised there's no . . . you know . . . pet odor."

Kat nodded, wishing Phyllis herself were here to respond to this. She could just imagine it—Phyllis in her housecoat with a Newport Light dangling from her lips. *Move your vulture butt on out of my house,* she'd say. *The only gut you should be focused on is the one that hangs over your mother's stretch pants.*

"And the idea of Phyllis Turner being a multimillionaire! It's completely insane! You can't make up this sort of stuff! Exactly how much was she worth when she died?"

Kat felt like bonking Julianna in the head with her folder for being so insensitive. "She was worth quite a bit. Excuse me a second."

Kat moved into the tiny dining area and stared out the sliding glass door. She missed Phyllis like hell. Kat missed her cackle of a laugh and her firsthand reports on the Baltimore City Council meetings, which she attended in person every Monday night and analyzed with zeal. Kat missed how

Phyllis would offer advice to anyone within shouting range on relationships, career, parenting, and managing the Baltimore Orioles—all subjects she'd had precious little personal experience with in her own life.

Around Highlandtown, Phyllis was known for her eccentricities and that's all, because that's where Phyllis wanted it to end. She didn't see the need for anyone knowing too much about her affairs, and the fact that the kids called her the Crazy Parakeet Lady just made her laugh. Only Kat and Cliff knew the whole story, and that's the way Phyllis liked it.

Julianna hadn't finished with the subject at hand, apparently. "My mother said Phyllis played the stock market and had four million when she died. Is that true?"

"Not quite." (It had been $3.8 million, not that it was anyone's business.)

"So what happened to all the birds?"

"We found homes for them."

"She was sure an unusual lady."

Kat put a palm up against the cool glass. What Phyllis had been was unusually kind—so much so that it took Kat over a year to trust her. Kat thought she was just too good to be true. She never called the authorities on Kat. Phyllis was quick to get Kat hooked up with everything she needed—prenatal care, GED classes, baby supplies, even a Social Security card. How many people would have done that? How many people would have welcomed a pissed-off, pregnant kid with a gigantic chip on her shoulder and asked for nothing in return? Who else but Phyllis Turner would have waited weeks before she even inquired about Kat's family? Who else would have simply let the gossip become the truth—that

Kat Turner was the orphaned child of Phyllis' second cousin, a girl who'd gotten herself in trouble and had nowhere else to go, and she'd be staying for as long as she liked.

Kat knew she'd owed Phyllis the truth about where she came from, who she was, and how she ended up hitchhiking to Baltimore, but she never found the courage to tell her. She convinced herself that it would hurt less if she just pretended none of it ever happened. So now, at age thirty-seven, Kat was left with lies *on top* of the hurt, which, as it turned out, had just been lounging around all those years, picking its teeth, waiting for just the right moment to pop up and slap her upside the head.

Apparently, that time was now.

"So, I'd like to talk price if we could."

Julianna's voice faded into the background as the weight of the situation hit Kat: Now that Riley Bohland knew how to find Aidan, it was only a matter of days—if not hours—before everything blew up. She had to get to Aidan before Riley did. She had to be the one to tell her son the truth, not a stranger.

Kat leaned her forehead against the sliding door and shut her eyes for a moment. There wasn't room in her life for fantasies anymore. She could no longer pretend. She'd gone back to Persuasion to get revenge and returned with the empty truth. Her mother was gone. Phyllis was gone. Kat and Riley had been stupid, horny kids—not each other's soul mates. And she would now have to right twenty years of wrongs with her son.

Clearly, Kat's basic approach to life was in need of the same level of "upgrades" as Phyllis' row house.

"How does that sound, Kat? Would you like some time to think about it?"

Kat gazed out at the tiny fenced yard, its summer lushness fading from the chilly nights and waning sun. Kat looked twice at the tangled hedge of rosebushes and wondered if Phyllis had been too tired in the spring and early summer to prune her beloved plants. If so, Kat hadn't noticed. Every time she'd asked if there was anything she could do, Phyllis would dismiss her offer and tell her to concentrate on her own life. *This old broad is still full of piss and vinegar,* she'd say. *You should be out there trying to drum up some excitement of your own while you're still young.*

Phyllis died sitting in her Barcalounger by the front window, *Good Morning America* on TV and the sports section of *The Sun* on her lap. A massive stroke, the doctors said. The parish priest assured Kat that Phyllis had left this world in peace. As they soon found out, she'd also left this world stinking rich. To Uncle Cliff and his family Phyllis bequeathed her Cal Ripken Jr. autographed baseball and a million dollars nobody knew she had. To Kat and Aidan she left everything else—the house, forty parakeets, and the balance of her money market accounts, stocks, mutual funds, and IRAs.

"I can't do this." Kat spun around in time to see Julianna's mouth fall open in surprise. "I just realized I can't sell. It's the only part of Phyllis that still exists. I'll fix it up and live here myself."

Julianna gave a little shrug and handed Kat her card. "The market is very unpredictable. And mortage rates may not—"

"I understand. I apologize if I wasted your time."

As Kat ushered Julianna through the small living

room and out the front door, her cell phone rang. She yanked the phone from her front pocket.

"Aidan! Finally!"

"What's up, Mom? Everything OK?"

"Fine. Hey, have you gotten any strange phone calls you want to tell me about?" The line went quiet. "Aidan?"

"Uh, does this one count?"

In her head, Kat let out a giant sigh of relief. "Funny," she said.

"So you and Nola survived the Big Apple?"

How could Kat explain to her son that they'd conquered Manhattan just fine but gotten their asses kicked in Persuasion, West Virginia? Aidan had no idea they'd driven there—in fact, Aidan didn't know there was such a place, that his father lived there, or that his life was about to be upended.

Kat steeled herself to do what was right. Starting today, everything would be on the up-and-up. Aidan would demand it. He deserved it.

"New York was great, honey. We're both gorgeous now, in case you were wondering. So can I take you to lunch?"

"Today?"

"Yes, today."

"I've got a two o'clock physics lab."

"It's only eleven. We'll grab something quick. I'd really like to talk with you. It's important."

"I guess, but . . ."

"How about we meet at the G and A? When's the last time you had a decent chili dog?"

It was barely noon, and the day was turning out to be one for the record books. Riley had a waiting room full of impatient patients. Carrie had been paging him all morning, asking for a few moments of his time. The clinic's new general contractor e-mailed to inform Riley that all the electrical work done by the old contractor was not up to code. And the short meeting Riley had tried to squeeze in with the loan officer first thing that morning had lasted an hour, and ended with a tidy, tri-folded legal document being shoved in Riley's hand.

It seemed the First National Bank of Persuasion wasn't pleased with his sporadic payment plan of the last six months and had decided to foreclose on the lien and put the Bohland House up for auction.

But no word from Kat.

Riley paced his office and groaned out loud in frustration. Kat coming back was a miracle and a mistake all at once. Why wouldn't she return his calls? What made her blow out of town without a good-bye, without a plan for how they would proceed with Aidan? Nothing made any sense, and Riley had spent the last two days in a state of agitation. Matt said he'd run into Kat and her friend in front of the house Sunday morning and that Kat had seemed goofy and nervous, but normally so. Matt had talked to Madeline at Cherry Hill and she said the women ate breakfast and abruptly checked out, but that nothing obvious had been amiss.

Once Virgil was out of recovery, Riley asked him if he'd heard from his daughter. "Why would I?" was his response.

So Riley was left wondering what had happened between the post-sex bliss and the burning-rubber way she left town. Was this some kind of compulsion for Kat? Did she run away as a hobby? Was this how she'd always been and would always be? If he tried to get to know her again, was this what he'd have to look forward to—sweet, hot love followed by this body-snatcher disappearance act?

There was a knock on his office door. Izzy poked her head in, and he held up a hand before his nurse could relay the obvious.

"I know. I know. It looks like I'll have to shuffle some appointments into next week."

"True, but I wish it were only that." A pained look spread across her face. "I hate to tell you this, but Dr. Mathis is in the waiting room, demanding to see you. She's making a bit of a scene."

"You've got to be joking."

"Knock-knock!" Carrie peeked over Izzy's head, and flashed her high-voltage smile.

Izzy looked like she was going to cry. "I'm so sorry, Dr. Bohland!"

"It's OK. Not a problem." Riley motioned for Carrie to come in, and she immediately closed the door and posed up against it, hands clasped demurely behind her back. She wore a black skirt and matching jacket, obviously custom tailored, because it fit so tightly, Riley figured he'd have trouble wedging a piece of dental floss between the fabric and her skin.

"You're a hard man to reach, Riley."

"That's because I'm not reachable." He leaned back in his chair and rocked, wondering what alternate universe he'd once called home, because he actually used to think Carrie Mathis was a warm, loving, and decent woman. He was almost ashamed to admit he'd fallen for that act not once, but twice—for their whole first year of med school and then again, three years ago, when Carrie started her statewide diabetes project and chose Persuasion as one of her data collection sites.

Maybe he was blinded by her smile. Maybe he'd given up on ever finding love again—the kind of love he'd once felt with Kat—and decided that settling for a successful, attractive colleague wasn't the worst fate in the world.

From her deathbed, BettyAnn Cavanaugh had saved Riley's life.

"What do you want, Carrie?"

She let loose with a throaty laugh. "Oh, now, that's a loaded question."

Riley shook his head. "I'm at a loss here. Help me out. What exactly do you need to hear before you understand it's over between us?"

Carrie looked offended.

"Because, from where I sit, it looks pretty cut-and-dry. I ignore your phone calls and pages because I don't want to talk to you. I tell my staff not to let you in the door because I don't want to see you. Would you prefer I hire a skywriter? Put it on a billboard by the highway? Place an ad in the *Charleston Daily Mail*?"

Riley watched her top lip twitch, its glossy surface catching the light. It amazed him that he'd once found her beautiful. Compared to Kat, Carrie seemed plastic.

"Pardon me, Riley, but I thought you might want to hear some good news."

"What?"

"I heard the clinic is going to be a funding priority this legislative session."

He narrowed his eyes at her. "I didn't hear the funding freeze had been lifted."

"It hasn't. Not yet. But when it is—"

Riley rose from his chair. Carrie had picked the

wrong day to try to screw with him. He walked around his desk and went toward her.

Three years ago, it was Carrie's enthusiasm alone that had conjured up state funding for the Persuasion Rural Health Clinic. Though he couldn't prove it, he knew it was her spitefulness that had gotten the funding pulled—it was no coincidence that the legislature reneged soon after Riley called off the wedding and broke up with Carrie once and for all.

Because of her, Riley had mortgaged everything he owned, and the clinic was still more than a million dollars short—and that was before he'd learned the whole place would have to be rewired!

God, what a stinking mess.

"Thanks for the update, Carrie. I'll have our lawyer make a few calls."

She shook her head, incredulous. "That's it?"

"That's it. Don't ever show up here again. Got it?"

Carrie's lips parted. Riley heard her let out a soft squeak of indignation before she turned on her high heels and left.

Kat watched Aidan start in on his third chili dog, all the while talking about how he might change his major to biochemical engineering.

"Mom, seriously. There is so much amazing shit going on in stem cell research—especially now that they've determined that other cells can yield the same kind of potent regenerative capabilities as in embryos. That will bypass the whole ethical debate and bust this field of research wide open!"

He sucked on the plastic straw sticking out of his old-fashioned Coca-Cola glass. "That's where I want to be in ten years—right in the middle of that revolution. Can you imagine all the diseases the world will finally have a way to fight?"

"That's wonderful, sweetheart." Kat stared at his five-o'clock shadow at one in the afternoon, and the way his mouth curved up so slightly at the ends. He was such a Bohland. Kat saw so much of Riley in her boy's face and body that she wondered what her contribution had been. He had Matt's smile. And, if she took away about a hundred pounds and a half a foot, she could see Big Daddy in there as well. Kat swallowed hard with the burden of all she was about to lay on Aidan, this boy who came from a long line of men he never knew existed.

She'd made such a horrible mistake.

"Alzheimer's. Parkinson's. Cancer." Aidan used a paper napkin to wipe away a drip of chili on his chin. "We're on the verge of being able to break apart the human genome inside a cancer cell and see exactly where it went off-track, then target each of those chromosomes with drugs developed to correct that particular defect. It would be like going after a fruit fly with an Uzi—that sucker just couldn't get away!"

Kat smiled at him, so proud of his passion and intelligence, so aware that his father had been just like him as a young man. She needed to change the subject in a hurry, before she lost her courage.

"Speaking of human genes, I have something to tell you, Aidan." She took a deep breath. "I need to talk to you about your father."

"My *whaaa—*" Aidan's entire body went still. His eyes—those intense blue eyes his father gave him—had gone huge. "What are you talking about?" he whispered.

"I haven't been completely honest with you. You need to know that up front. And I am asking you to find some way, at some point in the future, to forgive me."

Aidan dropped the last remaining bite of hot dog onto the chipped plate and stared at her. The enthusiasm that had been in his eyes just seconds ago had been replaced with what Kat could only describe as fear and dread. His mouth pulled tight. "You know who my dad is, don't you? You've always known."

Kat was busted. "That's true, technically. But it's a much bigger story, and I think you're old enough to hear the whole thing now."

"Oh, really?" Aidan took a sip of his soda, then slammed the glass down on the green Formica tabletop. He glared at her. "I've been old enough to hear the truth for about a decade now and you know it. You haven't told me because *you* couldn't deal, Mom. Not me. So don't go putting this all on me."

Kat was shocked. Aidan had never talked to her this way before. The anger she saw in him cut her to the bone, but she suspected she had it coming. Telling Aidan the truth was going to take more courage than anything she'd ever done in her life. In comparison, getting in that truck with Cliff Turner seemed like a snap.

"All I ask is that you put yourself in the right frame of mind to hear everything I'm about to tell you. Please. Just listen to the whole story; then you can decide how angry to be." Kat tried to reach out to touch his forearm, but he jerked it away. "You need to hear this, sweetheart."

Aidan nodded, then brightened up with mock enthusiasm. "I am the demon spawn of Troy Mikulski, is that what you're going to tell me? I always suspected it."

Kat thought she'd fall out of her plastic chair. "*What? Hell* no!" She reached out for her son again, but he made it clear he was off-limits. "Baby, Troy is not your father. He's just a guy I wasted two years of my life with!" Kat was horrified. "My God, Aidan. That was back when you were in middle school. Please don't tell me you've been walking around all this time thinking that bozo was your father?"

Aidan let loose with a bitter laugh, then shouted, "What the hell was I supposed to think?" He jumped up and kicked his chair. "I never had anything else to go on! Every time I asked about my father, you gave me some lame answer about your sordid past and you not even knowing who knocked you up and that it was all part of a life you wanted to forget!"

The grill cook turned around, hot-dog tongs in his hand and his face plastered with a hopeful grin.

"Keep your voice down, Aidan."

"No! This sucks!" He waved his arms around. "All you ever told me was that we needed to focus on the here and now, and that was basically nothing but a load of bullshit! You *lied* to me, Mom. You left me swinging in the wind. How bad can a parent be?"

"Sit your ass down, Aidan. *Now.*" Kat hadn't heard herself speak like that in years—not since Aidan came home at 2:00 A.M. from an alleged night at the movies, smelling like pot. She had grounded him for six months. But in this case, Kat knew she was the one who deserved to be grounded. As Aidan plopped back down in his chair, she saw his shoulders droop with despair.

"Sure. Why not?" he said flatly. "Let's have it."

Kat took a giant breath, searching her son's face

for an opening, an indication that he was ready. She encountered steady, smart eyes, filled with hurt that was her doing. "He was my childhood sweetheart, Aidan. I really thought we loved each other, and he never knew he'd gotten me pregnant, up until recently."

"He never knew?" Aidan was scowling.

"No."

"Why?"

"Because I never told him. I ran away without telling him I was pregnant."

Aidan let out a snort of disgust. "Brilliant move, Mom." He took another sip of his drink. He didn't look at her.

"But he found out last year, from my mother, just before she died. And he's been looking for you—for both of us—ever since."

Aidan's neck snapped in attention, and he stared at her. "Wait a minute. You told me your parents died when you were a teenager."

"They were dead to me."

"Wow. This is so incredibly fucked."

"Aidan."

"Seriously, seriously fucked." He shook his head. "OK, so you say this dude—my *father*—has been looking for me? Is that part the truth, at least?"

"Absolutely. I just saw him last weekend and told him all about you. He mentioned wanting to spend Thanksgiving break with you. I gave him your phone number. That's why I asked you earlier if you'd gotten any strange calls." Kat dug into her bag and pulled out Riley's business card. "Here. This is him. Look on the back."

She watched her son's hand tremble as he traced his fingertips along the raised black print.

"He's a freakin' doctor?" Aidan looked up, stunned, his whisper fading as he flipped over the card to read Riley's handwritten note: *I can't wait to get to know you, Aidan. Call me at work or on my cell anytime. Here's my home number, too. . . .*

"Shit, Mom. I don't believe this!" Aidan stuck the business card in her face. "But what's that last number there on the end? Is that a seven or a one? I can't read his writing!"

Kat laughed. "It's as bad as yours."

"Where the hell is Persuasion, West Virginia?"

"It's where I grew up."

Aidan's smile faded, and he pulled the card away. "I see. Yet another detail you lied to me about. You always told me you grew up in Martinsburg."

"Yeah. At least I got the state right."

Aidan shoved the business card in his front jeans pocket, shaking his head. "Anything else you lied to me about, Mom?" He folded his hands on the table, his face contorted with sarcasm. "Are you an alien? Are you really a man? Is your name even Katharine Turner?"

"Ah." Kat clicked her tongue on her teeth. "Actually—"

"No way—"

"It's Katharine Cavanaugh. I took Phyllis' last name, not because she was a distant relation, like I told you, but because I didn't want to be found. I wanted to protect you."

Aidan's face fell. Kat knew she was asking a lot of him. "Please try to understand, sweetheart."

"So my real name is Aidan Cavanaugh?"

"Well, if that's what you choose. Or Bohland, after your dad. I guess you can decide that later.

It's something we'll have to sort out legally, I suppose."

Aidan slowly shook his head, his eyes filled with sadness. "What the hell were you thinking, Mom? What could have possibly been so bad that you lied to me from the day I was born? What were you trying to protect me from?"

Kat didn't want to cry. She'd prided herself that no matter how rough things had gotten in all those years, no matter how she'd fought to keep it together with night school, work, bills, Aidan had never seen her break down. She was beginning to wonder if she'd done him a disservice by not letting him see how much she'd struggled.

"Well, what I was thinking was . . . I'd hoped to . . . I just wanted to protect you from—" Kat gulped down her sob. "From what happened to me, dammit! From getting rejected by those people, the people who tossed my pregnant ass out onto the street when I was sixteen years old!"

Aidan frowned as he listened.

"And I'm sorry if I made the wrong decision, but it was the only one I could make at the time. I thought it was best for my child."

Aidan stood up again, his mouth slowly twisting in grief. "News flash, Mom: It wasn't."

"Fine. We can talk more about this later, when you've cooled off." Kat stood up, too. "Do you need some money this week?" She reached into her purse, but Aidan placed his hand on her wrist.

She looked up at him. He looked down at her, the pain distorting the shape of his handsome face. "I don't need anything from you anymore, Mom," he said softly. "You've done plenty."

Aidan turned his back on her and walked out of the diner without another word.

Kat followed, perfectly aware of the way the grill cook checked her out as she went through the door.

She called Nola from her cell phone, watching Aidan's form disappear down Eastern Avenue. She could barely hear Nola's voice over the racket of delivery trucks and cars without mufflers.

"How'd it go?"

"Oh, just *super*!" Kat turned away from the street noise and back toward the diner but spun right back around when the grill cook winked at her.

"That bad?"

Kat sighed, raising her voice. "If I'm lucky, he'll forgive me by the time he's seventy."

"Oh, well, hon . . ." Nola sounded thoughtful. "You'll only be eighty-something, and you know what they say—eighty is the new thirty!"

EIGHT

Riley turned on the desk lamp, determined to power through these last few charts before he went home for the night. He hadn't eaten since breakfast and his head throbbed, but the sooner he finished, the sooner he would have time to call his son.

Riley reached into his pants pocket and touched the wallet-sized photo Kat had given him, with a cell phone number on the back. He'd already memorized it.

With a sigh of resignation, Riley clicked on the miniature tape recorder and resumed his dictation: "Patient is a forty-seven-year-old premenopausal female presenting with a variety of non-specific symptoms. . . ." He released the "record" button while he scanned the paperwork, then spoke into the mike again: "Dizziness, headache, body aches, joint pain, insomnia, depression—" He stopped, suddenly aware that he'd dictated these same words many times that day. Riley tossed the recorder to his desk.

"You weren't meant to live like this," he said, knowing the reprimand was more for himself than Mrs. Anita Prejean, the premenopausal woman tucked away inside that chart.

Riley rose from his chair and paced his office.

Riley figured that Mrs. Prejean's symptoms were caused by what was, in his opinion, the world's number-one disease—unfinished business. After six years as a primary-care physician, Riley could say that most people got sick because they lived a life of lies—a simple reality that was almost impossible to cure. The lies led to stress, which affected every organ system in the human body. He saw it all day, every day. And sometimes he thought of himself as nothing more than a lifeguard at an alligator-infested swamp, where all he could do was fix the latest flesh wound before he threw the swimmer back.

There were all kinds of lies, of course. There were the direct kinds, like marital affairs, dishonest business practices, and stealing what didn't belong to you. And there were the lies of omission and neglect—secrets never shared, anger never expressed, feelings shoved down so deep that people couldn't even put a name on what they felt. Patient after patient had come to him over the years with physical complaints he could trace directly to the accumulated stress of dishonesty. Lurking beneath the surface of their lives were silent burdens of guilt, shame, and bitterness, the inability to forgive oneself and others, and buried fears powerful enough to squeeze the joy out of the present day.

And nobody was immune.

Riley wandered to the exposed-brick wall of his office. He stared at everything displayed before him—the slew of diplomas, board certifications, awards. All the family photos.

His gaze fell on his parents' official wedding portrait. It was 1968, a summer of free love, race riots, and assassinations in the rest of the country. Not in Persuasion. From what he'd always heard, life had gone on like it always had around here, with mine strikes and unemployment worries. The only ripple was that every few months, word would come that another boy would not be coming home from Vietnam to exchange his camouflaged infantry helmet for a miner's hard hat.

Riley stared at his parents' young faces, amazed at the combination of innocence and resolve he saw there. He wondered what could have been racing through their minds the instant the camera flashed, what they feared, what they hoped for, whether they already knew which pieces of themselves each would have to keep hidden from the other in order to survive.

Big Daddy looked so fresh and handsome, the familiar crevices at his mouth and eyes not yet carved into his face. His Marine Corps head was shaved brutally close, and his jawline was fixed in seriousness, even on his wedding day. A week later, he would be off-loading from a Huey in a jungle clearing near Cambodia.

And there was Riley's mother, the former Miss Eliza Starliper, the town's great beauty. Her brown hair was teased ridiculously high, held in place by a tiny white bow that looked too dainty for the job. She had a sly smile on her lovely lips, as if she couldn't believe what she'd just pulled off. Eliza's beauty had meshed with Aidan Bohland's small-town prestige, and a new family had been born.

Riley's gaze moved toward the photo of Matt, Big Daddy, and himself fly-fishing in Wyoming the summer he'd finished his residency. A rumbling of regret moved through him. His own boy would have been about twelve that summer. He should have been with them. Instead, he was loose in the world, maybe playing baseball like all the Bohlands before him, doing homework, arguing with his mom, and thinking his father didn't love him. It was almost too much to bear.

There was a lot to make up for in that young man's life, and Riley knew he'd do whatever it took. He'd repair the lies. Erase the half-truths. He'd tell all the untold stories. He'd make sure his son didn't go another day with only part of the picture.

Not *his* son.

Riley backed away from the photos and stared out at Main Street. Who was he kidding? He was no superhero. He wasn't even courageous enough to be honest with his own brother about how he'd been paying for the clinic project. How was he going to be the kind of dad he wanted to be?

The door to his office creaked open without a knock, and Riley knew it could only be Matt.

"Did you find her?" Riley heard the impatience in his own voice as he spun around.

"Oh yeah. No problem." Matt stayed in the doorway, not moving inside. He frowned a little. "You think too much, Bro."

"Would you want a doctor who didn't?"

Matt chuckled. "You weren't thinking about medicine and you know it."

"Where is she?"

"She's at home in Baltimore."

"That's good."

"But do you want to hear the funny part?"

Riley raised his eyebrows. "There's a funny part?"

Matt chuckled. "The thing is, Kat was right where BettyAnn said she was, all along."

Riley jerked his head back in disbelief. "But we know she wasn't."

"And," Matt added, "she was in Baltimore at the same time. Let's get some fresh air and I'll tell you all about it."

Riley took off his white coat and tossed it over the back of his office chair. Once he turned off the lights and set the security system, he and Matt headed up Main.

"Did you eat?" Matt asked.

"No, I didn't eat. Just tell me what you found out."

Matt shook his head and laughed again, clearly relishing whatever it was that he was about to share. "Check this out, Riley. When BettyAnn was about to die, try to remember *exactly* what she said to you, OK?"

Riley stopped, glaring at his brother like he was nuts. How many hundreds of times had he gone over this with Matt—in hotel rooms, in breakfast joints, in the cab of the pickup on the road to somewhere else they wouldn't find Kat and the boy? BettyAnn had said that Kat and her son were in Patterson, California. She spoke the words and then she died. That information was the only thing Riley and Matt ever had to go on in the months that followed. It was all they could pass on to the private detectives and the police. It was the only thing that kept them going. And Riley remembered those words like BettyAnn had spoken them one second ago, not one year.

She was in the ICU at Davis Memorial. Her fight was over. BettyAnn had requested that she not be resuscitated, and the DNR order was slapped above the head of the bed like an orange neon beacon, impossible to miss.

By that time, all they could do was keep her as comfortable as possible until her body gave out. He'd come by on morning rounds and she was lying gray and listless with a white sheet tucked around bony ribs. Her eyes flashed when she saw Riley; then she sent Virgil out of the room with a weak flop of her hand. Riley was surprised to see Virgil leave without a word of protest.

BettyAnn motioned for Riley to come close. She whispered so softly he had to put his left ear down to her lips.

"You have a boy," she said. "Kat had a child."

Riley pulled back enough to stare into BettyAnn's sunken eyes. They were filled with sadness but something more. It looked almost like love.

His throat was suddenly so tight and dry he could hardly speak. "Are you certain?"

She nodded, the effort causing her to push the morphine pump for another dose of relief.

"Where did they go?"

In that surreal moment, Riley heard his own question and thought it sounded comically matter-of-fact, like he was asking BettyAnn if his little family had gone to a matinee or out to get ice cream. But his mind was spinning, his heart was ready to leap from his body, because Kat was somewhere with his child—*his child*—and BettyAnn was telling him this because she was dying. She was dying at that instant.

"Hang on, BettyAnn." Riley focused his eyes on hers, seeing how she struggled to stay with him. He gave her hand a gentle squeeze. "Please. Just tell me where I can find them."

She said something. He couldn't hear it. The anxiety ripped through him.

"Again, BettyAnn. Please *say it again*."

Yes, Riley remembered what she'd said. He stared at Matt, standing there on the sidewalk with that stupid grin on his face, and he humored him by reciting the exact words yet one more time: "BettyAnn said, 'Patterson in California.' "

Matt shook his head, his smile widening. "Not *exactly*."

"No?"

"Nope."

"Then what did she say? No more of this bullshit, Matt. What's going on?"

Matt put his hand on Riley's shoulder. "BettyAnn Cavanaugh said, 'Patterson *and* California.' It's an intersection in a working-class section of Baltimore."

Riley's mouth fell open.

"Kat and Aidan lived at 456 California Avenue until 1994, in a row house smack across the street from Patterson Park, in Highlandtown. She wasn't using her real last name—she took on the name of the woman she stayed with."

Riley stared at his brother for a long, silent moment, as the events of the last year of his life raced through his brain. BettyAnn's news. The wedding. The breakup. The private detective. The three-month leave of absence he took to find Kat and his son. Oregon, Texas, South Dakota, and a dozen more states that were all a blur to him now. Every single moment of that year was lived knowing he had a child he might never find.

And his son had been a five-hour drive away.

"Did you hear what I said, Bro?"

Riley nodded, awash in the randomness of it all, not knowing whether to laugh or cry. So he did a little of both.

It was impossible to sleep in this place. How was a man supposed to recover from having a balloon shoved into his groin if he couldn't get a decent night's rest?

Virgil lay awake in the hospital room, a sickening yellow night-light casting its glow on all the odd shapes around him. Somehow, being alone in the hospital felt a hell of a lot lonelier than being alone at home. At least at home, there were no nurses giving a play-by-play on how it was a shame he had no visitors or flowers.

Even his old bat of a sister hadn't bothered to come see him. She had called and spoken to the Chinese doctor, so at least it appeared she cared whether he lived or died. But Rita might have done that only for show.

Riley Bohland had stopped by, but that was probably required because he was Virgil's doctor. All Bohland wanted to know was whether Virgil had heard from Kat.

He had no idea what was going on with those two, but her showing up had obviously fucked with Bohland's head.

Virgil didn't know what to do with himself, trapped in here like a lab rat. He tried to read the paper but couldn't stay focused. He tried to watch TV, but it put his neck at an uncomfortable angle. And since sleeping was out of the question, that left him a lot of time to think.

He could see how having two heart attacks might make a man reevaluate things. It's unsettling when you almost die. Fortunately, there wasn't a damn thing he regretted about the way he'd lived his life.

But he couldn't stop thinking about BettyAnn and the secret she could have told Bohland. Virgil hadn't laid a hand on his wife in twenty years, so it couldn't have been that. It was something to do with Kat, no doubt, because BettyAnn never forgot that the two of them were sweethearts once. The whole business bothered Virgil.

BettyAnn used to try to hide the fact that she'd been crying about Kat, but other than that, the woman lived an open book. Virgil told her how much money to spend at the IGA, and she'd show him the receipt to prove that's exactly how much she spent. He told her what clothes to wear and what hairstyle to choose, and that's how she dressed and styled her hair. He told her who she could and could not associate with, and that's what she did.

She was a simple woman who needed his guidance to stay happy and peaceful. She'd long ago proven she couldn't handle freedom, so Virgil gave her the structure she craved. The idea that there would be anything in her head that he hadn't put there left him uneasy. BettyAnn was his plaything, his doll baby.

So how come his doll baby had something to tell Bohland just before she died? How come she specifically asked that it never be revealed to her husband, her king?

For the first time in twenty years, Virgil wanted a drink. It was no coincidence that the craving had returned the moment Kat did.

Madeline studied the low-cut, fur-trimmed neckline of Carrie's wedding dress and realized three things simultaneously—that it was not the same gown she had last year, that it really was stunning, and that Madeline never should have passed on those lies to Kat, because at some point in the very recent past, Carrie Mathis had become crazier than a hoot owl.

"Too much cleavage?" Carrie cupped her satin-supported breasts and sashayed her way to the kitchen sink and back to the table. "I'm pursuing an understated, sexy look, you know? Smokingly hot, but in a Grace Kelly sort of way."

Carrie swished until the white satin train swept around her feet. "I want Riley's eyes to absolutely bug out of his head when he sees this!"

Madeline nodded, not sure what to say, thinking that Carrie would have no problem getting Riley's eyes to bug out because he'd get one look at the woman he'd told to get lost a year ago, all dolled up in her wedding dress, ready for a secret wedding where he was expected to be the groom, and his eyes would bug out just fine. Madeline became vaguely aware of the nausea creeping into her belly.

"Hey, Carrie?"

"Hmm?" She was petting the strip of white fur at her wrist.

"Have you told anyone else about the wedding?"

Carrie's head snapped to attention and she flashed an over-the-top smile at Madeline. Carrie was gorgeous, with dark brown eyes and gleaming brunette hair, a flawless olive complexion, and that smile—that Miss Universe kind of smile that seemed to suck the energy from a room and shoot it back out like lightning. Madeline remembered how she'd actually felt nervous the first time Carrie checked into Cherry Hill, like she was meeting a daytime TV star or something. Then it hit her—she'd seen the woman on TV a thousand times, doing those public-health announcements for the State of West Virginia, and she'd actually been silly enough to ask for her autograph. Boy, did that seem stupid now.

"Does it matter who I've told?" Carrie continued to smile but raised a single eyebrow in challenge.

"It's just that . . . well . . . most brides have some kind of guarantee that there'll be an actual groom before they get into the nuts and bolts of the wedding. You know, like buying a dress."

Carrie sniffed, tossing her hair. "I'm not most brides."

"True enough." Madeline squirmed in the kitchen chair, trying to find a delicate way to talk some sense into her. "I'm only saying that—"

"What *are* you saying, Maddie?" Carrie scooped up the yards of satin and sat down in the kitchen chair across from Madeline. She folded her hands in her lap and lowered the wattage of her smile. "Are you questioning whether I know what I'm doing? Do you think for one minute that I don't have every contingency covered?"

Madeline blinked, feeling the sheen of perspiration beginning to form on her brow and under her arms. There was something unsettling about the lilt of Carrie's voice and the way her smile just hung there, unrelated to anything pleasant or funny. Madeline was nervous again, and it wasn't because Carrie was beautiful. It was because she was just plain weird.

"But Riley said he didn't want to marry you."

"Because of a personal emergency, not because his feelings had changed for me."

Madeline swallowed hard, knowing that she'd have to continue carefully. "You tried for months to get him to reschedule and he wouldn't do it, remember?"

Carrie glared at her.

"I remember you telling me that while Riley was out of town you called him every night, sobbing, and e-mailed him several times a day. He broke up with you, saying you were obsessive and irrational, remember?"

Carrie scowled.

"So, let's look at this realistically—not only did Riley not want to marry you; he didn't even want to date you anymore. I think you need to accept that, and move on."

"You are so very, very mistaken." Carrie crossed her arms under her breasts, showing more cleavage than Grace Kelly ever did. "Riley simply put our relationship *on hold,* Maddie. That's all. And I am only utilizing the laws of attraction—I'm attracting good into my life by preparing for it, making room for it, opening my arms to receive it, and what is good for me is marrying Riley Bohland."

Madeline's left eye started to twitch.

"Riley is most definitely responding. He's warming up, moving a little closer to me every day."

"You really think so?"

Carrie grinned sweetly. "I know so. I spent time with him just today, as a matter of fact. We had a wonderful talk."

With a nod, Madeline got up and took her teacup to the sink, turning away from Carrie to gather her thoughts, and her only thought was, *This woman is fuckin' nuts.* Maybe she should tell someone. How about Matt? Was Carrie weird enough that Madeline should alert the authorities? What could they charge Carrie with? Assault with a deadly wedding? Aggravated positive thinking?

Madeline rinsed the china cup under the faucet,

letting her thoughts swirl around with the water. Maybe she was just overreacting. Everyone was a little crazy in their own way. After all, half the town had told her she was insane to buy this old place and turn it into a B and B. And look at it now! Maybe it was none of her business what delusions Carrie operated under.

Madeline turned off the water and shook her head. She knew she'd made it her business the moment she allowed Carrie to manipulate her with the promise of conference bookings. She'd made it her business the second she told Kat just enough garbage to make her run out of town.

Besides, was it even possible to overreact these days? Madeline wiped her hands on a kitchen towel, thinking of the average night of network news—suicide bombings and schoolroom shootings, a killing spree here and a paranoid rampage there. Private delusions didn't always stay private. Sometimes they exploded all over the place, changing history.

Madeline turned around and gasped. Carrie was right up against her. How had she moved without making a sound, especially draped in all that fabric?

"I didn't mean to scare you," Carrie whispered.

"Oh. Sure. No problem." Madeline braced herself on the edge of the sink and leaned back to gain a few inches of distance from Carrie.

"It's not wise to pass judgment without all the facts, Madeline." Carrie said this as sweetly and as patiently as if she were showing a child how to use a salad fork. "As your friend, I'm just giving you that bit of advice."

Madeline tried to produce a smile; all the while her heart was thudding in her chest. "Thanks."

"You were not privy to the events that led up to the wedding's cancellation."

"OK." She tried to move a little to the left without Carrie noticing. It didn't work.

Carrie's eyes flashed. "Since you brought all this up, how about we just stay put and finish this conversation?"

Madeline nodded, mentally calculating how many steps it would take before she could lunge for the kitchen wall phone.

"You see, that girl—that Kat Cavanaugh—she is responsible for all this. She must have heard that Riley was about to marry me, and she used her poor dying mother to pass on the rumor about a baby, just in time to ruin everything."

Madeline jolted to attention, her focus moving from 911 to the word "baby." "What baby?"

Carrie laughed. "Oh, she claims that Riley fathered a child back in high school, a child no one has ever seen or met. She timed the rumor for maximum devastation, just in time to stop the wedding. She was jealous, no doubt." Carrie shook her head in disgust. "Then—this is the most despicable part—that woman led Riley on a wild-goose chase all over the country to find this alleged child. She did it to distract him, take his attention off of me, and ruin my life."

"A baby?"

"So she claims."

"Did he find it?"

"Of course not. There *is* no baby. That's my whole point—aren't you paying attention?" Carrie sighed with impatience. "Remember when Riley told everyone he was taking a leave to care for a relative out west? That was a lie—he was out searching for the non-existent child!"

Madeline hadn't heard anything this juicy since 1999, when Ralph down at the Sunoco had sent away for that mail-order bride who broke out in hives when she met him and cried for two weeks straight until he agreed to ship her back to Romania.

"So this is why Kat Cavanaugh came back here—without a child, you'll have noticed—just in time to ruin my plans for the second time!"

Madeline tried to shake off the confusion. Riley got Kat pregnant? But Kat said they hadn't seen each other since sophomore year, before she disappeared. But that would make perfect sense! Kat was pregnant when she left town! Oh, this was just too delicious! This made way too much sense!

"You have no right to judge me." Carrie's gaze drifted past Madeline's face to the window over the sink, where it seemed to settle in unfocused peace. "You don't know how much I love Riley and how I only have his best interests at heart. You don't know that I am only doing my job as his woman. I am taking care of him, don't you see?"

Carrie refocused on Madeline, cheerful again. "And when he realizes everything I've done all this time to protect him, he won't want to wait another day for me to be his bride! And here I'll be. . . ."

She stepped away from Madeline, beaming now, gesturing to her gown like a game-show hostess. "I'll have everything arranged! And, of course, you'll be a bridesmaid."

"I will?"

"I've ordered you a gorgeous red velvet gown with a flattering empire waist. I had to guess at the size—sixteen?"

Madeline felt her eyes go big.

"Now do you understand all this, Maddie?"

She gave a weak nod, sort of understanding.

"So just relax." Carrie gave Madeline's shoulder a friendly squeeze. "I'm not crazy. I'm just very, very efficient."

Riley pulled on a light jacket, took the cordless phone and a cold beer out to the front porch, and chose the sturdiest of the old wooden rockers for his purposes. Loretta plopped down at his feet.

"Listen up, girl," he said to the hound, pointing the phone in her direction. "This is just about the most important conversation I've ever had in my life, so keep the play-by-play to a minimum decibel level, if you please."

"*Aaahrooomfff,*" she said.

Riley set the beer on the porch floor and studied the wallet-sized photo of his son. In just two days, he'd handled the picture so often it had taken on the gloss of age. He flipped it over and stared at the phone numbers in Kat's handwriting. It was a small comfort, but he had to admit he was relieved to at least know where both Kat and Aidan were, and that they were both safe, even if she wouldn't answer his calls. As things stood, this thin scrap of paper was the only proof he had that Kat's visit had been real and not just the best fucking dream he'd had in twenty years.

He punched in the area code and paused, still not certain which of the numbers he should try first—the dorm phone or the cell phone? Probably the cell. All the students at Mountain Laurel had cell phones plastered to the sides of their heads all day, every day, and he figured it couldn't be much different for the kids at Johns Hopkins. He hit the numbers quickly and waited for the ring.

He got a busy signal.

Riley disconnected and had begun to dial the other number when his phone rang. He blinked twice in disbelief, because Aidan's cell number had just flashed on the caller ID. He was nearly breathless when he answered. "Hello, this is Riley Bohland."

The line stayed silent for an instant before a deep voice said, "Uh, this is going to sound totally strange . . ."

"Hello, Aidan."

"Or not."

A goofy smile spread all over Riley's face and he let out a laugh. It was all he could do. After all this time, his boy was on the other end of the line! And he sounded grown-up and strong. Funny. Smart. He sounded *real.*

"I just called you, Aidan. Your line was busy."

"Because I was calling you, I guess."

"Yes."

"Wow. Look, I just wanted to introduce myself. I, uh, this is pretty awkward, but I don't have any freakin' idea what to call you: Dr. Bohland? Riley? *Dad?* I mean, that just sounds totally surreal coming out of my mouth—I've never used that word in my life."

Riley closed his eyes and took a deep breath, saying a silent prayer of thanks for his boy's nervous rambling. It gave Riley a chance to savor the timbre of Aidan's voice and the rhythm of his words. It was the sound of pure joy pouring down on him, and Riley let a tear roll down his cheek without wiping it away.

"You can call me anything you like, Aidan. It's fine if you're not ready to think of me as your father. There's a lot to figure out between us—a lot to get used to."

"Cool," Aidan said. Then he went quiet again.

"Cool," Riley said, smiling.

"Uh, look. The thing is, my mom told me about you just today, at lunch. I never knew you existed until a few hours ago. It was kind of a shock, if you know what I'm saying."

Riley adjusted himself in the chair, uncrossing and recrossing his legs, rocking back and forth to relieve the tension. Whatever he did, he didn't want to push too hard, make Aidan angry, or make him regret what he'd learned that day. "It was the same kind of shock for me. I didn't know you existed until last year."

"Mom told me."

"It took a lot of courage for you to call, Aidan. And I thank you." Riley began to relax, believing they were off to a solid start. "I'm glad you're willing to talk."

Aidan sounded surprised. "Of course I'm willing. I'm your kid, I guess."

"You sure are," Riley said, shaking his head in amazement. "You have no idea how obvious it is. I saw your picture."

"You did? Which one?"

"Your mom gave me your senior class photo."

Aidan groaned. "God, I hate that picture."

Riley laughed. He'd hated his senior picture, too. A year or two after graduation, everyone did, no matter how they'd primped and agonized over it at the time. It was another rite of passage he'd missed with Aidan. One of thousands.

Riley felt a sudden sadness. Kat had never had a senior picture to hate. She should have had one—right there in the *Underwood Overview,* their high school's yearbook, the names "Bohland" and "Cavanaugh" separated by the same three kids who'd acted as yearbook spacers from kindergarten forward—buck-toothed Emily Bok, Travis "Butt Head" Butrick, and the pathologically shy Anna Callahan.

"So I look like you?"

Riley refocused on his son's voice. "Yes, but you look so much like my brother, it's scary."

"How many brothers and sisters do you have? Do they have kids? Do I have any cousins?" By the excited way Aidan asked, it was clear this was a new—and welcome—concept.

"No sisters and just one brother, Matthew. Your uncle Matt is the police chief of Persuasion. He's a few years younger than me, and he doesn't have any kids. No cousins."

Aidan remained quiet.

"My parents—your grandparents—have both passed away. My mother died when I was twelve. My daddy died about five years ago. You're named after him. Did you know that? His name was Aidan Bohland."

"No shit."

"It's true."

"OK. So I don't have any grandparents left at all?"

Riley stopped the back-and-forth motion of the rocker, struck by the pain in his son's voice. Here Aidan was, suddenly discovering at age nineteen that he came from somewhere and was part of a family, only to find out much of the family was gone. Riley swallowed hard, remembering how Kat had expressly told him not to mention Aidan to Virgil, but what about the other way around? Aidan was an adult. If he wanted to initiate contact with his grandfather, that was Aidan's decision to make.

Besides, Riley's son had just asked him a question that deserved an honest answer.

"I would ask that you get the details from your mom, but I will tell you that you do have a grandfather—Virgil Cavanaugh is his name. He's an artist and a retired college professor. He still lives here in town."

Aidan's silence made Riley aware of how cold that response must have sounded, how anyone would expect something more at the end of that sentence, such as, *and I'm sure he can't wait to meet you!* Unfortunately, Riley didn't know what Virgil wanted—or what he even deserved.

"Jeez," Aidan said sarcastically. "Is this where you tell me he was a quiet man, kept to himself, and no one ever suspected he killed squirrels in his basement?"

Riley let go with a big laugh, which was Loretta's cue to begin her howling harmony. He tried to shush her, but she was on a roll.

"What is *that*?"

Riley wrapped his fingers gently around the dog's gray snout, muffling the howls. "That's just Loretta. She's a talkative old coonhound." He patted her on her head and resumed his rocking. "And no, Virgil isn't a psycho killer, but he's not the nicest guy you'll ever meet, and I'm not even sure your mom would want me telling you anything about him."

When Aidan spoke, his words were tinged with disappointment. "Mom told me today that her mother died recently, but she didn't say one word about what's-his-name."

"Virgil."

"Right."

The loneliness Riley heard in his son's voice nearly broke his heart.

"Aidan, if there's one thing you take away from this conversation, you've got to know that I started looking for you the minute I learned you existed." Riley stopped and took a breath before the emotions could overrun him. "I tried to find you and your mom. It's a long story and I'll tell you all about it sometime, but the second I knew you were alive in the world, I went searching for you."

"I know. Mom told me."

Riley detected anger along with Aidan's disappointment, and he didn't blame him. "Look, I agree that your mom made a mistake when she chose not to tell you that you had a dad or I had a son. It was a whopper of a mistake."

"You could say that," Aidan said, laughing uncomfortably.

"I would have loved to have been your dad all this time."

"Yeah."

"But your mom had her reasons, Aidan. It's hard to see them from where we sit today, but Kat—your mom—she really believed she had no choice. Things weren't great for her here."

"Apparently not. But did that give her a right to keep me in the dark for my entire life? I mean . . ." Aidan paused and sighed. "It's just that I'm so fucking pissed at her right now, I don't know what to do."

"Don't cut her off, Aidan. Give it some time. You know, it took a lot of guts for your mom to tell you the truth after all these years, knowing how mad you'd be."

"But she totally lied to me."

"Yes, she did." Riley tried to soothe him without coming off as condescending. "She lied to me, too. I understand how you feel."

"No, you don't! You can't!" Aidan stopped, lowering his voice as he continued. "Look, this whole thing has just blown my mind—it's like waking up one day and finding out that nothing is what you thought it was."

"That's exactly what's happened—for both of us."

"Yeah. OK." Aidan took his time before he said anything more. "So what do we do now?"

Riley was wondering the same thing, and he smiled because he was so pleased with the person his son had turned out to be. He was articulate, sensitive, brave. But Riley was smiling mostly because his son had just asked him for guidance. He breathed deeply, images of Big Daddy steamrolling through his head. Sure, Big Daddy had done a lot of things right, but Riley would never bulldoze his kid the way his father had, and he'd always believed that, if ever given the chance, he'd figure out a way to be his own kind of father.

This was his chance.

"I think our next step is to get to know each other. I'd like to come to Baltimore to see you, if you'd agree to that. And I'd like you to come up here for Thanksgiving break, spend some time getting to know where you come from. Other than that, I suppose we'll figure it out as we go along. How does that sound?"

"Sounds good," Aidan said, his voice lighter. "I'd be up for that."

They talked for about an hour more, mostly about lacrosse, biochemistry, and a beautiful and brilliant girl named Rachel, whom Aidan had met in freshman physics class. Riley said good-bye to his son with a promise to talk again the next day.

Riley had just taken a long sip from his now lukewarm beer and settled back into the rocking chair when Loretta started up again. "Whisshhht," he hissed at her, but her rumble of complaint began to gain momentum. It grew louder as it moved up from her big barrel chest into her throat. Then she tipped her snout into the air and howled outright.

"I said stop it." Riley was just about to put her inside when he realized why the dog was howling. Loretta's keen sense of hearing had detected the car coming long before it made the corner. Riley got to his feet. He stared, his mouth opening in disbelief as Carrie's Volvo pulled in the drive.

He felt like tilting his head back and howling, too.

NINE

Just a year ago, Riley would have been checking out Caroline's legs as she sauntered up his walkway. Tonight, he checked for weapons.

Riley stood on the top step, more as a blockade than greeting. He didn't want her on the porch, let alone in the house. "I told you to never come back here again."

"I thought you meant the office." She flashed him a grin and stopped at the foot of the stairs, looking up at him sweetly.

"I was just heading out," Riley lied.

Carrie's eyes flickered toward the half-empty beer in his hand, and her tolerant smile revealed that she knew better. "I just need a minute of your time."

"Then we'll talk while I walk you to your car."

He took a sip from his beer and stepped down to the sidewalk, walking right past Carrie and catching a whiff of her perfume. She'd worn the same scent since their first year of med school, and when he was in love with her, he had associated that scent with joy. Nowadays it just reminded him of the nauseating cocktail of formaldehyde-phenol that had hovered over them as they dissected their anatomy lab cadaver, proving that love could not only make you blind, but it could fuck with your olfactory system, too.

"Could you put that dog away, please?"

Riley smiled to himself. He knew Carrie hated Loretta. It was mutual. "You won't be staying." He pulled open the driver door of Carrie's sedan and gestured for her to get behind the wheel. "Drive safely."

Carrie's hand covered his. "Please, Riley."

He yanked his hand away.

"How did this happen to us? We belong together."

Riley turned and walked toward the house.

"You are cruel!" she screamed after him. "You let a rumor completely destroy everything we'd planned! You went chasing after a baby that doesn't even exist! How could you do that to me?"

Riley made it to the porch, Loretta at his heels. "I'm calling the police."

"Why couldn't you give us another chance, Riley? Why?" Carrie ran up the sidewalk, falling onto her hands on the porch steps, where she began to wail. Loretta joined in. "Even though you basically left me at the altar, I was here waiting for you when you got back! But you just pushed me away! I love you! Why can't you understand that? Shut that dog *up*!"

Riley retrieved the cordless phone and began to dial, knowing that even if he did call the police, no one on the other end would be able to hear anything because of the surround-sound howling.

Carrie screeched louder than the dog, "Riley! Look at me! I insist you look at me when I'm talking!"

"Whssht!" Loretta strolled over to Riley at the command and sat at his feet in silence. "The day I canceled the wedding to go look for Aidan was the best damn day of my life."

Carrie's face collapsed. The tears stopped instantly. "Who is Aidan?"

"My son."

"You found him?"

"We found each other. Through Kat."

Carrie straightened up, dusting off her suit. "So that's why she came to town? To tell you about your son?"

"The police should be on their way," Riley said.

"She's just trying to ruin my life, don't you see?"

The pleasant lilt of her voice made the hairs on the back of his neck stand on end. He almost wished he'd actually made that call to the police. "What in the hell are you talking about, Carrie?"

"That Cavanaugh girl." Carrie ran a hand through her hair and smiled. "She's just trying to keep you from me."

Riley rubbed his jaw. Few things about the human condition surprised him anymore, but from a clinical perspective, Carrie's complete disconnect with reality was as fascinating as it was creepy.

"Well, Carrie, here's the thing. . . ."

"Yes?" Her eyes brightened.

"Kat is back in my life and Aidan is very much my son. That's where my attention is. Not you."

Her smile vanished. She began to slowly back away, retreating toward her car. Just before she ducked inside and drove away, she said, "You will live to regret this."

"Not likely."

Loretta let out a howl of good riddance.

He was hard as rock, but his flesh tasted sweet, tender, and as melt-in-your-mouth warm as freshly baked bread slathered in butter. Kat was operating on nothing but instinct, driven on by his wordless responses. When she flicked at the underside of his cock with her tongue, he shuddered. That probably meant he liked it. She nibbled along the length of him, cradling his flesh in her teeth while she looked up at his awestruck face. That move must have been a winner, too. When she accepted the swollen head into her mouth and sucked, his cock tasted salty and strong, and his hands went to the sides of her face, gently pushing her away.

"Baby, stop. Please. I'm going to come."

"That's OK," she said, truly meaning it. She was fascinated. She couldn't believe her little mouth held such power over his strong body. She wondered whether all girls had this talent, or if her gift was special. Either way, it amazed her that she'd already brought him to the point where he was panting and his eyes became so focused he looked angry.

But he wasn't angry—just serious. He tried to smile as he moved his hands to her hair and stroked, his groans becoming more desperate. Kat wasn't certain, but she didn't think he could maintain this excitement too much longer before he—

She jolted awake. The air felt strangely hot and humid, heavy with the smell of the ocean. Wherever she was, she was a world away from Persuasion's quarry road and the very first time she'd tasted Riley.

Kat tentatively opened one eye and found herself peering over the edge of a pair of dark sunglasses, only to be struck by light so bright it was painful.

"Would you like me to freshen your drink?"

Kat lolled her head to the left and encountered the smiling face of a blond guy she thought might be named Jeff. For some reason, she thought he might sell air conditioners for a living. Why would she think that? Why would she know his name? Her head hurt.

Then it all started to come back to her.

After a restless week in Baltimore, she and Nola had taken a last-minute vacation to the Cayman Islands. They'd flown first class, of course, and checked into a suite at a posh resort. And the night before—their first night on the island—they'd met four Connecticut businessmen at the resort disco. Kat vaguely recalled that Jeff over there, if that was in fact his name, was one of them.

Her body suddenly tightened in panic, her brain racing from one question to the next without pause: Why was this guy sitting next to her, sharing the same beach umbrella? Where was Nola? What had happened last night? Why was she dreaming of sex with Riley? Could she possibly have . . . Did this guy . . . ? *No!*

Without showing any of her anxiety, Kat used a fingertip to nudge the sunglasses down her nose, taking in Jeff's pleasant expression and his equally pleasant physique. She felt relief wash over her. The answer was no—of course she hadn't. She remembered now. She and Nola had made it back to their suite, quite late and pretty damn giggly, but without any men from Connecticut, the Cayman Islands, or anyplace else.

Jeff gave Kat a friendly smile and pointed to her half-empty cocktail glass. "You know what they say about the hair of the dog and all that."

Kat sat up in the cushioned chaise lounge, not wishing to appear to be lounging alongside Jeff. She quickly scanned the beach, and found Nola several umbrellas away, holding court with Jeff's coworkers.

"Are you staying with Mojitos today? Or did you switch to Alka-Seltzer?"

Kat ignored the guy's self-satisfied chuckle, glad that at least one of them thought he was funny. The tall, narrow bar glass on the table was sweating on the outside and its contents looked non-descript, but with a little effort, Kat remembered her cocktail of choice: two Excedrin with a ginger ale chaser.

"Thank you for the offer," she said to Jeff in the most pleasant voice she could muster. "But I'd prefer to pay for my drinks myself."

He laughed again. "You already have, cuteness. This is an all-inclusive resort."

"Right. I knew that." Kat wished this guy would get the hint. How rude did she have to be? She'd spent the last twenty minutes or so drooling on herself and dreaming about sex with the only man she'd ever wanted, who was about to marry someone else. She wasn't exactly encouraging Jeff's attention.

"Besides, I'm really enjoying your company," he added.

Behind the dark lenses, Kat rolled her eyes. "I've been asleep. I have a wicked hangover. You must be easily entertained."

He chuckled again. "Not particularly, but I think I'd enjoy watching you do pretty much anything."

Kat turned away, not sure if the sudden desire to heave was because of last night's Mojitos or Mr. Jeff. This guy was trying so hard that even if she were interested—which she wasn't—his approach would have made her run.

She stared hard at Nola in an attempt to will her to turn around and get back here to their umbrella. No such luck. Nola was enjoying herself, and whatever tale she was spinning had the men enthralled.

Then again, maybe their interest was in Nola's little red bikini and not her storytelling.

"You know, Kathy, you dodged all my questions last night." Jeff had turned on his left side so that he could gaze at her. He also managed to provide Kat with a full frontal view of himself. How thoughtful of him.

"It's Kat. And trust me when I say that you'd not like my answers."

He laughed again. Jeff sure was a cheerful guy. "I think I may have mentioned that I'm an engineer. We're down here bidding on a new resort construction project."

"Mmm," she said.

"I design commercial ventilation systems. My specialty is airborne contaminants."

"Really? How interesting."

Kat let her head fall back on the cushion, trying to figure out when she could safely take another dose of Excedrin as Jeff droned on about air volume and something called duct velocity, a term that struck her as unbelievably funny. Maybe she was still tipsy.

She sighed and folded her hands in her lap. It had been seven days since she'd returned from Persuasion and nearly that long since Aidan had spoken to her. She'd kept busy, of course. She'd accepted a bid for gutting the kitchen and bathrooms of Phyllis' row house and hoped to have it in move-in condition by the New Year. Also, she'd officially resigned her job at the florist, and though her boss was sad to see her go, she said she'd known it was coming. "If someone left me money, I'd run out the front door like the joint was on fire," she'd said.

Kat gazed out at the shocking blue of the ocean

and smiled to herself at the irony. Here she was—rich, single, and not burdened by the need to work for a living. Her child was grown and in college. She could do anything she wanted to do and go anywhere she wanted to go. She could start her own business or go back to school and major in any damn thing she felt like. She could live anywhere she wished. She could see the world, and, in fact, had already seen New York City and Grand Cayman Island.

So why did she feel so empty? Why did the prospect of any of those grand life adventures feel like a dreaded chore?

Riley was marrying somebody else, that's why.

"And you? What do you do? Are you married? Seeing anyone?"

Kat realized that Jeff had stopped talking about ducts and had moved on to her personal life. With a sudden jolt of inspiration, she looked him square in the eye.

"I should probably warn you that I'm on a truth kick," she said. "I've gone through some big changes lately, and I've decided that the only way to live from here on out is to tell the truth, no matter what. So you might want to take your towel and escape while you can."

Jeff tipped his head in interest. "How's that approach working out for you?"

Kat laughed. "It's a long story."

"I got time. Our presentation isn't until tomorrow."

Kat saw genuine interest on the man's face, but she shook her head. "I don't think so."

"Why don't you start at the beginning? That's usually a good place. Then you can just build on that."

Kat frowned. "You mean, like, with my childhood?"

"Sure."

"You have no idea what you're getting into."

Jeff shrugged. "Take me for an example. I was one of three kids, born and raised in Vermont. My dad was a middle school principal and my mom ran a day-care center. I went to Yale on scholarship and got my degree in engineering. I'm thirty-two. Never been married."

"Wow," Kat said. "I must have missed that sign-up sheet."

"And you?"

Kat reached for her watered-down ginger ale and drank every warm, fizzless drop that remained. "I was born in a West Virginia coal-mining town," she said.

He laughed. "That's a good one."

"It's not a joke."

"Oh." Jeff looked mortified. "Sorry."

"It was also a college town. My father was an art professor and a wife beater. My mother was a housewife who was scared of her own shadow. One Wednesday when I was sixteen, I found out I was pregnant, got thrown out of school, kicked to the curb by my boyfriend, and then went home to find my dad out in his sculpting studio, screwing the governor's wife. The state had commissioned him to do her bust, but I guess he decided to go ahead and do all of her."

"Damn."

"He saw me watching them. He sent the woman packing and then got in his car and drove off. My mom came home a couple minutes later. She'd been at the grocery. She found me out in the studio where I'd smashed the bust to a million pieces."

Jeff stared.

"My mom told me my dad would kill me when he found out. I cried and told her I was pregnant. She gave me all the cash she had hidden in the cookie jar and then kicked me out."

"Oh my God."

"So I hitchhiked on a lumber truck and was taken in by a woman in Baltimore who played bingo for a living and had up to forty-seven parakeets at a time. Her name was Phyllis and she helped hide me so my family could never find me. I had my baby. He's a sophomore at Johns Hopkins now. He wants to cure cancer."

Jeff's mouth hung open.

"I got my GED and then an associate's degree from a community college. I've worked as a florist for seventeen years, can you imagine? Then Phyllis died a few months ago and left me stinking rich. Apparently, she'd invested all her bingo winnings in communication and tech stocks. So I went with Nola there"—Kat pointed over her shoulder—"to Manhattan, where we got outrageous head-to-toe makeovers and then came up with the brilliant idea that I should go back to my hometown and get revenge while I still looked good, which we did about a week ago."

Jeff leaned toward Kat. "I've been meaning to tell you how much I love your cut."

"Thanks."

"So? What happened?"

"Well, my father had a heart attack when I showed up in town. Then I learned that my mother died a year ago. Then I realized I might still have feelings for my high school sweetheart—my kid's father—who is getting married to another woman in a couple months."

"No!"

"Yes. But we had incredibly hot sex while I was in town—before I knew he was engaged. In fact, I was just dreaming about him a minute ago, thinking how every time I've ever touched that man has been like magic. Even the first time. And we were just kids." Kat paused. "You know, I've only ever experienced sex and love together when I've been with that man. What is *wrong* with me? I mean, it can't be natural to be hung up on one man your whole life, can it?"

Jeff's lips parted like he wanted to speak, but nothing came out.

"Here's the really interesting part." Kat took a deep breath. "I'd always told my son that I didn't know who had gotten me pregnant as a teenager, that I was just another runaway hillbilly slut teenage mother."

"Get *out* of here!"

"So just the other day I had to tell him the truth—that he has a father, a father who wanted him all along. I had to tell him I've been lying to him his whole freaking life! And now he won't speak to me!"

Jeff suddenly sat up, swinging his feet over the edge of the lounge chair and shoving them into the sand. He hung his head in his hands and mumbled something that Kat thought ended with the word "nightmare."

"Yeah," she said, sighing. "It's a mess."

"But aren't you relieved?" When Jeff looked up, Kat saw tears in his eyes. "Aren't you at least glad that the truth is finally out? You'd been carrying the burden of lies for so many years that it's got to feel good to let it go."

Kat thought about that for a minute.

Jeff looked worried by her delay in answering. "It's a good thing, right?"

"Actually," Kat said, "it pretty much sucks."

"Oh God!" Jeff put his hands on either side of his face and looked nervously out to sea.

Kat was surprised by the level of his concern. The guy seemed broken up over her story. "Hey, I'll be all right," she said.

Jeff turned back and snapped at her, "This is not about you!" His outburst was obviously a surprise to him and he groaned. "Look, I'm sorry. I do want you to be OK and everything—you seem like a wonderful person—but I was thinking about *me.* My own lying, stinking mess of a life. I'm . . . well . . ."

Kat was having trouble following him. "You're what?"

"So completely gay," he whispered. "I've been hiding all my life, but I've finally fallen in love and I have to come out to my family, friends, even the guys I work with, or I'm just going to explode!" Jeff's eyes flickered toward the group down the beach. "But after hearing that god-awful account—"

Kat sat up too fast and almost lost her balance.

"Don't say that!" She placed her hand on Jeff's forearm. "My situation is just a little unusual is all. I'm sure the truth works out really well for most people."

Jeff stared down at his feet and wiggled his toes in the sand. "I don't know."

"By the way, why were you hitting on me so hard if you're gay?"

Jeff raised his eyes and stared at her incredulously.

"Fine, but if you plan to keep posing as a straight

man, you need to improve your game. Those were the worst pickup lines I've ever heard."

"Am I interrupting something?" Nola's voice had an edge of disapproval to it.

Kat turned, leaving her hand on Jeff. "Not at all. Join us."

"I should be going anyway." Jeff jumped from the lounge and grabbed his towel. "Maybe we'll all catch up later."

Kat was surprised when Jeff leaned down and kissed her cheek and whispered, "Thank you, sweetie." She smiled at him.

Nola wasted no time spreading her towel on the chair and taking Jeff's place. "He's cute. Is he any more exciting than the other three?"

"You seemed happy enough over there."

Nola shrugged. "I'd rather be getting my freak on than my geek on."

Kat laughed and lay back down, closing her eyes. "You say you're not looking for a man, anyway."

"I'm not, and ten minutes with those weenies reminded me why."

"Jeff was a very nice guy, actually."

"Yeah? Well, I bet Dr. Bohunk wouldn't like him very much."

Kat hissed. "He's gay, Nola."

"Riley is gay!"

Kat burst out with a laugh, which hurt her forehead. "I was talking about Jeff."

"Thank you, God."

"But don't say anything to his friends, because they don't know. Not yet, anyway."

"Well, all I'm saying is, I think you're glossing over the fact that Riley has been trying to reach you for days."

"There's nothing to say to each other."

"You really should talk to him—maybe he's had a falling-out with the future Mrs. Bohunk. Hey!" Nola shot straight up with excitement. "Maybe Riley was so happy to see you that he's called off the wedding!"

Kat closed her eyes, relieved to retreat behind the shades. Her head pounded harder, which wasn't entirely bad, because at least it gave her something to focus on besides the ache in her heart. *How could Riley be marrying someone else? He was supposed to be with me! How could he love anyone else—ever?*

"I've told you, Nola. Riley and Aidan know about each other and what happens from here on is between them. There's no future for me and Riley—even if I wanted one, which I don't."

Nola chewed on her lip. "You should at least hear what the man has to say."

"Can we just drop it for now? I'm on vacation."

"Technically, hon, the rest of your life is nothing but one long vacation." Nola stretched out on the chair with a deep moan of contentment. "Not that there's a damn thing wrong with that."

The presentation was titled *Diabetes Management in Rural Uninsured Populations—a Quarter Century of Failed Policy,* and Carrie's mind churned with fury. Oh, the injustice of it all! How could this have happened? How could something with so much promise be upended this way?

Kat Cavanaugh would pay.

Carrie sat front and center in the small statehouse auditorium, crossing her legs and pretending to listen intently. In just minutes, she would be expected to stroll up to the podium and comment on the ongoing study. But if the truth be told, she couldn't summon any interest in chronic disease management at this particular moment. While the presenter had droned on about community exercise classes and supervised meal planning, Carrie had been busy sending all of her positive, life-affirming energy toward Riley. Simultaneously, she'd been visualizing Kat Cavanaugh being run over by a garbage truck.

Carrie heard everyone in the auditorium clap, so she began clapping as well. She looked around, smiling pleasantly, trying to gauge how close the speaker was to wrapping it up. Carrie figured she had at least another ten minutes.

She would find Kat Cavanaugh's weak spot. Everybody had one. With a head start from Madeline and about three thousand dollars' worth of billable hours from a private detective, Carrie now knew quite a bit about the girl who'd been running around Baltimore using the last name Turner. Carrie had had a hearty laugh when she found out how Kat had gotten her money. It turned out she wasn't a call girl after all—she was a flat-out whore! Carrie could only imagine the elaborate web of deceit Kat had spun to get into that unsuspecting woman's will.

Kat's mother might be dead, but her father—a retired Mountain Laurel professor recovering from balloon angioplasty—still lived in Persuasion and might be worth a visit. And then there was the infamous child. Just as Riley said, his name was Aidan, and he'd somehow gotten himself accepted into Johns Hopkins on a lacrosse scholarship, which floored her. She herself had applied there for both undergraduate and medical schools and was rejected both times! It must have been because she was from out of state. And didn't play lacrosse.

Carrie checked her lipstick in a small compact and let out a big sigh. It really did take a lot of nerve to name that kid Aidan. She knew Big Daddy had to be rolling around in his grave at the insult. If Riley weren't so sentimental, he'd get a paternity test on the kid and move on. But Carrie was beginning to realize that Riley needed to believe the child was his. He had such a good heart. He had so much to give. He just wanted to be a father! *Oh, Riley,* she thought, closing her eyes to center herself, *I am open to receive your love. I say "yes, yes" to your love! And I will give you the son you so desperately want, a son who can carry on the Bohland family name without shame.*

Her mind drifted to the spat she'd had with the caterer earlier that morning. That diva actually said he refused to drizzle his hollandaise sauce on anything but the finest local or regional asparagus, which would be unavailable in December in West Virginia. Carrie had been stupefied. How simple could it be? She was the bride. She wanted fucking asparagus for the reception. What part of that arrangement didn't he understand?

Carrie felt a sharp jab on her upper arm and turned in shock to the person who'd obviously assaulted her.

"Wake up," whispered the man in the next seat. He jerked his thumb toward the stage. "They just introduced a Dr. Caroline Mathis. That's you, right?"

TEN

"Come on out, old girl."

Loretta jumped down onto the quarry road just like Riley ordered, immediately toddling off in search of an exotic scent, her snout to the ground and her white-tipped tail sticking straight up in the air like a furry periscope.

Riley grabbed his backpack and shut the groaning truck door. Matt sidled up to him and they began to walk.

"You know, I haven't been out here for recreational purposes since the night I left a huge hickey on Brendalee Larson's neck." Matt cringed at the admission. "I really felt bad about that."

"Yeah, well, every high school kid in Randolph County regrets something they did out here."

Matt was silent for a moment; then he said, "This was three months ago."

Riley laughed. Matt had always been more reckless than him. Maybe that was one of the benefits of being the baby of the family, but since birth Matt had seemed to breeze through life unruffled, blessed with a general sense that all would be well. Even when their mother died, Matt had bounced back faster and stronger than Riley did. Such confidence was probably a handy trait for a cop to have. It would likely be handy for anyone. All Riley knew was that he himself had missed out on the happy-go-lucky gene and doubled up on the one that coded for intensity.

He just prayed to God that Matt would bounce back when he told him about the mortgage. Riley took a breath and began. "Matt—"

"You talked to Aidan again?" Matt asked.

Riley must have looked unhinged, because Matt frowned at him and asked, "Is Aidan OK? Is something wrong?"

"Uh, no. He's great. We talk every day." Riley was relieved for the delay. "I was thinking of going down to Baltimore to see him this weekend."

"Want some company?"

Riley glanced sideways at his brother, suspicious of his sudden enthusiasm. "You still hot for Kat's friend?"

Matt grinned. "I'm just saying that I could take Friday off and we could drive down together. I'd give you your space with Aidan once we're there."

"Sure, Matt. It would be great for him to meet you."

"And, you know, while I was in town I could take the lovely Miss D'Agliano to a movie or something."

Riley chuckled. "Already track her down?"

"Not yet, but I'm workin' on it."

As they walked, the only sounds were the brush of Loretta's wide body parting the weeds, the beat of their hiking boots on the dirt lane, and the wind in the trees. Riley watched a hawk ride a thermal, effortlessly patrolling hundreds of square miles of old-growth forest and rolling mountains. He was enjoying this so much he decided to find another time for his confession.

"Does Kat know you'll be in Baltimore?"

Riley picked up a piece of quartz from the dirt, admired its shine, and then tossed it into the woods. "Aidan isn't talking to her and Kat won't return my calls, so I don't think she'd have any way of knowing."

"Hmm." Matt shoved his hands in his jeans pockets. "Sure is a dud of a way to reunite a family."

"How so?"

"Well, the mother—Kat—won't talk to the father, who is you, the son won't talk to the mother, and the mother not only won't talk to her own daddy, but doesn't want her son to have anything to do with his grandfather, which is probably good, because the grandfather doesn't even know he has a grandson."

"Sounds like your average American family to me," Riley said dryly.

Matt laughed. "All I'm saying is that y'all wouldn't get booked on *Montel* for one of those tear-jerky reunion shows."

"We'll survive somehow."

Matt kept his observations to himself for the next few minutes, and Riley concentrated on taking in the familiar beauty around him. The colors were unusually concentrated this fall, probably because of the ideal mix of rain and sun they'd had in late summer. Riley did love this place. Though the Monongahela Mountains of West Virginia were in his blood, a day didn't go by when he didn't see the irony—that all he'd ever wanted as a kid was to get out of Persuasion, yet here he was, to stay. He often wondered how differently his life would have unfolded if he hadn't gotten Kat pregnant, right here on the quarry road almost twenty years ago to the day, on a blanket spread out no more than a hundred yards from where he now hiked.

Back then, Riley had truly believed in the beach house and the Colorado ski retreat, the two kids he and Kat would have together, and the happiness that would come to them in due time. But on that October night, his need to be inside Kat was so blinding that it obliterated everything in its path—reason, dreams, and even Big Daddy's dire warnings. And in the following months, as they explored every corner of the sexual wonderland they'd created together, the desire to be with Kat only grew richer, deeper, more concentrated. He loved her. That was a given. But once the mind-blowing pleasure of sex was introduced into the mix, Riley was a drowning man—done for—and damn happy about it.

It was understandable that he'd never forgotten the rush of those first sexual experiences. What was inexplicable was that he'd gotten another taste of Kat just a couple weeks ago and it was as if time had stood still. His heart ignited at the sound of her voice. He wanted her more than ever. It was as if she'd branded his body and spirit with her own all those years ago and he'd always belonged to her, as if no matter where he'd been or what he'd done in his life, he'd only been waiting for Kat to reappear.

"I've got to get her back, Matt."

Matt didn't say a word in response, just kept his steps in sync with Riley's.

"I think I might still love her."

Matt swiveled his head around and glared at Riley. He opened his mouth to speak.

"Hold on before you start in on me," Riley warned. "I'm serious. I think I still love her. She fucked me over good—OK, I get that—but from where she sits, I fucked her over, too."

"That's some twisted thinking right there."

"Not really. The same afternoon Kat disappeared, she told me to meet her right here"—Riley pointed to the ground beneath his feet—"just to tell me she was pregnant. But she couldn't even get the words out before I broke up with her."

Matt stopped walking. "How long have you known that?"

Riley stopped, too. "She told me when she was here."

"And you believe her?"

"Why wouldn't I? She believed me when I told her I went looking for her and Aidan as soon as I knew."

Matt shook his head slowly, looking down at his feet as he dragged the toe of his boot through the rusty dirt. "You slept with her at Cherry Hill, didn't you?" When he looked up, his eyes were pleading. "Why, Bro? Why the hell would you go and do that?"

"I couldn't help myself."

Matt laughed loud enough to elicit a sympathy howl from Loretta, who bounded up from the creek like she was missing out on something. "Man, half the women in Randolph County are trying on a daily basis to give you a little sumthin-sumthin' and all you do is turn your nose up at the offers. But Kat comes back to town for a day and you suddenly can't help yourself? What the fuck?"

It was Riley's turn to laugh, which inspired Loretta to double her efforts. "You're way off-base, Matt!" he shouted.

"OK, three-quarters of the women, then!" Matt

yelled back. "But I'm telling you, there's plenty of no-strings-attached pussy out there for the taking. And you don't have to deal with crazy women like Carrie and Kat to get you some."

Riley didn't bother to hide how disgusted he was at Matt's last comment, and began walking again, this time at a faster clip.

"I was out of line," Matt mumbled as he caught up with Riley. "I know Carrie didn't start out totally psycho. I'm sorry for saying that."

"Apology accepted."

"But I still don't understand your obsession with Kat Cavanaugh."

"Someday you'll know what I'm talking about, little brother." Riley gave Matt a friendly slap on the back. "Someday there will be a woman who gets under your skin, and I mean all the way, and you won't want to hold back a thing—you'll want to give her everything you are and everything you have."

Matt shot Riley a doubtful look.

"It happened real early in my case. I knew who Kat was to me by the time I was twelve."

"Oh, please."

"It's true." Riley looked out into the woods, studying the rich spectacle that was the Monongahela Forest in autumn—the sunshine yellow of the Kentucky coffee tree, the dogwood's crimson, the post oak's pale brown. His gaze landed on the fused trunks of two old hemlocks growing near the walking path, and he wondered what extreme conditions were responsible for that twist of nature. Was it a single violent summer storm? Months of windy conditions? A mud slide? Whatever the cause, the two deeply furrowed trunks had created a single foothold in the earth, to be undone only with their death.

"Remember Mom's funeral?"

Matt seemed surprised by Riley's question but nodded. "Sure, as much as I can remember anything from when I was eight."

"Remember how Kat stood up in front of everyone and read that poem?"

Matt shook his head. "All I remember is Big Daddy telling me to stop my blubbering."

Riley nodded. "Well, Kat got up there with a voice as strong and clear as a church bell and read a poem by Shelley. It was beautiful—about how the dead live on in our memory—and the whole church went quiet when she read it." *How delicate she looked,* Riley remembered. Her small body was overpowered by the mountains of flowers behind her and she pulled the microphone down to reach her mouth. "I stared at her hands. She wasn't shaking one bit. And when she was done, she looked right into my eyes and I was so proud of her, so in love with her, even in my sadness. And I knew that she was the girl who would share my life with me, the one who would always have my back. There was no question in my mind."

"Right."

"We've been linked from childhood on up and we're still that way, even though we've spent more time apart than we ever did together."

Matt produced a doubtful grunt.

"Anyway, Kat's definitely not crazy—she just has a few issues to resolve."

Matt stifled a laugh.

"But you're right on the money about Carrie, man. She's been showing up unannounced again."

Matt swiveled his head around in surprise. "When?"

"At the office the day you told me you'd found Kat, and then later that night. She came to the house."

"Why didn't you tell me?"

Riley laughed. "There have been more important things going on."

"What did she want?"

Riley shrugged. "She gave me some bull about the clinic getting renewed attention in the legislature, and then gave another one of her Oscar-caliber performances, begging me to give her another chance. I'm telling you, she's totally crossed the line."

Matt nodded decisively. "We can have a protective order in twenty-four hours."

Riley chuckled. "Thanks, Chief, but Carrie isn't a physical threat. She's just living in a fantasy world. She really thinks that after all this time and after everything she's done, I would still consider getting back with her."

Matt shook his head. "That's ridiculous."

"Unbelievable."

"Yet that's exactly what you want to do with Kat."

Riley jerked his head in surprise at his brother's challenge. He was starting to regret inviting Matt to join him on his hike.

"The last year has been tough on you, man; that's all I'm saying." Matt placed a hand on Riley's arm. "I sure hope you know what you're doing."

Riley had no idea what he was doing. He didn't know what to say, what to do, or how any of it was going to feel. But he was doing it anyway. He was about to meet his son.

It was a pleasant Friday evening, and the Inner Harbor rocked with tourists and the after-work happy-hour types. Because he didn't spend a lot of time in the city, Riley paid careful attention to how he navigated the crowds, dodging, squeezing by, and mumbling his hellos when it would seem rude not to, considering that someone's face had just come within inches of his own.

The scene felt damn-near overpowering to Riley, which made him to smile to himself—he was such a country boy. The noise level was jarring. Two kinds of live music and at least three languages battled it out for the open airspace, and the shrill beeps of car horns were nearly drowned out by the lower, deeper complaints of sightseeing boats. His nose detected the competing scents of dozens of restaurants and taverns, but there was only one spot that would catch his fancy tonight—a seafood place called City Lights, where Aidan had suggested they meet.

Riley looked down at his watch and laughed at himself. Matt had been right—he'd left from the nearby hotel with so much time to spare that he'd arrived a full half hour early, even walking at a leisurely pace. So be it. Riley had been dreaming of this day for an entire year. He would finally get an opportunity to show his kid that he cared. This was no time to be even a minute late.

Out of the corner of his eye he saw the sign for the restaurant, then almost immediately spotted an end of a bench overlooking the water. Riley sat down, acknowledging with a nod the elderly African-American gentleman already headquartered there.

"Fine evening," the man said.

"Yes, it is."

"Visiting the city?"

"Yes, sir. I live in West Virginia."

The old man nodded with approval. "Now that's a beautiful state. Some of the prettiest scenery anywhere."

"Yes, sir."

"What brings you here? Business?"

As the words formed on Riley's tongue, he felt his face expand in a silly grin. He probably looked like a goof. "Actually," he said to the man, pausing to savor what would come next, "I'm in town to meet my son for a bite to eat. He's a student at Johns Hopkins—a biology major."

The old man lifted his chin. "One of the world's best schools. You must be real proud of him."

Riley looked out over the water, thinking to himself that he was proud of Aidan for being smart and disciplined enough to make it into Hopkins, surely. But Riley was most proud that his son had the courage to be here tonight, to meet him.

"I *am* proud."

"You know, I'm eighty-two years old, and I have to say that a job is just a job, but being a father is the best thing a man can do with his life." With that, he broke out into a goofy grin himself, revealing a shockingly white set of dentures. He slowly rose to his feet. "You enjoy that meal."

Riley stood to shake the man's hand and wished him well. As Riley watched his bent form make slow progress across the crowded plaza, something caught his attention. It had to be the shape of the chin, the set of the dark eyes. There could be no mistake.

It was Aidan.

He stood on the steps in front of the restaurant, leaning against the railing, one hand in his jeans pocket. Aidan was tall and lanky and looked nervous as hell as his eyes bored right into Riley's. Riley began walking, his mind blank and his pulse wild. His steps quickened, and he broke into a jog.

It took just a moment to reach Aidan, because he had raced down the steps and started running, too. They stopped in the middle of the crowd, their eyes the same level, their shoulders the same breadth. Riley wanted to shout and cry and throw his arms around his kid, but the last thing he wanted to do was scare Aidan.

So Riley extended his hand. "Aidan," he said.

Aidan swung his hand around and gripped Riley's, giving it a series of emphatic pumps. "You're early," Aidan said, still pumping.

Riley laughed. "I think I'm about twenty years late."

Aidan smiled, but his bravado didn't last. He threw himself into Riley's arms and crushed him with a hug. "God, I'm glad you finally made it," Aidan said.

Kat poked her head into the upstairs bathroom, watching as one of the workmen pulled up the faded pink tiles from the floor. She clearly recalled all the hours she'd spent staring at those tiles while on her knees, the morning sickness stretching into the afternoons and then the evenings.

Phyllis would stand on the other side of the door, asking after her, offering hot tea or a cold washcloth. As the days went by, Kat began to let her guard down, and she told herself that maybe there really were people in the world who were just decent and caring, and that maybe this Phyllis woman and her brother, Cliff, were two of them.

In those first months, Phyllis cooked for Kat, took

her shopping for clothes that would cover her growing lump, and made sure she got plenty of rest. Cliff stopped by when he came through town, and he'd always bring Kat a little something—a music box, some teen magazines, and a big box of chocolates for Valentine's Day. He called her Sunshine, because her hair and eyes were gold like the sun, he said. Kat always felt a little spoiled by Cliff, and wondered if that was the way it was supposed to have been with her real dad. She adored Cliff for that.

Phyllis got Kat into the health clinic. That initial trip to the doctor was the first time Kat had used the name Katharine Turner. Phyllis suggested it. "Just for now, until we get everything settled," she said. As the months went by and Kat's belly got bigger, Phyllis began to gently prod her, "Wouldn't it be nice to let your mama know you're OK?"

"No," was always her answer.

By her second trimester, Kat ate like a dockworker. She remembered having one particularly difficult conversation with Phyllis over a huge plate of Chef Boyardee spaghetti with meatballs.

"Are you sure you don't want to contact her?"

"Yes. Can I have some more milk?"

"Help yourself, hon."

Kat put down her fork and stared at Phyllis. Sometimes, depending on the light, there was something about her face that looked familiar and safe. Maybe it was the shape of her lips or the daintiness of her chin. Kat could never pinpoint it. But she thought that if Phyllis laid off the Toni home perms, put some meat on her bones, and didn't smoke so much, she'd probably be a pretty woman.

"I still don't get it. How come you're so nice to me? I'm nobody to you—just a girl in trouble."

Phyllis stubbed out her Newport Light and pursed her lips in thought. "It's like this, hon," she said. "Human beings have tiny little brains, smaller than parakeet brains if you ask me, and we don't always see that we're in this mess together."

Kat chewed another mouthful, frowning.

"See, people are connected like puzzle pieces, but because we can't tell what the overall picture's supposed to look like, we're walking around clueless about how we fit together, you know?"

Kat took a big gulp of milk and wiped her face with a napkin. "I have no idea what you're talkin' about."

Phyllis smiled kindly. "All I'm saying is that I know what you're going through, hon. It happens more than you think. I got pregnant myself when I was seventeen. I wasn't married to the boy, same as you."

Kat's eyes went huge. "No way!"

"Now, my story is set way back in 1964, mind you, so we ended up having to get married. Then I lost the baby—miscarriage." Phyllis immediately picked up on the fear in Kat's face and reassured her. "I was just a few months along and that's when most miscarriages happen. The doctor said you're doing great, remember? You're going into your sixth month and everything is fine."

Kat nodded, knowing Phyllis was right. "So what happened to your husband?"

"You done with this?" Phyllis picked up the milk carton without getting an answer and took it to the fridge. Kat watched her, knowing that she was avoiding the question. "You want a peach, Kat?"

"I hate peaches."

Phyllis stood at the kitchen counter with her back to Kat. "How about a banana?"

"No, thanks."

Phyllis returned to the table and placed a brown-freckled banana in front of her, and Kat didn't know if that meant she was supposed to eat it because it was good for the baby or because Phyllis hadn't paid any attention to her answer.

"What happened to him?" Kat asked again.

"Ever heard of the Vietnam War?"

"Of course I have," Kat said. "I got straight A's in history."

"Well, about a year after I lost the baby, Frank—that was my husband's name—Frank graduated from school and enlisted in the Army. He thought it would be our ticket to a good life, you know, see the world and all."

Kat nodded, already knowing where this was going.

"He finished his ordnance training up here at Aberdeen and they shipped him out. Three weeks later, he was dead as a doornail."

Kat fell back in her chair and rubbed her belly, not sure what to say. "I'm so sorry, Phyllis," was what she came up with.

"Me, too. Frank was a good boy. He loved baseball and believed in always paying cash—told me to never buy anything on time except for a house, and that's exactly what I've done."

"You never wanted to marry anyone else?"

Phyllis shrugged. "No one ever came along as good as my Frank. I figured I had me a good man once in my life and that was more than most women get, so why be greedy? It's like if I win two weeks in a row at the same bingo parlor, I don't go back to that location for three whole weeks. You never want to push your luck."

That's when Kat began to cry. Phyllis placed her hands over Kat's, which were still cradling her swollen belly.

"I hear you bawling at night sometimes, hon," Phyllis said gently. "I know you loved him. Did he love you, too?"

All Kat could do was nod as the tears dropped down onto their joined hands.

"Is he a good boy?"

Kat nodded again. "Yeah." She pulled a hand away from Phyllis and wiped her eyes. "He's real smart and funny and he plays every sport you can think of. He's always been respectful and kind." She looked into Phyllis' face. "Is that what you mean by 'a good boy'?"

Phyllis smiled gently. "Yes. That would make him a fine young man." She patted Kat's hand, then leaned back in her chair, studying her. "He don't know where you're at or that you're having his baby, does he?"

Kat snapped to attention. "Why do you ask that?"

"Because if he loved you—and knew where to find you and his baby—he'd be here." Phyllis tilted her head and smiled kindly. "That's what a fine young man would do."

Kat blinked, suddenly hearing Riley's last words to her, cold and empty and without one bit of respect or kindness: *Go away, Kat. It's over.* That's what had her crying at night—those horrible words, over and over in her head. Kat thought maybe she'd answered Phyllis too quickly. Maybe Riley had never loved her at all. Maybe she'd just been another ignorant girl whose head was crammed with wishes that would never become real. Maybe Riley had looked her square in the eye, kissed her, and lied to her just to get sex.

He wouldn't be the first man to ever lie to a woman; that Kat knew for sure.

"What's his name, hon?" Phyllis asked.

A bolt of fear shot from Kat's belly to the tips of her fingers. Phyllis was trying to get information from her that no one in the world could ever have. There was no one left in Persuasion who gave a damn about her, and nobody there would ever get to lay eyes on her precious baby, including Riley. He didn't deserve the baby girl Kat was certain she was carrying. It would be her baby girl and no one else's.

Kat could never again count on anyone in Persuasion for anything.

Kat's mind raced through blankness, grasping for any name to give Phyllis, just to get her to drop the subject. Her gaze fell upon the prized autographed baseball inside the dining room hutch.

"His name is Cal." As soon as Kat spoke, she felt like slapping herself in the head. How stupid could she be? Half the shit in that cabinet had Cal Ripken's name plastered all over it!

Phyllis picked up her Bic lighter and began tapping it on the tabletop, a strange grin on her face. "Remember when you first got here? You told me your name was Tina and you were from Ohio."

Kat froze.

"And it took you two weeks to tell me your real name was Katharine and you were from Martinsburg, West Virginia."

Kat kept her mouth shut.

"OK, hon. Cal and Tina it is." Phyllis got up from her chair. "Now eat that banana—it's good for the baby."

"Miss Turner, before we wrap up for the day, I need to tell you about a problem with the kitchen floor."

Had someone just said her name?

"Miss Turner?"

Kat spun around to face the remodeling contractor. She obviously had a crazed expression on her face, because the guy took a step backward. "Sorry to disturb you," he sputtered.

Kat laughed at herself, wondering how she'd managed to zone out in the middle of this much noise. The pounding and crashing coming from the two baths and the kitchen were so loud the contractor had to yell for her to hear him.

"No problem. I was just lost in thought," she said.

He nodded. "Well, we yanked up the kitchen linoleum and another layer of tile underneath, and it looks like you're going to have to replace the whole subfloor. It's rotted through."

Kat shrugged. "OK, I guess."

"And that'll change the estimate."

"I understand."

The contractor stuck a pencil behind his ear and sighed. "Once you start ripping away those top layers, you never know what kind of crap you'll find underneath."

She smiled. "Ain't that the truth?"

Riley hadn't laughed this hard or this long since he was a kid. The energy created by the three of them was magical, causing Riley to see the nature-versus-nurture argument in a far more personal way. Aidan hadn't known who he was until a week ago, and had been running around the planet using the last name Turner for all of his nineteen years, but that didn't change the fact that the boy was a Bohland through and through.

The stunned glances Matt would occasionally send Riley's way confirmed it.

The three of them had already covered a lot of ground that Saturday—literally. They'd gone to the National Aquarium, grabbed lunch at Asaro's in Little Italy, and were now watching the Ravens game on a huge high-definition TV screen at the ESPN Zone on the harbor. The day had started out perfectly and only improved from there, and Riley knew it was shaping up to be the best day of his life.

He and Matt had gone to Aidan's off-campus apartment to pick him up about nine that morning. It was a neighborhood made equally of the run-down and the remodeled, busy with college kids, people going about their business, and the occasional homeless person or empty crack vial.

As they neared Aidan's building, Riley watched as Matt felt for his service revolver out of habit and then groaned when he remembered he'd left it at home. "Aidan shouldn't be living here," Matt announced. "It's not safe."

Riley laughed at the mother hen Matt had suddenly become. "He's lived in the city all his life. It's his home." The men climbed up the two flights of stairs to Aidan's apartment.

"He shoulda been livin' in Persuasion."

Riley gave his brother a friendly pat on the shoulder. "Try not to act like a bumpkin from West *Virgin-eye-aye,* would you?"

"I'm a hick and I'm proud," Matt said.

After Aidan answered the door, all smiles, he and Matt studied each other in stunned silence.

"My God," Matt whispered.

"Kinda freaky," Aidan said. "You must be my uncle Matt."

Matt swallowed hard. "You got that right."

Though the three of them talked all day, Riley knew that he'd barely scratched the surface with his son. Riley had twenty years of day-to-day to catch up on, and he wanted to hear it all. He'd learned everything he never knew about lacrosse. He discovered the depth of his son's passion for biochemical research and the exotically beautiful Rachel Mishmurtha from Teaneck, New Jersey. Riley learned that Aidan's favorite meal was backfin crab cakes and Silver Queen corn on the cob, and that his mother had recently become a millionaire heiress.

That last bit was a minor detail Kat had apparently forgotten to mention when she was slumming in Persuasion.

"Shee-*it*!" Matt said at the revelation, the foam from his beer still clinging to his upper lip. "You're yankin' our chain, right?"

Riley leaned back in his chair and studied Aidan as he continued the story.

"Nope. Phyllis had been socking away thirty years of bingo winnings into stocks and bonds. When she died, Mom got about two-thirds of the money and all the parakeets."

Matt's eyes were as big as drink coasters. "Exactly how many millions—" He switched gears in the middle of his question. "How many parakeets we talkin'?"

Aidan laughed. "Well, Uncle Matt, we're talking

more than three million dollars and exactly thirty-six parakeets at the time of her death."

Matt nodded numbly, as if trying to process that information. "Better than the other way around, I guess," he said.

Riley didn't want to turn today into an interrogation about Kat, but his mind was burning with thousands of questions, many of which Aidan could surely answer. He told himself to be patient, to let the information come out when Aidan was ready.

Thank God Matt wasn't burdened by any such decency.

"So, did your mom ever marry? Did she date a lot?"

Aidan took a sip of his Coke and shook his head, seemingly unbothered by such a blunt question from his brand-new uncle. "She never married and didn't date all that much, though she had a few boyfriends over the years. She was famous for saying, 'The air is rare,' which Phyllis once explained to me meant that most men were assholes."

Matt nodded. "I like this Phyllis."

Aidan smiled sadly. "I do, too."

Riley couldn't stand it anymore. He leaned forward on his elbows and looked into his son's eyes.

"Where's your mom this weekend?" Riley knew his question sounded like the abrupt change of subject it was, but Aidan didn't seem to mind.

"She left me a message that she's back in town, probably at her place."

Riley tried not to let on how relieved he was to hear that. He knew where Kat lived, and he knew he was headed there as soon as they got Aidan back to the dorm. Riley had to see her. He couldn't come and go from this city without talking to her, finding out why she ran off like she did last week. It was his turn for a surprise visit.

"So," Matt said, obviously wanting to move the conversation away from Kat. "Did your dad tell about our road trip?"

Aidan frowned, shaking his head. "You mean your drive from West Virginia yesterday?"

Matt laughed. "Nope. I'm talking about last year, when we first found out about you. Just before she died, your mama's mama—BettyAnn—told your dad that you and your mom were living in Patterson, California. Or that's what your dad thought she said. So that's where we went looking."

Aidan cocked his head and Riley watched the comprehension spread over his son's face. Aidan let out a surprised laugh. "Phyllis' house is at the corner of Patterson and California."

"Yep," Matt said. "And if it weren't for that little misunderstanding, we would have found you a lot sooner."

"Damn!" Aidan's eyes sparkled. "So you went out west to look for us?" He addressed the question to Riley, but Matt was in cop mode and couldn't be stopped.

"You bet. I did all kinds of public-record searches and made some calls, but I couldn't find any trace of you or your mom, in California or anywhere else. Neither did the P.I. we hired."

"You really hired a private detective?" Aidan seemed incredulous.

"Sure did," Matt went on. "After he came up with squat, we decided to go see for ourselves. Your dad here—" Matt angled his thumb at Riley. "He took an unpaid leave of absence from his practice to look for you." Matt chuckled. "I flew out to help him on weekends and when I could get time off. We never found you, but we got to see a lot of the country, that's for damn sure."

Aidan's expression suddenly went serious and he turned to Riley. "I had no idea you did all that," Aidan said, obviously trying to hide the emotion he was feeling. "Thank you."

Riley nodded. "I just wish I would have done a better job."

"Don't listen to him," Matt said. "He followed every lead he got, and he got quite a few. It's amazing how many people said they'd seen a woman of your mom's description with a boy in tow over the years. How many states did we end up going to, again?"

Riley would never forget. "Seventeen."

Aidan's mouth dropped open. "You drove all those places?"

Riley nodded.

"Shit," Aidan whispered. After a long moment of silence, he started to laugh.

Matt laughed, too. "Yeah. You were probably sittin' around thinking your daddy didn't give a damn about you, right about the time he was staying at that health hazard of a motel in Montana, the one where the heater vent smelled like dead weasel. What town was that, again?"

"Helena," Riley said, carefully gauging Aidan's reaction to all this.

"Right," Matt said. "We put close to fifteen thousand miles on that old truck."

"Hey, Aidan," Riley said, knowing he needed to stop Matt before he began reminiscing about what they'd ordered for lunch in Cape Girardeau, Missouri. "All Matt's saying is, we tried our best to find you, and I was madder than hell that I had to come home empty-handed."

Aidan nodded.

"I'd do it all over again, too."

"Yeah." Aidan scooted his chair back. "I'm going to run to the men's room. Catch you in a minute."

Riley watched his grown son stroll through the cavernous old warehouse restaurant, shoulders square and straight as he moved. This was a hell of a lot for a kid to be taking in all at once.

"Is he all right? This has got to be a total mind fuck," Matt said, taking a sip of his beer.

"For all of us."

"Don't do it, Bro." Matt's expression went hard. "Don't go see her."

Riley shrugged. "I have no choice."

"Sure you do. We all have a choice."

"All right, so I choose to talk with her."

Matt rolled his eyes.

"Kat and I are nothing but one big ball of unfinished business and half-truths, and I'm not leaving here until we deal with some of it!"

Matt shook his head. "Remember that day I said you were too closed up and should talk about things more?"

"Sure."

"I liked you better that way."

They sat in silence until Aidan came back.

He looked calm, and smiled at both Matt and Riley. "This has been an amazing day. I mean, in some ways it feels like a dream, but I look at you guys and I know it's very real. It's just going to take some getting used to, I guess."

Riley smiled back. "The important thing is we've made a start."

Aidan nodded, pulled out a pen from his pocket, and clicked it open. "Got a piece of paper?"

Riley didn't, but he handed Aidan one of the extra bar napkins on the tabletop and watched him scrawl some numbers on it. Aidan shoved it back toward Riley when he was done.

"It's Mom's address and phone number."

Riley felt his pulse skitter. "Uh, thanks," he managed. "But I already have it."

Aidan grinned. "Cool."

"Hey, before you put that thing away—" Matt pointed at Aidan's pen. "Is there any chance you might be able to get me a number for Nola D'Agliano?"

Aidan let out a boisterous laugh and Riley heard the echo of Big Daddy in the cadence of it. "It's D'Agostino."

Matt nodded. "No wonder I couldn't find her."

"Oh, man," Aidan said, shaking his head.

"What?" Matt sat up straighter. "Not a good idea? I just wanted to ask her out for coffee or something."

Aidan snatched another napkin from the table and began writing on the back of it. "No, no, it's fine," he said. "I was just thinking that you're exactly Nola's type." He finished with the last few digits and handed the napkin to Matt with a sheepish grin.

"Oh yeah?" Matt waited for more details, but Aidan seemed to enjoy teasing him. "Come on, man; aren't you going to help out your old uncle here? What is it that makes me her type? My looks? My personality?"

"The fact that you're not Italian and you have a job. That about does it."

Matt's face went blank.

"See, she's always talking about how she's sworn off men, Italian men in particular. All her husbands have been Italian, and most of them either were unemployed at the time they married or got that way real quick. Nola earns good money as a paralegal."

One of Matt's eyebrows shot high on his forehead. "How many husbands were there?"

"Three."

Matt whistled.

"But none of them lasted very long," Aidan added, as if that would be reassuring.

Matt grimaced. "You're not saying they're all *dead,* are you?"

Aidan and Riley howled with laughter.

"Not that I'm aware of," Aidan said, catching his breath.

Riley patted Matt's arm. "This sounds like a match made in Hades."

"You should know," his brother snapped.

ELEVEN

Kat sat in the fading evening light, her legs tucked up underneath her, the mug of cocoa now cold in her hand. On the side table was the book she'd been reading, one she'd originally bought to enjoy on the beach, but mindless beach reading it didn't turn out to be. So now that she was back in the privacy of her own little city apartment, she'd spent most of the day with her nose buried in the print, reading about the psychology of suppressed memories—why they pop up when they do, how to handle them, and why people push them down in the first place.

She was hoping the book might help her remember everything that had happened in her dad's studio the evening she left Persuasion. It seemed impossible that the memory had ever existed in one piece in her brain, because she didn't even remember when she'd begun to forget. A week after she came to Baltimore? A month? Two years? She'd never mentioned anything about that night to Phyllis or Nola, because until recently she didn't realize there was anything to tell.

Kat rubbed hard at the back of her neck, pressing her fingers into the knotted muscles. The first snippets of memory about that evening had come when she and Nola sat in the ER of Davis Memorial, staring at Kat's father's limp hands. But the event didn't really come alive until the other day on the beach, talking to Jeff. When she'd said it out loud—telling him a story like it had happened to someone else—the memory had suddenly become real, taken root, and she'd been drowning in the emotional fallout ever since.

She needed a break. Kat got up out of the old chair and stretched, reaching toward the ceiling and then down to her toes. She shuffled to the bathroom and threw cold water on her eyelids, noticing the tanned but frowning face staring back at her from the mirror. She was thirty-seven now. She wasn't a girl running away anymore. She was nobody's victim and she wasn't hiding a damn thing from anyone. On top of all that, thanks to Phyllis, Kat would never have to rely on anyone for anything again for as long as she lived.

Whatever she had to deal with, she'd deal with it, whether it be something outside herself—like Aidan's fury—or something inside herself. Like her own buried memories.

Leaning closer to her reflection, Kat studied every fine line that fanned out from her eyes, every freckle that had survived the Fifth Avenue glycolic acid facial. She was still pretty enough. If she decided she wanted a man's company for casual dating, she could probably find a good one if she really put her mind to it.

Stranger things had happened.

Kat patted her face dry with a towel and headed into the kitchen to get a snack. On her way she flipped on the remote to her new Bose CD changer, and her apartment came alive with Bonnie Raitt's slide guitar and sweet lament. Kat sang along, slapping together a turkey and Swiss on rye as she wailed about good lovin' gone bad, and had just taken a large bite when she heard the banging sound.

Great. Kat tossed her sandwich to the paper plate. She'd been sitting down here quiet as a dead mouse the whole day, and the second she turns on some good music, Mrs. Brownstein starts pounding on her floor with her broom handle. Kat really looked forward to moving into the row house when it was remodeled. At least at Phyllis', there were no upstairs neighbors, and the shared walls were thick enough to give a person some privacy.

Kat turned the volume down until Bonnie's roar became a mewl, and took a seat at the dinette table. Just as she got another big bite into her mouth, the banging started up again. This time, it was her front door.

Kat was pissed. She'd lived under Mrs. Brownstein now for twelve years, and the older that woman got, the crankier she became. The broom had been plenty to get the message across. There was no need to come down here and make a fuss in person.

Kat flung open the door, already aligning her gaze to where she expected to find a pair of crinkly, angry eyes behind thick glasses. Instead, she encountered a man's chest. Not just any man's, either. She didn't need to adjust her gaze upward to know it was Riley.

"You've got something on your chin," he said, and because he said it in that unmistakable West Virginia baritone, Kat thought it was just about the sexiest sentence she'd ever heard in her life. She reached up to wipe away the mayonnaise, but Riley got there first, running his finger just below and to the left of her bottom lip.

She refused to look up at his face. She couldn't handle this. Why did he come here? He was about to get married! This was just torture! Oh, but she had to look—she knew he would be taking that dollop of mayonnaise and putting it in his own mouth, and she just had to watch! When it came to Riley Bohland, she'd always been so damn *weak*!

Kat raised her chin and dared to look at him. Riley was grinning, and his rich blue eyes were laughing, and he took that bit of mayonnaise and opened his gorgeous, soon-to-be-married mouth and flicked out his tongue to gobble it right up.

Kat thought she'd wet herself.

"This is so unfair," she whispered, not even realizing she'd said it out loud.

"It's about as fair as it gets. Now that I've dropped by unannounced the way you did, I'd say we're even."

Kat shook her head, overwhelmed at all the reasons that this was such a bad development, the most important being that Riley was engaged. Coming in a close second was that little complication that she hated him, followed by the fact that she was probably still in love with him. Really, all she wanted was to jump him right now, in her doorway, and give Mrs. Brownstein something to bang her broom about for once. But she wouldn't.

"Aren't you going to invite me in?"

Kat snorted. "I think not."

"Why's that?"

"I'm eating."

"I'll keep you company while you eat."

"No thanks."

"Then come out somewhere with me."

"I'm not dressed."

"Then put on those slutty fur-trapper boots I liked so much and let's go for a walk."

Kat's mouth fell open. "My *what*?"

"What you're wearing is fine, but if you're not comfortable for some reason, just put something else on."

Kat looked down at herself and laughed, knowing full well that her ratty cotton sweatpants and T-shirt weren't even fit for the Early Bird Tavern at the corner, an establishment famous for its complete lack of standards of any kind.

"I don't want to put anything on."

"That'll work, too," Riley said, grinning.

"This isn't a good idea," she said.

"C'mon now, Scout." Riley winked. "You know you're going to let me in."

At the sound of that ancient nickname, Kat gasped. She stared at Riley in wonder—yet another detail from her past she'd managed to shove down. Or maybe, if she believed the stuff she'd been reading in that book, she'd blocked the nickname from her memory because the idea that someone ever loved her like that—then dumped her—hurt too much to handle.

Riley continued to smile down on her, and she knew he was thinking of that day long ago, just like she was. They were ten years old, on the playground near the monkey bars. She was wearing her Girl Scout uniform—proudly—because her troop had a meeting after school, when Riley and a bunch of boys laughed and told her she looked stupid. "I'm a Scout," Kat had replied emphatically. "You guys are the stupid ones." The name stuck. But as time went on, Riley decided he was the only one allowed to use it. Travis Butrick called her that once, by the water fountain, and Riley had decked him. They both got detention.

Travis Butrick? They used to call him Butt Head, didn't they?

Kat blinked, dragging herself back to the present. "You need to leave," she said.

Riley slid one of his sneakers over the threshold. "I need to stay. We've got some serious catching up to do."

Kat tried to close the door, but his foot acted as a stopper. "Please, Riley. Don't do this."

"I just spent the whole day with our son, Kat."

All the strength drained from her arms. At that instant, Kat knew she would be letting Riley in, no matter how huge a mistake it was.

"Fine." She backed away and gestured him inside, then stooped to pick up last week's Sunday Baltimore *Sun*, which she'd left scattered on the rug before she went to the Caymans. "Obviously, I wasn't expecting company."

Riley stepped inside and she closed the door behind him. "Have a seat." She pointed to the armchair. "Would you like some hot cocoa? Tea?"

"No, thanks. I'm good."

She watched Riley enter her home and stroll around the room, taking in the combination of secondhand and self-assembled furniture that made up the main room of her apartment. His first stop was the set of bookcases that took up the whole far wall. He ran his fingers along the spines of the books.

"Eastern philosophy, archaeology, astronomy, Greek tragedies." He laughed softly. "I see you're still a bookworm."

Next, Riley stopped at the fireplace mantel to examine a series of photos of Aidan, from babyhood on up. Riley picked up a framed snapshot of their son at the zoo as a three-year-old. "He's so incredible," Riley whispered, placing the photo back where he found it and moving on to the next, and then the next.

"We can get copies made of all the photos," Kat offered from the kitchen doorway.

"That would be great." Riley moved toward the old chair where she'd been reading, the books scattered under the lamp on a side table. He selected the title on top, which Kat had left open, and flipped it over. A small piece of cardboard fluttered to the carpet.

"Repressed memory?" Riley frowned at her, then bent down to retrieve what had fallen. He read the print and his scowl deepened. "Is Jeff someone you're dating?"

"No. He's just a friend." Kat decided to skip the tea—and the small talk—and just get this over with. She left the kitchen and plopped down on the couch. "Riley, you shouldn't be here and you know it."

Riley returned Jeff's business card to between the pages and put down the book, but not before picking up the one underneath and reading the title aloud.

"*The Blunt Truth: How to Bust Your Life Wide Open with Honesty*. Hmm." Riley set the paperback on the table and made himself comfortable in the armchair. "Getting your degree in psychology?"

"Just getting my shit together." Kat told herself she would be all business with Riley, and in order to do that, she'd have to avoid looking at him, because every time she looked at him, her blood went hot and all she could think about was the hours they had spent tangled in the bed-and-breakfast sheets, his hard cock claiming its territory—which was her.

She took just a quick peek—God, that man looked good in a pair of jeans and a simple button-down shirt. Kat cleared her throat. "So how's Aidan? He's still not talking to me."

Riley smiled thoughtfully, continuing to check out her small apartment from his seat. "He's a wonderful young man, Kat. You should never have kept him from me, but you clearly were a good mom to him, and I thank you."

The sincerity in his voice made Kat soften. He was correct—she'd done many things right, and it was satisfying to hear him acknowledge it. "Thanks, Riley."

"Now, let's just get to the point. Exactly why is it that I shouldn't be here?" Riley rested his elbows on his knees and leaned in Kat's direction. "Because you started this, Scout. You rolled into Persuasion last week, fucked my brains out, made me remember what it feels like to be alive, then just disappeared without a word."

Any softness inside her just hardened up again. What kind of lowlife would be acting like he wasn't engaged? What had happened to Riley's decency? Wait—maybe it was the same old story—despite appearances, Riley Bohland didn't have any decency.

"And then you come back here to Baltimore and get so snooty that you won't even return my calls. You can't do that to people, Kat. You can't do that to *me*. And I don't know how far along you've gotten in this book right here, but we both know there isn't a speck of honesty in that bullshit, and I don't deserve it."

She stared blankly, not believing his audacity. "Oh, reeeally?"

"Really."

Kat produced a sweet little smile. "And what about your fiancée? I'm sorry, but I didn't catch her name."

Riley's face froze for an instant, and all Kat could think was, *Gotcha.*

He breathed hard through his nose a few times. "My *who*?" he whispered.

"The woman you're supposed to marry on Christmas Eve. That who."

Riley sat perfectly still, nothing moving but his Adam's apple.

"C'mon now, Riley. You're a very smart man—having gone through medical school and all—and I bet if you try hard enough, you can remember your betrothed's name."

Kat watched Riley's spine stiffen. After a moment, he collapsed back into the chair and crossed his legs. An expression of disgust washed over his face. "Where'd you get that information?"

"Does it matter?" Kat was becoming more annoyed by the second. Was he really going to sit there and deny it? He had become the kind of person she didn't even want to know, let alone be involved with, and she was beginning to regret bringing him into Aidan's life.

"Oh, it matters so much you wouldn't believe." It surprised Kat that Riley chose that moment to laugh, then shake his head. "So you met Carrie?"

"I don't know anyone named Carrie," Kat spat out. "Madeline Bowman told me about your wedding when I came in from a walk the morning after . . . after, well, after I fucked your brains out."

Riley looked stunned. "Madeline?"

"Yes. She dropped the bomb on me in the dining room, and . . . look, this is ridiculous." Kat got up from the couch and moved to the door. "What did I expect? I haven't spoken to you in twenty years, and it's not like all that stuff we used to tell each other as kids was *real* or anything. You're allowed to have a life. Now you're engaged. That's perfectly normal. I'm sure she's lovely. You don't owe me anything. It's no big deal. End of story."

Kat unlocked the door and cracked it open, then turned to him, suddenly energized. "But I'll tell you what is not OK, and that's how it didn't even matter to you that you were engaged! You didn't care about your fiancée *or* me that night in that ridiculously huge bed. The only thing you cared about was getting your freak on, as Nola would say, and when I look back, my God . . . I was so stupid! That's what it's always been about for you, isn't it? Maybe that's how it is with all men. I'm sick of men!"

Kat stopped, suddenly aware that Riley had left the chair and was standing near her at the door, glaring down at her. Without a word, he slapped his hand against the door and slammed it shut.

"Where's your bedroom?" he asked.

Kat couldn't breathe. Her head was spinning. She was so turned on that her legs were shaking. Why did this man turn her into human pudding like this? It wasn't fair.

"But—"

Riley grabbed a handful of her hair at the back of her head and calmly planted his lips right over hers, putting an end to whatever it was that she'd wanted to say. Which she couldn't remember now. Because he kissed her like he was entitled to her mouth. He held her in place by her hair like he had every right to do it. With his lips and tongue and teeth he put his brand on her, and through the fog of lust, all Kat could think of was the lyrics to one of those songs she heard at least ten times a week on the Oldies station in the back room radio at the flower shop: "If loving you is wrong, I don't want to be right."

Riley removed his lips and smiled down at her.

Kat was dizzy. But not too dizzy to do the right thing, because unlike Riley, she had a conscience. She fumbled for the door handle once more and pulled it open. "Good-bye, Riley. Have a happy life."

His smile didn't budge. "I'm not engaged. There is no fiancée."

Kat suddenly felt unsteady on her feet, like she needed to lie down. On her bed. With him. "No fiancée?" she whispered.

"There was one—Carrie Mathis—last year, right before I found out about you and Aidan." He began to brush his fingertips along the side of her face. "She became a little unbalanced when I canceled the wedding and broke up with her. I think she used Madeline to mess with you in a very big way."

Kat felt the hope begin to swell inside her. She could barely speak. "Is that the truth?"

"The blunt truth, Scout. And I'm thinking we're free to bust our lives wide open right about now, if you get my drift."

"The bedroom is down the hall to your right," she said.

Carrie didn't think he'd mind. After all, according to Madeline, Virgil Cavanaugh hadn't left his house since his wife died, except for his recent visit to the cardiac unit at Davis Memorial, so it wasn't like Carrie would be interrupting his busy schedule or anything.

She pulled her Volvo into the driveway and took a quick glance around. The place looked untidy. Obviously, hiring a neighborhood kid to rake up the leaves was not a priority for Mr. Cavanaugh. Then again, the way Madeline described him, maybe he couldn't pay a kid enough to do his yard work. She said the only person who could stand to be in the same room with him was his sister, who'd been doing his shopping and laundry since Mrs. Cavanaugh died.

Carrie smiled to herself as she climbed the front steps, thinking that she could handle one little old nasty hermit. She rang the doorbell. Nothing.

She rang it again. No sound of movement inside.

Carrie dug her finger into the doorbell and didn't let up. The hospital records indicated he'd been released five days earlier, but maybe he'd infarcted on his kitchen floor. She had just about decided to call 911 when she heard a faint rustling.

"Mr. Cavanaugh?" Carrie spoke in a voice loud enough to penetrate the door. "May I talk with you for just a moment? I'm Dr. Caroline Mathis, a colleague of Dr. Bohland's."

"I don't do house calls," said a scraggly voice from inside.

That made her laugh. "This is more of a social call, Mr. Cavanaugh. Please open up."

"I don't do those, either."

Carrie sighed and crossed her arms over her chest. This old geezer was a character. Unfortunately, he was beginning to irritate her.

"I'd just like a few minutes of your time."

The dead bolt turned. The wooden door of the tacky rancher opened, and from behind the ragged screen she saw an equally ragged face.

"Make it snappy," he said.

"Good evening, Mr. Cavanaugh. It's an honor to meet you."

The old man let out a wheeze of a laugh. "Charmed, I'm sure. Now what the hell do you want?"

Carrie blinked in surprise. No wonder Virgil Cavanaugh didn't have any friends. "May I come in?"

"You may not. Just state your business and then you can leave."

"Well . . ." Carrie looked around the unkempt front yard. "It's a rather delicate subject. Are you sure you want me to be standing out here in public?"

Mr. Cavanaugh craned his neck to look over her shoulder. "What public? What the hell are you talking about?"

"It has to do with your daughter, Mr. Cavanaugh. I need just a few minutes of your time."

Carrie observed, fascinated, as the old man's demeanor changed. His back straightened and his eyes cleared, like a heat inside him had just burned through the dullness of age, coronary artery disease, and what smelled like a fifth of Stolichnaya. She watched his cheek spasm.

"Go around to the back of the house." He slammed the door in her face.

"Can I just say how much I appreciate you not wearing a bra?" Riley yanked off Kat's T-shirt and buried his face in the heavenly succulence of her breasts.

"I'm happy that you're happy." While he kicked aside his shoes and socks, she pulled his pants off, then ripped off his shirt.

"Do you always go braless at home?" Riley inhaled the sugary aroma of her girl flesh.

Kat giggled, raking her fingertips through Riley's hair and pulling him tighter to her body. "I think I'm about to ruin some sort of man fantasy by telling you this, but no. I almost always wear a bra. I was just too depressed to put one on today."

"Ah. More blunt truth."

"Absolutely. That's all you'll get from me from here on out."

Riley groaned, enjoying how the tingles from his scalp were now shooting all the way through his limbs. He buried his nose deeper, inhaled some more, rubbed into her, then dragged his lips down from her cleavage to her tummy, where he grabbed the waistband of her pants and underwear, and yanked those off, too. He stepped back to stare at the vision in front of him—Kat Cavanaugh, naked. All pink softness. Real. A real Kat Cavanaugh all pink and naked and sitting on the edge of her bed looking happy to see him.

Riley fell to his knees in front of her. "Mind if I worship you?"

Kat laughed.

"I'm dead serious."

Her laugh died down. She played with his hair as a small smile crept over her face. "I wouldn't know what that feels like."

Her response shocked him. He and Kat hadn't talked much that night at Cherry Hill, but from what Aidan said, Riley figured that Kat had had a healthy love life over the years.

"How can that be?" Riley asked.

She shrugged. "Just never found the right man for the job, I guess." She ran a fingertip down the bridge of Riley's nose. "And you? How come no woman snapped you up in those moments you happened not to be engaged?"

Riley gently pushed her thighs apart. Not wide, but enough that he could see the tight red curls that guarded the entrance to a pussy that was already swelling and wet for him. He looked up at her and was greeted by eyes as warm as honey but shadowed by doubt. It broke his heart.

He wished he could say something profound, something that would satisfy that doubt once and for all. He wanted to wrap up all the pain and loneliness and mistakes and longing of the last twenty years and put all of it behind them. He wanted to wash them both clean, give them both permission to risk everything for another shot at happiness.

But since he didn't have a clue how to do that with words, he decided to rely on touch.

Riley leaned down and kissed the instep of her left foot, then her right. He slowly dragged his tongue along the inside of one of her ankles, then lifted her leg up and out so that he could nibble on the tender skin behind the knee. While he did this, Kat leaned back on her palms and let her head loll, moaning softly.

Riley noticed how she had instinctively begun to spread her thighs farther as his mouth worked its way toward the juncture of her legs. He could smell her—the same damp and rich abundance he'd nearly drowned in at Cherry Hill. Riley started to nip at her labia, press his nose into her clitoris.

"Seriously, didn't you date anyone after Carrie?" Kat asked.

"Mmmmm . . . I don't remember any dates with anyone," he said, dragging his tongue around his target, teasing, testing, then suddenly licking up and down through the wet seam of her sex. "But I can't remember much of anything right now," he mumbled.

Kat giggled, and Riley wasn't sure if she did that because she thought he was funny or from the vibration of his voice, but either way, her laughter indicated Riley wasn't exactly driving her out of her head.

"Why no women after Carrie?" she asked.

Riley stopped. He sat back on his heels so he could answer her properly. Her eyes were bright with interest.

"All I could think of was you," he answered. "You'd come back from the dead. I couldn't even *see* other women—it was like I had blinders on. I felt like my world was in limbo until I found you and my son."

"Oh, Riley . . ." Kat leaned down and kissed his forehead, then along the side of his face, and finally his lips. He closed his eyes with the decadence of it, all these gentle and loving kisses from the woman of his dreams, all for him.

His mind flashed with images from so long ago, how he and Kat had begun dabbling in sex when they were far too young to dabble. Riley remembered how she'd been so giving, right out of the gate, like she'd only been waiting for him to allow her to express her love. It was intense. Those nights on the blanket out on the quarry road were always heavy with emotion. It soon became apparent to Riley that he was Kat's lifeline as well as her boyfriend.

It must have killed her when he told her to get lost.

Riley's eyes flew open and he looked up at Kat. She smiled at him. Suddenly, the idea that any other man had ever been on the receiving end of Kat Cavanaugh's affections really bothered him. Suddenly, he hated himself for sending her out into the world thinking she wasn't wanted.

Yes, they'd wounded each other, but Riley knew without a doubt that he'd drawn the first blood.

"And you, sweet Scout? How come you never got married?"

Kat put her arms around herself, and Riley realized she was probably cold sitting there naked like that. He pulled her to her feet and wrapped his arms tight around her, gathering her close as he looked down into her eyes.

"No reason, really," she said with a shake of her head.

"Come on. Why aren't you in a relationship right this second? I would imagine you spend most of your time sorting through offers from men."

Kat tried to avoid eye contact, but Riley used a finger to tilt up her chin. She had no choice but to look at him. "Tell me, Kat."

She shrugged. "It's not a big mystery. I just had a hard time finding anyone I wanted to share my life with."

"Why?"

"I guess because I kept looking for . . . well, *you*, Riley. I kept looking for someone like Riley Bohland, and I never found him."

He let out a gentle laugh. "But you knew exactly where to find the real thing."

Kat laughed, too. "I mean I never found him in *Baltimore,* and there was no way in hell I was going back to Persuasion until I could show everyone I had made it without them."

Suddenly, the timing of Kat's return made sense

to Riley. He pulled back a few inches so he could study her. "You mean you didn't want to come back until you had a ton of money? Aidan told me all about Phyllis' estate."

"It wasn't about money," Kat snapped, pulling away a bit more. "I wanted to be strong when I went back to Persuasion. Strong and beautiful and totally together. I dreamed of the day I'd get to rub all your faces in my sheer *awesomeness*."

"Ahh."

"But then Phyllis died and left me millions, and I figured, hey, I'll just get a makeover and fake the rest."

Riley laughed. "You're not faking a damn thing."

"Ha!" Kat gave him a shy smile, then stepped out of his arms. She reached behind her to grab the down comforter and wrapped it tight around herself before she sat cross-legged on the bed.

Riley joined her. Once he got comfortable, he fished around inside the comforter until he found her small hand, which he kissed, then cradled in his own. "You really are all those things, you know."

"I will admit that there are times when I've been strong, together, or beautiful, but just not all at the same time, and that's what I wanted the day I went back to Persuasion."

"Give me this." Riley grabbed the comforter and pulled it away from her body, then swung her around so she was situated with her back against his chest, skin on skin. He wrapped the down blanket around them both and her small, warm body felt solid against him.

"Let me tell you a story about a girl I used to know," he said, talking softly in her ear. "She was always strong and together. She survived a childhood where her father would beat her mother, yet she had the presence of mind to nurse her mother back to health every time. She volunteered to read a poem at my mother's funeral, and she got up there in front of hundreds of people with steady hands and a calm voice."

She gasped. "I'd forgotten all about that."

"This girl was very smart, too. I always loved her take on things, whether it was music or school subjects or just normal everyday stuff. Her observations about people were funny and insightful. And sweet—my God, was she ever sweet."

"Do I know this person?"

Riley kissed the top of her head. "She was you. She *is* you, Kat."

She said nothing.

"After you disappeared, I used to imagine what it would be like if you were still at Underwood High. I'd picture you playing second base on the girls' softball team and getting on the honor roll every semester."

Kat whipped her head around in disbelief. "You remember what position I played?"

"Sure I do. I also used to imagine the dress you'd wear to homecoming with me, and how you'd be named 'Girl Most Likely to Succeed' in the *Overview* our senior year."

Kat snorted and leaned back into his chest. " 'Girl Most Likely to Get Pregnant Before She Earns Her Learner's Permit' is more like it."

"I don't think that was an actual category."

"Or how about 'Girl Most Likely to Live with Parakeets'?"

"Also not an option," he said, burying his smile in her silky hair.

" 'Girl Most Likely to Fuck Up Her Son's Life by Lying to Him from the Day He Was Born'?"

"Sssshhh," Riley said.

They sat quietly for many minutes. Their breath eventually fell into the same rhythm. Riley held her, rocked her, and kissed the side of her neck.

The phone rang.

"Don't get it," Riley said. "Please. Stay here with me."

"What if it's Aidan?"

"Then you can call him back."

They listened as the answering machine clicked on and a woman immediately launched into a squeaky tirade.

"Kat! Kat! You're not going to freakin' believe this!"

"It's Nola," Kat reassured Riley.

"The younger Bohunk brother is in town and he just asked me out! Should I go? Should I? Would you mind? I mean, I know Riley is an engaged asshole, but Matt seems decent."

Riley laughed to himself in surprise. *Did she just say "Bohunk"?*

Nola continued. "What am I saying? Of course I'm going to go—I already said yes. He's picking me up in fifteen minutes. What should I wear? And where are you? I thought you were just going to stay home and sulk today. Well, gotta go. I'll tell you everyth—" *Beep.*

"Wow," Riley said.

Kat began to squirm in his arms and he loosened the comforter so she could turn around. Once she threw her legs over his and got comfortable, Riley wrapped her tight again and smiled down at her.

"Yes," Kat answered before he could ask. "That's what Nola calls you."

"I like it."

Kat slowly shook her head. "She's gonna eat Matt alive."

"Oh, I think Matt can handle her."

One of Kat's eyebrows shot up. "You don't understand. Matt's just a small-town boy, and Nola's—well, Nola's been around the block so many times she's worn a groove in the sidewalk."

"Like I said, he can handle it."

"That remains to be seen."

A deep wave of comfort and ease flooded Riley. It was the combination of Kat's husky voice, her warm skin against his, the way their minds clicked. He kissed her softly on the lips.

"Have you noticed what we're doing, Riley?"

"Uhm . . ." He paused. "Is this a trick question?"

Kat laughed. "I just thought I'd point out that we raced in here to the bedroom, ripped each other's clothes off like wild animals in heat, and what did we end up doing?"

Riley smiled. "Talking."

She nodded. "Talking and snuggling."

Kat was right. "So what do you think that means?"

She bit her lip and gave it some thought. "I believe it means we've done things backward. It means we have a lot to hash out between us, a lot to understand about each other, and a lot to forgive before another night like Cherry Hill."

Riley studied her face, beautiful, strong, and together all at the same time. He laughed softly. "I have to say, as much as I'd like to have a Cherry Hill moment right here, right now, you're absolutely right."

Kat's eyes sparkled with pleasure. "I'm glad you agree, because I don't ever want to be left alone in the morning like that again, not knowing where things stand with us or what you're thinking or feeling, just sitting there holding one of your socks, not sure if I'm a complete moron or the luckiest girl on earth."

Riley let go with a raucous laugh and began to wrestle with her. "So you stole my sock!" he shouted. "Admit it, woman! Admit it, I say!"

They rolled around on the bed, laughing and kissing, until they rolled right off the edge and landed with a loud thud on the wood floor. They laughed even harder.

Riley suddenly cocked his head in alarm. He heard a loud banging sound that sounded like it was coming from the ceiling above them.

"What the hell is that?" he asked. Riley rolled Kat to the side to protect her. "Do you hear it?" The thumping started again.

"That's Mrs. Brownstein," Kat said, sputtering out a laugh. "She's just jealous."

Riley nodded. "Looks like now would be a good time to get a place with a little more privacy."

"Did I tell you I'm fixing up Phyllis' old row house?" Kat pushed herself up from the floor and offered her hand to Riley, the blanket draped over her shoulders like a queen's floor-length cape. "It will be a few more months until it's ready," she said, pulling him to a stand.

"Then come back to Persuasion."

The words had burst out of Riley's mouth before he even knew they'd formed in his brain, and the idea filled him with excited energy. "Come home,

Kat. Aidan can visit whenever he likes. Come back and stay for a while; see how it feels to have me in your life, rub my face in your awesomeness, get to know me all over again. Would you do it?"

Kat stared at him wide-eyed.

"I promise to give you all the time and space you need. But I'd be right there in town. We could see each other every once in a while. Have dinner. Hang out. No more Cherry Hills until we're both sure it's right."

She shook her head and took a step back. "I don't know."

"Why not? Is it Virgil?"

Kat hissed. "That old fart doesn't scare me anymore. In fact, one day I have every intention of marching right up to him and telling him everything I remember about my childhood, what he did to my mom and me, how we didn't deserve any of it. It might be therapeutic."

Riley dared to take this further. "You could register for classes at Mountain Laurel if you felt like it."

Kat's eyes flashed.

"We could get to know each other like real adult people in a real adult relationship."

A smile slowly spread over Kat's lips. "I'd want my own little place."

"There's always houses to rent near campus."

Kat walked back toward Riley with a regal gait, swinging her cape along the side of her nude flesh, all glorious, round, and firm *femaleness*. It was a vision he'd never forget.

She popped up on her tiptoes and locked her gaze on his.

"I am willing to try if you are," she said. "But you have to promise me a couple things."

"You name it."

"I want honesty."

"You got it."

"I want you to swear that if and when you want to break up with me, you'll find a better way to do it than the last time."

The knife went right into Riley's heart. "I swear. And will you promise me something?"

"Sure."

"Don't run away again, like you did twenty years ago and then again two weeks ago, because I'm man enough to admit that it scares the hell out of me to love a woman who has a habit of disappearing on me."

Kat plopped down on the balls of her feet, suddenly serious. "I thought you were engaged."

"I realize that. But humor me."

"Sure. I promise I won't run away again."

"And promise me you'll tell me should you ever again be pregnant with my child."

A sly little smile played on Kat's lips. She snaked her arm around the back of Riley's head and slid her fingers through his hair, pulling him down until his mouth was on hers. Kat kissed him hard and long.

It was a seal. It was a start.

TWELVE

Virgil rubbed his chin and frowned. "You sure look familiar for some reason."

"You recognize me from television, no doubt." Carrie smoothed her hair, waiting for it to dawn on him.

Virgil busted out with a hoot of laughter. "That's it! You're that self-righteous she-devil who gets on TV and tells people to eat right, exercise, and avoid smoking."

Carrie beamed. "That would be me."

"All right then," Virgil said, apparently satisfied. "Now what the hell did you want?"

Carrie was intrigued by her surroundings—and thrown a bit off-balance by the wiry, annoyed man who clearly ruled this strange kingdom. She stood next to Mr. Cavanaugh in a standard 1950s one-car garage that served as his studio. The walls were unfinished wood plank; the ceiling was bare wood beams with shelves built into the eaves. She could see where the garage door had been closed up many years before, the wood there a different grain and color, and how most of the entire back wall had been fitted with a picture window to let in the natural light. But it was twilight now, and the area seemed closed in. The shadows were stark. Ghostly shapes of what looked like unfinished sculptures seemed to sprout out of the concrete floor, surrounded by shapeless hunks of rock not yet touched by the artist.

Sharp tools similar to surgical instruments were scattered haphazardly on top of sketchbooks, tables, and the floor, along with heavy mallets and drill bits. Wooden stands had been tipped over on their sides, and a strange, thin stainless-steel contraption sat near the center of the room, arms askew. She took a step back. It reminded her of a huge praying mantis.

She shuddered.

Mr. Cavanaugh chuckled. "It's a pointing machine, honey. It's not going to bite you."

"A what?"

"It measures points three-dimensionally on a sculpture."

Stepping with caution, Carrie moved toward a plywood table and placed her business card on the edge, then reached above for the light fixture chain and pulled it. The sudden brightness didn't cheer the room—it only illuminated the mess.

"I didn't say you could turn on a light."

She refused to acknowledge Mr. Cavanaugh's rudeness. No one spoke to her like this. She would not allow it under any circumstances. She was a physician. She was beautiful. She was entrusted with developing policy that impacted thousands of lives. Carrie turned to face him. "I'm sorry, but I'm not familiar with your work. What kind of sculpture do you do, Mr. Cavanaugh?"

He grunted. "Whatever the hell I feel like doing.

I'll ask you one more time: What do you want? Why did you mention my daughter?"

"Ah. Well." Carrie looked for somewhere to sit. There was nowhere, except for a rusty, clay-splattered metal stool that he obviously used when he worked, and it looked as uncomfortable as this whole place felt. She folded her hands in front of her body and tried to smile politely. "It's about Kat and Riley Bohland."

The old man stared at her without breathing. Slowly, his lips curled into a grimace and he shook his head. "Whatever you're fishing for, you won't find it here. I don't talk to Kat. Haven't in twenty years."

That surprised Carrie. "I didn't realize the two of you were estranged."

Mr. Cavanaugh chuckled. "That's a fancy word for it." He offered her a sarcastic smile. "Now what do you want?"

"I want to know about her connection to Riley."

He waved his hand. "I go to Bohland because he's the only doctor in this town. Trust me, it's not because I'm a friend of the family. I never liked any of those idiots."

"I see." Now she was getting somewhere.

"But your visit has nothing to do with my health, does it?"

"No."

Mr. Cavanaugh nodded. He studied her as she studied him. Carrie took in the details of that sinewy body and hard face. Though he seemed surprisingly agile for a man who'd just had angioplasty, Carrie was struck at how his face had suffered from aging, the bones sharp under papery, blotchy skin.

She knew Mr. Cavanaugh was sixty-two, but he looked eighty, and the bitterness in him was probably responsible, along with his blood alcohol level. Carrie decided the guy was a walking, talking advertisement for the mean son of a bitch everyone said he was, and he seemed proud of it.

Suddenly, Virgil Cavanaugh shifted his cold eyes from Carrie's face to the rest of her. She shivered as his gaze roamed all over her, from her sling-back pumps, to the hemline of her skirt, to the delicate teardrop diamond pendant she always wore at her throat. She'd had the necklace made from the diamond engagement ring Riley had given her, which she rightly refused to give back. She did not appreciate the old man's gawking, and raised her fingers to touch the necklace, calming herself in the process.

"I need to know how to keep Kat away from Riley," she said. "Any suggestions?"

"I suggest you take off your clothes and sit for me."

Carrie felt her eyes bug out. *"What did you just say?"*

"You're going to model for me. I'm going to sculpt you. I've worked with my share of stuck-up brunettes over the years, and I need a new muse."

Carrie snorted in disgust. "I so doubt that, Mr. Cavanaugh."

He shrugged. "Your call, darlin'." He turned toward the door that led to the side yard and talked with his back to her. "Forgive me if I don't walk you to your car. It's been so long since I've had a visitor that it seems I've lost my manners."

Carrie's mouth fell open at the offensiveness of this wretched man. Who did he think he was? She tried to remember why she'd even thought it would be a good idea to come here and talk with him.

Kat Cavanaugh—that's why she was here. And she'd been correct to think that Virgil Cavanaugh was just the person to show her how to get Kat where it would hurt the most. The man was ruthless.

"Pardon my observation, but you really don't give a damn about your daughter, do you, Virgil?" It pleased Carrie to see him spin around as if she'd hit him in the back of his head. "It's none of my business why you despise your own flesh and blood, but it's convenient, because I don't like her much myself. So maybe we can help each other out."

Virgil stood riveted to the concrete floor, his expression one of tentative interest.

"You look surprised, Virgil. Can I call you Virgil?"

"You can call me Grover Cleveland if you get naked for me."

"If you tell me how to keep Kat from Riley, I'll do it. That will be our arrangement."

He let out a boisterous laugh, one so loud that it seemed too big for the bleak, tight space.

"My, my, my. What we have here is a regular old love triangle, isn't it? Is that what all the fuss is about?"

"It isn't a triangle," Carrie huffed, despising the way he'd just dismissed her dilemma with a soap-opera cliché. Her eyes fell on the praying-mantis thing. "What we have is two points on a three-dimensional masterpiece of true love—composed of myself and Riley—and your daughter is doing her best to get between us."

Mr. Cavanaugh laughed again, and this time it sounded downright gleeful. "You are a real pointy-headed piece of work." He scrunched up his nose like he smelled something unpleasant. "And how do you know Riley, anyway? You're not from around here."

"We met and dated in medical school. We were supposed to get married, but he called it off because of Kat."

A frown crept over Mr. Cavanaugh's brow. He tilted his head. "I don't follow."

"When your wife was dying, she told Riley about the baby. Right before our wedding."

The frown intensified, digging deep ruts into Virgil Cavanaugh's forehead. He clenched his teeth. "Go on," he hissed.

"Well, as soon as Riley was told he'd fathered a baby back in high school, he went searching for the kid. Out of a sense of obligation, of course. Guilt—that's all it was. I didn't even believe there really was a kid until just recently. And now Kat's come back to distract him all over again, and I won't stand for it. So, fine, I'll sit for you if you help me find a way to get Kat out of the picture for good. Agreed?"

Carrie waited a moment for him to say something. He didn't. But she watched the anger twist Virgil Cavanaugh's face until it turned flame red. It was the oddest thing how the man's fury sucked the air pressure right out of that cramped garage. An electrical charge passed through Carrie. Her skin tingled. Her sinuses pounded. Her pulse raced.

"Get . . . the fuck . . . out." He motioned for Carrie to exit the studio, and she did so without debate, not entirely sure what had just happened, but relieved to be stepping out into the fresh air. He locked the studio door, brushed past her, and disappeared inside the house.

Carrie stood in the yard, aware of her own too-fast breath, and it occurred to her that Virgil Cavanaugh hadn't known he had a grandson or maybe even that Kat had been pregnant when she ran away all those years ago. Cavanaugh's wife hadn't told him anything. No one had. How strange.

The wind kicked up. A handful of dry leaves skittered across her shoes. She shivered again. Then she ran to the car.

Carrie spent the first hour on the road trying to shake the feeling that she'd made a mistake by talking to Virgil Cavanaugh. The feeling wouldn't budge.

By the time she reached the Jennings Randolph Highway in Weston, she realized the encounter had left an icky scum all over her psyche. She decided that as soon as she got back to Charleston she'd take the hottest, longest shower of her life.

When she stopped for coffee in Sutton, Carrie began to ponder whether she should just let this whole mess alone. She had no business telling a sick old man his own family secrets. In fact, maybe she should just back off the Riley situation altogether. Clearly he was going to do what he wanted to do when it came to Kat. Maybe she should just let Riley be an idiot if that was his destiny, and she could stand back and watch his silly reunion fantasy blow up in his face.

Then he would come back to her. On his knees, crawling. Begging. She liked that.

An hour and a half later, Carrie rolled up her driveway, clicked on the garage door opener, and pulled inside the safe cocoon of her townhome. Only then did her hands begin to tremble. Only then could she admit that Virgil Cavanaugh was far more than just eccentric—she was damn lucky to be in one piece.

Kat's spine tingled with the expectation of pleasure as she hoisted the mallet over her head and brought it down with all her might. The wet clay imploded with a thud, splattering the floor with gray goop. It was satisfying to see how a single swing of the rubber-headed hammer obliterated the whole side of the woman's face, blew apart her left nostril, turned her carefully fashioned cheekbone and jawline into nothing but a pile of muck on the concrete floor.

Good. The slut deserved it. Kat only wished she could do the same thing to her father's face, the real one, the one made of flesh and bone.

She took another swing. And another. The rage came from the soles of her feet and poured out of her hands, liquid and scalding, never ending, always a new rush rising through her to give her the strength for another swing of the mallet. And another. The hate felt like it was cleaning her out, making things clear for the first time in her life.

Her fucking joke of a father had turned off the portable heater before he'd zipped up his pants and walked the governor's wife to her car, so by now the studio was quite cold. The sweat poured off Kat's face anyway.

Thud. Riley didn't want her anymore. *Thud.* She was three months pregnant. *Thud.* Her father saw her looking through the studio window—he knew she'd seen everything. *Thud.* Kat's life was over—she was only sixteen and it was fucking *over.*

"Stop! Oh God, child! Have you lost your mind?"

The voice seemed to come from nowhere and everywhere at the same time, inside Kat's own head and from another world, and it took her a moment to realize her mother was standing over her back, gripping her forearm so hard it hurt, screaming in her ear. But Kat couldn't stop the swinging.

"Katharine! Sweet Jesus, he'll kill us both. What have you done? Oh God, what have you done to his commission?"

Kat's fingers loosened. The mallet fell to the concrete floor with a thump. She blinked away a stream of sweat from her eye and focused on what she'd done, but it didn't make sense to her at first. It looked like a bomb had gone off in her father's studio. Clay was everywhere, and smack in the middle of the goopy mess was a pink grapefruit, stuck like a pig in the mud. A box of cornflakes lay on its side, splashed with white globs of cottage cheese that had spewed from the broken container at her feet.

Slowly, Kat raised her eyes, noting her mother's horrified expression. "You dropped your groceries."

"Sweet Jesus save us."

"I've ruined everything, haven't I?"

The spatula hit the kitchen floor, and Kat heard the clank of stainless steel against tile. She blinked. She was home, in her kitchen, in Baltimore. It was now, not then. She had made it out of there.

"It's not that bad."

Kat looked up to see the most shocking sight—Riley Bohland just out of the shower, all glistening olive skin and lean muscle, a white towel draped low on his hips, and a smile setting up residence on his handsome face. He walked toward her and scooped up the spatula.

Kat's mind scrambled to make everything sane

and normal and squeeze it back into the present moment. She was in her Baltimore apartment. Riley had stayed here with her last night, and they'd talked until the sun came up. She would be moving back to Persuasion.

Icy panic had begun creeping through her veins.

"I said you haven't ruined anything, Scout. The pancakes look great." Riley planted a quick kiss on her mouth and rinsed the spatula in the sink, wiped it dry, and handed it back to her. "Can I pour you a cup a coffee?"

Kat stared at him. "I'm sorry, what?"

"Coffee." Riley had reached into the cabinet for two mugs but stopped cold, his arm in midair. "Are you OK?"

"Yeah. I'm good." Kat shook her head. "Wait. No, I'm not. I remembered something. Just now. I was flipping the pancakes, and I remembered all the details from the day I left Persuasion. I—" Kat couldn't continue. She feared that saying any of it aloud would put breath and life into the events, making it real. "Something so terrible . . ."

"Come here." Riley took Kat into his arms, pulling her up against his damp chest. She clung to him. She breathed in the familiar yet exotic smell of his skin and rubbed her cheek against his warmth. She felt Riley reach around her back to turn off the stove, then guide her to the living room sofa. "Sit for a minute. I'll get us some coffee and you can tell me what you remembered. I want to hear everything."

Kat did what he said, not that she was capable of much else. Her head was swimming. She was shivering, but sweat was forming at her hairline. Was what she saw in her mind real, or was she making it up? And if it was real, how could she have forgotten so much of it for so long? What else had she forgotten?

She closed her eyes and concentrated. Maybe if she thought hard enough she could force all of it out of hiding—every one of the little ghost memories that she knew lurked inside her brain, just waiting to be named.

"Hey, Kat?" Riley returned to the couch and stood over her, looking sheepish as he reached down to gently touch her cheek. "I don't have a clue how you take your coffee."

"Two creams and a sugar, right?"

Madeline lifted the silver coffeepot and poured, keeping an eye on Matt during the whole maneuver. She'd made something she knew he loved—banana-walnut muffins—but he hadn't even taken a bite. The muffin just sat there on his plate, perfectly plump and golden, just waiting for the touch of his lips. He hadn't even noticed.

Madeline sighed. The women Matt dated had great boobs and/or flat abs. Her best assets were her baked goods. If Matt couldn't even muster up excitement for her muffins, then she knew with certainty that he hadn't dropped by to ask her out again.

Madeline placed the coffee cup in front of him and plopped down in the opposite chair, unintentionally letting out a heavy sigh. Suddenly, she was exhausted at every level—physically, emotionally, and practically.

"Listen, Maddie. I'm here to tell you to stay out of Kat and Riley's business."

Madeline tried to sit as straight as possible, but all she wanted to do was slump over the table and rest her head in her arms, the way they used to do in kindergarten after they'd had their crackers and milk. She needed a rest time. She needed crackers and milk. Instead, she reached across the table, grabbed Matt's muffin, and immediately bit into its fluffy, sugary, oversized cap.

This was all because of Carrie. Riding shotgun on Carrie's ego trip had turned out to be a giant mistake.

Bits of banana-walnut muffin dribbled onto her shirt, but Madeline didn't brush them off. Who cared? It's not like she had to worry about looking nice for Chief Matt Bohland ever again. Besides, what was she thinking? Did she really believe that a young hunk like Matt would be interested in a divorcée with kids? She'd always known better.

"I like you, Maddie. We've known each other forever," Matt said.

"Uh-huh." Madeline took another large bite. Honestly, these were the best damn banana-walnut muffins she'd whipped up in her life.

"I've got to be honest with you—what you did was way out of line."

She shook her head in agreement as she crammed the rest of the muffin through her lips. She realized she was going to choke unless she got some liquid into her as well. She reached for Matt's untouched coffee and slurped it down. "You weren't going to drink that, were you?"

Matt looked amused. "Nope."

"Good." Madeline drained the rest and put the empty coffee cup back on its saucer, right in front of Matt.

Matt sighed. "So, you had no right lying to Kat like that, telling her that Riley was getting married when you knew he wasn't."

With one hand, Madeline wiped her face with the cloth napkin. With the other, she held up the flat of her palm to stop him from continuing. "Let me make this easy for you, OK?"

Matt frowned, sinking into his chair. "That's all I needed to say, Maddie. There's nothing you have to make easy."

"Aren't you going to tell me why you never asked me out again after those three dates? That I'm boring? That I'm a weak, self-serving small-town gossip? That I have so little self-esteem that I have to go around playing Carrie's brown-nosing errand boy?"

Matt blinked at her in silence.

"Carrie said if I got rid of Kat, she'd book rooms for a spring conference here in Persuasion, so I lied to Kat and told her Riley was engaged. Then I called Carrie's assistant to confirm, and found out there is no conference."

"She bribed you."

"And I fell for it."

"Well, Maddie, you brought all this on yourself when you decided to tell Carrie that Kat was in town. You got her all stirred up."

Madeline laughed. "Hey, let's be real. Carrie was a little 'stirred up' *way* before Kat got here, and believe me when I tell you that you don't even have a clue just how stir-crazy that chick has gotten."

Matt crossed his arms over his chest and looked interested. "Really? How so?"

Madeline was about to give him the lowdown when she felt the weariness wash over her in waves. She had ten guests this morning. Two couples were going to be checking out any minute and the other six people would be here for dinner. She'd planned on making coq au vin with new red potatoes and needed to get back in the kitchen to start preparation. It was already 10:30. Plus, she had no idea where her next sex would be coming from. She could be looking at a dry spell lasting years, if not decades. "At least the sex was good with us, right?"

It was hard to believe, but Madeline had just embarrassed Matt Bohland. He was actually blushing, which she found charming.

"Yes, it was. You're a lot of fun."

"Good then. No regrets." Madeline got up and refilled Matt's coffee cup, then drank it down. "Anyway," she said, returning to the table, "Carrie's completely off her nut. She really is planning to marry Riley—as in, she's arranging an elaborate Christmas Eve ceremony and she really believes that Riley will be the groom."

Matt's mouth fell open. "Huh?"

"That's right. She's got the centerpieces ordered. She's hired a disc jockey and picked out bridesmaid dresses—which sound really pretty, by the way—and she's currently arguing with the caterer over the vegetable selection."

Matt's mouth opened wider, then snapped shut in anger. "Vegetables? What the fuck?"

Madeline laughed. "Yeah. She came over here to model her wedding dress for me. Seriously, Matt, she's one bad-ass Bridezilla. It's all totally sick if you ask me."

Matt knit his brows together, suddenly serious. "Where's this event supposed to take place?"

"I think I heard her mention something about a museum."

"I gotta go."

As she watched Matt stand up, grab his ball cap,

and pull it down over his dark curls, Madeline felt wistful. It was hard to believe that she'd once had the pleasure of rolling around in bed with that gorgeous man. He really was something. Generous, enthusiastic, and blessed with the stamina usually found only in battery-operated devices. If Riley Bohland was half the sex god Matt was, then it was no wonder Kat had to come back, even after twenty years. Madeline couldn't blame her.

"Hey, Maddie? You mind if I take a few of those muffins to go? I never even got a chance to taste them."

Madeline scurried to place five muffins in a white paper sack, a little embarrassed now that she'd eaten off his plate but truly flattered he was still interested.

"Thanks." He kissed her on the cheek. "You're all right, Madeline."

She followed Matt to the door, beaming from that kiss. Just before he walked down the steps, she said, "Hey, wait a second. How are you? I'm so tacky I didn't even ask you how you've been lately."

Matt turned slowly, holding open the heavy oak door as he twisted to face her. "I, uh, I'm good. Real good."

Madeline nodded, understanding immediately all that he'd left unsaid. "So, what's her name?"

"She's not from around here."

"Elkins?"

"Uh, no. Baltimore. I've only been out with her once, but she's really special."

Madeline saw the gone-fishin' look in Matt's eyes. She managed to plant a cheery smile on her face, but her body began to vibrate, raging inside with the unfairness of it all. She swore to God that if Matt Bohland stood there and opened his mouth to say he was dating Kat's friend Nola Something-or-Other, she would have to scream. That's all there was to it.

"Have I met the lucky girl?"

"Uh . . ." Matt glanced toward the parking lot as if to ensure that his cruiser was available for a quick getaway. "It's Kat's friend, Nola D'Agostino."

"How nice. Give me back my fuckin' muffins." She snatched the bag out of his hand.

At one point in his life, Riley had made the drive to Charleston to see Carrie at least twice a month, two hours down and two back up, half interstate and half winding, mountainous roads. He always enjoyed the solitude those weekend drives afforded him. It gave him time to let his thoughts wander outside the confines of work and the static of everyone who wanted something from him. Often, during those long, quiet drives, Kat would materialize in his mind.

Riley would concentrate on her memory intensely enough that he could taste her kisses, feel the softness of her hand in his, hear her husky laughter. He would sometimes imagine that she sat right there next to him in the truck. She would be all grown-up, smiling and laughing with the wind blowing her blond curls all around her head like a halo. She'd be telling him story after story about her adventures through the years and how wonderful her life had turned out, despite the rocky start.

He wasn't always optimistic enough to scrape up a happy ending for her. Sometimes, especially if he was driving at night, her absence would feel like a wound in the pit of his soul, and his mind would torture him with all the horrifying possibilities—she'd been raped and butchered before she even got out of Randolph County; she'd become a teenage prostitute and overdosed in a sleazy hotel room in some faraway city; she'd ended up with some beer-swilling asshole of a guy whose way with the ladies reminded her of dear old Dad. Why hadn't she ever called him just to let him know she was OK? It had to be because she wasn't.

Riley turned the windshield wipers up a notch and cranked the defogger. It was a cold and rainy afternoon, and he was missing a clinic board meeting, where there'd be nothing but more bad news. But he was on a mission that couldn't wait. Matt had practically begged to come along, just for the sport of it, but Riley stood firm. Putting an end to Carrie Mathis' fairy tale was no joke, and it was a job for him to do alone—along with the Jefferson County sheriff's deputies delivering the restraining order.

Matt had already done his part, anyway. Based on what he'd learned from Madeline, Matt did some investigating and painted Riley a full-color picture of just how *kee-razy* his former fiancée had become. The ceremony was to begin at 8:00 P.M. on Christmas Eve at the Juliet Museum of Art, reception immediately following. Calvin Klein tuxedos had been rented for himself and Matt and, by the way, the formal-wear shop needed their final measurements. A white stretch limousine would take the happy couple to a three-day retreat at The Greenbrier.

Riley shook his head at his own blindness. Yes, Carrie had always been a driven woman, and he'd liked that in her, as long as her obsession had been medicine. In fact, Riley had always been relieved that she was as consumed with her career as he was with his, that he didn't have to explain the demands of being a doctor. Only recently had Riley understood that that relief had been rooted in the fact that he didn't love Carrie and didn't particularly want to spend time with her.

Riley pulled into the parking garage at the state government office complex, jogged across Capitol Street, and took the elevator to the sixth floor. He walked right into Carrie's suite of offices inside the Department of Health & Human Resources.

"Hey, Alice. Nice to see you."

Carrie's assistant was an older woman with a sweet, round face. She stared at him for a second, obviously drawing a blank. Then she put a hand to her mouth. "Dr. Bohland? Oh my gosh! I haven't seen you in years! How *are* you?" She hopped to her feet.

"Is Carrie in?"

"Yes, but—"

"Thanks." He turned and headed down the carpeted hallway to the double doors of her office.

"Wait. Please!" Alice scurried up behind him. "I hate to be rude," she whispered, "but I just wanted to warn you that Dr. Mathis has been very distracted lately and she hasn't been herself. The strangest things have been going on. . . ."

"You got that right," Riley said.

Alice frowned in concern. "Is Carrie in some kind of trouble? Is it the stress of the wedding?"

Just then two uniformed deputies arrived. Riley greeted them, and asked that they give him about five minutes before they served the order.

Alice was beside herself. "What's going on? Someone tell me!"

Riley touched her shoulder. "There is no wedding. The deputies are going to serve Carrie with a restraining order."

Alice looked lost. "There's no wedding?"

"Never was one. Excuse me." Riley headed toward Carrie's door.

"But . . ." Alice's voice faded into a whisper. "Your everyday china pattern was so lovely."

Carrie's eyes shot up from her computer when he opened her door. She let out a startled gasp, but the surprise on her face quickly mellowed to comprehension. She rose from her chair and smoothed her skirt. "Hello, Riley," she said.

He made himself comfortable in one of the armchairs near her desk. "Hate to tell you this, but The Greenbrier is a little stuffy for my tastes."

Her eyes darted around the room.

"I'd like a few minutes of your time to go over the wedding plans, if you don't mind."

Carrie may have been a slight woman, but the size of her vanity could fill an empty airplane hangar, so Riley was fascinated to watch as she curled in on herself at his words, like she wanted to disappear. Riley figured he was witnessing her ego beginning to deflate. She sat down without a peep.

"Game over, Carrie."

She stared at him for a long moment. Eventually, she nodded. She made no attempt to argue or put any kind of spin on any of it. She just sat there, the woman he'd once thought he loved, dark-haired, perfectly groomed, and fiercely intelligent—with no fight left in her.

"I'm so sorry," she said in a flat voice. "I guess I got carried away."

Riley nearly laughed at the inadequacy of that statement but then noticed something near pitiful in Carrie's expression. His anger began to cool. Carrie was manipulative and self-centered, but Riley guessed that at her core she was just another person too scared to face reality.

He leaned forward. "Do you have somebody you can go see? Somebody to talk to?"

Carrie didn't seem the least bit offended by his question and calmly folded her hands in front of her on the desktop. "I've already made an appointment with Mark Gulledge—remember him from med school? He's got a private practice in town. I've heard a lot of good things about him."

Riley nodded. "He's a smart guy. I'm sure he can help you figure this out."

"It's pretty simple, really," she said with a shrug. "Erotomania, delusional disorder, obsessive-compulsive tendencies, maybe even borderline stalker typology."

Riley pursed his lips and nodded, thinking that was one scary-sounding laundry list of *DSM-IV* diagnostic criteria she'd just spat out, but it was probably spot-on. Carrie was always good with diagnoses. "When's your appointment?"

"Friday."

"You need to cancel everything related to the wedding. Immediately. How many people have you told?"

Carrie stiffened. "Just Alice and Madeline. Even my mother doesn't know about it. It was going to be an intimate affair, only about seventy-five guests. I was going to tell everyone it was a last-minute thing. But I've already canceled it all."

Riley couldn't help but think of the news stories about women who faked their pregnancy and, to keep their ruse intact, went out and stole a newborn when their alleged due date arrived. He shuddered to think what would have happened if, come Christmas Eve, the wedding had been a go, but there was no groom to be had.

"It's time you move on with your life."

She sucked in a trembling breath. "I am trying."

"And you won't interfere with my life or Kat's life ever again."

"All right," Carrie whispered.

"Sheriff's deputies are outside your door right now with a restraining order."

Her eyes flashed in alarm. "Please! That won't be necessary."

"You gave me no choice."

She stared at him, worried and embarrassed.

Riley didn't know what else to say. He hadn't expected her to be so malleable. She sat quietly, continuing to look at him.

"Did you put yourself on meds?"

"Of course not." She waved her hand to dismiss the accusation.

Riley wasn't convinced. He frowned at her.

"OK, maybe just a little Paxil to take the edge off, but that's it," she said. "I've been tossing around the idea of quitting my job, did I tell you? I'd like to give myself a chance to rethink things, see what I really want out of life. I don't even know anymore, because all I thought I wanted was you."

Riley stood up from his chair. It was time to go.

"This is the end for you and me—you understand that, right?"

"I do." After a few seconds, Carrie smiled, then laughed. "Hey! I got to say those two little words after all!"

Riley studied her, thinking that inside this very normal-looking woman lurked a churning chaos no one would suspect. It was sad, but he supposed that made her no different from everyone else.

"So why the sudden change of heart, Carrie?" Riley hadn't meant to ask that aloud, but his brain was practically screaming the question. "What made you decide to stop this bullshit now, after all this time?"

Carrie walked him toward the door, obviously weighing her response. "I was becoming such a self-righteous she-devil that I'd started to scare myself."

She opened the door. The deputies were waiting.

THIRTEEN

"Since when do you own a waffle iron?" Nola stood on a chair in front of the tall bank of kitchen cabinets, staring at the appliance in wide-eyed wonder.

"I've had it forever. I make waffles for Aidan nearly every Sunday." Kat straightened up, removing her head from inside the large packing carton, and corrected herself. "OK, I *used* to make him waffles, back when he could actually stand to have a meal with me."

"He'll snap out of it." Nola placed the gadget toward the back of the top shelf, next to the mixing bowls. "You're his mother. He loves you."

Kat let out a giant sigh. She'd been telling herself the same thing now for about a month, every time she called Aidan and got his voice mail, but the truth was, she was no longer her son's only parent. Aidan had Riley now, too, and from everything she'd heard, their relationship was growing more solid every day. Maybe Aidan didn't need her now that he had a father.

Reassuring herself that such thinking was total crap, Kat unwrapped the wooden salad tongs, placing them on the mound of utensils she'd have to run through the dishwasher before she organized the kitchen drawers. This was only the second time in her life she'd moved, if she didn't count running away, which she didn't. Her first move was from the row house to the apartment, which took two trips in Phyllis' little red hatchback to get Kat settled. This move was mind-numbing in comparison, and she'd had the movers pack up only her kitchen things, a few favorite framed posters and photos, clothes, books, CDs, linens, her TV, sound system, and computer. She left most of her furniture at the apartment and she'd shoved her beloved houseplants into the back of the Jag. Everything else would be brand-new and arriving that afternoon from an upscale mail-order company—two bedroom sets, a couch, chairs, ottomans, tables and cabinets, rugs, a dining set, and lamps. This little bungalow was going to look like a showplace.

She heard the front door creak open without a knock and a man's voice called out, "Hello? I'm looking for the hottest babe in West Virginia. Is she here?"

"In the kitchen, hon," Nola answered, giggling.

Matt poked his head into the archway, his face plastered with the kind of mischievous smile Kat had seen on Aidan's face a thousand times. God, how she missed her boy.

Matt took a quick peek at Nola's jeans-clad backside, then looked at Kat. "Need a hand? I'm on my lunch break and thought I'd check on you."

Kat tried not to laugh because Matt had already been kind enough to check on them first thing that morning, then check in with Nola three times on her cell, and had arranged to have them over to the Bohland House for dinner that night. It was like he couldn't bear to be away from Nola for ten minutes.

Fortunately for everyone in Persuasion, the day had been light on crime.

"Absolutely I can use a hand, Matt." Kat pointed to the half-unloaded cardboard box. "You can finish this one for me if you don't mind, and I'll take a quick break."

"No problem."

Kat winked at Nola as she left the kitchen, knowing full well that whatever happened in that room would be completely unrelated to unpacking. Almost immediately, Nola let out a playful scream of surprise and Matt was already murmuring under his breath.

Kat smiled as she headed toward the living room, once again appreciating her good fortune. Even stripped bare, the renovated house was inviting and warm. It had French doors, natural woodwork, and gleaming oak floors, not to mention high ceilings and two totally refurbished baths. But her favorite feature of the house was the stained-glass windows flanking the fireplace, now radiant with midday light and spreading a cheerful glow through the room. It was the second house Kat had looked at when she arrived in Persuasion last week, and she'd signed a year-long lease on the spot. She would use whatever she needed of the year to reacquaint herself with Riley and her own life story. If things didn't work out, she could leave and start over back in Baltimore, or anywhere else she chose.

She said a silent, *Thank you,* to Phyllis—up in heaven claiming the ultimate jackpot—for her generosity. What she'd bequeathed to Kat was no less than freedom itself.

She breathed deeply, her feet solid beneath her. She was now a resident of Persuasion by her own free will, and she planned to get to the bottom of the girl she was and the woman she'd become. The only heaviness in her heart was the knowledge that she'd have to go through Virgil Cavanaugh to get there.

A howl jarred Kat from her thoughts, and she looked out the picture window to see Riley and Loretta coming up the walk, the dog in the lead. Kat raced to the door to greet them. Riley displayed a large paper sack and an even larger grin.

"Brought us something for lunch." He stepped through the threshold as Kat held the door open. Loretta barked, sniffed the floor, then trotted toward the kitchen. Riley placed a sweet kiss on Kat's lips as she accepted the bag.

"Matt just brought Nola a little something for lunch, too, and he's in there giving it to her as we speak."

Riley closed his eyes and shook his head. "Looks like we're dining al fresco today."

After Kat grabbed a sweater, they opened the door and plopped down on a sunny spot on the porch steps, Riley immediately wrapping his arm around her shoulders. "I think Matt's got it bad," he said, whispering in her ear. "He's usually such a cool customer when it comes to women."

Kat snuggled into Riley's side, contentment settling in her bones. "Nola's pretty gaga, too. I'm trying not to get involved one way or the other. I can't stand the thought of either one of them getting hurt."

Riley kissed the top of her head. "I guess we're the last people on earth who should be advising anyone about how to run a relationship."

"Hmm," Kat said, pulling open the paper bag. "Maybe someday that will be different." She opened the top of the sack and was hit with the smell of grease and breading, and her eyes widened in glee. "Fried chicken and apple fritters? From the Sunset Diner? Holy hell, Riley—I hope you like plump girls."

"I like *you,* so eat up." He gave her rear end a proprietary pat and then fished out paper plates and napkins. He served her a big piece of chicken. "You look really pretty today, Kat."

She'd just ripped a chunk of white meat from the bone, caught off-guard by his compliment and aware she looked like the subject of a documentary on carnivorous jackals.

He laughed. "You're going to have to bear with me, because I'll probably be a real goof for a while, spending most of my free time sitting around staring at you until I'm convinced you're real."

"How long do you figure that will take?" Kat asked, trying not to talk with her mouth full.

"Decades, most likely."

She wiped her smiling mouth with a napkin, and then reached up to wipe his. She planted a playful kiss on his lips and pulled away, grinning at him. When their eyes met, time halted or it turned back or it never mattered at all—it was impossible to grasp—but for that suspended moment, Kat understood that their love was as ancient as it was brand-new. She understood that the fun-loving boy was still right there inside of Riley, alongside the lustful man, and she was destined to be the safe haven for both of them.

Riley smiled at her, and the smile was filled with so much tenderness and desire that she was overcome with longing for him. She wanted to comfort his soul, soothe the places of loss inside him, especially the ones she was responsible for. She wanted to get her hands all over his perfect tush and his silky chest.

Riley's eyelids grew heavy and his nostrils flared. "Your beds get delivered yet?"

Kat chuckled. "I can't believe you can think of sex when we haven't even touched the apple fritters."

"You were thinking the same thing and don't try to lie to me."

"Another day, another round of brutal honesty." Kat took a bite of chicken. "The beds should be here in the next couple hours, actually."

"Just planning ahead. No pressure."

They talked while they ate, Riley sharing with her the latest delays with the clinic, conversations he'd had with Aidan, and the fact that Matt had spent much of the morning preparing that evening's dinner for the four of them.

"Obviously, the man doesn't punch a clock," Kat said.

"He *is* the clock. It's the perfect career for Matt—lots of unstructured time to think about women and food."

Kat licked her fingers. "Would've been fun to be a fly on the wall during that job interview."

"What interview?" Riley laughed under his breath. "He got his criminal justice degree from Mountain Laurel and his last name is Bohland. He had his choice of being director of campus security or the town's chief of police, and one day he'll probably be mayor."

"Hmph." Kat rummaged around for an apple fritter. "Speaking of the college, I was looking at their catalog earlier, checking out classes I could audit."

Riley stopped chewing and his eyebrows went up. "Anything interesting?"

"Don't laugh." She looked out over the small front lawn, onto Laurel Lane. "Psychology. Maybe child psychology. It was just a thought."

Riley grabbed her hand. "Don't ever sell yourself short. You have a brilliant mind and you could do whatever you wanted to do. You've got the money and the time now—why audit classes? Have you considered working toward your bachelor's degree?"

"I think about it all the time."

"Then do it, Scout." Riley put a finger under her chin and raised her eyes to meet his. "I'll cheer you on in whatever you decide to do."

A loud crash came from the back of the house, followed by Loretta's howl. "We're good!" Matt called out, as if to prevent any sudden inspections of the kitchen. Within seconds, Loretta was using her snout to push at the front door, ready to retreat to a calmer location.

Riley got up to let her out. As he returned to his perch, he said, "You'll never guess who I ran into at the diner."

"Carrie?"

Riley shot Kat a sideways glance as he rooted around inside the bag for his fritter. "Don't even joke. Nobody's heard a peep from her since the protective order was issued, and I'm praying it'll stay that way."

"Who then?"

"You dad's sister, Rita."

Kat put the pastry down. "Oh yeah—I was going to go rip her a new asshole when Nola and I were here last month, but I just didn't get around to it."

Riley's eyebrows arched in surprise.

"She was the first person I told about being pregnant that day. I went to her house right after I got the test results, and do you know what that woman told me?" Kat shook her head, remembering how it had stung. "She said I'd have to drop out of school the minute I started to show. Then, as my aunt and not my principal, she told me that whatever I did, I should not tell my father anything about my situation."

Riley shook his head. "Jesus, that's brutal." He tossed the half-eaten dessert back into the bag and sighed. "At least there are agencies working to keep girls in school nowadays, unlike your experience, but the pregnancy rate here is still a huge problem. In fact . . ." Riley looked at Kat without finishing his thought.

"What?"

"Well, I wanted to start a reproductive health outreach center as part of the clinic. It's kind of pie in the sky at the moment, but I'm hoping we can find a way to make it happen." Riley scooted closer so that his long, lean thigh pressed up against hers. "Hey, Kat?"

She nodded.

"Whenever you're ready to talk to Virgil, I'll go with you. Promise me you won't go alone."

Kat looked up at those bottomless blue eyes and was caressed by the earnestness and love that lived in them. Suddenly, hope filled her up, and it was the kind of hope that was big enough to spread wide and wrap its arms around both of them. No wonder she'd never found a man like Riley in Baltimore or anywhere else—there was just one of him, and he'd always been right here, waiting for her to come home.

The door opened behind them.

"Got a possible drive-away at the Sunoco," Matt announced, weary with the burden of authority.

"A what?" Kat asked.

"That's when a motorist fills the tank and drives off without paying," Matt explained. "Been happening a lot more lately with gas prices the way they are."

Kat was appalled. "You mean you don't have pre-pay in this town? You still actually trust people?"

Matt laughed. "Maybe not for much longer." He clomped down the porch steps. "See y'all tonight! Bring your appetites!"

Nola appeared a moment later, the part in her thick brunette hair askew and one earring missing. "I'm moving to Persuasion," she mumbled.

"Because you don't have to pre-pay?" Riley asked with mock innocence.

Nola stared out toward the street, her eyes unfocused. "No, because your brother is ass-kickingly hot."

Kat winced, knowing it was her duty to remind Nola of her convictions, since she seemed incapacitated at the moment. Kat turned to Riley and asked in a loud, clear voice, "Does Matt have a beer can collection by any chance?"

Riley looked nonplussed. "It's bottles. Why?"

Virgil hadn't come up with a decent piece in more than twenty years and he knew it. Sure, the lamebrains down at the gallery took whatever he gave them, and they'd sell something every once in a blue moon, so they were happy enough. But he knew he'd been producing nothing but trash for decades, resting on whatever renown he once had. There was no longer any flow in his work, no essence, no energy, and it didn't matter if it was marble, wood, or even that fiberglass-reinforced fake cement shit that he could usually pawn off to the gallery—nothing had been good in his art, or his life, since January 1988.

His last truly beautiful creation, his only near masterpiece, was the clay model and rough-cut marble bust of Eleanor Erskine. She was the D-cupped wife of West Virginia's goofy governor, who happened to be the brother of Mountain Laurel's chancellor. That's how Virgil had gotten what was to be the biggest commission of his life—the twists and turns of coincidence. When the state wanted a bust of the big-busted first lady and was willing to pay $250,000 for it, the Mountain Laurel art professor got thrown a bone. He took it happily, and got to bone the governor's wife as a bonus. Unfortunately, Kat saw him do it.

Virgil fidgeted with the business card in his hand, staring at the name of that dipshit doctor who'd bulldozed her way onto his property a few weeks back. He should call her. Get her to come out here and sit for him right this minute. He wanted to see a beautiful woman completely naked one last time before he died, and she'd reminded him a bit of Eleanor, anyway. If she was anything like the governor's wife, the doctor was haughty because deep down she was naughty. Virgil smiled at his clever turn of phrase and sighed with pleasure. Eleanor Erskine had been a good lay; maybe the doctor would be, too.

He put down the business card and looked around him at the debris, the graveyard of his career. He didn't even know why he bothered coming out to the studio anymore. Nothing more than habit, probably, and the need to get away from the TV for a while. Too much violence. Virgil rose from the stool and wandered toward the back of the garage, looking for something in particular. He knew he'd put it on a cart back there somewhere, back when BettyAnn had first gotten sick. He never wanted her to see it.

His hands encountered the cool, smooth surface of the form of his daughter. He wheeled the cart to the worktable, and sat back on the stool. It was always better to work from a live model, of course, because there were nuances in the personality and expressions that a sculptor could get only from life itself. But he'd remembered so much of Katharine. With the old photos BettyAnn thought she'd hidden away, and his many detailed memories, he hadn't done a half-bad job.

Katharine had been a beautiful baby, and he remembered being deeply relieved by that. She'd been born with blond curls and flawless pink skin and those strange citrine-colored eyes. He'd always thought they looked feline, and they made him vaguely uncomfortable. BettyAnn had reassured him that Katharine would grow out of the unusual eye color. She didn't. Luckily, people accepted them and even thought they were lovely, and didn't question who among the Cavanaughs had such coloring.

From what he could tell from her short visit in the ER, Katharine had grown into a stunning woman. What was she now—thirty-seven? She still had a sexy shape for a woman her age. She'd always had a nice curvy and petite shape.

Virgil shook his head, as if to knock some sense into himself. He stared at the unfinished bust and decided he would complete it. He'd make her all grown-up. He'd give her that smirk of disdain he'd seen on her face in the studio window twenty years ago, the same one she'd shown in the hospital room just last month. Next, he'd flesh out her cheeks and thicken the fall of her hair. But he'd leave her throat just the way it was, dainty and vulnerable.

God, he hadn't meant to, but he'd beaten the shit out of BettyAnn that night. It was like he couldn't stop himself. He'd come home to find her trying to scrape up his $250,000 commission from this very floor. Then she lied to him, saying she'd accidentally knocked it over. He knew better. He'd seen the betrayal in Katharine's eyes as she peeked in the window, and he knew she'd ruined the clay model to get her revenge.

BettyAnn was hysterical, begging for him not to go after their daughter. *Take it out on me!* she screamed. God, he hated when she got like that, so protective, like he was some kind of monster, like he'd ever hurt his daughter. He was a good man! A damn good father! And that little cat-eyed bitch had been ungrateful from the day she was born, because she didn't know the truth. *She just didn't know.*

Virgil let his head fall into his hands. He reached blindly for the tumbler of vodka he'd left on the worktable, brought it down to his lips, and sucked down half of it. BettyAnn had made it out of surgery just fine, and the scars around her eyes eventually healed up so they were hardly noticeable, especially if she wore that special mail-order makeup. But as ridiculous as it sounded now, he'd actually ended up spending three nights in jail, where he'd been forced to endure a visit from the King of Persuasion himself. Aidan Bohland had put his finger in Virgil's face and told him that if he ever touched BettyAnn again, he would lose everything—his tenure, his home, his reputation. Virgil hated that holier-than-thou bastard. What did he know about keeping a wife in line? Nothing, obviously—Eliza Bohland was known for making a complete fool of herself when she'd had a little too much to drink, which was daily.

Then Big Dopey Bohland had the balls to inform Virgil that Katharine was a special young lady who deserved more attention from her father. Virgil had laughed because it was just so damn ironic, and told Bohland to fuck himself.

Virgil got out of jail on a Saturday. With BettyAnn in the hospital and then laid up at home—and with all the legal rigmarole that had gone into getting the charges against him dropped—it was a good two weeks before they reported their daughter officially missing.

And now, twenty years later, she finally found her way back to Persuasion, unashamed of the fact that she couldn't keep her legs together any better than her mother could. Just today, Rita told him that Katharine had rented a house off-campus and that some expensive furniture and whatnots had already been delivered.

Virgil stared at the pretty clay face frozen in time and felt the old craving course through him. It surprised him how strong it was, considering the lid had been on it for twenty years. It was the vodka. The vodka always triggered his urges. And his urge for Katharine had always been the strongest.

He drank what was left in the glass, feeling the heat lollygag through his bloodstream. He allowed himself to remember how it used to be. Oh, how he'd enjoyed the act of hitting BettyAnn. It was a sweet, sweet agony. A taboo rapture. And it was the only way he'd ever found to dampen the flames, since it wouldn't be right to touch Katharine the way he longed to.

He looked down at his pants and laughed. By God, he was getting peckerwood! He didn't even think that was possible anymore, what with all the medicine he was taking.

Suddenly, he was certain she was spying on him again. His eyes shot to the window, but there was nothing—no blond curls, no cat eyes. Then he realized it was the bust on the worktable that was mocking him.

Virgil raised his tumbler, found it empty, and threw it against the wall. BettyAnn had betrayed him. She'd always known Kat left here pregnant with Bohland's child. That was BettyAnn's big secret the day she died. Virgil had spent the last few days systematically ripping the house to shreds in search for what else that ungrateful bitch might have kept from him. He found nothing.

Virgil cried. A man needed to know he controlled some part of his life, and Virgil's life's greatest pleasure had always been the absolute knowledge that he controlled dumb little BettyAnn absolutely. But she'd been fooling him all along. Underneath it all, she was a lying slut, just like all the rest.

Virgil studied the unfinished bust through his tears, circling around the table, looking from every angle. Something about the way the image danced and distorted in the teardrops made him smile. Then he began to laugh. It was incredible! A miracle!

In the eleventh hour of life, he'd finally found the inspiration for his masterpiece.

Kat stepped out into the crisp morning with a smile on her face and determination in her heart. Today was going to be all about school—when she'd finished the registration process at Mountain Laurel she planned to pay a little visit to Principal Cavanaugh.

Kat chugged up the hill to campus, struck by the charm of its Gothic limestone spires, its ornate wrought-iron front gate, and its tidy fall landscape. It looked magical to her that morning, and welcoming.

Things went smoothly in the admissions office. She picked up a class schedule and orientation package, and though Kat was told it would be several weeks before all her transcripts were transferred, it would leave her plenty of time before winter quarter began in January.

While there, Kat ran into no fewer than five women she'd known in school. She chatted briefly with each of them, giving each enough to satisfy her appetite for gossip. They all wanted to know where she'd been and if she'd come back for Riley Bohland, and she gave them the basics, adding that she was looking forward to catching up with old friends, including Riley. She knew every word of it would be all over town by supper time.

As Kat wandered the campus, it became painfully obvious that everyone there was Aidan's age. Her heart suddenly felt like it weighed a thousand pounds, a big, thousand-pound stone of loneliness for her son.

It was almost comic now. Every morning she

would call Aidan and talk to his voice mail. He never answered and he never called back. As Kat strolled down the hill toward town, she decided it was time for her daily exercise in futility.

She got Aidan's voice mail, of course, and had readied herself to leave another message about Thanksgiving dinner at her house when she heard a real, live voice.

"Hey, Mom."

Kat froze. She looked around for a place to sit and chose a small stone planter in front of a hair salon, where she managed to prop herself. "Sweetheart," she said. "Are you all right?"

"Look, Mom, I just need some time. I've been doing a lot of thinking. I'm fine, but I need some space."

Kat nodded in silence, realizing that she'd asked Riley for the exact same thing, for the exact same reason—forgiveness is a process, not something you can pick up at the drive-thru. She dared not say another word. She didn't want Aidan to know she was crying.

"I know you're crying, Mom. Don't try to hide it. It's time to stop hiding shit from me, OK?"

"I know. I know." She sniffed. "I miss you so much!"

"Well, I miss you, too. Look, I'm late for class. We'll catch up later."

"All right, Aidan."

"Hey, Mom?"

"Yes?" Her heart began to pound with anticipation.

"I'm bringing Rachel up over break. Dad said that would be OK, so if I decide to accept your dinner invitation, she'll be coming along."

Kat punched a fist into the air, stomped her feet, and mouthed a silent, *Woo hoo!*—all of which was witnessed by four ladies gawking from under their hair dryers. This, too, would be around town by supper time.

"Rachel is always welcome," she answered Aidan, trying to sound casual.

He laughed, almost as if he'd witnessed her little break dance of joy. "You're too much, Mom. Talk to you later."

"I love you."

He'd already hung up, but she didn't care. She'd talked to her boy. He was coming. And he'd just referred to Riley as "Dad"!

With the bounce restored to her walk, Kat headed south on Main and stopped in the coffee shop, a long sleek space with modern bistro tables, colorful couches, and some kind of Latin jazz floating down from the ceiling. Every student in the place was on a laptop and/or a cell phone. The rich smell of roasting coffee filled her head.

This was Persuasion? Kat laughed out loud.

She got a café au lait to go and headed north. She hadn't called Rita in advance but figured if she wasn't available she could still have a look around Underwood High for laughs. She walked at a leisurely pace, catching little changes in the town that she hadn't noticed the last time. The clock tower on the square actually displayed the correct time. The sidewalks on Main Street were twice as wide as they once were, and trimmed in a fancy redbrick basketweave pattern. Streetlights designed like old gas lamps lined the length of the shopping district, each one sporting a hanging basket of autumn annuals. Kat hummed to herself in approval.

As she reached the intersection with Forest Drive, she stopped cold, all the cheerfulness gone in an instant. She dared herself to look.

It was just a house. A squat, ugly, yellow brick ranch house with a tacky 1950s door and a trashed yard. Her eyes flickered to the garage studio, and the sight opened a gaping hole in her belly.

One day soon she would go back there. She would open the door to the studio and look her father in the eye and say her fill.

Just not today.

She moved along for six more blocks, knowing her sights were set on a smaller fish. Kat opened the door to the school, followed security warnings for visitors to report to the office, and encountered the same secretary at the same desk, wearing an outfit Kat swore was right out of 1987.

Kat felt awful because she couldn't remember the secretary's name. As it turned out, she didn't have to.

"She's here!" the woman called over her shoulder.

Within seconds, Kat's aunt appeared, offering her hand and a courteous smile. "I've been expecting you, Katharine," she said.

"You owe me."

"You sound deranged," was Carrie's reply. "I'm concerned for your well-being."

Madeline began laughing so hard she thought she'd pee her pants, considering that that came from a woman who had pranced around in a wedding dress in this very kitchen not even three weeks ago, holding up her boobs and saying she looked like Grace Kelly.

When Madeline could finally stop laughing, she

tucked the phone under her chin and methodically scraped the cake batter in the Bundt pan. She was trying a new recipe that called for a dash of amaretto, which she thought would be lovely.

"Well, here's the deal, Carrie—you manipulated me, lied to me, and made a fool of me in front of the Bohlands. And now you owe me. It's pretty simple."

"I'm very busy these days. Now that the wedding is off, you'd be amazed how much time I have to pursue other things. I'm taking tai chi. I'm in therapy."

Madeline snorted. "That's just great. So, how do you plan to do it?"

"Do what?"

"Make it up to me?"

Carrie let loose with a giant sigh of exasperation. "I really don't have time for this kind of thing. I'm testifying in front of the legislature next week on domestic violence prevention initiatives."

Madeline let loose with a snicker.

"Besides, I'm turning over a new leaf. This junior-high stuff you seem to bring out in me has got to stop. At any rate, you ratted me out to Matt. You're a gossip, and that is a crippling dysfunction. I would recommend a Co-dependents Anonymous meeting."

Madeline rolled her eyes, reaching into the pantry for the confectioners' sugar and the roasted almonds she'd be using to garnish the cake.

"I really have to go," Carrie said cheerfully. "Take care."

"Oh no, you don't." Madeline dropped the baking supplies on the countertop. She was never going to take this kind crap from Carrie Mathis—or anyone else—again. It was time for Madeline Bowman to be on top. "Maybe I'll go straight to the state medical board with your secret to weight loss."

Silence.

"I know all about your problems, Carrie. I cleaned up after you every time you were a guest here, remember? I'm not stupid. I snooped around in the garbage and in your luggage, too, which helped flesh out the overall picture, no pun intended."

Carrie gasped.

"If the big boys in the statehouse knew they had a bulimic, laxative-munching ephedrine addict like you in charge of changing the freaking *copier toner* at the health department, they'd kick your skinny ass all the way to Kentucky. But you're the state's poster child for wholesome living, Carrie! You're on TV every damn day, telling the entire state of West Virginia how to be healthy! Can you *imagine* how embarrassed that will make your bosses?"

"Don't you dare threaten me," Carrie said.

"Then just do what I ask. It's your turn to do some of the dirty work around here."

"That's blackmail."

"No," Madeline said matter-of-factly. "Blackmail would be if I threatened to let everyone know you're a stalker by telling the Charleston newspaper about a little ole restraining order that's tucked away up here in the Randolph County Courthouse files."

Carrie gasped. "How did you hear about that?"

"The county clerk is my former sister-in-law."

"What do you want?"

"I'd like you to use all your considerable talents to get Matt Bohland's new girlfriend to dump him flat. And I want it done by Thanksgiving."

FOURTEEN

Kat sat in the passenger seat of Rita Cavanaugh's sedan, not recalling a time in her life when she'd felt more awkward. Rita had always reminded Kat of Virgil in the way she held her head, the slight hunch of her back, and the vibe she gave off that she couldn't stand to be in the same room with Kat.

"So you've been living in Baltimore all these years."

Kat nodded wearily. "How did you know I was coming to see you today?"

"From what I understand, you were supposed to come see me the evening of January seventh, nineteen-eighty-eight," she said with a laugh. "That's what your mother told you to do."

"I didn't feel like it. You'd just thrown me out of school, remember?"

Rita shook her head. "Oh, Katharine, you're still the same smart-alecky know-it-all you were in tenth grade, only hearing the parts you choose to hear."

Kat felt like screaming.

"What I said to you that day was that you could attend classes until you began to show. I didn't kick you out. Those are two different things."

"Right. My mistake."

Rita drove on in silence while Kat gained the courage to do what she'd come here for.

"I think your response was unbelievably cruel, Rita."

She looked sideways at Kat with irritation.

"I was a child," Kat continued. "I was scared to death. And all you cared about was how it would reflect on you."

"The whole family, Katharine. I cared about how it would reflect on your parents as well."

Kat shook her head. "This is Persuasion we're talking about. Even if I never set foot in school again, everyone would still know I was pregnant."

"I'll tell you what the real tragedy is, Katharine—that an intelligent girl like you couldn't keep her drawers on a bit longer."

That was enough. "Stop. I'm getting out of the car."

"Oh, please." Rita waved her hand to dismiss the request. "This won't take but a second. I just want to give you a few boxes of your mother's things that she wanted you to have. As soon as I heard you were in town, I brought them down from the attic."

Kat propped her elbow on the edge of the passenger's-side window and held her forehead in her hand. She wondered what things her mother could have possibly wanted her to have. Sentimentality was never a quality Kat had associated with BettyAnn Cavanaugh.

"Have you spoken to your father?"

"Only briefly at the hospital."

Rita nodded. "You really should have a talk with him. It would be good for you both. I know he would appreciate it."

Kat laughed at that one. "He hasn't appreciated a single thing I've done in my life."

"He won't be around forever, you know, and once he's dead, that's it."

"Just like my mother," Kat said.

Rita turned down the street where she'd lived as long as Kat could remember. "Come grab one of the boxes," she told Kat.

The moment she stepped inside Rita's foyer, Kat became nauseous. Something about the smell of the home caused Kat's throat to tighten and her stomach to cramp. She felt panicky. Rita looked at her like she was crazy, so Kat picked up a carton and carried it to the trunk, talking sense to herself, recalling how she'd read somewhere that smell was the most primitive sense, hardwired to the brain's memory center. Kat got another box and repeated the process, and this time the sensation hit her even more strongly. Thankfully, Rita carried the last box.

When they were back in the car, Rita looked at Kat and asked, "Is something wrong?"

"No more than usual," Kat answered.

"Well then, do you remember Joanna Loveless? She was a year ahead of you, I think."

"I guess."

"She's the editor of the local paper now, and she inquired whether you might agree to be interviewed for a holiday feature article—a kind of a homecoming thing."

"Ugh."

"That's what I told her you'd say."

Rita pulled up in front of the bungalow on Laurel Lane, which made Kat laugh.

"I didn't tell you where I was living."

"You didn't have to."

Rita waited in the car, staring out the window at something way down the street that must have been fascinating while Kat carried the boxes inside, one by one. *Cold, cold, cold.* That was all Kat could think as she moved the cartons. It was more than a word, though. It was an image, a feeling, and it wasn't just about her aunt's lovely personality. The feeling was so severe that there wasn't room in Kat's senses for anything else but all that freezing *cold.*

Rita drove away with a casual wave and Kat entered her own comfortable retreat. That's when it dawned on her—it was a taste she was remembering, not a smell, and it was steadily rising from the depths of her childhood and placing itself right on her tongue.

Kat felt heavy and weak. When the front door opened, she didn't have the energy to look up to see who it was.

"When you shell out for premium leather furniture, you don't have to sit on the floor anymore, hon." Nola breezed in. "And I thought we finished unpacking a long time ago. Did you find more boxes?"

Kat felt awareness returning to her body. She was in the middle of her living room floor, sitting cross-legged on the new rug, with her left foot asleep. She still had her coat on. She looked up at Nola.

"Oh my God! What's wrong?" Nola collapsed down on her knees in front of Kat. "Darlin', are you all right? What happened? Are you hurt? You've been crying." Nola touched Kat's cheek, then the wet lapel of Kat's corduroy jacket. "I'm calling Riley."

"No." Kat's eyes began to focus. She must really be in bad shape if Nola looked that horrified. "I'm OK."

Nola unbuttoned Kat's jacket and peeled it off her arms. She hoisted her up and got her to lie on the couch. "I'll heat some water for tea. Stay right there. Don't move."

All this hullabaloo was about ice cream, for God's sake—homemade peach ice cream. Kat slapped her own cheeks. What kind of woman had to lie down on the couch to recover from thinking of peach ice cream? At least it now made sense why Kat had hated the taste and smell of peaches her whole life. Funny how those things worked.

Nola returned, moving Kat's legs so she could sit down next to her. "Riley's on his way."

Kat shut her eyes and groaned. "That wasn't necessary."

"What's going on, hon?" Nola reached out and moved a strand of hair back from Kat's face. "You didn't go see Virgil, did you?"

Kat shook her head. "His sister."

"That trifling principal bitch."

Kat laughed, reaching to touch Nola's arm. "Thanks for having my back."

"Always."

"So how did the interview go?" Kat knew that Nola had interviewed for a job as a paralegal at the town's only lawyer's office.

"I got it, of course. Where are they gonna find someone like me all the way out here?" A grin spread over Nola's face. "And Matt's going to be thrilled."

Kat sat up slowly, feeling a little better, and not wanting Riley to walk in and find her stretched out like an invalid. "That's great news, Nola."

"So what happened with your aunt?"

Kat shook her head. "I feel ridiculous. All I do is whine to you and Riley about all this stuff about my past, and I'm sure you're both sick of it by now."

"Nope." Nola stroked Kat's arm. "Coming back here is just flogging your memory is all. It's perfectly natural."

Kat smiled. Her friend might have chosen the wrong word, but she had the right idea—Kat's brain did feel like it was being flogged. "Thanks," she told Nola.

"Now spill it. What did you remember? More about the sculpture? Your mom?"

Kat folded her hands in her lap and decided she'd just tell it straight and get it over with. It was such a stupid thing, really.

"I was at my aunt Rita's for some kind of summer picnic. I think I was about seven. I kept asking my dad when I could have some ice cream—somebody had churned a big batch of peach ice cream." Kat took a moment to steady herself. "My dad told me I had to wait until he said it was time, but I just kept bugging him."

"I think I remember this."

Kat jolted at the sound of Riley's voice. He stood in the entrance to the living room looking handsome and worried. His hands were dug deep into his pockets.

"Do you?" Kat asked.

"Parts of it, anyway. It was your mom's birthday."

"Seriously?" Kat had tried to extract that particular detail but couldn't.

"My mom was the one in charge of the ice cream," Riley said. "Big Daddy was there and Matt was just a toddler running around." Riley walked into the room, stepped over the boxes, and sat on the couch on the other side of Kat. He took one of her hands and Nola took the other.

Kat had to laugh. "This is not a huge deal, guys. Really. I'm not going to need to be resuscitated or anything." They didn't budge.

"Tell us what happened next, Kat." Riley's voice was particularly gentle.

"You probably already know."

"Tell it anyway."

Kat took a breath. "My mom told him not to be so hard on me, that the other kids were getting their ice cream, so I shouldn't have to wait."

Riley nodded.

"Virgil was drunk. He started yelling at my mom." Kat's blood began to pound and black spots jumped in her vision, and she found it annoying that her body considered this so much more frightening than her common sense did. "I remember being ashamed. I don't remember exactly what my dad said, but I couldn't believe he would talk to my mom like that in front of people, because I thought it was only supposed to happen at home."

"I know exactly what he said." Riley put an arm around her shoulders. "Can I tell you what I remember from that day?"

Kat nodded.

"Virgil told your mother she was stupid and that she had no right to question how he raised you."

Kat stared at Riley. "Oh my God. You're right. That's what he said!"

"What a prick," Nola contributed. She gave Kat's hand a firm squeeze. "What happened next?"

"Well, this is where it gets really weird." Kat

paused, telling herself that she'd get through the rest without stopping. "The next thing I know, my dad's got me in his lap and I'm looking straight up at the clouds, and there is this sudden pain in my throat, and I tried to scream, but no sound would come out because . . . because . . ." Kat choked on the words.

"You can do this," Riley whispered to her, holding her tightly around the shoulders. "He can't hurt you now."

Kat clung to the cadence of Riley's words and the safety of his arms around her. She told herself he was right—she could do this. Her entire body began to shake.

"That fucker shoved a big spoon of ice cream down my throat and told me to enjoy it because it was the last ice cream I'd ever get! It hurt so much! He hurt me! It was freezing cold and sharp inside my throat and I couldn't . . . I couldn't breathe—I couldn't *breathe*! Oh God! Why did he have to be so mean all the time?"

Kat buried her face in the heat and safety of Riley's body and cried. After what felt like hours, she willed herself to take slow, deep breaths and pay attention to the voices floating around her. Riley's soft baritone promised she was safe and loved—over and over he promised her that. Nola was right in the middle of a long list of Balmerese obscenities when Riley asked her to chill out. Then Matt walked in and added his own words of comfort.

Kat eventually sat up, her insides feeling scraped out like a jack-o'-lantern's. Nola handed her some tissues. Everyone stared at her, worried.

"I'm going to be fine," she said, knowing it was true. Virgil couldn't hurt her anymore. Neither could Rita or anyone else. Kat was a grown-up now, and had control of her own life. She had her own place. Kat turned to Riley and gave him a shaky smile, aware that the biggest difference of all was that now she wasn't alone.

"Big Daddy pulled Virgil off of you," Riley added as an afterthought, his hands rhythmically stroking Kat's hair as he talked. "Then he escorted your dad by the shirt collar and put him in the car. The two of them drove off and never made it back to the party. I always wondered what happened."

Matt laughed. "Doesn't take a hell of a lot of wonderin' if you ask me."

"Hey, Kat?" Nola's voice sounded small.

"Yeah?"

Nola looked like she was going to cry, so Kat rubbed her knee. "I really am OK, Nola."

"Hell yes, you are," she said. "I just need to apologize for ever questioning why you ran away." Nola shook her head. "That guy was bad news. You probably saved your life and your baby's life by leaving this town, plain and simple. And do you know what that makes you?"

Kat shook her head.

"A freakin' *hero,* hon."

Kat allowed the warmth of that word to spread through her. Maybe Nola was right.

Without warning, Matt squatted, pulled out a penknife, and sliced open one of the boxes. "I'll unpack these last few for you," he said.

Virgil felt energized and brave. The buzz of power raced through his body, down his arms, and into his hands, where he would use it to give form to the raw beauty of the stone. Virgil had long understood that working with marble was the opposite of dealing with women. Marble was at its best when the artist respected its essence and found a way to coax its inner beauty out into the open. Women, Virgil knew from personal experience, must be molded to fit an outer structure.

Marble needed to be set free. Women needed to be managed. And any man who didn't understand that was a fool.

Even through Virgil's earplugs, the tapping of his heavy chisel against the rock sounded like an elaborate orchestral movement to him, the music of making art. He was working free-form today, not sure what had possessed him to risk it, without even a rough pencil sketch on the stone to guide his way. He knew instinctively what lay at the core of this solid, creamy pink block of Italian Carrara he'd been saving for over a decade—for what, he'd never known. Not until today. And his hands were flying and his mind was spinning and he was releasing, releasing, releasing the feminine from this rock, more than one face, more than one mouth, more than one set of eyes. He was releasing all that had been haunting him. All those women. Those breasts. Those buttocks. Those thighs.

Virgil suddenly stepped back, ripped off his goggles and paper mask, and walked back toward the door to get a better look. The dust was flying. His chest was tight.

He couldn't die now—not fucking now!

He replaced the goggles and mask and went back to work. He picked up a point chiseler, a riffler, and saw them all coming at him—weak BettyAnn, lusty Eleanor, know-it-all Katharine, and so many other faces. Then there was the doctor lady. He'd dreamed of her again last night, naked and willing and silent.

And all these women blurred together into one vision, and it flew out of the stone and into his brain, through his fingers, back into the stone, and back into his brain again. He was easing the beauty out of the big chunk of marble while still managing to keep all those women in line. It was a delicate balance, but he could do it. He was the only sculptor who could.

Virgil stopped again, the old craving running so hard through his body that he felt faint. He wanted the doctor lady. Right here. Her smooth skin and dark hair. He needed to see the tops of her breasts, her clavicle, the slope of her thin shoulders. He needed to have her sit for him. He wanted to get his hands on her, choke the haughtiness right out of her.

Because he wasn't allowed to touch Kat.

His chest tightened again.

He refused to die before he'd brought his exquisite vision to life.

Matt pulled the flaps of the cardboard box apart, and a fold of red fabric poked through the opening. Kat gasped. Riley looked at her face and knew that whatever was in that box, she wanted nothing to do with it.

"Stop right now," she said sharply.

Matt glanced up with surprised eyes, his knife poised over another box. "You don't want me to unpack these?" He sounded hurt.

"I'll take care of it later." Kat tried to sound casual. "I'm just pretty tired right now is all."

Matt shrugged. "You kick back and relax then, and I'll just—"

"No. Leave it."

Riley watched Kat smooth over her abruptness with Matt, and soon she had Matt and Nola talking excitedly about Nola's new job at Richard Keefauver's legal office in town. Riley wasn't sure how he felt about the two of them moving at the speed of light like this—Nola had already given her notice at her job in Baltimore—but he gave her a big hug of congratulations as she and Matt headed out the door. Matt and Nola were adults. Just because Matt put the "wild" in Wild, Wonderful West Virginia and Nola had collected one husband per decade of her life didn't mean the two of them couldn't discover something that could last. One thing was for damn sure—Riley had no place judging anyone else's love life.

"I need a distraction," Kat said. She paced in the foyer, running her hands through her hair in exasperation. "I need to get my mind off all this crap for a little while. In fact, I think I might need to hit something." She looked up at Riley. "Got any ideas?"

"I certainly do," he said, with the wag of an eyebrow.

Kat exhaled in disbelief. "Sex? How could you want to have sex with me? I'm haunted by my childhood. I'm a nut job. I have visions. Pretty soon the voices will be telling me to do things. I'm an emotional slop heap. I'm crazy. And this turns you on?"

Riley moved closer to Kat and put his arms around her, laughing. He planted a sweet kiss on her mouth. "I wasn't even thinking about sex, but obviously, you were, and here's a little secret we doctors usually don't share with the civilian population: If a person says they may be going crazy, they're normal. The ones who believe that all is well are the ones you've got to watch."

"Hmph."

"But I do think I've got something for you," he said, kissing her again. "You're gonna sweat a little, learn a few new tricks, and you'll be exhausted when you're done. How does that sound?"

"It sounds like what we did at Cherry Hill."

"Well, it's not."

Kat looked down at herself. "I bet I need to change, don't I?"

Riley surveyed her outfit—a pair of gray dress slacks, high-heeled boots, and a sweater set in a nice soft pink. She looked sexy as hell, but it wasn't suitable for what he had in mind. "Remember how you used to dress in eighth grade?" he asked.

Kat looked at him with suspicion. "That wasn't my best year."

Riley laughed. "It's nobody's best year, Scout. Just put on some jeans and a sweatshirt, OK? Then you won't have to worry about your clothes."

Kat's eyes lit up and she smiled, and it was like a jolt of lightning went through him. Of all the sights in the world, Kat smiling and happy was the most beautiful he could imagine. "Be right back!" she said.

Riley watched her run up the stairs and was tempted to follow that beautiful little ass of hers to the bedroom but thought better of it. He could put the few moments alone to good use right down here on the first floor.

Riley went to the boxes. The blue ink had faded so much that it was hardly visible, but written on each box in an unsteady cursive hand were the words *For Katharine.* A chill went through him at the sight of BettyAnn's handwriting. Riley squatted near the open box and, carefully, he pulled a flap away from the red fabric and brushed his fingers over it. He thought he recognized this, and when he lifted a corner to see the black velvet trim and buttons, there was no room for doubt.

Kat had worn this coat when she was little. He remembered it. He remembered her in it. His heart clenched.

Not sure continuing was the right thing to do—but knowing he would anyway—Riley reached under the heavy coat and lifted. He saw a stuffed rabbit, a few books, and several pieces of kids' artwork. Riley swallowed hard, wondering how these things had gotten to Kat and how their presence in her home was connected to her painful memory.

He heard her bounding down the stairs, so he put everything back in its place and met her in the foyer. She wore a pair of torn jeans and an Orioles sweatshirt. She looked so good he wanted to eat her alive.

"I'm not ready to look inside those boxes yet," she said casually, opening the hall closet and choosing a fleece jacket.

"How did they get here, Kat? Are they from your mom?"

She nodded. "Rita gave them to me. I went to see her at the school today and we stopped by her house." Riley helped Kat get her arms in the jacket sleeves. "She said Mom gave them to her to give to me one day."

Riley hummed in thought. "You know that's your old coat in that box, right?"

"Yeah." A sad smile spread over her face. "What else is in there?"

"Books. Crayon drawings. A stuffed animal."

Kat's eyes darted to the living room floor, then back at Riley.

"Let's get out of here," she said.

After a quick stop at the Bohland House, where Riley threw a change of clothes in the truck along with Loretta, they took off toward the west side of town. Within minutes they were at the clinic construction site, and Kat was shocked at the progress made since she'd shown up that day more than a month ago, with revenge at the top of her to-do list.

"It's looking wonderful, Riley," she said. Kat saw that the blacktop had been poured in the parking lot and the curbs and sidewalks put in. She watched one cluster of people unload rolls of carpet padding and vinyl flooring from a delivery truck while another group readied the ground for landscaping.

"We've been working in shifts," Riley explained. "There's a community sign-up sheet down at the Independent Grocery, and a bunch of the college sororities and fraternities have been helping for community service credits."

"That's amazing."

Riley brought the pickup to a stop near the front sidewalk and he looked at her with a frown. "It is. The problem we've got now is the cost of the interior supplies and furnishings. Do you know a single exam table costs about six thousand dollars? It's ridiculous!"

Kat suddenly felt guilty—she'd paid that much for her leather couch.

"We've got some county funds. Plus, I've squeezed out a dozen or more sponsorships from the business community, and a whole bunch of in-kind donations, but it's not like Randolph County is an industrial powerhouse."

"How about the mine?"

"The operation is a shell of what it used to be, but they did pony up something. The bank came up with about a hundred thousand, and it was much appreciated, but I'm having to do some real creative financing to make all this happen."

Kat's brain started to gallop ahead of her. She was suddenly thinking of a hundred ways she could help get Riley's clinic up and running, and one of them was a huge cash donation. "I've got a few ideas, Riley. Let's sit down and look at the numbers later, OK?"

He shook his head. "Hell no, Kat. I don't want your money. That is not why I'm telling you this."

"I know that," she said.

"I wouldn't take it, anyway. It's yours."

She strained to reach Riley over Loretta's large body but only managed to plant a kiss somewhere near his cheek. "First of all, it's Phyllis' money, not mine." Kat saw the doubt in Riley's eyes. "She had a giving heart and would love this idea. Let me talk to her brother and see if maybe we can do something."

Riley shook his head. "I can't ask for that."

Kat smiled at him. "You didn't, my sweet man. I offered." She smacked her palms on her jeans. "Besides, that's not my only idea. I think I know how we can get everyone to come together for one last push so you can open by Christmas."

Riley's face was flooded with a combination of relief and joy. It occurred to Kat that he'd been carrying this burden by himself a long time, probably because he hadn't trusted anyone to share it with him. "Tell me what happened with that grant money from the state. You never did explain that to me."

He nodded, sliding his hands together so they met at the top of the steering wheel. "Carrie—I told you she was the head of rural health policy for the state, right?"

Kat nodded. "I meant to tell you I saw her on a TV public-service announcement the other night—she's stunning."

Riley let out a groan. "She sure screwed me over in a stunning way."

"What did she do, exactly?"

Riley took a minute before he answered Kat, and she could tell he wanted to choose his words with care. "I can't prove it, I have to say that up front, but right after I called off the wedding and broke up with her, everything went to hell. One day we were told the money was ours, and the next day it was as if nobody knew a thing about it. By the time I realized what was going on, the legislative session had ended. I hired a lawyer, who's been trying for a year now to bulldoze his way through a mountain of bullshit. I eventually took out a personal loan just so we wouldn't have to scrap it."

"You *what*?" Kat's mouth fell open.

"I took out a second mortgage on the Bohland House."

Kat's body hummed with agitation. "How much, Riley? How much was the state supposed to give you? A couple hundred thousand?"

He shrugged. "A little more than that."

"How much, Riley?" Kat was suddenly filled with trepidation. "How much do you owe?"

"They say real estate is location, location, location—well, the location of the Bohland House is the middle of nowhere, obviously, but it has some serious value because of its architecture."

She knew he was stalling. "Just tell me how much you're in debt."

He shook his head. "A little too much, I have to admit."

"Brutal honesty, Riley. You promised me."

He looked at her and chewed the inside of his cheek. "About one-point-five million dollars."

Kat thought she'd throw up. "Oh my God," she said, looking back and forth between Riley and the single-story stone-and-siding office complex. "What does Matt think about this?"

Riley shrugged.

"Is he in the position to help you pay it back?"

Riley laughed. "I'm sure if he knew, he'd double up on his weekly Mega Millions tickets."

"No way." Kat thought her eyes would pop out. "Please, please, *please* don't tell me you did this behind his back."

Riley's face fell. He couldn't look her in the eye, so looked down at his hands on the wheel. "I've been meaning to tell him. I really have. And now I have to."

"Really? Why? Did you suddenly grow a conscience?"

Riley looked stunned. "Ease up, Kat. I made a serious error in judgment and I'll take responsibility for it. I'll tell Matt what I've done and I'll get his share of the money to him somehow."

She stared at Riley blankly as the realization hit her—he was capable of large-scale dishonesty with his own brother. What would Riley hide from her if given the opportunity?

"I really thought I could pay off the loan without Matt ever being the wiser." Riley leaned his head against the seat back. "I kept hoping the state money would show up somewhere. But it didn't, and I missed several payments and was short on others. I'm trying to hold them off, but the bank says it's going to file for foreclosure. I need to tell Matt—I don't want him to hear it from someone else."

"How noble of you."

"You know, I feel plenty disgusted with myself all on my own."

"Did you know about the foreclosure before you persuaded me to move back here?"

Riley's head shot up. "Yes. But what are you—?"

"You're absolutely certain you didn't bring me up here for my money?" The second Kat said it, she regretted it, but there it was.

Riley's mouth went hard. "One of the reasons I got so behind is because I cleaned out my savings and investments and lost three months of income running around the country looking for you and Aidan."

Kat nodded, fury engulfing her. She reached for her purse and began fumbling around for her checkbook with shaking hands. "Here, let me reimburse you. What are we talking—gas, hotel, food, and three months of salary? Can you give me a ballpark?"

"I don't want a damn check."

"Oh, but I damn sure want to give you one. I need us to be even. I don't want to be indebted to you for a damn thing."

"Please, Scout. Don't do this."

Kat scrawled out the check. "Don't call me Scout."

Loretta began to whimper.

"I see." Riley let go with a bitter laugh. "I wasn't aware I was the only imperfect human being in this truck. Thanks for setting me straight."

Kat's head shot up. "What is that supposed to mean?"

"Haven't you ever made a decision you now regret, Kat?" Riley paused, waiting for some kind of answer. "You know, maybe something like denying a man his right to be a father, all because of pride and spite?"

Kat ripped the check from the checkbook and threw it in his face. "You didn't even have the guts to tell Matt what you'd done! It's been months!"

Riley nodded. "It took you twenty years to tell Aidan your little secret."

"Oh . . . my . . . God." Kat could barely breathe. "This is perfect. This is why I *knew* I shouldn't have any more sex with you! There's no forgiveness here. You can't forgive me for the mistake I made when I was just a scared kid! If I don't have that from you, I don't have anything. *We* don't have anything."

Riley laughed. "And how about you, Kat? Have you forgiven me for my mistake when I was a scared kid? Or how about the mistake I made getting this loan, which I am now admitting to you? Can you forgive me for that? And how about the mistakes I'm going to make in the future, which will all be real whoppers, I'm sure. Will you be able to forgive me for those?"

Kat said nothing. Her heart pounded in her chest.

Loretta's whimpering intensified.

"Let's look at the bigger picture while we're at it!" Riley shouted, raising his voice in competition with the dog. "The last twenty years of your life have been fueled by resentment—you didn't even *consider* finding a way to forgive your parents, me, your aunt, the town, the whole *world*—yet you have the nerve to be impatient with Aidan because he hasn't immediately forgiven you for a lifetime of lies? And then you demand forgiveness from me, like I'm defective if I don't forgive you in the exact way you'd prefer, in the exact time frame?"

They sat in the truck and glared at each other, breathing hard. The blood roared in Kat's ears so loudly she hardly heard Loretta's howling.

A friendly face appeared outside the driver's-side window, and a man knocked on the glass to get Riley's attention. Riley rolled down the window.

"Travis! How's it going?" He reached out to shake the man's dirt-covered hand.

"It's time to stop yer yakkin' and get to workin'." The man produced a big smile, then looked over to Kat and touched the bill of his ball cap in greeting. "Heard you was back in town. Remember me?"

Kat stared at the guy, the adrenaline pumping through her veins. She was at a loss. She didn't know what to do. Where to go. What to say. She didn't know how she felt. About Riley. About herself. About what he'd just said. About anything.

And she sure as hell didn't know this yahoo in the window.

"Come on now. Think hard."

Kat squinted, attempting to picture the man minus twenty extra years, and the name "Travis" finally registered in her brain.

"Hey, Butt Head," she said. "How've you been?"

FIFTEEN

Kat woke with a jolt, aware that the vivid red of her childhood coat had dominated a whole string of dreams. They were dreams of velvet, blood, red ink, and anger. Her stomach was in knots.

She threw off the covers, sat on the edge of her bed, and turned on the light. She looked down and stared at her dangling bare feet. In her half-awake state they looked so strange hanging there in the air, fragile and translucent, the thin bones crushable and the skin easily cut. It suddenly struck her as odd that these were the only two feet she'd ever get. Like her two arms and two legs and one set of lungs, one heart, and this one life, just like everyone else. In fact, she was one person in a sea of billions, and she was making her way through this life holding two baskets—one filled with her problems and another with her blessings. Just like everyone else did.

Kat wiggled her toes and breathed deep. It was a hard thing to admit, but she'd been an ass the day before. Riley was right—ever since she'd shown up here looking to settle the score, it was all about how other people had wronged *her,* what they owed *her.* And when you went through your days like that, you always wanted more and more from people. You were always keeping score, checking that nobody else ever got the bigger slice of cake.

She hopped off the bed and padded across the wood floor of her bedroom, wondering how she could have thought it was OK to beg for forgiveness out of one side of her mouth and deny forgiveness out of the other.

Kat ran a brush through her hair. Riley had chosen the only option he thought he had to save the clinic project. He'd made a stupid assumption that the state money would eventually reappear. But it wasn't like the millions were going to bankroll a life of extravagance. The money was used for examination tables, an X-ray machine, medical laboratory equipment, bandages, a playroom for children.

Riley's mistake had been withholding his plan from Matt. He was aware of that, and was doing a fine job beating himself up without Kat's help.

She'd asked Riley for the truth and he'd given it to her. It couldn't have been easy for him to admit that he was broke and wallowing in bad debt, but he'd told her anyway.

And now everything felt wrong.

She'd come to Persuasion to sort out her past, true. But the real reason she was here was Riley. She was here so they could learn about each other, see if there was a place for the two of them, in each other's lives and in the world. How were they going to discover that if they didn't talk to each other? She'd hopped out of his pickup at the construction site yesterday and walked the two miles back home, full of righteous indignation. She'd refused his phone calls all evening and into the night.

And it felt all wrong.

Still wearing her pajamas, Kat tied her sneakers,

ran down the stairs, and reached for her fleece jacket. She was out the front door in seconds.

As her feet hit the sidewalk and the cold darkness rushed by in her peripheral vision, she knew which route she'd be taking. Kat made it down Laurel to Birch and then to Main. She ran past Forest Drive, passing her father's home without even a curious glance, and retraced the rhythm of her childhood.

Who lived in these houses now? She had no idea. But as she ran past them, the long-ago names floated into her brain like a forgotten language—the Missonis, the Ballingers, the McClintocks, and finally the Wilmers, where she encountered the chain-link fence. Though a little winded, Kat had enough air to thoroughly laugh at herself. Once upon a time, she could vault this barricade without a second thought, hardly even slowing from a run. Tonight, she came to a full stop, grabbed the fence post, gingerly shoved the toe of her right shoe into a link, and prayed she could pull herself over. She felt a rush of pride when she hoisted her leg above and landed on the ground near the cedars. *The old girl still had it!*

Like always, Kat ran across the lawn to the side of the house, where she pulled herself onto the central air-conditioning unit to reach the porch railing. In her youth, this same railing had seemed as wide as a diving board. Tonight, under the porch light, it felt more like an emery board. So she held her breath and raced across it with a quick tiptoe before she could lose her nerve. Kat gratefully found her way along the ledge of the dining room bay window, then held on to each of the three equally spaced window frames on the turret to reach the roof of the carport.

It was there she had second thoughts. She must be crazy! She was a thirty-seven-year-old woman with thirty-seven-year-old bones. What if she fell? And besides, it wasn't like Big Daddy was patrolling the premises anymore. She didn't have to sneak inside, did she?

Kat was about to climb down when it dawned on her that she didn't have a key, and Riley might not be in the most gracious of moods after their argument, throwing open the front door to welcome her. She was almost there anyway.

Kat took a deep breath, steadied herself, then remembered the loose tiles. Sure, they'd probably been fixed at some point in the last twenty years, but she did her best to steer clear anyway, just to be safe. She was crawling along on her hands and knees when the tile she'd chosen to hold her weight gave way. She started to slide, and in a panic, she reached out and prayed that her fingers found the edge of something sturdy. Her foot hit the gutter and the slide stopped.

Kat closed her eyes for a second, steadied herself, and slowly, so slowly, climbed her way back up the carport roof.

She said a silent prayer of thanks as she reached the window, then, as quietly as she could, raised the wooden sash, feeling inside to see if a screen or storm window blocked her way. She found neither, and silently balanced her rear end on the window ledge, then swung her legs around.

She was in. Quickly she closed the window and tiptoed toward the bed. She'd never really asked Riley if he still slept in his childhood bedroom, but there was most certainly a man sprawled out on the bed in the darkness, breathing deeply, and since Riley was the only current resident of the Bohland House, she figured it was mission accomplished.

Almost.

As soon as she took off her shoes and slipped out of her coat and pajamas, she realized how cold she was. With a shiver, she pulled away the comforter and slipped her naked body into Riley's private cocoon. It made her smile to see that he still slept on his right side, and she curled up against his back and pressed close. He was warm. His body hair tickled her. She nuzzled her nose into the nape of his neck and breathed deep.

"Hey there," said a sleepy voice. Riley flipped over to face her. "What took you so long?"

Kat giggled, noticing right away that he was naked, too—gloriously, fabulously naked. "I'm middle-aged. I don't run as fast as I used to, and scaling the roof was a bit dicey," she said.

With his fingertips, Riley began to stroke her cheek. "Middle age looks real good on you, in case I haven't mentioned that, but I did leave the front door unlocked for you." Kat could see his wicked grin.

"What?" She smacked his biceps and laughed. "You mean I didn't have to risk life and limb to get to you?"

"Nope." He left little kisses all over her face and neck. "But you got to admit—it's pretty damn hot that you did."

He was right. It was damn hot. Kat grabbed his head and brought her mouth hard against his. She wanted to inhale him, eat him alive, melt into his flesh.

Riley groaned in pleasure, extending the kiss down to her throat. "You do know that this has been my primary sexual fantasy for the last twenty years—Kat Cavanaugh coming through my window, curling up against me, begging me to make crazed, unrestrained love to her—right?"

She giggled. "How about having a crazed, unrestrained heart-to-heart talk with her?"

Riley stopped kissing her throat. "That was always a close second."

"I want another chance with you," Kat said suddenly, before she lost the nerve.

"OK—"

"I want to get to know you again—as the complex grown man you are, not the kid of my memories. I want you to know me, too, all of me, including my darkest mistakes and my brightest hopes."

"I want that, too," Riley said, his voice warm and gentle.

"I want to see if there's a future for us. I'm so sick of wondering and guessing and fantasizing about you and me—I just want there to *be* a you and me." Kat's eyes began to fill with tears. "Riley, I know I was stupid and selfish yesterday and—"

"You sure were."

She laughed in surprise. "Yeah? Well, you were stupid and selfish, too."

"My God, I certainly was."

"I'm sorry, Riley."

"I'm sorry, too."

The tears streamed down the sides of Kat's face. Riley wiped them away. "Kat, there's something I want to say. I need to get it out there."

"Let me go first. Can I go first?"

Riley kissed her gently, smiling at her childlike enthusiasm. "Sure."

Kat took a giant breath. She wanted to get through this without too much blubbering. "I ask that you forgive me for keeping Aidan from you all this time out of spite. You were right—that's exactly what it was—and I'm so ashamed to admit that." Kat squeezed her eyes tight; then, when Riley tried to speak, she shook her head to convey that she wasn't done. "Forgive me . . . oh God, Riley, please forgive me for taking away your right to be a father."

Kat opened her eyes again and stared at him expectantly, swallowing hard as she waited for his answer.

"I forgive you, Kat. I truly do."

She mouthed a silent, *Thank you.* When she closed her eyes in relief, a whole flood of tears was released.

"Please forgive me for sending you away like I did." The words broke from Riley's throat in a scratchy whisper. "Kat, forgive me for not even giving you a chance to tell me you were going to have my baby. I understand now how much you loved and needed me, and I know it must have killed you when I told you I didn't want you anymore."

She nodded quickly. "It did. But I forgive you, Riley. From the bottom of my heart, I forgive you."

Riley placed a gentle kiss of thanks on her trembling lips and breathed in the relief of the words they'd spoken to each other. He'd always heard that forgiveness was just as healing to the person doing the forgiving as the person being forgiven. Now, as they both basked in a double shot of forgiveness, he knew how right that was.

Riley gently cupped her face in his hands. "Here's my promise to you—we will be able to handle anything the world throws at us, as long as we face it together."

She smiled. "I like that."

"Who do you love, Kat?" he asked, his eyes on fire in the darkness.

"That's an easy one," she said. "I love Riley James Bohland, forever and ever, the way I've always loved him."

"And who does Riley Bohland love?"

"Katharine Ann Cavanaugh, forever and ever."

"What kind of car do you want?"

"A loaded Jaguar that I drive right off the lot, paid for in cash." She started giggling.

His hand landed on her bare butt. "And what's the first house you want to buy?"

"A run-down row house in Baltimore."

Riley laughed. "How about the one after that?"

"Maybe a beach house. Or a ski chalet. Or maybe we can find an old Victorian rat-trap to get out of hock."

"Ugh," he said. "Moving along . . . how many kids do you want?"

"One is good—and I already got him. His name is Aidan."

"Yes, it most certainly is." Riley paused and lifted Kat's chin so he could look intently into her eyes.

"Thank you for my son. Thank you for loving him so much and keeping him safe."

"Thank you for accepting him into your life the way you have." Kat stroked his solid biceps, his hard chest. "He's a lucky kid. And he talked to me yesterday! I didn't even have a chance to tell you! He answered my call!"

Riley gathered her in his arms and held her tight, his hands caressing her from her shoulder blades to her upper thighs. It felt so good to her, she groaned out loud.

"I knew he'd come around," Riley said, smiling. "And now I have a little favor to ask."

"Anything."

"Would you be willing to give me one more?"

It took Kat a moment to realize what he'd asked for, but when she did, she broke out in a smile. "I can't think of a single reason why we shouldn't."

"Me, either, Scout."

"I think we should start trying right away."

"You do?" He gulped.

"I'm ready for a Cherry Hill repeat."

"Oh, thank God." Riley said it half-laughing and half-serious.

He kissed her, then let his lips slide down to her full breasts. All the while he moved his hands along her sides, across her rounded belly, to the crux of her smooth thighs. With his fingers, he read her, listened to her, heard exactly what she wanted and needed.

"I need you to fuck me," she said.

"I'm getting there," he said, smiling to himself at her greedy request.

"Don't tease me, Riley," she panted.

"I'm trying to please you, so just lay back and enjoy."

With the gentlest pressure, he sank his fingers into her wet slit, then moved them up and down the length of her opening until she was writhing on his hand. He rubbed the swollen head of her clitoris, feeling it plump up further under his fingers, knowing he was bringing her close to coming.

"This is the rest of my fantasy, just so you know."

Kat's laugh immediately turned into a gasp of surprise when he introduced two fingers all the way inside her. He found her ready for him, as usual, but she felt particularly hot and swollen. The feel of her inner flesh on his fingers made him crazy with need. "I'm going to take you now, sweetheart. I'm going to come deep inside you and give you a baby. Will that be all right?"

She came on his hand, a strangled squeak of pleasure all the answer he needed.

Riley jumped up from his position on his side and kneeled in front of Kat. He put his hands on her ankles and widened her legs, then pushed her knees back toward her chest. She looked up at him with pure longing. She knew this was the way it was supposed to be for them.

He positioned himself before her and was about to push himself in when she wrapped her little pink hand around his cock and whispered, "I want to do it."

Riley saw a mischievous glint in her eye, like she was egging him on. He didn't need egging. That was the last thing he needed. When she placed the head of his cock at her entrance, Riley shut his eyes and submitted to the pleasure of the slow, tight slide into heaven. When he opened them again, he saw Kat already halfway gone again, her eyelids heavy, her chest splotchy with the deep pink of arousal.

He didn't know which was hotter—the look of abandon on her face or the way his cock went in and out of her pussy—so he went from one insanely hot vision to the other, back and forth, in and out, suddenly aware that he could see all this beautiful vision because the sun was rising.

The light spilled in the window onto Kat's body. His woman. His love. She began to pant, then her eyes flew wide, and she said, "Oh, Riley. This is just right. You feel so right."

Immediately, he felt her flesh contract and shudder as she orgasmed, and he waited it out, went for the ride, until the moment came when his own gates flew open and everything he was and everything he ever wanted to be poured out of him and into her. He called out her name as his being went rigid, peaked, then came crashing back to earth, to Kat.

Riley told himself that if they were blessed to have fifty years to make love together it would never get old, that it would always be a destination for his soul, the glue that held his life together. It would always feel just like this.

Kat sat at the dining room table with her laptop, phone, pens, paper, calculator, and three large poster boards. She had four projects going simultaneously, and the strain of organizing everything had given her a dull headache.

But she had no complaints. She had Riley. She had Aidan. She had everything.

Looking at what was spread before her, Kat realized that the simplest of the projects was working with Cliff to create a charitable foundation in Phyllis' name to contribute to the clinic. It took no persuading—he'd loved the idea from the start, and he and Kat had had a long and enjoyable chat.

Her second project was figuring out a way to halt foreclosure proceedings on the Bohland House. It turned out the loan officer was happy to restructure the mortgage, admitting to Kat that the bank would be relieved not to continue with legal action—taking on the Bohlands was publicity they didn't need. Over dinner the night before, Riley said he'd tell Matt everything that very week.

Next on the agenda was Thanksgiving dinner for twelve, and so far everything was moving along smoothly. Kat was planning the traditional menu of turkey and dressing, along with a ham, all the usual sides, and three kinds of pies—pumpkin, apple, and pecan.

Her guest list included herself, Riley, Nola and Matt, her uncle Cliff and his wife and two granddaughters, who would be traveling from Cumberland, Maryland, Aidan and his girlfriend, Rachel, and Jeff the duct specialist from Connecticut and his out-in-the-open partner, Richard. The idea of having so many people in her new home filled Kat with joy, and only the smallest twinge of nervousness.

The last project was considerably more complicated, but once she'd gotten Riley's OK to hold a volunteer extravaganza at the clinic the day after Thanksgiving, things had quickly fallen into place. Kat took that as a sign that she'd hit on an idea that was meant to be. It also helped that she'd enlisted anyone and everyone she could think of to help her pull it off.

The printing shop had whipped up flyers and delivered them all over town. Nola was reading one, tapping her foot in agitation:

Work off that turkey by pitching in at the
GIVIN' THANKS BENEFIT

for the
PERSUASION RURAL HEALTH CLINIC!

Bring your tools, paintbrushes, your know-how, your elbow grease, and your checkbooks and credit cards—our hometown state-of-the-art medical facility will open by Christmas only if YOU do YOUR part!

A JOB FOR EVERYONE!

Live Music!	Free Gourmet Coffee!
Food!	Free Child Care!
Games!	Pony Rides!

PLUS . . . YOU COULD WIN A DATE WITH POLICE CHIEF BOHLAND!

Friday, November 23, 10:00 A.M. to 6:00 P.M.

Nola's foot-tapping escalated. "OK," she said, placing the flyer on the table and looking at Kat expectantly. "Explain to me again why this shouldn't bother me."

"It's for charity."

"But it's a date! Matt's selling himself for a date! It's like he's a gigolo or something!"

"It's not a real date," Kat said, then went back to answering e-mails.

"Oh yeah?" Nola seemed truly agitated. "Who says?"

"He says." Kat stopped what she was doing and noticed that Nola looked close to tears. "Honestly. We just figured it would be a good way to get people to come in from other towns—Matt knows a lot of people in Randolph County."

"He knows a lot of *babes,* is that what you're saying?" Nola pointed to the flyer again. "Where do you think this band came from? Well, Matt got them to donate their time, and do you know why they agreed? Because he used to date the lead singer, that's why! It's an all-girl country rock band! I think I'm about to blow a gasket!"

Kat tried not to laugh.

"I've already moved in with that man! He shouldn't be dating other women!" Nola jumped up from the dining room chair and disappeared into the kitchen. "I'm starving," she said from the interior of the refrigerator.

"No, you're not starving; you're anxiety-ridden!" Kat called after her. "And I just read an article that said you should never eat when you feel anxious because the stress hormones turn the calories directly into abdominal fat."

When Kat got nothing but dead silence as a response, she glanced up to check on Nola. She was leaning against the kitchen pocket door, arms crossed defensively across her chest.

"So you're saying I'm fat?" she whispered, incredulous. "First you make my boyfriend the prized stud at the county fair, and now you tell me I'm *fat*?"

Kat would have busted a gut laughing if Nola didn't look so forlorn. "Have you talked to him, like I suggested?" Kat led Nola into the living room and sat her friend down on the love seat.

Nola sighed. "Yeah. I talked to him last night."

"And? What did he say?" Kat's cell began ringing, but she didn't answer.

"Aren't you going to get that? And you never did reassure me that I wasn't fat." Nola was clearly in a huff.

"The phone can wait. You're not fat. What did Matt say?" Kat sat down next to her.

"He said not to worry, that it's just an auction thing where people can bid to get him out of jail and then go out to eat with him. It sounds stupid and harmless, but I'm just a little freaked about it."

Kat smiled at her. "I understand. But you can bid, too. You could be the one to pay his bail and get the date."

Nola's eyes lit up. "I could, couldn't I!"

The doorbell rang. Over her shoulder Kat called out, "Come on in!"

Nola sighed and went on. "I just don't want that big-ass breakfast-in-bed owner to get her hooks in him again, that's all—*ohmigod*."

Kat watched as Nola's eyes widened and she sank back into the love seat.

"Hello, ladies," Madeline said. "I hope I'm not intruding. I did just try to reach you on your cell to say I was coming up the walk."

Madeline was tempted to take the fresh-baked pumpkin loaf she held in her hands and grind it into Nola's face. If it weren't for the fact that the bread was far too light and fluffy to inflict any harm, Madeline would have thrown it at her.

"Hey, Madeline!" Kat got up from the sofa. "Come on in. We're doing some planning. Join us."

Madeline took a tentative step inside Kat's house, thinking that it must be nice to have the kind of money that made it possible to order absolutely everything being sold between pages 1 and 100 of the Pottery Barn catalog. Even the rug was gorgeous. "Thanks," Madeline said, following Kat through the living room, keeping Nola in her peripheral vision. "I brought you a pumpkin loaf. It's just a sampling of what I might be able to whip up for the fund-raiser."

Kat reached out and accepted the gift from Madeline. "That was very nice of you. Would you like a cup of coffee and maybe a slice of this obviously delicious bread?" Kat put her nose to the cellophane and hummed with delight.

"No, thank you," Madeline said, taking a seat and pulling a clipboard from her shoulder bag, pleased that at least Kat knew fine baked goods when she saw them. "What kind of crowd are you expecting at the benefit?" Her eye caught Kat's Thanksgiving to-do list.

"I'm hoping five hundred, but you know, Madeline, before we get started, I was wondering if we could clear the air between us." Kat took her seat. "We're going to be working together for the greater good, and I just live a block from Cherry Hill, so I was wondering, are you willing to meet me halfway? Can we just let bygones be bygones?"

Nothing Kat Cavanaugh could have said would have stunned Madeline more. It took her a moment to pull herself together. She surprised herself with what came out. "The fault is mine, Kat. I'm the one who should be apologizing."

Kat didn't say anything. Nola did, however, which shouldn't have been a shocker. "Well, now's your chance, hon," she said, passing through the dining room on her way to the kitchen.

Madeline pursed her lips and made doodles on her clipboard, so irritated with Nola What's-Her-Face that she could spit. "I am happy to apologize to *you*, Kat." Madeline glared in the general direction of the kitchen before she returned her eyes to Kat. "It was wrong of me to tell you that horse-hockey story about the wedding. Carrie kind of pushed me in that direction, and it was a horrible thing to do. I hope you accept my apology."

Kat gave her a smile. "Apology accepted."

"You don't have to do everything she tells you to, Madeline," Nola said, suddenly deciding to return to the table. She carried a thick slice of the pumpkin loaf on a plate.

Outwardly, Madeline ignored the comment. Inwardly, she sharpened her claws. If she'd known Nola would be the one snarfing down her loaf, she'd have added a half cup of ground glass.

Madeline picked up the benefit flyer and read through it, trying to calm herself. When she reached the line about Matt putting his affections on the auction block, her stomach did a somersault. Carrie made *excellent* money. She could bid for Matt, take it right up to the stratosphere, then lay some lovin' on thick for Nola to see.

When Madeline looked up, Nola was staring at her. She gave her friendly smile, then returned to the flyer. True, the event was one day after Carrie's Thanksgiving deadline, but hey, Madeline was flexible if she was anything.

"Let's get started then," she said. On her clipboard she began to divide the benefit food into categories. "I've already committed to the desserts," she told Kat. "My team will do the cakes for the cake walk, of course, and a dozen or so each of pies and dessert breads, but mostly we plan to focus on quantity and ease of presentation, as opposed to haute cuisine."

"Rice Krispies treats?" Kat asked.

"You know it." Madeline went down the list in great detail. "I've got at least six women on each committee, except for meats, which has more, and breads and rolls, which has fewer. I'm afraid there'll be some store-bought items from that crowd, since none of them are handy in the kitchen."

"Whatever you say." Kat looked overwhelmed.

"Is there anything we might have missed?"

Kat's mouth fell open a bit. "Madeline, I just called you two days ago. How in the world did you get all this done so fast?"

"This sort of thing is right up my alley," she said, actually feeling good about contributing to the event. She packed up her bag and got ready to go. "So, have you decided whether you're going to let Joanna Loveless do her annual Thanksgiving Day feature on you?"

Kat blinked. "Uh . . ."

"She's the head of your meat committee, you know." Madeline told Kat that in the hopes that she'd understand the gravity of that particular responsibility. It appeared she didn't, so Madeline broke it down for her. "Joanna's got twenty women on her team, and you can only imagine the cost involved in something like that—we're talking ribs, smoked hams, turkey breasts, pit beef, steamers, sausages . . ."

"That's lot of meat, hon," Nola said to Kat.

Madeline smiled as she left. As soon as she hit the sidewalk she was on the phone with Joanna, telling her the Thanksgiving article was a done deal and that Kat would be hosting a houseful.

Riley was on call and had an admission in Elkins that night. Kat was tired but filled with the feeling that she could accomplish whatever she set her mind to. After a long, hot shower, she got into her softest cotton nightgown, matching robe, and warm slippers and headed to the end of the upstairs hallway.

She opened the door and retrieved the open box from the bottom step of the attic stairwell, where she'd left it. She carried it to the floor of her bedroom, and told herself to breathe.

It had taken her more than a week to get the courage to look in here. She knew this box would be the easiest because Riley had told her what she'd find. But even without surprises, she knew when she laid her eyes on these things from her past—touched them and smelled them—it might be overwhelming.

The coat was on top, folded lengthwise and then in half. When she pulled it out and saw the little sleeves and the black velvet collar and buttons, a deluge of emotion washed over her. She remembered how she would poke her arms inside the sleeves, fiddle with the buttons, and try her best to keep it Sunday clean.

She remembered that her mother had been smiling the day she bought this coat. That's what made that day seem so special to Kat. BettyAnn seemed lighthearted, glad to be out enjoying the day, alone with Kat. The day had been infused with magic.

Kat raised the coat to her nose and breathed in. Yes, she got a noseful of dust, but she detected the slightest hint of something else—her mother. Her perfume clung to this fabric, and it struck Kat with awe. Had BettyAnn actually held this little garment close before she packed it away in this box? Had it meant that much to her, too?

Kat hung her head and let the tears pour out of her, right onto the red velvet. She cried and cried, clutching the coat to her heart and face, trying to get inside the scent of BettyAnn Cavanaugh.

Suddenly, Kat straightened. The tears stopped. With a sense of wonder, she saw the pieces fall together in her mind without the slightest bit of effort—*bam, bam, bam*—and there it was, the reason that day had been so extraordinary. Virgil had been out of town! It was one of the few times he'd left them alone overnight. They celebrated their freedom by going shopping, then dined on root beer floats at the pharmacy soda counter. Mama bought Kat a charm bracelet at the five-and-dime. Then they went home, got in their jammies, and played Uno until it was way past her bedtime, and Kat remembered being fascinated by how the bracelet sparkled under the dining room light fixture.

She recalled falling asleep in her bed that night feeling loved. Safe. Completely sure there would be no hitting and screaming and shouting that night. Because it was just her mother and her.

Kat sat for a long while cross-legged on the floor, realizing that BettyAnn might have been free to be herself with Kat only when Virgil was away. Kat's heart constricted with sadness—it must have been hell to be so squashed by a man like that. To think, BettyAnn couldn't even express love to her daughter without facing his jealous rage. Why didn't BettyAnn leave? Why wasn't she ever strong enough to leave and take Kat with her?

But she had saved all these treasured mementos of their time together. She'd loved Kat. She really had. And being able to see that calmed Kat's spirit. Gingerly, she draped the coat over her shoulders and went rooting through the rest—her prized one-eyed stuffed bunny that she'd inexplicably named Cher; drawings from kindergarten all the way to Kat's tenth-grade autumn art show, where she'd done a mixed-media collage that she had to admit wasn't half-bad. Maybe she'd get it framed. Other than that, the box was chock-full of old books. Except for something shiny she noticed at the very bottom.

Her charm bracelet, from that very same day! It dangled with a roller skate, an LP, a paintbrush, a telephone, a softball, and a heart. With trembling fingers, Kat worked diligently to get the bracelet around her adult-sized wrist. It fit.

She was charged up by these amazing discoveries, and curious what the other two boxes contained. With the coat still draped on her shoulders, she grabbed a pair of scissors and returned to the attic door. She sliced open the box on the second step, peered inside, and found school yearbooks, records and tapes, and every report card she'd ever brought home. It all made Kat smile, but in her heart she also felt disappointment—obviously, the box containing her coat had been the one filled with a personal message from mother to daughter.

Suddenly, she felt tired, and told herself she'd get to the last box some other time. With her charm bracelet dangling on her wrist and the dusty red coat and one-eyed Cher clutched tight, Kat climbed under the covers and slept. No nightmares. Just blessed sleep.

SIXTEEN

"Are you sure about this?" Riley's legs were much longer than Kat's, but he had to walk at a fast clip to keep up with her.

"Oh, I'm positive," she said, barreling up Main Street.

Even though it was a Sunday, the downtown was busy with students and locals, and many of them had stopped to ask Kat questions about the upcoming clinic benefit. Riley was flabbergasted at how Kat had whipped together something so complex in such a short time. From what he could tell, half the town was involved. He wondered if maybe Kat should ditch the psychology degree and just go straight to being the president's chief of staff.

"You were right, Riley," she said, gaining steam as she headed to the intersection of Forest Drive. "He can't hurt me anymore, and I can't believe I've been here almost three weeks and I'm just now believing that!"

Riley didn't have a good feeling about this. "I take it he has no idea we're coming."

"I don't think he's gonna have many scheduling conflicts," Kat said sarcastically.

Riley didn't respond. They kept walking. He

glanced over to Kat, shoulders back, head up, feet a blur. Eventually he figured he should bring up another possibility. "He might not be feeling well."

Her eyes flashed.

"He's missed two appointments now. The guy's had an angioplasty and needs follow-up care with his cardiologists but refuses to go."

"Have you called Rita?"

Riley nodded. "She told my nurse that she's happy to drive him and has offered to do so, but he tells her he's too busy."

Kat laughed. "It guess it takes real time and effort to be the biggest asshole in the state of West Virginia."

"Kat." Riley reached for her arm, stopping her.

She shrugged away from his grasp. "Yes?"

"Are you sure you want to approach him like this?"

She put her hands on her hips and looked peeved. "What do you mean?"

"Look at you—you've been going non-stop lately and now you're charging over there to tackle your father like he was just another item on your to-do list."

She blinked at him. "If you didn't want to come with me, all you had to do was say so."

Riley looked up to the sky to ask for patience. When his gaze returned to earth again, Kat's demeanor had changed. She took his hand.

"You're right, Riley." She brushed her fingers over the tops of his. "I am pretty jazzed right now, but I think it's time to start talking with him. As Rita said, he won't be around forever." Kat looked up at Riley with sadness in her eyes. "Please come with me," she said. "I could use your support."

Riley gave Kat the tightest squeeze he could without cracking her spine, lifted her up, and kissed her. "It's a deal," he said, putting her back down on the pavement. "All I ask is that you take it slow. You don't have to try to right every wrong in one visit."

"I hear you," she said.

A few minutes later they stood on the walkway leading up to the front stoop. Kat took several steps forward, pulled the storm door away, and knocked firmly on the wooden door. When she got no response, she knocked again, this time somewhat more firmly. The third time was a straight-out pound.

"Kat?"

She didn't answer Riley. She let the metal storm door slam shut, its spring mechanism busted.

Riley was about to suggest they try the back when Kat headed across the yard toward the back gate. Riley jogged to catch up before she reached the kitchen entrance. This time, she skipped the warming-up knock and went straight to the pounding.

The door flung open. They both gasped. Riley wasn't sure what he was seeing, and reached for his cell to call EMS.

"What do you want?" Virgil looked like a ghost. His face, neck, chest, arms, and hands were covered in a coating of fine white powder. His eyes seemed to pop from his colorless face, pink-rimmed and crazed.

Kat turned to Riley and said matter-of-factly, "Marble dust."

Riley put his phone away.

"Well?" Virgil looked at each of them like they were strangers. "I'm on lunch break. I'm busy. What the hell is it?"

"I wanted to talk to you for a minute," Kat said.

"Ever hear of calling in advance?"

Riley noticed that Virgil's hands shook and he was unsteady on his feet.

"Would you have answered?" Kat asked.

"Fuck, no."

Riley knew that if Virgil had decided to pick up the bottle again after twenty years of sobriety, he'd be a human grenade with the pin already pulled. Not only did he get violent when he drank; he also was on a laundry list of meds that would lose their efficacy when combined with alcohol, if not create a toxic soup in his bloodstream. His third heart attack would be just around the corner.

"Did you ever stop drinking, Dad?" Kat asked the question with such innocent disappointment that it broke Riley's heart.

Virgil grunted. He wrapped his white claw around the door and stepped outside, then took a wobbly step toward Kat. "I don't know. Did you ever stop being a whore?"

Riley was a nanosecond from kicking the old man's feeble ass when Kat quietly moved closer to her father and reached for his hand. Riley hadn't known what to expect, but what Kat did was the last thing in the world he would have imagined—she leaned in and kissed Virgil's cheek. He was as stunned as Riley was.

"I was really hoping we could talk some things through," Kat continued. "I have some questions I wanted to ask you about what happened when I was a kid. I even thought—" Her eyes flashed to Riley as if to warn him that she was pulling out the big guns. "I thought if the talk went well, and if you felt up to it, you could join us for Thanksgiving dinner."

"Oh yeah?" he asked. "Well, a fine howdy-do to you, too, Mother Teresa, but I think I'll pass."

Kat sighed. She turned toward Riley, her face a mask of sadness, and he reached out for her hand. "Let's go," she said.

"You fucking bitch!" Without warning, Virgil threw the door wide and lunged for Kat. Riley got between them and grabbed Virgil firmly around both of his thin upper arms, pushing him back against the side of the house. He felt as light and hollow as a bird.

"Virgil, get hold of yourself. This is not what you want to do right now." Riley made sure Virgil was focusing on him and not Kat. "You're going inside to sleep it off. If you don't, I'll get the ambulance here and they'll take you back to Davis and I'll admit you."

"Fuck you, you fucking *Bohland*."

"Let's go." Kat tugged on Riley's sleeve.

"Stay and fight like a man!" Virgil screamed, the spit flying everywhere. Riley guided him back inside the kitchen door, then shut it.

The walk back to Kat's was much slower. It was also completely silent except for the phone call Riley made to Rita, informing her that her brother was in a drunken rage and needed to be taken to the hospital.

When they reached Kat's place, she took Riley by the hand and headed upstairs. She led him to the bed, peeled off his coat and then her own, and brought him down to lie next to her. "Please hold me," she said.

He did. They fell asleep in their clothes.

Grinding, grinding, sanding, sanding . . . the faces of women were emerging from the stone now, women who'd pleasured him, women he'd controlled, women he wanted to control, women who pissed him off or turned him on, women who got him so angry they deserved to be pushed out of windows, women who made him feel lucky to be a man.

To most sculptors, this part of the process was the least enjoyable—all the work, hours and hours of dipping silicon carbide sandpaper in water, slowly working your way from the coarser to the finer grits, wearing down the marble in an imitation of the ways of nature, the millions of years of rain and wind and dust and light and heat and cold it would have taken to get the same gloss. But Virgil loved it. He loved the physicality of it. He loved how he got to be God in human form, how the baseness of his effort—hunched over and pushing, pushing, pushing the sandpaper over the rock—resulted in such beauty.

Grind, grind, sand, sand . . . the women exposing themselves to him, just as he knew they would. And they were exquisite, every one of them.

"Good Lord, that's the most hideously ugly thing I've ever seen in my life."

Virgil didn't even bother looking up. "Then stay away from mirrors, Rita."

He hoped that if he just kept working, she'd go away, but instead he sensed her moving closer.

"There should be a limit to how many heads can go on a single sculpture."

"Get out."

"Riley called me," she said.

"So what?"

"He said you were in a drunken rage and needed to go to the hospital. So I'm here to take you."

"Do I look full of rage?"

"You look very ill, Virgil. You've just had a heart procedure. And obviously, you've been drinking."

"Fuck you. Fuck the procedure. Fuck Bohland. Fuck *everyone*."

For some inexplicable reason, Rita decided that that was her invitation to sit down on the sculpting stool and cross her varicose-veined legs like she was getting settled in for a nice long visit. Virgil ignored her. He dipped. He hunched. He sanded.

"Did Kat say anything to you today?"

"Yeah. She invited me to Thanksgiving dinner, if you can believe that."

Rita was quiet. Virgil looked out of the corner of his eye to see her staring in disbelief. Finally, she said, "I'm sure she was crushed to hear that your dance card was full."

"I told her to fuck off."

"At least you're consistent."

"Go away."

"What I meant was . . ." Rita's voice trailed off. "Well, I was wondering if Kat said anything about her childhood, you know, anything about BettyAnn or you."

Virgil threw the 150-grit sandpaper sheet onto the studio floor, right at Rita's feet. "I am working. I don't want you here. I don't want to discuss my dead wife. Now, get out."

"It's just that Riley's office has been badgering me," Rita persisted. "They said you really need to get back to the cardiologist."

"I don't want to go to that foreigner! Leave me alone!"

"You're killing yourself," she said, like she was his principal, the principal of the world.

"If I die, I die." He was growing really tired of

this conversation. "And up until that moment, I'd like to work in solitude."

Rita groaned.

"This is my masterpiece."

"It's a piece of something, all right," she said.

Virgil tried to stand up tall, but his body began to sway. "Rita," he said, pointing at her with a wavering arm, "you're an ugly old-maid schoolmarm who couldn't get laid if her life depended on it, and forgive me if I don't see the value in your critique, but you don't know shit about art or life or passion or . . ." He staggered, catching himself on the edge of the worktable. "Anyway, you're ugly. Get out."

With a deep sigh, Rita stood up from the work stool. Her lips were pursed, and Virgil noticed how old she looked. When did that happen?

"I hate you," she said flatly. "I always have. I don't know why I ever moved to this town to be near you. You may have been my only living relative, but you are a waste of humanity. I'm sorry for every kind thing I ever did for you, because you deserved nothing." Then she turned her back on him and headed for the door.

"Not as much as I hate you, you wrinkled old cow."

"By the way," she said, clearly about ready to deliver her parting shot. "That's no masterpiece—it's a freak show. I hope you rot in hell."

Thank God she was gone. He could get back to the lovely ladies. Virgil knew they'd missed him.

"I absolutely refuse to do that," Carrie said.

"You have a better idea?"

"Yes, in fact, I have a great idea, Madeline—how

about you just drop it? How about you get over yourself? Find a hobby? I can tell you from personal experience that it feels fabulous!"

"Uh-huh."

"I've met someone!"

Madeline couldn't resist. "So, when's the wedding?" she asked.

Carrie said nothing at first, but when she did speak, her words came out clipped. "I want you to stop calling at work or at home. I think this borders on harassment, and I will get a protective order if I have to."

Madeline laughed so hard she had to stop pinching the edge of the piecrust.

"You were never really my friend, anyway," Carrie continued. "I just used you."

Madeline tossed the rolling pin down on the counter. "Yeah. I'm real clear on that. But obviously, you're not so clear on the situation we have right here, right now."

"I'm hanging up."

"Fine. Then I'll be sending out some e-mails as soon as I get these apple pies in the oven. I think I've got everybody I need, but tell me if I'm missing anyone important. Let's see—the director of the state's Department of Health and Human Resources; the chairman of the state medical board's committee on impaired physicians; your assistant, Alice; your parents, Charlie and Verna Mathis of Beckley, West Virginia; the chairman of the legislative committee on whatever it's called—"

"You wouldn't!"

Madeline laughed. "Carrie, just do it, for crying out loud. Come to Persuasion for the Thanksgiving benefit and bid on Matt—you'll make a donation for a good cause and you'll get me off your back. I can't see the harm in that."

"And you'll drop this?"

Madeline did a silent victory dance. "If you make Nola visibly jealous and work her into a tizzy, I'll drop this. It's a promise."

Carrie didn't miss a beat. "But I have no control over whether Nola goes into a tizzy, or even what constitutes a tizzy."

Madeline supposed Carrie had a point, which made her pout. "Do it or I hit the 'send' button."

"Fine," Carrie said with finality. "I make Matt's bail in the charity auction and I'll make sure everyone thinks I'm hot for him, and you'll back off. Agreed?"

"Agreed."

"What time is the auction?"

"Two."

"That seems an odd time, right in the middle of the day like that, but OK." Carrie sighed with defeat. "After the auction, I want nothing to do with you. You will never tell a soul about my, uh, shortcomings."

"The fund-raiser takes Visa," Madeline said.

Thanksgiving Eve was here, and Kat's heart was filled with love and gratitude as she studied the faces of those gathered around the fireplace. Aidan had come. That alone sent Kat bouncing off the walls with happiness. He'd brought his girlfriend, Rachel Mishmurtha, who Kat could tell was trying her best to overcome her shyness. There was Matt and Nola. And Riley, of course. Loretta was snoozing near the hearth.

Everyone was enjoying delivery pizza, beer, and hot apple cider while the heavy sweetness of baking pies permeated the house.

"Calzones absolutely taste different than pizza," Nola said, defending her position. She and Matt were snuggled together on the end of the couch involved in an intense discussion.

"How could they, baby?" Matt asked. "You make pizza dough. You smear pizza sauce on it. You add meat and cheese and whatever else you want; then you flip the crust over on itself. You bake it. It comes out a deformed pizza."

Nola was not giving up. "I am an Italian," she said, waving her hands around in case no one believed her. "I know my Italian food. Calzones taste different than pizzas."

Matt shrugged. "All right, but why anyone would want to do that to a perfectly good pizza is beyond me." He took another drink of his beer.

When Kat glanced in Riley's direction, he was already looking at her, his face lit up with relaxation and happiness. She was astounded at how different he appeared lately. That day she saw him walk into the ER room to check on Virgil, Riley had looked dog-tired, on the surface and deep down in his soul. She now knew that's exactly what he'd been, because he hadn't been able to find her and Aidan, and had just put himself in hock for the rest of his life in order to save the clinic.

Tonight, everything was different for Riley. His woman and his child were right there with him, and Riley was about to come clean with Matt.

"Matt, there's something I need to tell you."

"Hmm?" Matt and Nola apparently had reached a truce and then reached for each other.

"Look, I just wanted to tell you I did something stupid recently—I took out a second mortgage on the Bohland House and got into some trouble with the payments."

Matt dragged his gaze from Nola and blinked at his brother. "You don't say."

"Yeah. I took out a . . ." Riley stopped. He glanced quickly toward Kat, then frowned at his brother. "You already *know*?"

Matt shook his head, leaving his nest with Nola and moving to the very edge of the couch. He leaned his elbows on his knees. "I've been waiting for you to come to me about it."

Riley looked baffled. "How did you find out?"

Matt laughed. "Bro, half the women down at the bank used to—" He straightened up. "Be my friend."

Riley narrowed his eyes. "You're not angry?"

"Ha!" Matt slapped his palms on his knees. "I'm pissed as hell, man, but I figured it was for the clinic, and that you'd find a way out of the mess somehow. I have total faith in you."

Riley narrowed his eyes and Kat watched his brain working. "You know how much money we're talking, right?"

"Sure. One and a half million."

"Jesus-Snowboarding-Christ," Nola whispered. The room went silent.

"How many people will be here for dinner tomorrow, Miss Turner?"

Kat thought Rachel had done a nice job of changing the subject. She was a strikingly polite young woman.

"Fourteen in all. And just so everyone knows, I've agreed to let Joanna Loveless come over and take a few pictures for the local paper, kind of a back-in-town feature story she's doing."

"That sounds nice," Rachel said, smiling.

"We're very glad you could come up and join us," Riley said.

Rachel's face became animated. "Oh, wow, me, too. It almost didn't happen." Then her eyes went big and she looked to Aidan as if to acknowledge that she'd made a mistake.

Aidan cleared his throat. "Yeah. Her parents aren't all that excited about Rachel dating me. I'm not Indian, obviously, and it's kind of a sore spot with them."

Kat nodded. "I see."

"But they like him," Rachel added quickly, looking at both Riley and Kat. "They're, well . . ." She glanced at Aidan for his blessing.

"Obviously, we tell it like it is around here, Rach. Go for it."

She laughed uncomfortably and looked down at her mug of apple cider. "Well, it's just that my parents are very old-fashioned, from a small city in northern India, and they have their hearts set on me finding a nice boy from my culture."

"What's wrong with American men?" Matt asked.

"It's just that they'd rather I date someone with a similar background. They think Americans are, well . . ." She swallowed hard. "They think Americans are undisciplined and lack a moral foundation."

The room went quiet again, the only sound the crackling of the fire. Rachel was visibly embarrassed. "I am very sorry. Like I said, they're old-fashioned, and they embarrass me sometimes."

Matt cleared his throat and tapped his service revolver under his waistband. "Well, you can reassure your folks that I'm always packin' my moral foundation right here."

"He's just joking," Aidan reassured her, then planted a tender kiss on her forehead, right in front of everyone. Kat was touched by the sweetness of it.

"I'll heat some more apple cider," Kat said. "Be right back." Within moments she heard a man's footsteps in the dining room, and she figured it was Riley. She turned to greet him and encountered Aidan.

His eyes were filled with concern. "Hey, Mom. You OK?"

"Oh! Sure. I'm great."

He stepped close to her, a smile playing at his lips. "This is a really nice house, Mom. And Rachel's totally in love with it."

Kat knew that was his way of breaking the ice. "I hope you two spend a lot of weekends out here."

"Yeah. We could do that."

"I know your father would like that, too."

After a second's pause, Aidan burst out laughing. "Do you have any idea how weird that sounds coming from you? It's like a line from *Leave It to Beaver* or something." He shook his head in amazement. "I never would have pictured this in my wildest dreams."

"I love you, Aidan."

"Ah, Mom." He put his arms around her, and it had been such a long time since she'd felt her son against her that it was a shock to her system. She tried not to cry. She wasn't successful.

Aidan rubbed her back as he talked to her. "I'm

sorry for all that trash talk that day at the G and A, Mom. I said some horrible things and I apologize. You just totally blew me away is all."

"I know." Kat didn't loosen her grip on him. "And I am profoundly sorry for keeping this world a secret from you."

"I know you were only doing what you thought was right."

Kat patted her son on the back and stepped away, leaving her hands on his strong shoulders. "But you were right about a lot of things, Aidan, especially that I was protecting myself, not you. It's embarrassing to admit that I couldn't handle the idea of coming back here, not until Phyllis died and left me her money."

"A security blanket," Aidan offered. "A sense of power."

"Yeah. I guess." Kat looked at her son's face—so much a man but still a trace of boy. "And now you need to know something else." Kat craned her neck out the pocket door and looked through the dining room to the living room. She wanted to make sure she had a few moments alone with him.

Aidan looked terrified.

"It's about my father," she said, which seemed to reassure him. "Since I've been back and had a chance to talk to your grandfather, I'm positive I made the right decision to leave here. He is a very unstable man, Aidan—an alcoholic who beat my mother and treated me like I was nothing but an annoying neighbor kid. He was emotionally abusive to me, and I always believed that sooner or later I'd get the physical part, too."

Aidan's face fell. "I had no idea."

"I know you didn't, sweetie, but I'm telling you

now. There will be no more secrets between us, all right?"

A smile curled his lips. "That would be great."

"So what I'm saying is that keeping you as far away as possible from Virgil Cavanaugh was the smartest thing I ever did. Turns out I did something right."

"You've done lots of things right, Mom." Aidan inclined his head toward the voices coming from the living room. "Getting back together with Dad is right up there, too."

Kat felt her face blossom with happiness. "You think?"

"Oh yeah. He's . . ." Aidan stopped, clearly overwhelmed with emotion. "I couldn't have dreamed up a better dad. Or a better mom. And now I look forward to having both of you in my life at the same time. I'm finally going to know what having a whole family feels like."

Kat burst into tears and grabbed her boy, never wanting to let go.

"Everybody OK in here?" Riley hung back in the dining room, not quite entering the kitchen, not sure that he was welcome.

Kat separated from Aidan and wiped her eyes. "I just had a mother moment," she said, grabbing a piece of paper towel from the dispenser and blowing her nose. "It's kind of surreal having Aidan here."

Riley nodded.

"I'd like to try something," Aidan said. "You guys up for it?"

Riley and Kat looked at each other, and then at their son.

"Sure," Kat said.

"Come here, Dad," Aidan said, holding out his

left arm. Riley stepped into his son's embrace. "Come here, Mom," he said, holding out his right. Kat pressed up against him, then instinctively brought her arm around and grabbed on to Riley. The three of them stayed in a huddle like that for several long moments, their heads touching in the center, a feat that required both men to bend way down to meet Kat.

Eventually, Aidan pulled away. "In-friggin'-credible," he said, shaking his head. "I will never forget this night as long as I live."

SEVENTEEN

Carrie hit the road early on Thanksgiving Day, figuring there would be serious northbound holiday traffic. She wanted to get this distasteful errand over with. She brought along a book to read in the coffee shop because she knew she'd get to Persuasion with hours to spare.

She shook her head, merging onto the highway. It was beyond her why Riley and his crowd decided to hold a fund-raiser on Thanksgiving Day, a day that was supposed to be sacred, spent in the company of family and cherished friends. It pissed her off to no end that she'd had to leave Kenneth behind in Charleston, especially since his parents had extended an invitation to join their family for dinner.

Carrie sighed. Kenneth was gorgeous and brilliant. Not like Riley, of course, but in his own way. He was a financial analyst. He'd grown up in Morgantown and gone to Ohio State. He played squash and racquetball, and he dressed tastefully. His kissing needed just the teensiest bit of work, but Carrie was up to the challenge. And he had nice eyes. Kind of plain, really, not the knock-me-on-my-ass kind of eyes like Riley had, but *nice.*

She was aware that she'd have to stay more than a hundred feet from Riley at all times, just as the protection order said. She would not speak to him or Kat. She would show up at this stupid event, bid for Matt, rub her leg against him or do something equally distasteful for everyone to see, and then she was out of there. That would have to satisfy Madeline's taste for revenge because that was all she was getting. As far as the money went, Carrie had set a five-hundred-dollar limit for herself. She absolutely, positively would not go a penny higher.

She'd decided that once the legislature was back from holiday recess, she'd undo the clinic-funding mess. The last few weeks had been filled with soul-searching, and she realized that withholding the clinic money had been a mean-spirited thing to do. Carrie had breathed life into the project by calling in every political favor owed to her. She wanted Riley to adore her. Be in awe of her. She wanted him to propose to her, and it had worked. How embarrassing it had been to go back to the same people a couple years later and beg them to make the money go away! She did not even want to think about how humiliated she'd be returning yet again, wanting the funding restored. The whole town would think she was nuts.

Carrie shivered. She dreaded going back to Persuasion, because the last time she was there was for her encounter with the foul Virgil Cavanaugh, closely followed by being slapped with the protective order. It was pretty obvious that her meeting with Virgil had been a harbinger of disaster, a blatant signal to Carrie that she was on the wrong path and needed to clean up her act. If it weren't for the fact that she was driving, Carrie would've closed her eyes right then and taken a moment to connect to the positive energy flow of the universe.

No matter how much she cranked the heat, she just couldn't seem to get warm.

Kat greeted the day happier than she'd ever been in her life. Today was going to be the kind of Thanksgiving she'd dreamed about since she was a little girl—delicious food on the table and a bounty of forgiveness, honesty, and love in the hearts of those gathered together. She had much to be thankful for.

The first thing she did that morning was call Riley.

"Happy Thanksgiving," a groggy voice answered.

"I love you, Riley Bohland."

"Mmmm," he replied, still half-asleep.

"I wanted those to be the first words I said today."

"That's really sweet, Scout." She heard him roll over in bed.

"Are the young lovebirds still asleep?" she asked.

"It's not even seven yet, so I'd say it's likely."

Kat opened the drapes in her bedroom, and looked out over the quaint scene of Laurel Lane in the morning. She hoped that in each of those houses there would be peace today.

"I'm sorry for waking you, but I'm just so excited!" Kat padded down the stairs and into the kitchen. "I'm going to begin all the turkey prep work and start some of the side dishes."

Riley chuckled. "You really are enjoying this, aren't you?"

"It's my home and my family and my chance to do things differently, so, yes, I'm enjoying this."

"I love you, Kat. Do you know how much I love you?"

"A lot?"

"You got that right. Now, would you mind if I go back to sleep?"

She giggled. "Of course not. Be here around noon, OK? Please don't forget the six extra chairs."

"We'll bring 'em in the truck. Bye, sweetie."

Kat spent the next several hours in glorious solitude, puttering around her kitchen, drinking coffee and listening to her music as loud as she wanted. With Aidan and Nola both here in Persuasion today, she didn't feel the slightest internal pull east toward Baltimore. And once Phyllis' donation made her part of the clinic forever, she'd be here in Persuasion, too, in spirit.

Cliff had called about ten o'clock last night to let Kat know that he, Barbara, and the grandkids were checked into Cherry Hill. He told Kat how much he was looking forward to the visit. Jeff and his partner, Richard, arrived earlier yesterday evening, and Jeff couldn't stop raving about Cherry Hill—he thought it was absolutely charming.

Jeff sounded cheerful, but Kat had gotten to know him since the Caymans, so she was able to detect the hint of melancholy in his voice. He was in Persuasion because his own family in Vermont had reacted coolly to his coming out and told him they were uncomfortable having Richard for the holidays. When Kat invited Richard and Jeff, he had leaped at the offer. She looked forward to seeing him again.

By ten, Kat had everything under control and had

showered and dressed. She'd chosen her outfit with the newspaper photos in mind, selecting a subdued eggplant turtleneck and a pair of black dress slacks. Nola arrived by ten-thirty, bringing a huge pan of lasagna "in case there wasn't enough turkey to go around."

For the next hour or so Nola and Kat put the finishing touches on the table, including setting out the floral centerpiece she'd whipped together using asters, gerberas, mums, cranberries, and sprigs of dried wheat. Nola made a fire, opened the blinds, and ran the vacuum. When they were done, the two of them stood in the dining room and pronounced that it was good.

"Martha Stewart can kiss my fat Italian ass," Nola said.

Kat draped her arm around Nola. "I told you—you are *not* fat."

"Who cares? Whatever I got, Matt likes it."

After admiring their handiwork for a few more moments, Kat studied her friend and, in all seriousness, asked, "Are you enjoying life in Persuasion, Nola?"

She looked at Kat like she was insane. "I've never been with a man who treats me as good as Matt does. It's an adorable town. My job is mellow and my boss is decent." Nola looked pensive for a moment, then said, "It's sad in a way—I'm thirty-seven years old and I don't think I ever really knew what being happy felt like until now."

"I know what you mean," Kat said.

Nola smiled thoughtfully. "Do you remember the night you found out your mom had died, and we were back in your room at Cherry Hill?"

Kat nodded.

"Do you remember what I said about how you came back here for revenge, but you might come away with something even better?"

Kat laughed. "My God, you really did say that, didn't you?" She gave her friend a squeeze. "How'd you get to be so wise?"

Nola shook her head. "It can only be one thing—after all those years in front of the TV, I guess I've finally earned my D.O. degree."

"What's that?"

"Doctor of Oprah, hon."

The marrow of his leg bones ached. Sharp pains shot through his shoulders and back. His neck seemed to be stuck in one position. And he couldn't remember what month it was or the last time he'd bathed or slept. But the beauty—the beauty he'd created—made all the discomfort meaningless.

How many weeks had this taken him? He had no idea. All he knew was that he'd never worked with such sharp focus or sense of purpose in all his life. It was as if he'd been resting up all these years, putting out worthless junk in order to eat while every aspect of his body and soul prepared itself for this singular masterwork.

It would be called *Woman, Thou Art a Whore—Italian Carrara marble, by V. L. Cavanaugh, 2007.*

He wept. He let his fingers play on the perfection of each of those female faces. He fancied doing an entire series of such sculptures. Perhaps each would focus on just a single female body part. It was sheer genius, but who was he kidding? The tightness in his chest was intensifying. He didn't remember when he'd last taken any of his medicines. He knew where he'd stashed the revolver, and thought maybe he should hasten the inevitable. He was dying.

And unless he went out with a bang, nobody would even notice he was dead. Nobody would give a fuck.

Cliff, Barbara, and the grandkids—Erin and Stephanie—were the first to arrive. Kat was overjoyed to see Cliff and hugged him with all her might.

"How's my sunshine?" he asked. "Everything OK with you?"

"Oh, absolutely, Cliff. I'm great."

The slightest look of confusion crossed his face.

"I am, Uncle Cliff. I am incredibly happy." She hugged him again before she chatted with Barbara and got the girls situated with the Macy's Thanksgiving Day Parade on TV. Matt came in next, and Nola did the introductions with the Turners. Aidan, Rachel, and Riley came right at noon, with six chairs and one large hound, and Rachel did her best not to appear overwhelmed by Cliff's loud and gregarious voice. Jeff showed up with Richard a few minutes later, his arms filled with wine and flowers.

"Kat!" He hugged her quickly before he introduced Richard, and Kat saw the pride and love in Jeff's face when he did so.

Soon, everyone was comfortable with wine or some other drink and the house was rocking with laughter and conversation. Riley snuck up behind Kat as she stood at the kitchen counter, and he slid his arms around her waist and put his warm lips on the side of her neck.

"This is fabulous," he said, whispering in her ear. "And you are beautiful."

Kat leaned back into Riley's solid body and closed her eyes. She wanted to feel all of it, all at once, if only for a second. She wanted to let the completeness of the moment imprint itself on her spirit so that she could carry it with her, always.

This made no sense whatsoever. Carrie had done a drive-by at the clinic and the place was deserted, not a bit of preparation in place. Thinking maybe she'd gotten the time wrong, she drove into town. The coffee shop was closed. Every business on Main Street was empty and locked. Even the Sunoco was dark. There was nobody out, anywhere, except for the occasional lonely college kid whose ride home hadn't materialized. Madeline had talked up this day like it was going to be second only to the Second Coming.

Carrie began to get a very bad feeling about this.

She drove back to the clinic. She parked in the utterly vacant lot and walked to the glass double doors in front, the spike heels of her boots echoing in the emptiness. She read the flyer. The damn thing was *tomorrow,* not today! She was going to kill Madeline!

Carrie took hold of both the door handles and shook until the entrance rattled. She screamed out her fury until her throat hurt. She stopped only because she tripped the security alarm.

She ran to her car and drove off. She had just wasted four hours of her life in holiday traffic! She could have gone to Kenneth's family's dinner! She was stuck in Persuasion for Thanksgiving and she had nowhere to go, nowhere to stay! What kind of cruel joke was this?

Carrie called Madeline at the B and B. Then Carrie tried her cell. She didn't answer that, either, so Carrie drove over to Cherry Hill, only to find the parking lot full. She had to drive about a block away down a side street before she found a spot.

She stormed down the sidewalk, painfully aware of the food aromas wafting from every single little house on the street—roasting turkey, gravy, stuffing, potatoes, pumpkin pie . . .

She'd eaten one rectangle of shredded wheat and a half cup of skim milk for breakast, and that was six hours ago. She was so hungry it felt like her stomach had given up waiting for food and had just started digesting itself. From one of the houses she heard raucous laughter.

She was going to strangle Madeline with her bare hands.

By two in the afternoon, Matt had made it back from a false alarm at the clinic, everyone was seated, and all the food was served. Riley said grace—a simple prayer of thanks for fellowship and possibilities—and then each person around the table named one thing they were thankful for.

"No school for a week," Stephanie said.

"Ice cream," Erin said.

"Family," Barbara said.

"The fact that God's hand is in all things," Cliff said.

"My mom and dad," Aidan said.

"Open minds," Rachel said.

"Nola," Matt said.

"Matt," Nola said.

"I like what Rachel said," Richard said.

"New friends," Jeff said.
"Love," Riley said.
"Forgiveness," Kat said.
"Let's eat!" Matt said. And they did.

Virgil's chest hurt. He called Rita, but she didn't answer. What day was it? Wasn't some sort of holiday coming up? He couldn't remember. He went into the kitchen to see if there was anything to eat. The TV was on and there was some sort of parade. Then he remembered it was Thanksgiving.

Carrie walked right on through the front door of Cherry Hill. It wasn't locked. She clicked her way down the hallway, past rooms Madeline had given pompous names such as "the parlor" and "the library." Carrie came to a halt at the entrance to the dining room.

Every seat at every table was taken, and guests were lined up like pigs at the trough trying to get to the buffet. She scanned the room for Madeline but didn't see her.

"Excuse me," Carrie said, pushing her way through the line to get to the kitchen door.

"I think that's employees only," an old man told her.

"I'm an employee," Carrie said, slamming her hand against the swinging door.

"In that case I should probably tell you we're low on yams."

Madeline was sitting at her kitchen table, wolfing down what looked like half a key lime pie. She stared up at Carrie like she was coming face-to-face with an alien.

"What in the world are you doing here?" she asked, wiping crumbs off her chin.

"Does it give you some sort of perverse thrill or something, screwing with my life like this?"

Madeline looked around the kitchen, like there might be someone else with whom Carrie was conversing. "Huh?"

"Look, I'm sorry I was less than honest with you, all right? But you're fucking with my peace of mind now, and I won't stand for it."

Madeline wiped her mouth on a napkin. "What are you even doing here today? The fund-raiser's tomorrow!"

"Ha! Funny. I am here because you told me the fund-raiser was *today,* you fat, dateless innkeeper!"

Madeline stood up from the table, throwing down her napkin like it was a gauntlet. "I never told you it was today, you bulimic bitch!"

"You did so tell me it was today!"

"I did *not*!"

The kitchen door opened. It was the old man. "We're waiting on those yams," he said.

Madeline scurried around the kitchen. "Coming!" She ran out to the dining room. While she was gone, Carrie hooked her finger and dragged it through the top of the key lime pie and ate the stuff right off her finger.

Madeline came back. "Look, I'm kind of busy right now. So, if you don't mind . . . ?"

"Mind what?" Carrie asked.

"Leaving."

Carrie huffed in disbelief. "And go where? Nothing's open in this ridiculous town! It's Thanksgiving Day! I don't have anywhere to go!"

"Then go home and come back tomorrow."

"No! I . . . well, no! I'm not driving all the way back to Charleston tonight, then back up tomorrow, and back down again tomorrow night! That would be an entire day of my life completely wasted!"

Madeline shrugged. "Then go get a hotel room somewhere."

"I'll take my usual suite here."

"Oh yeah?" Madeline stopped what she was doing and stared at Carrie. "You'll be rooming with Mr. and Mrs. Cliff Turner of Cumberland, Maryland, and their two lovely granddaughters. Let me get you a key."

Carrie felt like she was cracking into tiny pieces. Many people might see this mix-up as a minor inconvenience, but on top of everything else she'd been through in the last few months, it was too much.

"Then just forget it," she told Madeline, sick of the whole business, sick of her whole life. She was tearing up. "You go ahead and e-mail anyone you want. Tell everyone that I make myself puke a few times a day—I don't think it will cause the state government to come to a screeching halt. I just don't care anymore. I was going to quit anyway." She turned to leave.

Madeline sounded just as tired. "OK. Great. Whatever."

Carrie was about to exit the swinging door when her empty stomach twisted in on itself. "How much is the Thanksgiving buffet?" she asked.

"Everything is fabulous," Jeff told Kat. "You've done an incredible job."

Heads nodded all around while the forks kept moving. Kat beamed.

"Sunshine?"

She turned to her uncle, who was seated at her

left elbow. "Ready for more turkey?" she asked him. As soon as she said the words, she saw that something was wrong. In fact, she'd been so busy that she hadn't admitted that something had been a little off all day. Cliff was acting worried. He seemed uncomfortable when he talked to her, which was not like him. Kat glanced at Barbara and saw the same discomfort in her expression.

Kat's heart fell to her stomach. "Is something wrong?"

It was probably the cadence of her voice, so unlike the laughter and lively conversation that had filled the house all day, but as soon as she asked her question, everything came to a standstill.

Cliff looked around the table, horrified. "I . . . uh, it can wait, I guess."

"Oh, Lord," Barbara mumbled.

Kat looked back and forth between them. "Would somebody please tell me what's going on?"

Barbara gestured to Cliff. "I told you to wait until the end of the day if she didn't bring it up, but no, you had to say something right in the middle of dinner."

Cliff looked guilty.

"What?" Kat put her napkin in her lap and waited. "Is it something about the charitable gift?"

Cliff shook his head in the negative, dragging the tines of his fork across his gravy, making a serpentine design. Finally his eyes met Kat's. "Did you look in all the boxes Rita gave you?"

Kat was about to answer when a powerfully charged current of dread passed through her. It took her a few seconds to ask the most pressing question, which was, "How the hell do you know Rita?"

Cliff looked to his wife. She nodded for him to continue.

"Did you open the boxes?"

"A couple of them, yes. Why?"

Cliff began to grind his teeth.

"Oh, Lord, Cliff!" Barbara sighed. "Kat, honey, I guess you didn't find anything in the boxes that you'd like to discuss with Cliff, would that be accurate to say?"

Kat was baffled. She looked at Riley and he shrugged.

She put her napkin on the table and pushed her chair back. "What are you talking about? How do you know about my mother and her boxes? Or Rita? Or that Rita gave me the boxes?" Kat's heart began to beat wildly.

"Where are they, Kat?" Cliff asked in a calm voice.

"On the attic stairs. But you're not answering me!" Tears began to well in her eyes. "Why aren't you answering me? What's going on?"

Cliff looked pained. "What did you find in the boxes you did open?"

Kat had a feeling her hard-won peace was about to be blown to hell. "Books, an old coat, a charm bracelet, art projects."

Cliff frowned. "But there was a box you never opened at all?"

Kat swallowed hard, nodding.

Cliff said to Aidan, "Do you think you could go find that one and bring it on down here?"

Aidan's mouth was pulled tight and he flashed his eyes at Kat in disappointment. "I thought you said there weren't any more secrets, Mom."

"There aren't!" she yelled.

"Well, that's not entirely true," Cliff said. "How about you go get that box, son?"

Aidan left the table. Nola stared at Kat with giant eyes. Matt buttered a roll. Rachel sat straight and stayed quiet. Barbara looked sad. Jeff and Richard were huddled together, whispering. The kids looked bored. Riley put his hand on Kat's shoulder in a protective gesture. "I think you better explain what this is all about, Cliff," he said.

Cliff nodded, the seriousness etched in his kind face. "Everything she needs to know is inside that box."

Virgil staggered around the kitchen, the lack of sleep and the physical demands of the last few weeks finally catching up with him. He found a box of saltines in the cabinet and ate a few. There was a vanilla pudding cup on the shelf, so he ate that, too, but had to use a dirty spoon because Rita hadn't been over to clean in ages. Then he poured himself a jigger of vodka and slugged it.

He knew where he was headed next, and it pained him. It really did. He'd hoped that that working on the sculpture would soothe the urge. It hadn't. His body was dying, but the urge was alive, and it swirled through him, driving him on, making him suffer. He remembered how it would go, back in the day, how, when he'd feel this unholy desire for Katharine, he'd just take it out on BettyAnn. It was always pure relief, damn near rapture, and when he was done, the world was back in balance and the fire would mellow to a glow.

But Kat had come back to rub his face in it. She knew what she was doing. She knew how parading in front of him had always tortured him.

The time had come. He had no choice but to extinguish the source of his misery, once and for all.

He walked out to the studio, noticing with a kind of removed curiosity that his feet were scraping the ground, that he couldn't lift them up and place them down the normal way. Just another sign that the end was near, he supposed.

He put his hand in the bottom drawer of the worktable, reached beneath a stack of worthless sketches, and got the handgun. Sad to say, but the day he'd bought this gun over at the pawnshop in Bowden, he'd been a vital man, still handsome, still able to get the ladies when the need arose. Now, he was just an old man, sick, and so very tired of all of it.

Virgil stuck the gun in his pants pocket and set out for Laurel Lane. At this pace, it was going to take a while.

EIGHTEEN

By the time Aidan made it downstairs with the box, everyone except Matt had relocated to the living room. Matt was still eating.

Aidan put the carton in the middle of the floor and Kat moved closer. It was then that she noticed something for the first time—there was writing on the side of this box, in blue ink that had faded almost to he point of it being unreadable. She leaned in closely. *Open this box first* was what it said.

"Great." Kat crumpled to the rug. She was afraid. When she looked up, she saw everyone staring down at her with a combination of curiosity and pity.

"Put down your fork and get out here, Matt!" Nola called. "This is a family thing we've got going here!"

Still chewing, Matt sauntered up to the crowd.

"You might want to make sure it's not ticking," he advised.

"Give me your pocketknife," Riley said, not amused in the slightest with his brother. Riley then bent down and sliced the box open. "We're all here, Kat. Whatever it is, we'll deal with it together." He kissed the top of her head.

"Thank you." Kat's eyes darted to Cliff.

"It's all going to be fine. You'll see," he said.

Madeline had denied Carrie's request to take a quick trip through the buffet. Of all the nerve! Cherry Hill was the only restaurant serving food today, and Madeline knew it—yet she'd kicked Carrie out! That meant a stop at the McDonald's in Elkins on the way out of town, and she hated to throw up in public restrooms unless she absolutely had no choice.

She began to walk toward her car. The afternoon was bright and cheery. She smelled food coming from *everywhere* and her thoughts turned to that creamy, thick key lime pie filling, just the right combination of tart and sweet. She hated Madeline, but the woman sure could cook.

Out of nowhere, a blast of cold collided with Carrie's body, and she was chilled to the bone. *Probably from starvation,* she told herself. She pulled her coat tight. Then ever so slowly, her skin began to crawl, and something told her to be on alert.

"I knew you'd come back to me."

The voice came from her right. She whipped her head around and froze. The ghost of Virgil Cavanaugh lay in a pile of brown leaves in someone's yard. It glared at her through sickly pink-rimmed eyes, and an otherworldly smile was pasted on its face. Then it coughed. But ghosts didn't cough, did they?

Carrie's pulse tripped. This was exactly why she'd opted for a job in health-care policy instead of clinical work. Clinical work required her to touch everyone who came to her for help, no matter how frightening or dirty or wretched they were. Her mind spasmed—she'd taken the Hippocratic oath as a physician and this was a human being who needed her help, but, honestly, she wanted to bolt.

For a long moment, she stared at him.

"Did you come to sit for me, darling?" he asked.

"I am going to call an ambulance," she said, getting out her cell phone.

"Wait!" Virgil tried to push himself up to a stand. Carrie waited to make sure he didn't fall, and was grateful that he'd managed on his own. "I was just catching my breath. I'm going in right there." Virgil pointed a shaky finger toward the house behind him, a beautiful two-story bungalow that Carrie had often admired in her visits to Persuasion.

"I've been invited to dinner in there. Would you mind helping me up the sidewalk?"

A white envelope sat on top of what looked like a stack of photo albums. *For My Darling Daughter* was written in shaky handwriting in the same blue ink. Kat picked it up, a million questions fighting to get attention in her head, the first one being, "This is for me?" She'd said it out loud.

"It is," Cliff said.

"How do you know my mother?" Kat asked, and somewhere in the bottom of her gut, she knew the answer.

"Look through everything. All your questions will be answered."

Kat picked up the first photo album and cracked open the plastic cover. This couldn't be. The first page was filled with photos of Aidan as a baby. In fact, she recognized many of them. Either she or Phyllis had taken them. Kat was shocked and looked up to Aidan with a sense of helplessness.

"What in the hell is going on?" Aidan asked. He dropped to his knees next to Kat and she grabbed his leg.

"Look through this one." She handed it to Aidan and picked up the next—Aidan's kindergarten graduation, Kat in a sun hat in the backyard helping Phyllis with the roses, several Ocean City vacations . . .

"She knew about me," Aidan said, whipping through the album in his hand. "Phyllis must have sent these to her."

Kat thought she would faint. She picked up the last album and started with the final page, crammed with photos of Aidan's lacrosse matches. Kat began to sob. "I don't understand," she wailed, looking up to Cliff. "What is all this shit? I don't get it! Phyllis knew my mom?"

Cliff nodded gently. "She sent pictures to Rita through the years, so Virgil would never know. You'll have all the time in the world to go through the albums, but you should probably read the letter." He caressed Kat's shoulder.

Kat tried to tear open the flap but ripped the entire envelope in her anxiety.

"I'll do that for you, hon," Nola said.

Kat gladly handed it over, then accepted the three-page handwritten letter Nola handed back. Kat stared at it, her eyes swimming and her whole body shaking. "Read it for me, please." She handed it back to Nola.

Aidan's arm went around Kat. He pulled her to her feet and took her to the sofa. He sat on one side of her and Riley sat on the other. She clutched at both of them as everyone found a place to sit. Jeff and Richard brought dining chairs into the living room for Cliff and Barbara. Nola propped herself on the arm of the love seat, directly in front of Kat.

"Wait. I need a beer," Matt said. He was back in seconds, but Nola greeted him with a glare when he returned. She cleared her throat.

" 'My Dear Daughter,' " Nola read aloud. "You do want me to read aloud, right?"

Kat nodded, so stunned she wasn't sure she'd hear a word of it.

" 'This letter is an apology and an explanation. I hope you read it in good health.

" 'I did some very stupid things in my life. First off, I did not tell you the truth when you were a child, and I suppose you've lived all this time knowing something was wrong, but you couldn't put your finger on it. Forgive me, Katharine. I was ignorant and so afraid, and now I'm going to be facing my maker soon and I don't have the strength to come see you in person. That's why I'm writing this down. I will give it to your aunt Rita to give you, once I'm gone.' "

Nola looked up. "You OK, hon?"

Kat blinked. She turned to Riley, hoping he'd have the answer to that question.

"Do you want to go on, Kat?" he asked her.

She nodded.

Nola continued. " 'Your real father was a very nice young man from Cumberland, Maryland—'

"Wow—holy shit!" Nola shouted. "Sorry, that part was mine."

Kat's eyes flew to Cliff. He smiled at her. Kat felt the strangest combination of rage and relief begin to churn inside her.

" 'I met him at the Randolph County Fair when I was a junior in high school. He was there with a group of students, and he came back often to see me. By my senior year I was pregnant with his child. Virgil Cavanaugh was older and smarter than me, a visiting lecturer at the college, and he married me even though I was pregnant with another man's baby. But I paid a high price. He never let me forget that he took me in when no one else would have me. He used it against me all of our marriage. For whatever reason, I was never able to give him his own child, and it enraged him. When you were four years old, Virgil caught me answering a phone call from your real father. That's when the hitting started. What was I supposed to do? Your real father was married with a family of his own and it wasn't true love between us, anyway. I had nowhere to go. No job. No place to live. I decided to stay and take whatever Virgil dished out so that you'd have a home.' "

Kat squeezed her eyes shut. She felt Aidan and Riley tight against her sides, which was a good thing, because she really thought she might shatter into a million pieces if they weren't there.

Nola stopped reading. "Maybe I should end it here." Her question was directed to Riley, but Kat raised her head.

"Let's hear it all," she said.

Nola cleared her throat and continued.

" 'I know I made the wrong choice. I should have grabbed you and taken my chances in the world. My dear daughter, forgive me. I was a scared woman when Virgil married me, and I stayed scared all my life.

" 'You may have already figured this out, but it's no accident that Cliff Turner picked you up on Route Three. Cliff is your real daddy, Kat. Rita called him the instant I sent you away and told him to get here as fast as he could and find you and get you out of town. Cliff's wife didn't know about you until recently. She was very understanding. And, as you can imagine, I feel indebted to Phyllis. I know she was a better mother to you than I could ever be.' "

"Those are nice things for her to say," Barbara whispered.

"Does this go on much longer?" Erin asked.

"Where's the bathroom?" asked Stephanie. Rachel got her started down the hallway.

" 'I bet you've always been amazed at how lucky you were that Cliff picked you up that night. You *were* lucky, but not for the reasons you thought. You were real lucky that nobody picked you up before Cliff got there and that your real daddy cared enough to make sure you were safe. You were always loved, Katharine. You were always wanted. My beautiful grandson was always wanted, too.' "

"My God," Aidan said with a sigh.

Rachel went over to him and sat at his feet.

" 'If you're reading this, it means I'm dead and you somehow got my things without Virgil standing in the way. If it was Rita who managed this, then God bless her. She's really not so bad, Kat. She was scared of Virgil, same as me.

" 'Now let me tell you about Riley—he's turned out to be a fine man and a wonderful doctor. He's taken real good care of me. Now, I've wanted to tell him for years about you and your boy, but I never did because I knew if Riley brought you back to Persuasion, Virgil would try to get his hands on Aidan. I probably made a mistake with that, too, and I hope someday you'll find a place in your heart to forgive me and all my weaknesses. I know I was real weak.

" 'Love, Mother.' "

The silence was shattered by Loretta's howl.

"Somebody put her outside, please," Riley said, his eyes on Kat. Matt excused himself and came back promptly, a fresh beer in hand.

Cliff began to speak, but Kat's hand flew up to stop him. "Nobody say a word. I need to sort this out." The first person she turned to was Aidan, still right next to her. He looked surprisingly cool. "Are you all right?" she asked him.

He nodded. "Are you?"

Kat thought about that for a second, and then she shook her head. "No, I'm not all right. I'm just . . . amazed—amazed that my life has been nothing but a big stinking pile of lies, from day one. Everyone kept the truth from me because they thought they were doing me a favor! My God! How stupid can people be!"

Cliff tried to interrupt, but Kat wouldn't have it. "You!" she cried. "You knew all along that I was your daughter, but you didn't have the guts to tell me?"

Cliff's face fell and he looked toward Barbara. "My life was a lie, too, Kat. I hated not being able to share that with you, but I swore to your mother that I would never say anything. She never budged on that, even after I came clean to Barbara and there was no reason to hide it anymore."

Kat nodded. "I see."

Cliff inclined his head toward the letter still dangling in Nola's hand. "BettyAnn always said she'd tell you in her own way someday, and about a month before she died, she told me about the letter she wrote and that she'd packed it up along with other mementos and gave the cartons to Rita for safekeeping. So when you told me you'd come back to Persuasion, I figured it was only a matter of time until you knew."

Kat felt numb.

"So Virgil is not my father." Kat's head hung with the weight of that news. It was pure relief. It explained why he'd never loved her—she wasn't his and his wife couldn't give him a child of his own. He'd seen Kat as a burden. And none of it was ever her fault—it was his.

"It's interesting that your mom did the same thing with you as you did with me," Aidan said. There wasn't a trace of anger in his words, just the wonder of seeing the connection. He smiled at Kat. "She did the best she knew how, Mom. She was protecting her child. Same as you."

"Yee-haw!" Matt said, raising his beer. "Welcome to Dysfunction Junction, West Virginia!"

Rachel made a little squeak of alarm from the floor near Aidan. Her eyes were as round as plums.

"What?" Aidan asked.

"I, uh . . ." Her eyes flashed up to Kat. "I'm just so glad my parents aren't here for this."

Loretta continued to howl. Riley said, "Will somebody find out what's wrong with that damn dog?"

"It's probably just a squirrel," Matt said.

"So you're my grandfather!" Aidan looked across the room at Cliff and his face broke out into a huge grin.

"Oh my God," Kat said. "You're right." She looked to Cliff. "Phyllis left me all that money because I really was her niece, didn't she?"

Cliff's face softened. "Sunshine, she left it to you because she loved you and Aidan more than anything in the world."

"This is all good news," Nola said, perking up. "Think about it—you don't have to go through any of the hassle of changing your name back to Cavanaugh or anything, because you really are a Turner."

Kat laughed in astonishment. "I need a drink."

"And you don't ever have to worry about Virgil again, 'cause he's nothing to you," Matt pointed out.

Kat stared at the fire, knowing there was something that gnawed at her. It was Phyllis. "Even Phyllis lied to me," she mumbled, incredulous. Then she spoke up, looking around the room. "No wonder I went through most of my life unable to tell truth from lie. No wonder I could lie to myself so well that I could actually forget big hunks of my life! I come from a dynasty of bullshit!" She looked at everyone in the room, then shouted, "When I showed up here last month, I wouldn't have known the truth if it bit me in the ass!"

"That's pretty much what it did, hon," Nola said.

Barbara got up and gathered the grandkids. "Now's a good time to have some pie," she said, practically dragging them out of the room.

"I'll take a piece of the pecan while you're out there," Matt said. "No whipped cream."

"I hope you can find a place in your heart to forgive me someday, Kat." Cliff's face was red and wet from tears. "Try to forgive your mother and Phyllis, too. We just wanted the best for you and Aidan."

Riley squeezed Kat's hand to get her attention. Kat had almost forgotten he'd been right next to her. She looked up into his face and he gave her a private smile. Then he kissed her.

"You know, Virgil knows I'm your father," Cliff added. "We met once, before you were born. He told me if I ever showed my face around Persuasion again, he'd kill me where I stood."

Loretta's howls continued from the backyard.

"What is *wrong* with that dog?" Riley asked.

There was a pounding at the front door.

"I'll get it," said a woman who stepped out from behind the foyer archway. Kat had no idea who she was.

"Is that woman your aunt Rita? I'm totally lost," Jeff said.

"No," Matt said, shaking his head and laughing. "That right there would be Joanna Loveless, from the newspaper."

Joanna Loveless? Kat didn't know Joanna Loveless was there. She jumped to her feet in horror. How long had the newspaperwoman been standing by the door? Had she heard the whole sordid tale of Kat's existence? Had she even bothered to *knock,* for God's sake?

Kat didn't have time to explore those questions, because as soon as Joanna opened the front door, Virgil staggered in, supported by Carrie Mathis.

"Look, before you say anything, I just want everyone to know that I am not intentionally in violation of my restraining order." Carrie glanced frantically around the room. "Riley, help me get him to the couch. Matt, call EMS. You . . ." Carrie blinked as she looked at Aidan. "Oh my God! Wow. You've got to be Aidan—get some blankets."

"Nobody fucking move!" With a wild swing of his arms, Virgil clipped Carrie in the face with an elbow. She fell with a thud. In his left hand he held a gun, and though he swayed unsteadily, he aimed it right at Kat.

"Everything's your fault," he said to her, and began to pull the trigger.

All that flashed through Kat's mind was, *I can't die. My life just started.*

Madeline knew it was a brazen thing to do, but she'd decided to walk on over there with this chocolate-cranberry torte, like a good neighbor, and wish everyone a happy Thanksgiving. She dressed up her old metal tart pan with a bit of clear plastic wrap and a festive red bow.

Yes, she'd see Matt and Nola together, but truly, Madeline was exhausted from all the petty jealousy. That stupid catfight with Carrie in the kitchen had been a new low. Madeline was disgusted with herself, with both of them. It pained her to admit it, but Carrie was right—it was time to grow up and move on. Life was too short to spend it meddling in other people's affairs.

Besides, Madeline wanted to see how Joanna Loveless was coming along with her article.

Madeline walked briskly up the sidewalk, pausing only to give a quizzical glance at what was obviously Carrie's Volvo parked at the curb. Where had she gone? Madeline wondered if, after she'd kicked Carrie out of the buffet line, the poor woman had gone door-to-door through Persuasion, begging for a cup of green bean casserole. Madeline sighed, promising herself that if she ran into Carrie, she'd invite her back to Cherry Hill. There was plenty to go around.

Madeline headed up the walk. Oddly enough, the front door to Kat's house gaped wide open, so Madeline poked her head in and gave a polite holler to announce her arrival.

It was then she noticed a room full of people cringing in terror, Carrie's body sprawled out on the welcome mat, and an unsteady Virgil Cavanaugh, who that second whipped around in Madeline's direction. The wild insanity in his eyes and the gun in his hand was further proof that she'd come at a bad time.

Madeline screamed. She raised the tart pan in front of her face and winced. Virgil fired the gun. The tart pan bent from the zing of the bullet and clattered to the floor. So did Virgil Cavanaugh, who was then tackled by what looked like an entire football team's worth of men.

Matt Bohland topped the heap, using his cell phone to call for an ambulance and report a twenty-seven-eight in progress, whatever that was. Joanna Loveless fainted, and her spiral notebook slid across the foyer floor.

"Thank you, Madeline. For everything."

Finally, after about six hours, Kat had stopped trembling. The cup of herbal tea Madeline just placed in Kat's hands already had begun to cut through the chill in her bones. Loretta lay snoring at her feet. "I appreciate you opening up your home like this."

"It's nothing. Half the group was staying here anyway, and you couldn't exactly relax in a living room roped off with police tape."

That was true. In fact, she didn't know when she'd be able to relax in that house, if ever.

Madeline once again disappeared into the kitchen, but the B and B buzzed with activity. The parlor and library swarmed with police of every jurisdiction, plus the county medical examiner, reporters from as far away as Morgantown and Charleston, evidence technicians, and a host of Persuasionites who had no reason whatsoever to be there except to share in the excitement and eat Madeline's leftovers.

Rita sat across the room, huddled with the funeral director. Kat had overheard Rita tell him how she wanted Virgil's remains cremated once the body was released after autopsy. Rita added that there was no need to select a style of funerary urn, because no one would be taking the ashes.

"That's an unusual twist," the mortician said.

"He was an unusually twisted man," Rita replied.

Virgil had died of a gunshot wound. The bullet from his own gun had apparently ricocheted off Madeline's baking dish and hit him right between the eyes, killing him instantly.

Everyone else who'd been in Kat's house was well and accounted for. Carrie was fine. She was in the library at that very moment flirting with a TV reporter. Poor Joanna Loveless had been admitted to Davis Memorial for observation but was listed in good condition. The girls had been sleeping for hours, but Cliff and Barbara had only moments ago gone upstairs for the night. Cliff was a good man, simple and direct. He told Kat he'd understand completely if she hated him. With a tight hug and a kiss on the cheek, she assured him she didn't.

Unfortunately, Aidan was already on his way back to Hopkins. Though Kat worried about him driving at night, Rachel was inconsolable and said she needed to go back to Baltimore, where it was safe. Kat had a feeling their love might not survive the events of that night, but Aidan seemed upbeat when he left.

"I'll come home after finals. I love you, Mom," he said, hugging her tight.

Nola came through the parlor with another tray of desserts and stopped to check in on Kat. "Madeline said the fund-raiser's already been rescheduled for next month—it's a done deal and everyone's been notified, so no worries there."

Kat nodded with relief. "She's incredible."

Nola laughed. "I haven't seen anyone kick ass in the kitchen like that since Grandma Tuti. I'll be back in a sec, hon."

Kat smiled. It was fascinating how life just seemed to go on. Earlier that day, her universe had been blown to pieces, yet it had already started to put itself back together again, in an entirely different form—its true form. She now understood the cryptic comment Phyllis had made that day so long ago, while Kat chowed down on a plate of Chef Boyardee. Phyllis had said that everyone was in this mess together, connected like puzzle pieces even if they couldn't see the big picture.

Kat finally got her big picture. Her mother had loved her. Her father had, too. And she'd always had a family who, whether she knew it or not at the time, were looking out for her.

At that moment, Riley and Matt came bursting through the B and B's front door. Kat noticed how Matt immediately scanned the rooms for Nola and Riley for her. "Let's get out of here," Riley said, helping her from the chair and motioning for Loretta to come along. "Now."

"Is something wrong?" Kat asked as soon as they were all in the pickup.

"Yeah." The tires squealed going around the corner. "I need to be with you. Alone. We need to go over a few details."

Kat sighed. "Like where I'm going to be staying."

"That one's easy. You're staying with me." Riley whipped the pickup into the drive at Bohland House. He went around to her side and opened the squeaky door and reached for her. Without a word, Riley picked her up in his arms and started up the walk toward the porch. He managed to open and close the door without putting her down, then practically ran up the stairs to his bedroom.

He gently placed Kat on the bed. He took off his clothes, then, in silence, removed everything Kat had on. He laid her down and got under the covers with her.

"OK. This is good," he said. "I can breathe now."

Kat smiled and snuggled into him, realizing that for the first time in many hours, she could breathe, too.

"Who do you love?"

The urgency she heard in Riley's question concerned her, and Kat answered in a gentle voice, "I love Riley James Bohland, forever and ever, of course. Who do you love?"

"Katharine Ann Turner, forever and ever." Riley's body suddenly shuddered. Kat heard a cry come from the deepest part of him. "I could have lost you," he choked out. "My God, Kat, I could have lost you forever."

"I'm not going anywhere." She soothed him with her hands and her kisses. "Riley, sweetheart, I'm home. I'm really, finally, home."

EPILOGUE

Two Years Later

The only sound came from the night forest around them. Tree frogs buzzed and a soft breeze teased the leaves of Indian summer. Kat and Riley lay on their backs, hands clasped, sharing the view of stars framed by old trees.

"Isn't it remarkable that we were right here in this exact same spot when we were kids, looking at these same stars?" Kat turned her head toward Riley.

"Aidan was made right here."

"He was." Kat's smile shone in the darkness. "Promise me we'll come back to this place on our wedding anniversary every year until we're too old to get up off the ground."

Riley squeezed her hand. "I promise, Scout."

"Do you know this is the most romantic night of my life?"

Riley chuckled. "Now I'm sure you've been living in Persuasion too long, baby."

"Sssshhh," Kat warned him, trying not to giggle. She lowered her voice to a whisper. "If we're not quiet, this little party's going to be over before it starts."

Riley craned his neck to see past the flickering candles at the blanket's edge to the occupants of the open SUV. He seemed satisfied that all was well and said, "Loretta's still under the car seat snoring like a backhoe, so if that hasn't woken her, nothing will."

Kat sighed with what sounded like deep contentment. "Fiona's exhausted. She must have been held by half the town today." Kat reached up to brush a fingertip along Riley's jawline. "How about you? Did all the excitement exhaust you, too?"

"Nope."

"Good. 'Cause I'm not done making out with you yet." Kat rolled over until she lay directly on top of Riley, and he groaned with delight. The feel of her soft female body, stretched out full-length along his, filled him with pleasure. He wrapped his arms around her in awe and gratitude.

"I love you so much, Kat."

Her lips moved softly on his. "I love you, too, my sweet husband. Thank you for giving me such a happy life."

"Thank you."

Riley pulled her close, holding on as tight as he could, his eyes shutting with the intensity of the moment. He'd been filled to capacity with love and contentment lately, like his heart had been pried open to make room enough for the whole world. Kat was responsible for that. She'd opened his soul with the gift of herself, Aidan, and now their two-month-old daughter, Fiona. Riley grinned to himself, thinking that all this was quite a turn of events for a guy whose own brother once compared his emotional range to that of a zombie-assed robot.

"I think Phyllis would be proud and happy," Kat said.

"I know she would."

They'd just come from the official opening of the

Phyllis Turner Center for Reproductive Health, the latest addition to the clinic complex. Riley hoped it would turn the tide on the region's teen pregnancy epidemic and eventually attract the town's first full-time ob-gyn. Between that and the clinic's domestic violence outreach center, life for women in Randolph County had taken a sudden turn for the better.

That, too, was all because of his wife.

The original cash donation from Kat and Cliff had only been a beginning. With Kat's dedicated efforts—and Carrie's assistance—the state finally ponied up, and the idea for the reproductive health clinic was born. Kat and Rita came up with the bright idea of selling Virgil's final sculpture, the vile thing he'd finished right before his death. To this day, no one quite believed what had happened next—art critics raved about it, calling it a masterpiece of madness, and a fancy New York auction house got close to two million for it. Every penny of profit went to pay for domestic violence prevention right here in Persuasion. Kat was finishing up her degree in clinical psychology and worked at the center three days a week.

"Did you hear that?" Kat whispered, going still in Riley's arms.

A soft whimper came from inside the truck, and Riley cocked his head to decipher the meaning of the sound. Was Fiona awake? Was she hungry? Did she need to be changed? Did she open her eyes in the darkness and need her parents? Riley waited for another hint, and heard a muffled howl followed by the sound of dog nails churning on carpet.

"Loretta's dreaming," Kat whispered, trying not to laugh.

Riley looked into his wife's beautiful, smiling face and said, "Truth be told, sometimes I think I am, too."